MAYFLY HOLLOW

ANNE LUCY-SHANLEY

MAYFLY HOLLOW
Copyright © 2021 Ninth and Aries Publishing
EBook ISBN: 978-1-7366907-0-3
Paperback ISBN: 978-1-7366907-1-0
Editing by EnCompass

Look for Anne online at: www.AnneLucyShanley.com

For my husband, my very own book boyfriend

CHAPTER ONE

WRAPPED IN A TOWEL AND HER CHESTNUT-COLORED HAIR STILL dripping from her shower, Kate silenced the staccato alarm clanging from Ben's phone. The sky showing through the slats in the window blinds had transformed to something between charcoal and pewter gray, signaling she was behind schedule. She nudged him impatiently. "Get up. I gotta get to work."

"My head's killing me," Ben grumbled, nestling further into his pillow like a hibernating bear. Kate flung back the duvet, prompting him to groan and flip on his back.

Grabbing her comb from the bedside table, she ran it through her hair then gathered it into an elastic band. "Hope you're not getting that flu everyone's talking about."

Ben stretched, as if savoring the delicious feeling of the morning after a well-deserved screwing. "Too much wine last night, more like." Hauling himself up, he sat at the edge of the mattress and rubbed his sleep-smudged eyes, his shaggy hair disheveled.

Kate selected a printed blouse from her closet. As she thumbed through the stack of laundry on a chair in the corner of her bedroom for jeans, she said, "Last night was fun. Same thing next week?"

"Sure. I'll even let you be on top."

Kate snorted, side-eying him. She scooped up Ben's tee and sweatpants from the floor and lobbed them at his head. He ducked, snagging his clothes with his fingers but not losing his grin.

Zipping her blue jeans and stepping into loafers, Kate peeked at her cell. Wincing at the time, she hastened to locate her purse and keyring on the dresser. She said over her shoulder as she left, "Lock up when you leave, stud. If you stop by the shop later, I'll buy you an éclair."

Her partner was at Buttercream Bakeshop when Kate arrived, a catchy pop song blasting over the speaker of her smartphone. Blonde-haired and blue-eyed, at forty Rosie was a decade older than Kate but exuded the perkiness of a college co-ed. She bopped to the music as she leveled flour in an eight-cup measure, adding it slowly to the whirring commercial mixer with practiced movements.

Kate projected her voice to be heard over the din. "Good morning, Rosie. Sorry I'm late. What are you working on?"

"The shortbread for Les's catering order." Rosie lifted her chin toward the ovens. "I've got the pies going for LuAnn."

"You're a lifesaver!" Kate went to the staff coffeemaker on the worktop and poured a cup of coffee. Blowing on the surface, she took a sip then grabbed the spiral bound notebook from its place beside the coffeepot, consulting her to-do list. She put a line through *Pies—three peach, three apple, three mixed berry, three cherry* for LuAnn's standing order at Corner Market and set about assembling the pâte à choux pastry for the éclairs to go along with Les's shortbread.

Over the next hour, the two women mixed and baked doughs and batters in tandem without speaking, operating with efficiency honed over years of sharing a workspace. When the rolling metal racks were filled with trays of cooling confections, they sat for a quick coffee break, sharing the reject pieces of shortbread that had broken during cutting. Popping the last morsel in her mouth with relish, Kate savored the buttery taste. "You want to deliver orders or open the shop today?"

"I'm in the mood to deliver." With a swift look at the wall clock, Rosie pulled the elastic netting from her head and fluffed her bangs. "It's almost six! I've got to get those pies boxed and loaded into the van. When I get back, I'll run the dishwasher and bake the cookies and cupcakes."

Resigned, Kate stood. "And I need to get the case stocked before Bud pounds on the door for his breakfast. I could set a watch by that guy."

Kate yawned as she replaced her stained beige baking apron with the pristine bubble-gum pink serving apron embroidered with a cupcake logo. It was the same graphic as on the pink-and-black striped awning above the street entrance to the bakery. Pulling off her hairnet, she ran a shrewd glance over her appearance in the mirror inside the swinging kitchen doors, wiping a smudge of flour from her nose.

The trays of blueberry, banana nut, and apple cinnamon muffins were artfully arranged in the glass case beside decorative stands piled with shortbread, éclairs, and croissants. On her way to the front door to turn the *closed* sign over to *open*, Kate pushed the power button on the boxy three-burner Bunn coffeemaker on the counter behind the case. The rich, nutty aroma of brewed French Roast mingled with the hint of sugar in the air. She straightened the chairs around the half-dozen bistro tables in the shop while listening to WPAL's morning show broadcast on the wall-mounted TV.

Through the plate-glass window the tangerine orb of the sun peeked above the horizon, the sky infused with lavender and fuchsia. Kate didn't need to hear the forecast to know it would be a pleasant spring day. The international news briefing had just begun when the bell above the door tinkled. Bud Bradley, her favorite customer, entered the café.

The pouches under Bud's eyes were pronounced and his greeting less robust than normal. "Mornin', Katie girl."

"Hey, Bud. Rough night?" Kate poured his coffee and used plastic tongs to put a blueberry muffin on a paper doily-lined plate. He wearily lowered his large frame to a chair at his designated spot overlooking Main Street.

"Whoa," Bud muttered, putting his hand to his temple. Kate's forehead wrinkled in concern as he abruptly got to his feet, his actions erratic. He put a palm up to discourage her from bringing his order. "All the sudden I'm not feelin' too bright. I'm gonna have to pass on breakfast, kiddo."

"Yeah, that's probably a good idea. How 'bout I lock up shop and drive you home before you keel over?" She hurried around the counter to help Bud, untying her apron as she walked, but he waved her away before she reached him.

"No—don't get close to me. Maybe I'm comin' down with that nasty flu I heard about on the news." He jerkily pushed his chair in and went to the door. "I'm gonna crawl back into bed, where I 'spose I oughta have stayed to begin with."

Bud's face became ashen, and his fingers trembled on the doorknob as he gripped it. Kate's tone revealed her alarm when she protested, "I really think I'd better drive you—"

"Now, Katie, don't fuss! I'll be right as rain tomorrow mornin' and ready for my muffin first thing."

Mouth pursed, Kate watched as Bud staggered out to his rusted pickup and drove away. She sanitized everything he'd touched, her attention cutting to the anchorwoman on WPAL-TV saying, "Concerning reports coming in this morning as the yet-unidentified strain of influenza cases grew exponentially the last twenty-four hours…"

CHAPTER TWO

STILL DISTURBED BY BUD'S DEPARTURE, KATE WORRIED WHETHER SHE should've insisted on driving him home. Shaking off her lingering misgivings, she wrote the day's offerings on the shop's chalkboard wall above the coffeemaker. She had just stepped down from her stool when she heard the bell above the door. Turning, Kate tucked the chalk marker in her apron pocket and pasted on a welcoming smile.

Her smile slipped when she saw Dierdre Harcourt making her way across the shop.

"Kate, darling!" Dierdre was in her seventies with smooth face-lifted features. Her blue-black hair was arranged in a chignon, and she wore riding pink that made it seem as if she recently dismounted from a thoroughbred horse. "I'm desperate for your assistance!"

Irritation rose in Kate's breast, crowding out the unease that nagged at her after viewing the morning news. "Let me guess... catering order for bridge club?"

"No, Ladies Circle. Millie was to hostess, but she's under the weather, so the task falls to me, I'm afraid."

Kate's focus shifted when she noticed Ben's green Jeep Cherokee parked in front of Buttercream Bakeshop. He emerged, freshly showered and shaved, wearing his customary dark suit. When he came into the bakery, Kate briefly met his eyes. "Dierdre, do you remember when I told you last time that I'd have to upcharge last minute orders?"

"I know, and I surrender myself to your mercy..." Dierdre appeared properly chastened, glimpsing over to Ben where he joined her at the display case. His fair brow was furrowed as he studied the chalkboard, like he was trying to decide between a muffin and a pastry. "Benjamin, how are you, dear?"

"Good day, Dierdre," Ben replied, mouth quirking, the dimple in his cheek surfacing. "I'm just fine. Thought I'd grab breakfast on my way to court. I have a hearing in a half-hour."

"Please, do go ahead of me. You absolutely must if you're in a hurry. My insignificant gathering pales in comparison to the magnitude of your vocation as a public defender."

Ben and Kate met eyes again. She could tell he was amused by the way the corners of his eyelids crinkled. He swept a hand in a gallant gesture. "Ladies first."

Dierdre flashed him a coquettish look and said to Kate, all business, "No sheet cake. The Ladies Circle gals are a discerning bunch."

"Uh..." Kate's heart sank. She knew what that meant. "Not macarons?"

"I hoped for an assortment of macarons, truffles, and petit fours. Two dozen of each."

Kate suppressed her displeasure and thought fast. "I can do chocolate truffles, and white cake for the petit fours, but I'm only able to do two flavors of macarons. What were you thinking?"

"Pink and yellow."

"So strawberry and lemon? A dozen each? And pink and white icing for the petit fours? I'm afraid it'll be quite costly at this late hour, Dierdre." Kate threw out an astronomical figure, but Dierdre didn't balk at the price. She clapped her immaculately manicured hands in delight.

"Accommodating as ever. You've swooped in and saved the

day, Kate. You'll be sure to deliver to my house by ten tomorrow morning?"

"Certainly." Kate grabbed an order pad and hastily scrawled Dierdre's selections. The woman was notoriously *forgetful* about paying the invoices Kate sent via mail. "However, new bakeshop policy dictates prepayment on catering orders."

Dierdre opened her designer handbag and rooted around, producing a matching wallet. "Can I get one of your delicious croissants to take away as well?"

When the shop door closed behind Dierdre, Kate rolled her eyes. Ben roared with laughter, leaning across the counter and lacing her hand in his. "What was she wearing? There can't seriously be a fox hunt planned in Clayton's Corners."

"All she needs is a riding crop."

"Tally ho and all that rot," Ben said in an exaggerated British accent. "Our very own Lady Grantham."

"Lucky us."

He lifted a shoulder. "At least you'll make bank on her order, luv."

"I'll also be here all night," Kate groused, nonchalantly pulling her hand away. "I promised you an éclair, didn't I?"

"Yep." Ben's voice was neutral, but she sensed his disappointment as she plucked the pastry from the case with tongs. She avoided his gaze while putting it in a pink wax paper bag adorned with the shop's stylized cupcake logo.

Ben was three years ahead of her in high school, so they'd known each other only superficially then. Last year, they'd met again at a local bar called Cahoots and hit it off. Their friendship-with-benefits suited Kate to a T.

"Coffee?" Kate lifted a pink-and-black striped to-go cup, and he nodded.

When she handed him his coffee, Ben pinned her with a serious look. "When are you going to let me take you out on a proper date?"

Kate bit back a groan. She scanned his fair hair, slicked back neatly from his forehead, to his handsome, boyish face, and his broad shoulders encased in his power suit. Most women would be thrilled to date Ben. He was a catch and on a fast track to a successful private practice. He was a hell of a nice guy to boot— Kate just wasn't interested in dating. Her heart fluttered as she searched for the right thing to say. "It works. Why complicate things?"

"Because I *like* you," Ben murmured, his sapphire eyes sad. "I want more than a once-a-week-roll-in-the-sack."

"Please. Let's not get into all that..." Kate realized she fidgeted. She seized the spray bottle of cleanser and a paper towel and set about swabbing at the already spotless countertop. "You know I'm a loner."

"Yeah. I get it." Ben's fingers tightened on the wax paper bag he held, but his face remained impassive. "See you Thursday."

Conflicted, Kate observed him leave. His stiff shoulders and ramrod straight posture made his frustration clear.

Ben had a huge family. Sisters and brothers and nieces and nephews. They went to church together. Planned birthday parties and hosted ham suppers. Ben's folks had been married forty years. He'd said more than once that he wanted the same for himself someday and couldn't fathom why Kate didn't. Raised by her older sister after their parents' death, Kate didn't know how to act around Ben's family—what to say in their presence. How to belong.

Anxiety closed her throat when she contemplated explaining *why*. Could she verbalize how she felt like an actress tripping over her lines? That she was a fraud? Kate shook her head. Nope. That's why she didn't do families. It was easier to be alone. Her past was too complex to dissect.

If only Ben would accept her wishes.

"Deliveries are *finito*," Rosie said as she came through the swinging kitchen doors, tying her baking apron over her sweatshirt. "Something unusual though. Corner Market was shuttered. I tried LuAnn on her cell, but she didn't answer. I let myself in with the key she keeps hidden by the service door and left the pies on the counter with a note."

"What? Corner Market isn't open for business? That's not like LuAnn." Kate put her hands on her hips and worried at her lip with her teeth. "You don't think she's sick with that flu going around?"

Rosie volleyed her a blank look as she affixed a hairnet over her blonde curls. "What flu?"

"Instead of streaming music, you ought to listen to the news occasionally, Rosie," Kate chastised, picking up the TV remote by the cash register to choose a cable news channel. "Maybe the media is making a bigger deal of it than they should, but Bud looked awful when he came in earlier. He was so sick he had to turn around and leave."

The TV host interviewed a taciturn epidemiologist who said, "The origin of this particular strain remains unknown. The WHO is tracing patient zero somewhere in Southeast Asia. Details remain murky. There's been conjecture that it originated as few as thirty-six hours ago. Since it's already here, we know it's highly contagious and aggressive—"

The broadcast was gone, and the president appeared onscreen, seated behind his desk in the Oval Office. "My fellow Americans, it's with great gravity I address you today. Last night citizens began falling ill in massive numbers along the southeastern coast. I've spoken with state governors, and we are coordinating a nationwide shelter-in-place effective six o'clock Eastern Standard Time. I urge you to refrain from panic buying—"

Rosie's cell phone trilled from her trouser pocket. Still watching the TV, she fished for her phone. She glanced at Caller ID, then at Kate, paling. "It's the middle school."

Alternating between the president's address and Rosie's conversation, Kate's guts turned to ice. Perhaps all the hubbub was justified—she'd seen enough disaster movies to be worried. Propelled by Rosie's unsteady hands as she spoke to the school nurse, Kate moved to lock the shop door and flip the *open* sign to *closed*, adrenaline making her wobble. She had shucked her apron and was flicking the power switch on the coffeemaker when Rosie ended the call.

The distress Kate felt was mirrored in Rosie's eyes. She whispered, "I've got to fetch the twins. Robbie's got a fever of a hundred and four, and Jeff's asthma is kicking up."

CHAPTER THREE

KATE STOOD IN THE MIDDLE OF THE KITCHEN, TAPPING HER THIGH with an index finger. She was at a loss. Rosie had flown out the back door to go pick up her twins from school, but Kate couldn't focus on any one distinct task.

Her stomach gurgled, which made her think about food. She didn't have many groceries at her townhouse. Should she go to Corner Market? Take provisions from the bakery? She'd have to transfer the baked goods from the display to the freezer first. Kate consulted the clock. It was nearly eleven. She grabbed the pad of paper from the worktop and made a list. The first thing was *freeze items in display case*. Once that was done, she called Dierdre.

Voicemail picked up on the sixth ring. Kate explained that due to the shelter-in-place mandate, she'd put a refund in the mail for Dierdre's catering order. Sealed envelope in hand, Kate was unlocking the front door when her cell rang. It was Ben. "Where are you?"

"Still at work. Why?" She stuck the envelope partway in the pink mailbox attached to the black-painted brick storefront.

It was like Kate was invisible. People strode by, frowning, their steps purposeful. A woman brushed Kate as she went by, saying crossly to her companion, "At least we have some time to shop before the lockdown nonsense. Talk about overreacting."

Ben asked, "You know I'm friends with Jocelyn Stein, the Deputy Commissioner at the Department of Health, right?"

Kate latched the door then leaned a shoulder on it. "You've mentioned Jocelyn. What does she say about this flu? Is it really *that* bad?"

"Worse than bad. People are dropping like flies." Ben sounded rattled, which wasn't like him at all. That gave Kate pause.

"But people die of the flu every year, don't they?"

"Within hours of contracting it?" Now he was annoyed, even angry. "You have to understand—we have a vaccine for seasonal flu. We don't for this strain. Joss says they think this stays airborne for at least an hour. *An hour.* You need to wear a mask when you leave the bakery—do you have one?"

"I don't think so. I have a scarf, somewhere, that I can tie up... God, this is *surreal*."

"Wear it. And wash your hands. Or use hand sanitizer, in a pinch. You can wear gloves as long as you're careful not to cross-contaminate." There was commotion over the line and then dead air.

"Ben? You there?"

"I'm here. Driving. Fuckin' insanity on the road. Idiot almost broadsided me!"

"Be careful," Kate urged. She craned her neck to witness the activity at the end of the block. It was Mr. Gonzalez from the Mexican Grocery and a middle-aged ash blonde woman with a stiff, helmet shaped hairdo. It was hard to tell what was happening, but he was trying to take something from her. Had she stolen from his store? She kneed Mr. Gonzalez in the groin before running off. He crumpled to the sidewalk in a fetal position. Pedestrians scurried past without helping. "Some lady just attacked Mr. Gonzalez! Let me see if he's alright. Hold on."

Phone held to her ear by her shoulder, Kate unlocked the

door but stilled when Ben shouted, "Don't! I mean it. Don't interact with anyone. They could be asymptomatic. Fuck. I'm swinging by for you. We're going to my parents' farm. My family is rallying there."

Predictably, Kate's first instinct was to withdraw. She said emphatically, "No, Ben. I can take care of myself."

"I don't want to argue about this. Now's not the time to assert your independence."

"If I go anywhere, I should drive to Colliers Junction to be with my sister." Quarantining with twenty strangers was out of the question. Even dealing with her stuffed shirt brother-in-law would be preferable.

"Colliers Junction?"

"Upstate New York."

"Oh, right. Where you grew up. But that's hours from Clayton's Corners. You'd have to take I-81. Could be dicey. I'd use back roads, but what if you have a breakdown or run out of gas?"

"I filled up yesterday..." She heard raised voices outside the bakery. An Asian fellow no less than eighty quarreled with a middle-aged man whose arms were filled with packages of toilet paper. The elderly man wagged a finger at him but was prodded aside with an elbow as the younger man plowed by and continued down the sidewalk. The fellow massaged his sternum with the heel of his hand, scowling. He caught Kate's eye and shook his head in disgust.

"Kate?"

"Two men were arguing about *toilet paper* outside Buttercream," Kate murmured, chewing her thumbnail. It was inconceivable. People were acting like animals!

"Get away from the windows. You don't want to draw attention to the bakery. I've heard reports of looting on the radio." Ben paused. "Look, I'm about to turn off Route 9. I need to know whether to turn left to come get you or right for the farm."

Kate hustled through the kitchen to the matchbox-sized office she and Rosie shared, her mind racing. "You go on to your folks' place. I'll manage."

Ben exhaled noisily. "Stubborn as usual. Promise me you'll drive straight to your townhouse. That you won't leave unless absolutely necessary."

She put her hand behind her back, crossing her fingers. "Sure. I'll text you later, okay?"

Kate found the emerald-green pashmina she'd bought because it matched her eyes hanging on the back of the office door. Her whole body was shaking—her blood sugar must be low. She went to the commercial fridge in the kitchen and chugged orange juice from the carton.

Think. Think! She pulled out plastic bags with handles from the supply shelf and filled them with items from the fridge and walk-in freezer. Frozen juice and frozen fruit. Eggs. Heavy whipping cream. She scrounged through the cabinets and found nuts, seeds, dehydrated fruit, chocolate, granola.

Folding and tying the scarf over her face, she loaded the bags in her black minivan. The alley was silent, but voices echoed from a block over. Somebody screamed. Heart hitching, Kate went back inside and washed her hands with soap. The urge to move was overwhelming. She thought about the men fighting over the toilet paper and carted the unopened packet from the supply closet to the van.

Kate hefted a fifty-pound bag of flour and wrestled it into the trunk of her van, followed by a smaller sack of sugar. *Boy, I'm gonna feel dumb if I have to bring this stuff back once things settle down.* Still, erring on the side of caution, she snagged a box of vinyl gloves and the economy-size bottle of hand sanitizer when she left.

She pumped sanitizer into her palms and rubbed them together before getting behind the wheel. Slouching in the seat for a minute to gather herself, Kate pulled the scarf down and took a deep breath. She was starving. Tearing open the bag of granola from the passenger seat, she scooped a fistful and shoveled it in her mouth, washing it down with a half-full bottle of water she'd left in the cup holder the day before.

Kate started the van and tuned to radio WVIA. Half-listening to the news, she drove to the end of the alley. The streets were nearly deserted now—barely anyone was about. She turned right onto Main Street. Bud lived on the outskirts of Clayton's Corners, east of the Save-A-Bunch discount store. Kate wanted to check on him.

The westbound highway was much busier than her eastbound side. Kate wondered why. Traffic clogged as she approached Save-A-Bunch. She braked so the car ahead of her could turn into the shopping center. Vehicles queued at the gas station on the other side of the street, extending into the roadway and obstructing the flow of traffic. People filled not only their automobile tanks but gas cans. Drivers in line were impatient as they waited, laying on their horns and yelling out their windows.

Kate's mouth parted. At Save-A-Bunch's double doors, crowds of shoppers swayed like weeds in the wind as they pushed and shoved. A truck beeped behind her. Starting, she gave the driver an apologetic wave, but with a roar of his engine, he veered around her, using the grass shoulder and kicking up dirt and rocks. He gave Kate the middle finger as he edged in front of her van.

Trembling, Kate put her foot down on the accelerator, anxious to reach Bud's house, and ultimately her own. She'd never been to his place, but she recalled him telling her about his distinctive mailbox on Sprindle Avenue. There it was! The metal cat-shaped mailbox was painted bright orange. The plaque that hung from its neck read *Bradley*.

At the end of a lengthy gravel lane was a boxy ranch with faded tan siding. Bordered by overgrown greenery, the dwelling had a neglected air. Bud's pickup sat in front of the attached garage. Parking, Kate tied the scarf over her face and slid on a pair of vinyl gloves from the bakery.

She pounded on the front door, peeking through the glass inserts. She could see into the living room, but there was no sign of life. "Bud?"

On impulse, Kate tried the doorknob. It was unlocked. The door squeaked on its hinges as it swung inward. She hesitated before stepping over the threshold. It felt wrong to enter uninvited, like she was an intruder. The house reeked of wood rot and mothballs—and something unidentifiable. Foul. "Bud?"

He lay prone in the hallway. His skin was waxy. Coagulated trails of blood and mucus oozed from his eyes, nose, and mouth. There was a puddle of slimy liquid on the cracked linoleum floor beneath him. A repugnant stench drifted up, unlike anything Kate ever smelled before. Saliva and gastric juices pooled on her tongue. She tried to swallow them away.

Staggering out of the house, Kate yanked her scarf off. Bending at the waist, she retched into the grass. Partially digested granola projected from her mouth and nose in vile, viscous chunks. Kate's eyes watered and her sinuses and throat burned from the acid. Her abdominal muscles painfully contracted until there was nothing left to heave.

CHAPTER FOUR

"Oh my God. Oh my God. Oh my fucking God," Kate gasped. Her cheeks and chin were wet with tears and snot and bile. The world spun. She fell to her knees and dug her gloved fingers into the soil to keep tethered to the earth.

A cool breeze stirred, ruffling her hair. She tilted her head back and squinted at the sun. In the leafy canopy of the trees surrounding the property, goldfinches flew from branch to branch and twittered. Kate felt fuzzy, disconnected, like her soul was floating. If she pinched herself, would she wake from the nightmare?

What do I do now?

Think, for crying out loud!

She hadn't seen anything as grisly since discovering her parents' bodies. Bud's lifeless form triggered flashbacks of memories long repressed.

Kate screwed her eyelids shut, hyperventilating. She was unable to quash the mental picture of her mother's body on the living room floor. Momma's head missing above her jawline. Her brain matter splattered on the wall. The rank odor permeating the air.

With a sound of anguish, Kate stripped off her gloves and

delved into her jean pocket for her phone. Her fingers fumbled when she punched Nine-One-One.

A robotic voice intoned, "All circuits busy. Please hang up and—"

"Shit," Kate panted. She redialed but received the same recording. Putting the heel of her hand to her forehead and rubbing, she understood. She was on her own. "Okay. Alright."

She stumbled to her van and got another pair of gloves from the box, then fastened her scarf over her mouth and nose. Straightening her shoulders, Kate reentered the house. She grabbed the crocheted afghan from where it lay folded lengthwise on the back of the couch, ignoring her nausea and covering Bud. She whispered hoarsely to his corpse, "I'm so sorry."

She needed to find Ollie. Bud had often talked about his wife's deaf tabby and his pledge to nurture the cat when she'd passed. Kate wouldn't leave without him.

Ollie was curled up on the guest bed, blissfully unaware anything was amiss. He was raw-boned, his ginger-colored coat ratty from age. She put him to her breast. Blinking at her with rheumy eyes, he sagged into her and purred. Kate wasn't a cat-lover, but she couldn't help pitying him. Now that Bud and his wife were gone, Ollie was like her—an orphan. She murmured to him in a soothing tone, making her way around the bed to the hall. Kate looked thoughtfully at the gun cabinet by the closet as she went by.

Latching the sliding door to her van, she gnawed on her cheek, warring with herself. Was Nine-One-One jammed from generalized chaos or downright anarchy? The desire to possess a firearm was an alien concept, but Kate had seen people's outrageous behavior. Though the thought of firing a gun made more bile rise in her throat, she was no fool. She needed to be able to protect herself. To be prepared.

Taking things without permission wasn't in Kate's comfort zone, but practicality won out. Bud wouldn't begrudge her. Decision made, she marched back inside and opened the cabinet.

She figured some were rifles and some were shotguns but couldn't distinguish which was which. There were handguns too, and boxes of ammunition. In her eagerness to flee, Kate hurried to load her van.

The drive back to Clayton's Corners was nerve-wracking, rendering Kate edgy. She blasted the vents to rid the putrid scent of puke and death from her hair and clothes. WVIA's special coverage was interrupted at intervals with recorded transmissions. "This network has issued an emergency notification for the state of Pennsylvania. This communication is at the request of the Pennsylvania State Police and Department of Emergency Management in cooperation with the federal government and The Center for Disease Control. The local authorities have issued a warning for the subsequent counties..."

Kate's mouth became dry as she listened.

"Columbia, Luzerne, Lackawanna..."

"Fuck!"

"An unknown virus has now spread nationwide. Symptoms include but aren't limited to vomiting, headache, fever, body aches, fatigue, nausea, joint stiffness, and discharge of mucus from the ears, nose, and throat. Hospitals are overwhelmed. Social unrest has been reported."

As time inched closer to six when the lockdown was officially set to begin, the palpable charge in the air became increasingly frenzied. A sedan beside her van cut off an SUV, and the SUV's driver gunned his engine, giving chase. Kate watched in horror as both vehicles pulled to the shoulder. When the SUV's driver beat the other with a tire iron, she looked away, her intestines knotted.

Clinging to the steering wheel, she slammed on the brakes as a fuel tanker swerved in her path. Her van shuddered and fishtailed. Once she'd regained control, Kate considered Ollie on the passenger's side floorboard. The ancient cat slept, unconcerned. Her armpits prickled at the close call.

Societal collapse within a day. How could it be? It was incomprehensible.

She had to get home—she was pressing her luck being out this long. Kate drove as fast as she dared. Only when she was parked in her garage did she relax. Her chest hurt from holding her air. She released it in a giant *whoosh*. God, she felt drained. Reclining her head on the headrest, Kate's eyelashes fluttered.

She jolted awake several minutes later when Ollie jumped on her lap. *Jesus Christ!* Kate put a hand to her temple in dismay, blinking. She'd fallen asleep without turning off the van. She could've gassed herself!

While unloading the food, supplies, and weapons, Kate cursed her carelessness. Understandably, the day had taken its toll, but by the time she'd unpacked everything, her brain buzzed. Stripping off her clothes in the garage and chucking them in the garbage bin, Kate walked naked through the house. She turned the shower on as hot as she could stand. She felt defiled. The rancid perfume of death and vomit seemed permanently bonded to Kate's nostrils—she couldn't get clean enough.

Toweled off and cloaked in her robe, Kate switched the living room TV on to WPAL and propped her elbows against the breakfast bar. Like earlier on the radio, the coverage alternated between breaking news reports and an Emergency Alert System broadcast. The newscasters looked as shell-shocked as Kate felt.

"This is unlike anything we've ever seen. The rate people are getting sick and dying is… it's unprecedented." The anchor shook his head and raked a hand through his hair. "The CDC's amassing data as I speak, but they posit this highly contagious strain has a mortality rate of…" He gulped. "Seventy to eighty percent, or more."

Face graying, the man faltered and wilted to the floor. Offscreen, somebody cried out. His coworkers rushed to carry him away.

A young woman dressed in a t-shirt and khakis took his place. "I'm afraid I'm the only one left here, besides the cameraman." Tears glistened in her eyes as she read a teleprompter. "Those who aren't infected are lawless, scavenging for supplies. Their only objective—survival. The panic isn't confined to the US. Major cities overseas are also filled with mayhem." Images flashed on the screen of looting and violence in the streets of Paris, Rome, London, and Sydney, amongst others.

"Oooh," Kate muttered, gaze glued to the screen.

"County General is urging the infected to isolate at home." Onscreen, quick snippets of images panned. A doctor consoling a keening nurse. Dead bodies drooping in waiting room chairs. Just beyond the emergency room entrance, an ambulance was on its side. A close-up of a paramedic still in the driver's seat showed bloody mucus staining his uniform. Kate turned off the TV and paced, hands clasping and unclasping.

"Connie. I've gotta call Connie." She dialed her sister's number but there was only a rapid busy signal. Kate typed a message instead. *Con, call me ASAP!* The text wouldn't send. Powerlessness washed over Kate, and she put her head in her hands. Tumbling down to the kitchen floor, she sobbed until Ollie nudged her with his nose.

Kate wiped her face on the sleeve of her robe and situated the cat on her lap. "Poor thing. I didn't mean to scare you. Bet you're hungry." Then it occurred to her—she'd forgotten to search for cat food or litter at Bud's house.

After mincing deli ham on a plate, Kate filled a bowl with water. While Ollie ate, she emptied a box she found in her closet and shredded a newspaper she hoped he'd use in lieu of proper litter. The idea of going out for cat supplies was unthinkable. She would worry about that later.

Once dressed in old sweats, Kate coiled her hair into a clip. Nervous energy propelled her to clean her townhome from top to bottom. She mopped, vacuumed, washed linens, and sanitized surfaces. Sporadically, she'd peek out the front door spyhole to the sidewalk and her driveway, but everything was tranquil.

Craving fresh air, Kate stepped out the balcony doors to her second-floor deck overlooking the complex's courtyard and pool. The security lamps threw light on the concrete patio and the moonlight reflected on the placid surface of the water. Nothing moved. Beneath Kate's unit was storage, and the home on the left side was vacant. She speculated about her neighbor on the other side, Mrs. Ferguson. Typically, Kate heard the hum of her TV through the bedroom wall, but tonight there was nothing. Did Mrs. Ferguson lay dead in her bed?

When she felt faint, Kate realized she needed to eat. She assembled a sandwich, Ollie on her lap while she ate. After eating she turned on WPAL, but the cameras rolled on a deserted studio. Kate was beginning to nod off when her phone rang. She leaped to snatch it from where it charged on the counter. The Caller ID read *Constance Halloran Metzger*.

"Connie? You okay? The baby?"

"Yes. Seth and I are quarantining. And you? Are you symptomatic?"

"No, thank God, although I was exposed." Kate swallowed, throat clogging with tears. "How can this be happening? And so fast? The virus is *everywhere*."

"TV reports are done, probably permanently." Connie paused. "Look, it's no secret you and Seth aren't bosom buddies, but I think you best head up to Mayfly Hollow, Kate."

CHAPTER FIVE

ANNOYANCE SURGED AT THE MENTION OF SETH. ANXIETY AND weariness made Kate short-tempered enough to snap, "I'll bet he's eating this pandemic up with a spoon. You guys may just be able to put that bunker to use after all."

"You'll benefit from our prepping, too," Connie pointed out. "Don't be a brat."

Kate swallowed. *Why am I acting like this?* She mumbled, "Sorry, Con."

"He isn't an easy man, but give him some credit. Despite your ugliness, Seth says as your brother-in-law he has an obligation to you. You're pretty damn fortunate if you ask me."

"I said sorry." Kate sat down on the sofa. "Did any of Seth's family come to the farm?"

"No, they have their own contingency plans. When you get here, we have a cabin for you to quarantine in. Seth says fourteen days is mandatory."

Seth says, Seth says, Seth says. If Kate had a nickel for every time Connie uttered those words, she'd be a billionaire. "*If* I come to Colliers Junction, you mean."

Connie mewed in aggravation. "Why wouldn't you?"

"You know I take care of myself." Kate tried not to come across bitchy. It was the truth, wasn't it?

"You're like a broken record with that lone wolf BS."

"Well, facts are facts. I learned early on in life that the only one I can depend on is me."

"I was only eighteen when Momma and Dad died. I did the best I could raising you," Connie lamented. "Can't you ever forgive me?"

Kate bit her lip, trying to curb her resentment. Why was it bubbling up now? "How many fifteen-year-olds have to hunt their sister down at her dealer's house? How many have to pull a needle from her arm and call an ambulance because she's overdosed for the third time?"

"Now you see why I rarely call," Connie said. "Kate. I was young. I made mistakes. I've apologized for my shortcomings and turned my life around. What else can I do? You ought to be grateful Seth came into our lives and created order from the chaos."

Kate didn't speak. Talking about Seth ordinarily made her irrational, but now the notion of dealing with him was unbearable. She thought she'd grown enough to put her past behind her but perhaps not. Teardrops spilled from her eyes.

"You there?"

She couldn't get the image of Bud's dead body from her mind. When Kate answered, her voice quavered. "I-I found my friend dead today, and I'm not coping so good."

"Seth says this is end times. A plague. He says we must prepare ourselves for the worst." Connie paused. "I don't want you to stay in your townhome all by yourself—you should be with your family. Come to Mayfly Hollow. Please."

After the call, Kate curled up on the couch. She was able to send texts to Rosie and Ben but got no response. Falling into a drugged slumber, Kate didn't wake until she heard the insistent bleep of the EAS from the TV. Wiping the crust from her eyelids, she blinked at it, but it was the same recording as earlier.

When she woke again, the sun was high in the sky, and Ollie yowled for food. Kate chopped the last of the ham for him. She ate dry cereal from the box and drank milk from the carton. Peeking out the deck door as she chewed, Kate found the grounds undisturbed. When she turned, she pursed her lips. Ollie squatted on the kitchen floor. "Guess you don't love your litter box, huh? Great."

That wouldn't do.

After cleaning the floor, Kate consulted her phone to see if she had any texts from her friends. There were none, but the internet was functioning.

Bracing herself, she sorted through Bud's firearms until she found a handgun. She did an online search for how to load and use a handgun for beginners. Scrolling through the results, she clicked on an instructional video discussing a gun like Bud's. There was plenty of talk about slides, rounds, and magazines. The bullets required for her gun were nine-millimeter. Organizing the boxes of ammunition she'd stacked on top of her fridge, Kate was relieved to locate a full box.

The gun was on the counter where she'd left it. Kate replayed the video. Hands damp, she picked up the gun and mimicked the instructor's actions. Kate learned how to remove the magazine to assess it. It was loaded with nineteen rounds. She pushed the slide backward and inspected the chamber to make sure it was clear, replacing the magazine. The guy on the screen said not to rack the slide until she wanted a bullet in the chamber and not to put her finger on the trigger until she was ready to fire. Kate eagerly flipped on the safety and put the firearm back on the counter. Would she have the cojones to fire it if necessary?

I guess I'll find out...

THE HANDGUN LAY on the passenger's seat of her minivan. Kate backed out of her garage slowly, scanning the complex. There was no movement other than the wind rustling the leaves in the trees. The ten-minute drive to LuAnn's Corner Market lasted forever. Kate had to negotiate around stalled vehicles along Highway 12. Many were unoccupied, the doors left ajar. Some contained dead bodies. Kate avoided looking too closely.

Downtown Clayton's Corners showcased destruction. Dead lay on the street and on the sidewalk. The shell of a torched truck sat outside Mr. Gonzalez's shop, black smoke curling in the air like a question mark. The hardware store across from Butter-cream had obviously been looted. The door stood open, broken merchandise spilling outside. The plate-glass windows were shattered. The streets were like a film set for an apocalypse movie. As a kid, Kate had seen spooky episodes of *The Twilight Zone*. What if she was the sole survivor? She smothered the panic such thoughts brought and compartmentalized.

Kate had one goal—to get the needed supplies from LuAnn's Corner Market and get the hell out of Dodge.

The main entrance of the market was shuttered. Kate circled the building. Reassured she was alone, she parked in the alleyway by the delivery entrance. Affixing her scarf, Kate timidly placed the gun in her purse before getting out of her van. She eyed the alley, afraid to be snuck up on.

Finding LuAnn's spare key in its usual hiding spot, she slipped inside, turning the deadbolt. Kate hesitated. It wasn't the first time she had been there when the store was empty—she'd often made early morning deliveries, but this was different. Weird. Not intending to dawdle, Kate didn't bother turning on the overhead lights.

Wheeling a cart past the customer service desk, she noted the stacks of pies Rosie had left there yesterday. She went down the pet aisle and loaded up cat supplies. Kate hurried to gather groceries. After packing her purchases in her van, she returned her cart to the corral by customer service. The place was creeping her out.

Kate abruptly halted when she heard a thud and shuffling

coming from the manager's office beside the customer service counter. Mouth parched and sweat beading her lip, Kate made her way to the closed door. She squeaked, "LuAnn?"

Kate took a steadying breath. Hoping it wasn't the stupidest thing she'd ever done, she brought her hand to the doorknob.

CHAPTER SIX

SOMETHING BLOCKED THE DOOR. KATE PUT HER SHOULDER TO IT, forcing it open. She stilled when the stench assaulted her sinuses. She knew that smell. The same stink had emanated from Bud's corpse. Gagging, Kate reeled back.

The bumps and thumps coming from the office hadn't ceased. Something was *alive* in there. Kate identified the shuffling as footsteps. "LuAnn? I-is that you?"

A figure appeared in the doorway, its steps stiff. The carrot red hair and flowery muumuu belonged to LuAnn, but it wasn't LuAnn. In the dim light Kate saw the colorless, mottled skin. The dried mucus and blood.

The foul odor misted like fog, infusing the air.

An involuntary wail of terror left Kate's throat. LuAnn swiveled her head. Her irises were no longer brown. Now they were milky and bloodshot.

Squatting, the creature moved into position like a high school track and field sprinter. She vaulted forward toward Kate. With a squeal, Kate turned on her heel and ran, the beast in pursuit. She rounded the corner of the bread aisle and dove behind the butcher's case, heart ratcheting painfully against her ribcage.

The beast banged into a shelf, knocking loaves of bread from an end cap. She made snuffling grunts, like she was trying to trace Kate by scent. *What the fuck?* Crouching down, Kate duck-walked to the other end of the meat cooler, gingerly lifting the hinged counter by the produce section. *If I can just sneak through here and get back to the alley delivery door...*

The hinges squeaked just enough to make Kate's heart ram into her throat. She paused, listening.

It happened in slow motion.

LuAnn went airborne, her body landing on the top of the glass meat case with a thunderous clunk. She crouched like a gorilla, swinging her head back and forth while delicately sniffing the air. Her snapping teeth made terrifying clacks. Stifling a scream, Kate raced past the produce section, digging in her pocket for the door key as she ran. She was keenly aware of the loud wallop as the creature plunked to the floor and gave chase.

She didn't dare take time to look over her shoulder to gauge LuAnn's progress. Kate was so focused she nearly didn't see the towering pyramid of stacked soup. Inspiration struck. She swept an arm across the display as she sped past. Cans crashed and skittered on the tile, rolling in every direction. Then there was the satisfying clatter of the creature tripping and floundering.

Frantically twisting the deadbolt to unlock it, Kate escaped to the safety of the alley. She forced the door shut. With frenetic fingers, she rammed the key into the lock and secured it just as the beast hurtled into the door. In the glass insert on the upper portion of the door, Kate got a close-up view of what once had been LuAnn.

Fascinated, Kate examined the creature. Behind the window, LuAnn snorted and drooled, lifting her nose. From the corner of Kate's eye, she caught a flash of something and turned to look, her chest rising and falling as she wheezed. A mob of infected shambled at the mouth of the alley. She recognized the portly figure of Mr. Gonzalez in the crowd, his apron bloodied. His head spun, his teeth knocking together. His companions froze.

"Oh, you've got to be kidding me," Kate gasped, scrambling for her car keys. Where was her purse? Lost inside. The gun was in it, but she'd clipped the keyring to her belt loop.

Hysteria tearing at her throat, she unlocked the driver's side door to her van. Diving into the seat, she jammed the key into the ignition, her gaze on the rearview mirror. The hum of the engine spurred the creatures. They sprung into the alley as if on pogo sticks. Mr. Gonzalez led the pack as they tore toward the van. Kate threw the shifter to drive and burned rubber. They got closer and closer, until she turned onto Main Street. She put distance between them, and, by degrees, they got tinier in her mirror. The pack came to a standstill.

She'd outfoxed them.

With a cry of relief, Kate swiped a hand across her lip to wipe away the moisture beaded there. The scarf! It was gone. She whimpered. Maybe she was already infected. She'd end up just like LuAnn. She'd be a sniffing creature. Feral. Savage. Animalistic. Clicking her teeth as she killed indiscriminately.

Kate gripped the steering wheel until her fingers ached. She was spiraling out of control. *Knock it off. Get your shit together.*

Southbound on Highway 12, Kate drove on the shoulder. She kept her speed low, avoiding stalled vehicles. She was alert for any sign of life. In the cars, dead people clamored against the seatbelts restraining them. From the road, a hulk of a man rose shakily to his feet. Suddenly supercharged, he flung himself onto the hood of her van. He battered on the windshield, and Kate shouted, yanking the wheel and hitting the gas. He clung on by the wipers.

She slammed a foot on the brake, and the van shimmied until it was motionless.

The ghoul somersaulted from the hood, taking a wiper blade with him. Gritting her teeth, Kate accelerated. The vehicle bounced over the corpse. She squinted at the rearview mirror to make sure he didn't get up.

Returning to her townhome on autopilot, Kate struggled to

comprehend the events at Corner Market and those on Highway 12.

This can't be happening!

The dead were rising.

What about Bud? Had he become one of them?

Her complex was as noiseless as when she had left it. Kate parked in her garage stall, confirming the door safely shut behind her. She pinched her cheek between her teeth, biting down to keep from shrieking. *Plan, Kate, plan.* She'd pack and head to Colliers Junction. It was getting late. She'd better move. Pulling her cell from her jean pocket, she tapped out a text to Connie to let her know she was on her way. The text didn't send.

With a growl, Kate exited the van and put her phone back in her pocket. She stood with her hands on her hips, getting her bearings. She had a three-hour drive ahead of her. Making a mental list, Kate popped the hood. She checked the fluids—oil and windshield washer—topping them off.

Thoughts centered on her next task, Kate hurried from the service door up the stairway to the kitchen. At the landing, she halted. It was *in* her house—the reek she was beginning to know all too well. Anguish made tears well in her eyes. Kate swallowed hard, cautiously stepping into the kitchen.

Ollie's lifeless body lay on the kitchen mat in front of the sink, blood and mucus seeping into the fibers.

CHAPTER SEVEN

It was late afternoon by the time Kate departed her deathly still townhome complex. Turning right onto Meadowood Terrace, she shivered with loathing, thinking of how she'd failed Ollie. After bundling his body in a garbage bag, Kate had put his remains in the bin in the garage. *Poor fucking cat.*

She shook her head. Dragging a hand through her hair, she entered the northbound lane of Highway 12 and watched for any sign of the infected. Kate dreaded the lengthy voyage ahead —she knew she'd have to be constantly vigilant.

I-81 was bedlam. Abandoned cars littered the roadway. Contents of coolers and suitcases were scattered across the asphalt, impeding her progress. Corpses trapped in stalled vehicles detected Kate's van and launched toward windshields and windows, trying to break free. She kept the van to the berm instead of weaving through the melee, on the lookout for any creature that may be loose. It was slow going.

Two hours passed before she crossed into New York State, and her head pounded. She ate a cereal bar and washed it down with a warm soda, but the headache persisted.

Kate hoped to pick up a station, but there was nothing but static when she fiddled with the radio. She turned it off and dug in her pocket for her phone, speed dialing Connie's number. Busy signal. Stowing her phone, Kate almost didn't see the woman in her path. She frantically waved her arms, her face beseeching.

Teeth clenched, Kate debated what she should do. Her conscience tugged. "Shit."

Ensuring the doors were locked, Kate slowed. The woman trotted to the van's driver's side door. Her clothes were torn, her brunette hair was mussed, and she had a bloody nose. Kate cracked the window. The woman clawed at Kate's door, her eyes wild with fright. "Please! You've got to let me in! My husband—he's not my husband anymore. He attacked me—"

There was movement in the grassy area between the north and southbound lanes, then the van juddered as something smashed into it. Yelping, Kate stared open-mouthed. The woman slithered like a snake down the window, the horror etched on her face branding Kate's soul. Fingers scratching and scrabbling at the door handle, she disappeared from view.

Bloodcurdling screams filled the air.

Kate squashed her cheek against the glass to see what was happening.

A creature in a polo shirt fell upon the woman, jaw clicking as his teeth ripped into her neck. The muffled sounds of the woman's wet gasps and the creature's chewing amplified in Kate's ears. Blood spurted from the woman's jugular, spraying the side of the van. Then, she stopped moving.

Go!

Kate mashed her foot on the accelerator, and the van rocketed. When she hit a pothole, the steering wheel wrenched from her fingers. She seized the wheel, overcorrecting. The van fishtailed. Putting both feet on the brake, she pressed with all her weight. The back of the van skidded off the shoulder, shuddered, and stopped. The passenger's side tire teetered just over the edge of a drainage ditch.

Polo Shirt had gotten to his feet, blood from his kill dripping down his chin. He zeroed on the van. Kate's breathing hitched, and perspiration dotted her brow. "Ohhh."

Kate tapped the gas, trying to ease the van back onto the pavement. The front tires spun, unable to gain traction.

I'm dead!

He squatted, ready to pounce. Sending up a prayer, Kate punched the gas pedal to the floor. The engine roared, and the van found purchase. Lurching forward, it nearly plowed into a station wagon.

Kate drew a breath. Clumsily guided the vehicle to the hard shoulder. In the side mirror, she saw Polo Shirt leap toward her van, his arms outstretched. With a shriek, Kate took off. The tires squealed on the pavement. Missing the van by inches, he smacked facedown on the ground.

It took several minutes afterward for Kate to subdue her thoughts. Her whole body vibrated from the rush of adrenaline. Grabbing her soda from the cup holder, she swigged it, her gaze never straying from the motorway. She tried to come to terms with what just happened. *Idiot!* Kate knew she was making foolish choices. She was bushed. She'd need sleep—soon.

The sun dipped below the horizon, heralding nightfall. To her dismay, the low fuel light pinged. Normally a full tank was enough to get to Connie's, but the trip was taking twice as long as usual. *How did I not notice the gauge hovering above empty?*

An upcoming exit promised fuel, and Kate took it.

The gas station appeared deserted, but she didn't trust appearances. Everything was lit up—evidently electricity still functioned. She parked, leaving the vehicle idling and the door ajar. Wary for any sign she wasn't alone, Kate pumped gasoline. The station was bordered by thick forest, and the gathering twilight cast eerie shadows. Seconds lasted hours. Feeling exposed, she scanned the perimeter, her heartbeat painful in her ears. Tapping a foot, she willed the pump to hurry. "Come on!"

At last, the van's tank was full. Kate holstered the nozzle. She screwed on the cap, hearing footsteps running across the parking lot.

Without looking, Kate darted back into the van and put the shifter to drive. A group of creatures jumped on the van as she pulled out of the station. Some fell to the blacktop, but she heard the thumps overhead as one scuttled like a crab across the roof. Growling, Kate floored the accelerator until she was on the frontage road, and then stepped on the brake. "Get off, motherfucker!"

The beast sailed across the hood of the vehicle headfirst to the asphalt. Kate grasped the steering wheel as she trampled over it and continued on her way.

She drove for another hour. The high beams of the van's headlights cut a wide swathe of light in the inky darkness, but Kate's eyes were strained. She took a hand from the wheel to rub them. Her body begged for sleep. She bit her cheek to stay awake. She was still a good thirty minutes from Colliers Junction in normal driving conditions.

Her eyelids lowered, and Kate twitched awake. She had to find a secluded place to park for a few hours.

Taking the next exit, she traversed French Boulevard until she found a turn-off. The road looked like an old logging thoroughfare. In case Kate had to leave in a hurry, she turned the van around so it faced French. The windows sealed and the doors locked, she switched off the ignition and reclined her seat, succumbing to slumber.

When she opened her eyes again, it was dawn. Wondering what had woken her, Kate peered out the driver's side window. A grizzled man aimed a gun at her, its muzzle to the glass. Moaning, Kate sat up and put her hands in the air.

The man's voice came through the closed window. "Open the door."

She shook her head, incapable of speech. Was this how things were going to end?

"I'm commandeerin' your vehicle. Do you want me to kill

you? 'Cause you bet your titties I will. Git out." His voice was deadly calm. She knew he meant every word.

I'm fucked. It's over.

Tipping her head, Kate sighed. She slowly opened the door. Keeping her hands in the air, she slid from her seat, stumbling to the rutted ground. Numb with resignation, Kate said, "Don't shoot, please."

"I won't if you do what I say, lady."

She met his eyes and tried to appeal to his sense of decency. "You cannot just leave me in the middle of nowhere with no weapon. Let me drive you to where you need to go. Please."

"Nope. No dice." He scoffed, moving his head from side to side, "You think I trust you?"

Tears pooled, but she blinked them away. "I'm trying to make it to my sister... we can help each other."

His mouth compressed into an unyielding line. Gesturing with the gun, he motioned her to the rear of the van. "Move it or lose it, sweet cheeks!"

"If you leave me here, I'll have to walk," Kate cried. "How can I fend off those monsters with no weapon?"

"Here," he said, putting one hand to his belt. He unhooked an ax from a loop, lifting it to show her. He threw it past her into the weedy overgrowth. "Go git it."

Helpless, Kate stayed rooted in place. The man backed away, the gun still leveled at her sternum. Shoulders sagging with defeat, she heard the driver's door slam. Before the van turned onto French Boulevard, a window lowered, and a box of black-berry-flavored cereal bars and a bottle of water were tossed out.

"Thanks a lot, buddy," Kate muttered, spinning on her heel to comb through the weeds for the ax.

CHAPTER EIGHT

Hands wrapped around the ax handle, Kate rotated in a circle, deliberating. The air was cold and damp. Watery sunlight cut through the trees, making the dew glisten on the grass and the brush. The only sound was birdsong and her own breathing.

Burrowing into her pocket, she pulled out her phone. Full signal and plenty of battery. Tapping Connie's address into the phone's search bar, Kate selected hiking directions. She was in Upper Bremer, and Colliers Junction was eighteen miles away.

"Six fuckin' hours. You've gotta be joking," Kate said. Bending to snag the bottle of water and the cereal bars, she stuffed the bars into her jean pockets and wedged the water under her bra strap through the neck of her shirt. Abiding by the onscreen directions, she hiked parallel to the boulevard—off the pavement and just out of sight of any passersby.

As she walked, Kate fumed. Her transportation—gone. Her food, water, and supplies—gone. And Bud's weapons—gone. All her work for naught. Her carjacker really hit the jackpot with her. Her unluckiest day was that bastard's luckiest. All her efforts—a complete and utter waste. Kate wanted to weep but wouldn't allow herself the luxury.

Poky little houses painted in pastel hues were adjacent to the highway. Kate gave them a wide berth, keeping behind the scrubby brush and pine trees at the base of the gentle slopes of the Allegheny Plateau. When she came to more built-up areas, she sprinted from building to building, her pulse drumming in her throat.

Three and a half hours into her travels, the GPS directed her to walk through Mergenville, a town with a population of fifteen thousand people. "*Hell* no," Kate murmured. She skirted it, which added another hour to her journey.

Mid-morning, she took a break in a heavily wooded copse just beyond the highway. She plopped down at the base of a scraggly fir tree, her breath ragged.

Ax across her lap, she opened the last two cereal bars. They were smooshed from being in her pocket. She ate them off the wrapper, then drank half the water. After pulling burrs from her jeans, she rebraided her hair and got to her feet.

A twig snapped. Kate clutched her ax like it was a life preserver. She shrank against the tree trunk and swept her gaze over the woods. Not daring to breathe, she listened. Pine needles crunched. A shambling figure appeared, wandering through a thicket of brambles. The prickly overgrowth snagged his olive drab green uniform—he had been a forest ranger. Now, he was an *it*.

Kate tiptoed backward out of the glade and toward the road. It was too late. He had caught her scent. The creature lifted his nose, huffing the air. She figured he couldn't see her, but could he hear her? She stopped. Waited. When his teeth clacked, Kate gasped and ran.

He gave chase. Kate wove through the trees, hoping to trick him. She locked on a grouping of boulders in the distance, clustered like a rocky outcrop. He was gaining on her! Legs thrusting and heart banging, she made for the boulders. Afraid to waste time appraising his progress, she clambered to the top of the outcropping, the ax in her fist.

He stopped short at the base of the boulder Kate stood on.

The odor she now recognized reached her sinuses. She swallowed a gag, chest heaving and belly protesting. The creature stiffened, snuffling into the air.

Kate got into position. With a grunt, she brought the ax down on his cranium with all her strength. The blade cleaved clean through the skull, splitting it in half. Black blood and slimy brain tissue landed on her jeans and sneakers as he crumpled to the grass.

Kate chewed back her vomit. Her legs like jelly, she half-crawled and half-fell from the boulders. Panting, she wiped the ax blade on a bed of weeds to clean it then jogged out of the clearing.

When she had collected her wits enough, Kate took her phone from her pocket, assessing her progress with trembling fingers. Eight miles to Colliers Junction and her phone battery was near flat. It was all she could do to keep from dissolving into tears. Wearied and combat scarred, Kate's only option was to soldier on.

She trudged along highways and on dirt footpaths, past homes and through woodlands. All seemed peaceful. It was early afternoon when she came across a tan sedan next to the wooden welcome sign. *River Heights—A Little Town With A Big Heart. Population 6,000.* Seth and Connie lived just a couple miles north, and she'd been through the town many times before. Driving, she'd be to Connie's in minutes, but Kate had at least another hour's trek. She reckoned her feet were a bloody, blistered mess by the way they pained her.

Making sure the sedan was unoccupied, Kate sat in the driver's seat, securing the door behind her. There was a key in the ignition, but the car wouldn't start. Though the blood and brain matter were mere splatters on Kate's clothes, the unsavory fragrance overwhelmed the enclosed space. Her stomach grumbled with hunger anyway. Kate scoured the car for something to eat or drink—her mouth was dry as a desert. With a triumphant smile, she took the unopened can of cola from the passenger's floorboard and popped it open. She drank it all in one go. Wiping her lips with her sleeve, Kate squared her shoulders. If she ever wanted to get to Connie's, she had to *move*.

She'd avoided towns up until then, but Kate didn't have time for more detours. Nightfall was growing near. Knowing she was close to Colliers Junction gave her a second wind. She ignored the way her sneakers rubbed her heels and toes with each step. Ax in hand, she marched into town.

Kate observed a small horde of infected a block ahead by the post office. To keep space between them, she stole into an alley. Glancing over her shoulder to confirm they hadn't tracked her, she wasn't aware of the creature next to the dumpster until she was upon it.

She came to a swift halt, a scream caught in her throat. Dropping into a balanced stance, Kate readied the ax. It had been a chubby middle-aged woman with glasses. She wore a neon floral-print blouse and a black skirt. With a disinterested sniff, she bumped into Kate as she shuffled past. Suppressing a shiver of revulsion, Kate watched, mouth gaping, as she left the alley.

It was as if Kate were invisible.

A possibility hit Kate like a bolt of lightning—did the foul gore on her jeans and shoes cancel out her scent? Flabbergasted, she slouched against the building for a minute. If she could wear infected blood like camouflage, it would be a game changer. Kate decided she'd need further testing of her theory before she could put faith in it.

Making her way through the hushed downtown business district, Kate's gaze clapped on a familiar black minivan with a pink cupcake logo outside a pawnshop. She blinked. Could it be? Or was it a mirage?

Carefully creeping by storefronts, Kate advanced to the pawnshop. Crashing came from inside the store. She was willing to bet her carjacker was looting the place. Kate crouched low and dashed to her minivan. Sidling her way around the tailgate to the driver's door, she pulled the door handle. Locked.

She slunk back to the rear of the van. Poking her arm under the bumper, Kate glided her fingers over the dirty metal until she found what she sought—the magnetic key holder she'd secreted there months earlier for emergency use.

Kate opened the holder and snatched the key fob before sticking the holder back in its hiding spot. When she pressed *unlock* on the fob, the lights flashed. Wincing at the response it was sure to bring, Kate slipped into the driver's seat and jammed the key into the ignition. As she reversed, the carjacker materialized in the pawnshop doorway, gun in hand. Color high in his cheeks, he bellowed, lifting the firearm and aiming.

Whacking the shifter to drive, Kate put the pedal to the metal. He fired.

The back window shattered. Shrieking, Kate ducked. She whipped down Magnolia Avenue. In the rearview mirror she saw creatures encircle the man, and he fled into the shop.

Kate laughed, the thrill of victory surging in her chest.

Fuck you, dude.

CHAPTER NINE

"It's me. Kate."

She sounded as drowsy as she felt. Waiting for an answer from the intercom outside the mechanized iron gate, Kate regarded the fence with tired but inquisitive eyes. By design, the compound was at the end of a narrow, overgrown lane. It had been years since she'd been there, but the gate was new, as were the spotlights and sophisticated-looking surveillance cameras.

The intercom crackled to life and Connie said in her formal way, "I've been anticipating your arrival. Seth says he has your quarantine lodging set up. Come through, and hang a right until you come across cabins. Yours is the first one. Go directly there, and we'll chat with the walkie-talkie that's on the kitchen counter. Hurry. We don't like vehicles loitering at the entrance." Then she was gone, and the gate slid smoothly open.

Kate watched to make sure nothing followed her in as she pulled forward. When the gate latched, she bore right. Seth and Connie lived in the 1800s brick farmhouse at the apex of the ridge. The house was surrounded by outbuildings, a large red-painted barn behind it.

The van crunched on the gravel for about an eighth of a mile before Kate came to the row of three log cabins with solar-paneled green metal roofs. She parked at her assigned cabin and turned off the ignition.

For the first time in days, she felt truly safe. Hair tangled, outfit soiled with carnage, and feet throbbing, Kate got out of her vehicle and kneeled to kiss the ground.

Swiping away a tear, she sat back on her heels and closed her eyes for several seconds.

Her sneakers cut off her circulation as she hopped to the cabin's miniscule porch and pulled herself up the steps by the railing. The door was unlocked. Smelling of mildew from being closed up, the cabin's setup was similar to an old-timey roadside motel. The queen-size bed covered with a blue quilt dominated the room. A primitive-style timber desk and chair were tucked into an alcove by a compact bathroom with a fiberglass tub. In the other corner was a basic kitchenette with an apartment-sized fridge and stove. The walkie-talkie rested on a stack of clean clothing.

Kate opened a cabinet to find a drinking glass. She filled it at the tap, drank it down, and refilled it. Snagging the walkie-talkie, she went out to the porch. Carefully lowering her aching bones to a green plastic chair, she depressed the button on the side of the walkie and brought it to her mouth. "Con?"

"Did you see the clothes on the counter?"

"Yes."

"You're about to topple over, aren't you? Shower, and I'll send someone down with a plate of hot food. They'll leave it outside the door."

Kate recalled the black blood on her clothes. "Uh, my outfit got some blood on it. What should I do with it?"

Connie's tone was alarmed. "Blood? Are you hurt?"

"I-it's not mine. It's a long story, but I think we better throw my outfit and shoes away."

There was a moment of silence before Connie answered. "There are garbage bags under the sink. Put everything in one, and tie it up. I'll see to it that it's burned."

"Okay." Kate swallowed the sudden lump in her throat. Her voice was husky when she spoke. "Con... thanks. I mean it."

"I'm only doing what a sister should. Now go shower. The food will be there in fifteen minutes. Then rest. We'll talk tomorrow."

Kate finished her water and put her glass on the porch floor. Loosening the shoelaces on her sneakers, she tried to wriggle from them, but they were incredibly tight on her swollen feet. She had to brace her shoe on the edge of a stair and hold onto the wooden railing to force it off.

Her socks were crusted with dried blood at the heels and toes. When she peeled her socks from her feet, patches of skin came off. Breath hissed through Kate's teeth. She limped inside, each step agony, shutting and locking the door behind her. Stripping down, she put her clothes in the plastic bag from the roll under the sink. Her feet pained her so badly tears swam in her eyes. When Kate stepped into the shower, the water hitting her wounds made her cry out. She was glad nobody was there to hear her whimpers.

Draped in a towel, Kate went through the stack of clothing. Sweatpants, tee, sports bra, underwear, socks, and leather moccasins. There was a tube of lotion in the medicine cabinet. She lathered her feet with a thick layer of it before putting on the socks. Kate dressed fast, running the comb she'd found in the bathroom vanity through her hair before opening the door to drop the garbage bag of dirty clothing she held daintily by her fingertips. There was a tray on the doormat with a glass of milk and a plastic dome covered plate like the ones used for hotel room service. Kate's mouth watered as she brought it to the desk. Connie was an excellent cook, and she couldn't wait to see what was sent.

Slices of meatloaf were arranged on a hearty serving of mashed potatoes. There was a scoop of corn and a buttered roll. Kate lifted the fork on the tray and dug in. She made little noises of pleasure as she ate, demolishing the meal within minutes.

Crawling into bed, Kate fell into a deep sleep.

It was dark when Kate jerked awake. She was drenched in a cold sweat and disoriented. Where was she? Her feet protested when she sprang up. She fell back on the mattress. "Ow! Son of a bitch."

That's right. Mayfly Hollow. Kate shook her head. What day was it?

Tentatively, she stood and shuffled out to the tiny porch. The bag of sullied garments was gone. She took a seat in the plastic chair. The air was cool and silky smooth. It entered and exited her lungs effortlessly. Soon, her heartbeat slowed to a normal rhythm. Kate put her head back and considered the twilight sky. Indigo satin scattered with stars like moondust. She heard the lowing of cattle in the distance and nothing else.

Eyelids growing heavy, Kate crossed her arms over her torso and allowed herself to nod off, knowing she was sheltered by tall fences and security cameras. When she woke, it was dawn, and her clothes and hair were damp with dew. Mouth opening wide, Kate yawned. Male voices carried from the barn. It must be the hired help tending the animals.

Feet still tender, Kate hobbled around the kitchenette, heating a pan of water on the stove for the instant coffee she'd found in a cabinet. She took her mug and the walkie-talkie outside to the porch. After sipping some coffee, Kate felt more like herself. Running fingers through the tangles in her hair, she pressed the button on the walkie. "How many hours did I sleep?"

Connie's voice came on a minute later. "I don't know. Thirteen? How are you feeling?"

"Groggy, like I slept thirteen days. You wouldn't happen to have a jar of medicated salve or something, would you? My feet are like bloody stumps."

"Why would they be like bloody stumps?"

Kate's laugh was dry and humorless. "That's another story, Con."

"Hmm. I have a tincture of meadowsweet and calendula I made last summer with a homesteader friend. I'll send it down."

"Thanks. How are you? How's the pregnancy?"

"I'm fine. Twenty-nine weeks on Friday." She paused. "Imagine waiting years for the right time to start a family—then this crap."

"About that. You guys are cut off here. Do you... know what's going on?"

Kate heard Connie murmuring to someone else before she said, "Seth says he's heard some rumors over our ham radio. He says it's outlandish stuff."

"Listen, Connie—"

Seth came over the walkie. "Kathryn. I want to make something crystal clear from the outset. Everybody here contributes. There's no room for people that don't."

"Don't call me Kathryn." Kate counted to three before adding, "How about you give me a chance to contribute *or not* before coming at me, Seth?"

As if Kate hadn't answered, Seth continued, "We've got a bag of clothes needing repair. You can manage darning socks and sewing buttons on shirts, can't you?"

Pompous ass. "Yeah, I think I can *manage* sewing on a couple buttons. If you want to talk about contributing, I've got non-perishables, supplies, and guns in my van. Take 'em. They're yours. I wouldn't want you to think I'm taking advantage of your hospitality."

"Where did you secure guns?"

"I have my ways."

Seth seemed less antagonistic when he said, "Very well. Your contribution is noted, Kathryn—Kate. After your quarantine period ends, we'll have other jobs for you."

"Fine. But before you go any further, I think we need to talk about something else."

"What's that?"

"Connie says you've heard some rumors about what's going on out in the real world?"

Seth said, "Yes. Ridiculous yarns. I won't entertain such nonsense."

"You better entertain it, pal. With my very own eyes, I saw a corpse rip into a woman's jugular. It happened right in front of me..." When Seth didn't answer, Kate's lips screwed into an ugly smile. "Still believe it's nonsense?"

CHAPTER TEN

"Think I'm lying?" Kate demanded and then waited. Dead air. Typical. When challenged and unwilling to debate, Seth simply turned mulish and shut down. No amount of cajoling would make him engage if he refused to. It was one of the more irritating things about her brother-in-law. She gnashed her teeth. "You'll just have to learn for yourself."

"Are you experiencing symptoms?"

"No. I was exposed numerous times. Based on what I've seen, if I was going to get sick, I would've within a day of exposure. A two-week quarantine seems stupid, in my opinion."

"You could be asymptomatic and infectious. I won't allow you to break quarantine."

"Did I say anything about breaking it, Seth? Just deliver what needs mending to the front porch. Give me back to my sister."

There was silence, then Connie came on, saying gently, "You know he means well. He's troubled. Not only does the obligation of me and the baby wear on him, he's got six others—now seven, with you—to protect. It's all on his shoulders."

Kate got up and tottered inside so whoever was coming wouldn't come in contact with her. "I get it, but I saw things that you couldn't begin to fathom. Seth burying his head in the sand is gonna bite him in the ass—maybe literally."

"The minute we heard about the virus, we hunkered down. The only interaction we've had with outsiders was either over the phone or the radio..."

"That's precisely it! I. Saw. It. I'm not sure if everyone who dies comes back, and I don't know how quickly they do, but it's apparently damn quick!"

"Please," Connie implored, "calm down. You've been through some terribly distressing things, and you're not rational—"

Kate growled. Frustration, powerlessness, and anger gathered in her chest, as if in competition. How could she warn people if they refused to listen? "You know what, Connie? I wish it were all in my head. Maybe, like Seth, you need to see things for yourself. Until then, why don't you piss off?"

She threw the walkie onto the mattress. It bounced, tumbling to the floor. Kate flopped on the unmade bed and put her head in her hands. Images flashed through her mind, unbidden—Bud on the buckled linoleum. LuAnn's corpse stalking her through Corner Market. The lady on I-81 pleading for aid. The horror in her eyes haunted Kate.

Gasping, Kate fought for air—guilt and grief an icy band constricting her ribs. Why hadn't she understood the urgency? Why hadn't she let her into the van right away? *Next time someone begs me to help I will—*

Footfalls sounded on the porch stairs. Kate tiptoed to the window and shoved the gingham curtain aside. A tall, rangy man wearing a N95 mask placed a black garbage bag and a cardboard box on the doormat. As he pivoted to leave, he noticed her in the window. Tipping his brown Stetson, he stepped from the porch. He wore a western-cut flannel shirt and dark denims, his loose-limbed gait confident.

What was his story?

Kate brought the bag inside, then the box. Setting it on the desk, she rifled through it. A sewing kit, an assortment of paper-backs, a tea saucer of brownies covered with cling film, and a folded note. *I'm sorry. I do love you. Remember that. Con.*

Sniffling, Kate unpacked the garments, sorting them into piles.

DURING QUARANTINE, time moved at a sluggish pace. After Kate put the bag of patched garments on the porch, it was days before she got another task. She had the feeling Connie told Seth to go easy on her. There'd been no discussion about anything of substance—all conversation had been superficial. Nobody asked about the guns or supplies in her van. Kate read the paperbacks and ruminated. The safety she'd relished faded as she began to feel incarcerated.

When sacks of soil, cardboard egg trays, and packets of seed were left on the porch, Kate jumped at the opportunity to be productive. Planting the seeds in the trays, she tended them until seedlings grew. Then, she carefully placed them on the grassy patch in front of the porch, so they could be picked up.

Once her feet healed, Kate took evening strolls. She was careful to stay within sight of her cabin. The farm was situated on a cleared parcel of land where glaciation occurred hundreds of thousands of years earlier. The land wasn't particularly good for farming, although Kate knew Seth grew hay for his livestock. A short distance from the rear of Kate's cabin, the iron fence served as a barrier at the base of the rounded hills.

Late at night she would hear a dog's bark or a horse's neigh carry from the barn. The farm was in a bubble, insulated from the reality of the new world. It was easy to be lulled into a false sense of security.

Near the end of her confinement, Kate was woken by her cell phone ringing. She'd left it on the nightstand plugged into the spare charger from her minivan's glove compartment. The display said *Ben*. She accepted the call with frantic fingers.

"I've tried calling so many times. I can't believe I finally got through." His voice was weary. Flat. Emotionless.

She gripped the phone and propped against the headboard, nerves making her tummy somersault. "The internet doesn't work on my phone anymore, but occasionally I get bars. When I dial out trying to call you or Rosie, I lose service."

"Mine's working. The electrical grid's functional, too—but we're on borrowed time. There isn't anyone to maintain infrastructure anymore." He paused. "I'd assumed you were injured... or worse."

"I'm okay. I'm at my sister's. How are *you*? How's your family?"

Dead air. She held her breath, concerned they'd lose the connection. "Something's happening, Kate. Something I don't understand. It defies logic. I-I..."

"I know. I've seen them up close and personal." A shiver whizzed through her. "My trip up here was a goddamn nightmare. It took forever. Those *things* almost got me."

"At first, there were only a couple here and there. My brothers and I were able to fend them off, but in the last three days— they're organizing. Gathering." Ben coughed as if he were fighting tears. "My folks, two of my sisters, a niece, a nephew... they're gone. They got sick and died within twenty-four hours. M-my nephew got up and attacked my brother. I had to put him down."

"Oh no. Jesus. Where are you?"

"We're still at the farm. What's left of us. We boarded up the windows, but I see them outside through the slats. I tell you, Kate, they are gathering into hordes!"

The line crackled again. She rushed to say, "Listen to me— I've mentioned my sister's place." Kate rattled off the address. "If you can get up here—"

The signal was lost.

CHAPTER ELEVEN

IT TOOK KATE A LONG TIME TO FALL ASLEEP AGAIN. SHE FELT saddled by what Ben had told her. A millstone hung from her neck. She knew that smothering feeling—it was one she'd always avoided whenever possible—duty. Burdensome responsibility, both to Ben *and* those at the compound. This time, Kate couldn't ignore it. She was seriously contemplating driving back to Clayton's Corners, though the thought of it made the blood in her veins run cold. No doubt it would be a harrowing trek, one which may cost her her life.

What had Ben meant when he said the creatures were organizing? Did that mean they were capable of communication with each other? Was that why they clacked their teeth before attacking? Were they attracted by noise? There were so many unknowns. Anxiety licked at Kate's spine. Aware the only thing that would tame it was preparedness, she found her scrap of paper on the nightstand and added *practice shooting Bud's guns* to her list.

Water heated on the stove for coffee when Connie's voice came over the walkie. "How are you today?"

"I'm alright." Kate hesitated to tell her sister about her late-night phone call. When she tried talking to Connie about anything beyond the farm, Connie merely changed the subject.

"Tomorrow's the big day. You can come up to the house first thing and have breakfast with everyone. Then I'll show you around."

"Let me see if I can recite their names," Kate said. "There's Otis and his wife, Peggy. And Jamie and Judy and their daughter... What's her name?"

"Nora. She's ten. Judy homeschools her. Teller's our youngest hired hand. He's your age—thirty. Tomorrow afternoon you can help me bake bread. I do that twice a week. We go through it fast around here."

"I'll drive the van up. I've got those supplies I want to give you. What are you up to today?"

"Canning. I've got a bushel of tomatoes—over fifty pounds worth—to process."

Kate frowned. "Where did you get tomatoes this time of year?"

"We have a hydroponic garden in an outbuilding. We set it up last year."

"Hydroponic?"

"The roots grow in water. We use LED lights and that way we have fresh produce year-round. I planted a root vegetable garden out back, too. You'll see tomorrow."

―――

KATE FINISHED IRONING patches on the hole-y knees of jeans. She neatly folded them back into the milk crate and lay the cool iron on top. Opening the door, she put the crate on the porch, catching sight of the gangly man in the flannel shirt she'd seen before. He no longer wore a mask. Clean-shaven and handsome in a nonconventional way, he ambled down the gravel road as if he hadn't a care in the world, an Australian Shepherd trailing behind. As he came toward the cabin, Kate leaned on the doorjamb.

He stopped at the bottom step, tipping his hat in greeting. The dog mounted the bottom stair but froze and settled on his haunches when the man commanded, "Heel, Ace."

"You Jamie or Teller?"

His irises were the bluest blue she'd ever seen. They blazed against his suntanned skin. "Teller."

"I'm Kate Halloran. Connie's sister."

"I know. The baker. Stubborn and hard-headed. We've heard all about you." Teller's grin was crooked, and he spoke with a lazy drawl. When his gaze swept over her, Kate blushed.

She narrowed her eyes before answering. "Seth been bitching about me?"

Teller chuckled. "Seth is Seth, but Connie talks about you all the time."

Kate didn't say anything for a minute. "Really."

"It ain't like that." He didn't lose his grin. Putting his hands up, Teller said, "What I'm wonderin' is if you're as great a baker as your sister promises."

Kate's mouth quirked. There was something about his laid-back, unruffled disposition that drew her in. "You play your cards right, and maybe you'll find out, cowboy."

He lifted an eyebrow and inserted a thumb in a belt loop. "Wanna go for a walk?"

"My quarantine's not done yet."

"Shoot, it will be in the morning anyhow. What difference can twelve hours make? C'mon." He waited while she slipped into her moccasins. Slamming the cabin door, Kate joined him. Ace wagged his tail, nudging his nose into her hip. Teller said, "You can pet him. He won't nip."

Kate shook her head without meeting his eyes. "I saw a cat get infected and…"

"Kate." It was the first time he said her name, and she looked up to discover him focused on her. "Chances are fairly good you're not contagious, right? At some point, you gotta stop giving into fear."

"It's good to have fear. It keeps you alive," Kate argued, but she sank to her heels and caressed the dog's velvety ears.

Ace trotted between them as they made their way down the gravel road toward the property's gated entrance. Kate slanted her head toward the cameras as they passed them. "We're in a George Orwell saga."

"You get used to 'em. Your brother-in-law's mighty proud of his fancy schmancy security system."

"Did you know his whole family are hardcore doomsday preppers? They gave Seth and Connie a bunker as a wedding gift when they got married." She stopped, drooping against a tree, reflective. "I never thought I'd see the day where they may actually need such a thing."

"Gotta admire their self-sufficiency."

"Connie told me Seth's great-grandfather lost everything in the stock market crash in the late nineteen twenties. Since then, prepping is like religion to his family. I shouldn't have been so critical of it." Kate shrugged. "Your accent says you're not native to New York State."

He bent to stroke Ace. "I grew up in Texas. Killeen. Once outta high school I got on the rodeo circuit. I traveled all across the states and into Canada in my early twenties. It ain't an easy life. I decided to throw in the towel when I about ended up paralyzed."

Teller resumed walking, and Kate tagged along. "What brought you here?"

He gave her a half-smile over his shoulder. "A girl, what else?"

Laughing, Kate asked, "And where is she?"

"Probably shacked up with one of the guys she cheated on me with. Or dead." Teller's tone was nonchalant, but Kate sensed there was a story there. Nosy enough to want details, she kept her mouth zipped, not wishing to pry. He'd confide at his own pace—or not at all. She figured there was a lot more to Teller than met the eye.

They continued down the lane, side-by-side, not speaking. A bluebird flew past. The only sound was the buzzing of insects and Ace panting as he loped good-naturedly beside them. The sun had begun its descent, telling her it was nearing suppertime.

Teller followed the fence line where it curved. He led her into a densely wooded area where there was no pathway. Kate hesitated. "Where are we going?"

"You'll see."

Kate squinted her eyes at Teller suspiciously, waiting for instinct to tell her the right thing to do. No alarm bells clanged. "I hope I don't regret this."

"You won't."

A few minutes later, they entered into a small clearing. A brook meandered around a bend until it was out of eyeshot. Teller lowered onto a log positioned on the grass, and Kate did the same. The pleasing scent of fabric softener and hay wafted from him. It seemed so innocuous and homey, she instantly loosened up.

Ace scampered to the stream and lapped thirstily. The late afternoon sunshine kissed his freckled coat and glistened on the water as it swirled around moss-covered rocks. They were surrounded by sloping hills densely packed with verdant green pine trees, which gave the glade the intimate ambiance of a secret garden. The air was soft, humid. For a moment, Kate indulged in pretending everything was normal.

"When I have a hankerin' to escape, I hide away here. It's a haven for me," Teller murmured, turning to her, his blue irises like dazzling aquamarines in the sunlight.

An unexpected ember of attraction kindled as Kate studied Teller's face. "I can see why. Real life seems a million miles away, doesn't it?" Ace came up to her, his muzzle wet. He gave her a doggy grin and relaxed at her feet. Kate laid a palm on his head.

Teller cleared his throat. Surmising he was building up to

something, Kate fixed him with an expectant look. His manner was somber when he said, "I heard some bizarre things on the radio. The others here dismiss it as rumors, hysteria. *You've* been out there. The blood on the windshield of your van—the missin' back window. Obviously, you've survived some shit."

Kate bit her lip, frowned, then ran her fingers through her chestnut hair. "How much do you want to know?"

"All of it."

Where to even begin. She held his gaze. "You sure? You won't like what I have to say."

"Tell me everything."

CHAPTER TWELVE

"By the skin of my teeth, I made it. And here I am."

Teller didn't comment. His mouth hung open. His chest rose and fell in measured beats. Kate scrutinized him in the gathering dusk. The sun had long set. It was chilly and cave-like, reminding her of a grotto.

Kate rubbed her arms with her hands to warm up. Was he going to tell her she was out of her mind? "Say *something*, Teller."

He shook his head, snagging his cowboy hat off before scratching his neck. His hair was dark and cropped close to his scalp. "What can I say to all that?"

Kate's voice came out brusque when she suggested, "How about you believe me?"

"Heck, why do you think I'm speechless, girl? I do believe you."

"Why? Nobody else has."

"The rumors on the radio were the first inklin'." Teller's brows pulled together. "Why would you lie?"

"I wouldn't. I'm not a liar."

"I'm just tryin' to process all the info. Dang, you're prickly."

"That's part of my charm."

"And wary as hell."

"Which is a valuable survival skill."

Teller didn't respond.

"My warnings to Seth and Connie have fallen on deaf ears." Kate angled her head back and inhaled deeply. She whispered, "You have no idea the responsibility I feel being the only person here who knows what's really going on outside the fence."

A frigid wind picked up, making the tree branches sway. Teller asked, "Know what that is?"

Kate perused the trees but saw nothing. "No. What?"

"The winds of change are a comin' for the skeptics. The folks here won't be able to ignore reality forever."

Kate shivered.

Teller unfolded from the log and stood, brushing his palms across his seat. He held his hand out to her to help her up. She took it. It was big and calloused. Comforting.

Silently, they headed back to the gravel road, Ace following behind. The sky darkened as night fell, blanketing everything in shadows. The light on the front porch of Kate's cabin was like the North Star, guiding her home.

When she opened the cabin door, she paused, examining Teller. The rosy glow of the porch light blurred the planes of his profile and made him look like a different person. Harsher. Mysterious. Kate couldn't help questioning how much of his persona was genuine. Nevertheless, he intrigued her. "See you at breakfast."

"Thank you for lettin' me in, Kate. I have a notion it don't come without reservations." With a whistle to Ace, he tipped his hat and disappeared into the night.

LATER IN BED, Kate's brain wouldn't quiet. Teller. The little trill of attraction she'd felt at the brook disturbed her. Although good-looking, he was unlike her usual type. Something about him got under her skin. What was his deal? Could he be trusted? She replayed their conversation, picking it apart, and getting nowhere fast.

Teller had homed in on the fact that Kate wasn't a person who shared confidences freely. When Ben encouraged her to be vulnerable with him, she'd refrained. So why had Kate been so unguarded with Teller? Her thoughts naturally turned to Ben, a ball of dread forming in her stomach. Was he okay? Should she drive to Clayton's Corners?

In the wee hours of the morning, Kate gave up on sleep and sat on the plastic chair on the porch. She was still there when the crowing of a rooster floated from the barnyard. Of the many things going through her mind, meeting a new group of people at breakfast niggled at her. It was daunting. And she'd have to deal with Seth.

Kate pursed her lips. The dreary overcast sky foretold rain. She'd used masking tape found in a desk drawer and garbage bags from beneath the kitchen sink to cover her van's broken window. It would never outlast a torrential downpour, but there was nothing else she could do. Deciding to change and head up to the farmhouse, Kate went inside and pawed through the apparel Connie had sent down the day before.

She removed some weapons and supplies from her van, stashing them in the cabin—just in case.

Getting behind the steering wheel, Kate started her van. She maneuvered around the bend in the road and past outbuildings. She parked behind the house, next to the kitchen door. When Kate got out, she was mindful of the chickens pecking about. A clucking brown hen approached her.

"That's Amy. I'll be right back," Connie said from the screen door. She returned with a strawberry. She kneeled down and Amy waddled over to eat the berry from Connie's hand. "She's my favorite Speckled Sussex. Such a sweetheart. My best layer, too."

Amy flapped her wings before wandering off. Connie clumsily got to her feet, groaning. She wore a plain, faded tee and yoga pants. Her shoulder-length chestnut hair was threaded with steel-colored strands and needed trimming. All her extra weight was in her baby bump. Thinner than Kate ever remembered seeing her, she possessed the flattened facial features heavily pregnant women often get.

After a stiff hug, Kate stood back. "You look worn-out."

Connie opened the screen door, and Kate accompanied her into the old-fashioned kitchen. "I am. You know I've never been the lady of the manor type. Even with hired help, there's plenty to be done. I'm happy you're here. I really need someone who can cook."

Neat rows of stewed tomatoes in blue glass jars lined the butcher block counter. Kate slouched against the fridge. "The canning must've been a lot of work. Didn't Judy or Peggy help?"

"Peggy's out in her flower garden or tending her bees most days, and Judy's got Nora. Technically, they don't work for us. Their husbands do. Judy was employed as a doula in town before the virus." Connie lowered to a chair at the head of a rustic trestle table and heaved a sigh. "She'll come in handy when the baby comes. She's expecting too, but she's only in her first trimester."

Kate watched her sister, noting the swollen ankles peeking from the hem of her pants. Concern wormed around her intestines and squeezed. "Do you want me to get a tub of cool water so you can soak your feet? I can cook breakfast."

Connie's grateful smile hinted at the pretty woman she had once been. Glancing at the wall clock, she said, "I don't need a tub, but I have a French toast bake in the fridge. Would you mind preheating the oven?"

Kate twisted the dial on the antiquated electric range and took the prepared casserole from the fridge. She sat it on the counter. "What else?"

"I planned to serve it with homemade yogurt. Nothing else

needs to be done for a bit. It's still early. Why don't you pour us a cup of joe, and come sit with me?"

The metal stovetop percolator was a throwback, similar to the one they'd grown up with. Kate brought it to the table with two cups, knowing Connie preferred her coffee black like she did. She poured for them then lifted her cup, her eyes shrewd on her sister over the rim. "Where's Seth?"

"He's in his den, fiddling with the radio. He's been trying to connect with his family this week, but..."

Kate swallowed. "They very well could be dead. The day I drove up here I came across two people. *Two.*"

"It's possible everyone is barricaded in their homes, isn't it?"

"Maybe." Kate paused before continuing, "I had a call the other night from a friend." She briefly described her and Ben's conversation. When she brought up the subject of the creatures, Connie paled. "Do you think I should go back to Clayton's Corners and make sure he's okay? I could check on Rosie, too."

"Are you joking? Didn't it take you six hours to get up here?"

Kate admitted, "Way more than that. And it was perilous. I— I'm not sure I can justify staying here and doing nothing."

Connie blinked. Her hands trembled on the coffee cup.

"Here I thought you didn't believe me. You're just scared, aren't you?"

Connie didn't answer. She looked out the window.

"Con."

Her voice shook when she said, "Seth says—"

"Enough of what Seth says. What do *you* say?" Kate put her hand on Connie's. It was ice-cold, although the kitchen was warm from the preheating oven.

"I-I don't know."

"Kathryn." Seth stood in the entryway to the kitchen, and Kate tamped down the rush of irritation seeing him brought. His hands were parked on his hips. To look at him, one would never guess he was a prepper. Short, chubby, and balding, Seth wore wire-rimmed spectacles and a prissy countenance. *Mild mannered accountant by day and doomsday prepper by night.* "You look well."

"I'm dandy. Connie says you haven't been able to contact your family." The oven beeped, and Kate went to put in the casserole.

Seth took a mug from the cupboard and poured the remainder of the coffee from the percolator then sat on a bench at the wooden trestle table. "It's possible they're en route to the family bunker a mile from Crestview."

Kate set a wind-up timer, frowning. "Why would they go there?"

"Perhaps it's unsafe at the farm." He shrugged, saying to Connie, "Today I'm going out with the guys to supervise the repair of barbed wire fencing in the back forty. I want to get the livestock through the security gates and out to pasture there soon. Can you make up a cooler with sandwiches and a thermos of lemonade? We won't be back 'til supper."

Connie began to stand, but Kate snapped, "Sit down, Con. Seth, can't you see she's beat? She's been working too hard." Seth's blank expression caused anger to bloom in Kate's chest. *He's fucking clueless.*

"I'm fine," Connie protested, but Kate lasered her with a look.

"*I'll* pack the lunch while breakfast bakes. Get me the cooler, Seth."

Annoyance crossed his face, but he did as Kate bid. She poked around in the fridge, pulling out cooked chicken breast, lettuce, and mustard. A sliced loaf of homemade bread was on the counter. She assembled the sandwiches. After rummaging in the cupboard for a thermos, Kate filled it with lemonade. There was potato salad in the fridge, which she doled out into reusable plastic containers. She turned to Seth. "Can you go out to my van and find the granola? I'll send some in the cooler."

Wordlessly, he left the room, his mouth tight. Connie chastened, "You shouldn't talk to him like that."

"Like what? It won't kill him to fetch granola," Kate drawled. "You've spoiled him. Do you want to end up on bed rest? I'm no doctor, but—"

"It was being on my feet canning all day yesterday, that's all." When Kate opened the freezer for ice packs, Connie volunteered, "They're in the chest freezer in the laundry room."

The laundry room floor was heaped with dirtied clothes. Before looking for the ice packs, Kate loaded the washer. When she came back into the kitchen, the granola was on the butcher block, but Seth was nowhere to be found.

Kate bit back the bile that threatened to spew from her as she portioned the granola into zipper bags and added raisins. *Ick.* She'd never be able to tolerate granola again.

Connie was at her elbow when Kate secured the lid on the packed cooler. She asked, "Are you okay? You look funny."

"I'm alright… just go relax." The timer went off. Kate gulped away the saliva collected in her mouth and checked the casserole.

"Everybody will be coming in shortly. I can help dish the yogurt," Connie said, but Kate shooed her away. She found the coffee grounds and got another pot going then laid the table. Intending to serve family-style, she put the crock of vanilla yogurt in the center of the table with bowls of berries, granola, and nuts.

She'd just pulled the French toast bake from the oven when Teller came in, freshly showered and wearing a linen shirt and denims. The scent of soap drifted to Kate. She felt his gaze, and a blush crept over her. Calling out a greeting, he took off his hat and had a seat at the table.

A loud squawk of feedback drifted from down the hall, followed by the sound of a woman's voice. Connie said, "Seth's radio!"

Kate hurried from the kitchen, Teller on her heels. Seth met them at the open door to his den. His eyes were wide behind his glasses, making him resemble an owl. The voice over the speakers of the sophisticated equipment was high-pitched and panicky.

"Please! Somebody! This—Audrey Davies in River Heights—I—I'm—people are trying to get in—they should be dead—please, I—help! Blue house with—swans—Oak Street!"

CHAPTER THIRTEEN

Seth's skin drained of color at Kate's meaningful look. His gaze shifted away.

There it was—she felt the zap of it—vindication. Recognizing it for what it was, Kate snuffed the grim self-satisfaction that came along with it. She said coolly, "Kinda sounds like what I encountered on my trip up, doesn't it?"

Looking perplexed, Connie clung to Kate's arm. Her lips trembled. "What should we do, Kate?"

"Absolutely nothing. It's not our affair," Seth said, diving for the doorknob to the den. Kate put her foot forward to stop the door from latching.

"I guess I feel different. You can communicate with your radio, right? Let's try to reconnect with her." Kate attempted to step into the den, but Seth wouldn't yield passage.

"No! We aren't getting involved."

Kate glowered at Seth, then at Teller, then Connie. Both Seth and Connie avoided her scrutiny, but Teller was watchful. He exuded impartiality. Kate had told herself she wouldn't refuse assistance the next time she was asked, hadn't she? She felt bad enough she wasn't helping Ben—she certainly wasn't going to disregard someone a town over! "How can we turn our backs on her? What if it was one of us begging over the radio?"

"But it's not," Seth snapped. "Evil lurks outside Mayfly Hollow—"

"We need to get on the radio," Kate insisted, "or drive to River Heights to investigate."

There was the sound of the screen door opening and closing. A tall ebony-skinned man around Seth's age—mid-forties—and an older Asian woman dressed in a flowy caftan and Birkenstocks met them in the hallway. Otis and Peggy, Kate presumed. The man had milk chocolate brown eyes and a reassuring way about him. He asked, "What's the ruckus about? We heard quarreling all the way outside."

Seth explained about the radio transmission as another younger couple came in and lingered in the entryway, their unease apparent. A little girl with the same golden-blonde hair and cornflower blue eyes as her mother peeked around the corner. They must be Jamie and Judy and their daughter, Nora. Kate cut her attention from the new arrivals, her gaze skittering back to Otis. She argued, "There aren't many people left out there. We have a duty to—"

Seth shook his head. "Beware false prophets! I won't allow us to be bewitched from safety."

"I'll ask her if she's got symptoms. We can isolate her, like you did with me. There are empty cabins next to mine—"

"It's deception, Kathryn. A ploy."

"A *ploy*?"

"The wicked will use their wiles any way they can. Satan—"

"What?" Kate scoffed. "You're talking crazy."

"Now, let's all simmer down," the dark-skinned man said, coming to stand in front of Seth, facing Kate. "You must be Connie's sister. I'm Otis."

She nodded, puzzled by Seth's words. He was always a pain in the ass, but she'd never heard him spout off in such a way— was he off his rocker? "There's no time for introductions, Otis.

We've gotta try the radio or get motoring. I saw a creature fall on a lady on the interstate—it tore into her jugular. She bled out within seconds."

Judy gasped, whipping around to cover Nora's ears with her hands and hustling her from the house. Kate looked at everyone in turn. Seth—mumbling to himself indignantly. Connie—ashamed. Peggy—stunned. Otis—disturbed. Jamie—bemused. Kate huffed, then met Teller's steadfast eyes. She threw him a beseeching look, and he dipped his chin. "Kate's right. We need to decide *now* what we're gonna do. There ain't time for squabblin'. Should we open a dialogue with that gal?"

Seth focused wrathful eyes on Kate, his mouth clamping shut.

"Shall we put it up for a vote?" Connie asked weakly.

Kate threw her hands in the air. "So, is that how it works around here? You all *vote*? Majority decrees whether that poor bitch gets a chance?"

"Kate, please," Connie broke in. "If it's really that bad out there, I don't know if..."

"I've tried telling you what my friend said, Con, but you don't want to hear it—those *things* are rallying. The time to help people is now. That woman could be us someday."

"Never! My fence is like the walls of Jericho—" Seth began.

Kate snarled, "Are you for real? You better reread your Bible. Even *I* know the walls of Jericho eventually crumbled."

"Nonetheless—"

"Seth, you haven't seen them in action! I have. I can only describe them as... as... well, zombies."

There were audible gasps. Kate knew it was a mind-boggling concept, and she hadn't wanted to use that word. It conjured images of shambling figures from B movies—but that was what they were. Zombies. The others remained silent, regarding her as if she were a lit fuse on a stick of dynamite. She asked Teller, "Do *you* know how to work the radio?"

Teller looked to Seth, as if he were unwilling to openly defy him.

Kate hissed, "Seriously? I appreciate your misgivings. I do. Really. But I'm going to River Heights, even if I have to go by myself!"

She pushed her way through the corridor. Teller followed, grabbing her arm before she got far. "Kate. You're actin' pigheaded here. You're lettin' your emotions rule instead of common sense. I know you feel sorrow about not savin' that gal on the interstate—"

And Ben. Tears coursed down Kate's cheeks. She flicked them away with impatient fingers. Teller put his arms around her and hauled her to his chest. At first, she resisted, but he smelled so good. Soothing. She leaned into him for a moment. When she pulled away, Kate was dry-eyed and in control. "Will you help me?"

She could see Teller caving. Seth stalked past them and went outside, banging the screen door and ranting to himself. Teller shrugged with resignation. "Alrighty then."

He led her past Connie, Otis, Peggy, and Jamie, where they loitered, and into Seth's den. Plopping into the rolling chair, Teller adjusted the knobs on the equipment before speaking into the apparatus. There was feedback but no response from the woman—or anyone else—no matter how many times he tried.

Kate moaned. "I feel half-inclined to go anyway. Should I, Teller?"

Teller's mouth curved into a lazy smile. "You got a lotta grit, girl."

She raised her eyebrows. Nobody had ever said such a thing to her before. "You think so?"

"Know so. But rushin' in is foolhardy," he cautioned. "I can't have you goin' alone. I'll run you to River Heights."

Kate breathed and smiled, feeling not so alone for the first time in days. "Thank you."

"But I'm famished. Get us a snack and drinks, and I'll bring my truck 'round."

Teller rushed from the house. Kate hastily grabbed sandwiches and the thermos of lemonade from the cooler. The others eyed her warily as they sat at the table, half-heartedly eating breakfast. Kate didn't say anything as she left the room, her jaw tight.

Judy stood outside near the steps, smoking a cigarette. When she saw Kate, she flinched guiltily, throwing her cigarette butt to the gravel. She ground it with her shoe. "I know I shouldn't be smoking. It's nerves."

Kate readjusted the thermos under her arm. Remorse flickered. "Judy?"

The woman was Connie's age with a peaches and cream complexion. She hugged her arms around her midsection, pinning her blue eyes on Kate.

"I didn't mean to traumatize your daughter. I-I'm sorry."

Judy was reserved. "Connie says you've been through a lot."

Kate remembered Otis and Peggy's reticence. They didn't appear to like her much, and Kate couldn't blame them. She'd made quite the first impression. "Still, I promise I'm normally pretty cool-headed."

Teller pulled up in a shiny dark 4x4. He jumped out and took the sandwiches and thermos from Kate, stowing them in the vehicle. Kate bit her lip before stepping away. "Sorry again, Judy."

Judy gave her a polite smile.

Before Kate climbed into Teller's truck, she jogged to her van and opened the passenger's side door. There it was. She wrapped her fist around the handle of her ax and hastened to join Teller.

On their way down the lane, they saw Seth pacing in front of an outbuilding with his hands on his hips. He watched them drive by, wearing a scowl.

Tearing her gaze from Seth, Kate murmured, "Nobody else

seemed overly concerned by his fire and brimstone diatribe. Is that his typical behavior?"

"Seth has his moments, but he was downright hostile towards you."

Kate rolled her eyes. "What would dystopia be without a religious wacko."

At the gate, Teller pressed a remote control clipped to his visor. The gate slid smoothly open. He swiveled in his seat, fixing Kate with a subdued look. "I think we're *both* on Seth's shit list now."

CHAPTER FOURTEEN

WHAT TELLER SAID DIDN'T SIT WELL WITH KATE.

The atmosphere was tense during the trip into River Heights. With no other option, Kate concentrated on the task at hand. Knowing she needed sustenance for what was to come, she picked at her sandwich.

When Kate caught sight of the white-painted welcome sign tagged with graffiti and splattered black blood, she sucked in a breath. What little appetite she had gone, Kate packaged the remnants of her food, not meeting Teller's eyes.

Slowing the truck, Teller chewed the last bite of his sandwich. He wiped breadcrumbs from his shirt, matter of fact. "Like a bad omen, ain't it?"

"You want to forget it? Go back to the farm?"

"Naw."

"Alright then," she said shakily. "Let's locate the blue house with swans on Oak Street."

Teller lowered his window so they could listen for anything unusual as they coasted through town. He wrinkled his nose. "Peuw. What the hell is that rancid stench?"

"Zombies—zombie blood, viscera. Told you it was horrible,"

Kate muttered, inhaling through her mouth rather than her nostrils. Her stomach churned.

Everywhere they turned was destruction. Decomposing bodies cluttered the streets. The business district was like a war zone—burned out cars, broken windows on storefronts, and evidence of looting. Kate recognized the pawnshop where she'd recovered her stolen van.

Teller whistled. "Holy shit."

"What?"

He stopped at the curb in front of the post office. A man and two women lay motionless on the sidewalk in a puddle of crimson. "I know gunshot wounds. They're riddled with 'em. They ain't been dead long neither."

"The blood—it's red. Not infected," Kate murmured. "So, *people* killing *people*?"

"Unless your zombies know how to shoot a twelve gauge."

"I don't even think they can see." She shook her head. "On top of everything else, now we have to worry about roving bands of criminals, too?"

Teller quickly put the truck in park, then rotated in his seat. He grabbed a weapon from the gun rack mounted on the back window. Setting it crossways on his lap, he rooted under the bench seat for a box of ammunition and loaded several cartridges. "I ain't bein' logical. We should have done this before comin' into town. Know how to use this?"

It reminded Kate of the gun she'd found on the floor by her father's corpse. She recoiled. "No."

"Dang. We're really flyin' by the seat of our pants here."

She wrenched her attention from the firearm and cleared the lump from her throat. "I'll stick with my ax."

"Ax ain't gonna cut it. Listen, this here is the bolt. You push it forward before pulling the trigger." Teller demonstrated for Kate, his gaze intent on her as if to make sure she understood. "After you fire, you pull the bolt back to release the spent cartridge. When you need to reload, push it forward. The rifle holds four bullets in an internal magazine. Got it?"

She frowned. "Uh…"

"It's the simplest long gun I got. Just press the bolt forward, aim, and shoot." Teller shoved it in her hands, forcing her to take it. "We gotta get goin'."

He put the truck in drive and headed to the residential section on the west side of town. Kate held the firearm like it was a coiled viper ready to strike. Focusing on street signs was a battle.

Teller turned left onto Maple Street. The houses were poky, rundown ranch-style homes. Kate urged, "Stop a sec. And put your window up. I saw something at the end of the block."

He complied, and they squinted out the windshield. There were probably twenty-five of them, a mixture of men, women, and children. They entered Maple in an unorganized, shuffling horde. Intermittently, they lifted their noses to the air. Teller asked, "What are they doin'?"

"They're trying to catch a whiff of us. That's why I told you to shut the window."

"You said they can't see?"

"Their irises are white—they seem blind, but they *can* hear. I just don't know how well. I think they primarily track by scent."

"If it wasn't for their mottled skin and the way they stumble about, you'd reckon they're alive."

"I know. Once they fix on you, they'll bash their teeth together. Then watch out."

Teller made a sound in his throat. "They're movin' this way. What should we do?"

"Before they get any closer, back out of here very slowly."

"Hold on." Pushing the shifter to reverse, Teller put an arm along the back of the seat. One hand on the steering wheel, he piloted them out to the main thoroughfare.

Kate never glimpsed away from the pack. "They don't seem to notice us, luckily. Let's get out of here."

Three blocks away, Teller exclaimed, "Hot dog!"

"What?"

His smile was lopsided when he indicated the green street sign one block up. "This here's Birch. *That's* Oak."

Hanging a left on Oak, Teller said, "Everything looks kosher down yonder."

"There's a blue house, but no swans..." They passed tan, yellow, and white houses.

He angled his chin toward a cobalt blue ranch. "Does the bird on the welcome flag count as a swan?"

"Looks like a goose to me. Let's keep searching." At the other end of Oak, there was a house with peeling robin's egg blue paint. "Swans!"

Cheap plastic swan-shaped flower planters were spaced evenly apart in the front rock bed. Teller shifted into park. "That's got to be it. Should I leave the keys in the ignition?"

"Better not," Kate said, thinking of her carjacker. She passed the rifle back to Teller. The breeze kicked up. Tree boughs rubbed together, making a peculiar noise. Crows pecked at bodies strewn on front yards and sidewalks, but otherwise the street was still. "I'm more at home with my ax. C'mon."

Exiting the vehicle, Kate pushed the door gently until it just closed, Teller following suit. He motioned a hand toward the front porch. "This is your pleasure cruise, girl."

"Gee, thanks," Kate muttered. Swinging her head left and right, she confirmed the coast was clear before charging across the scrubby yard. She vaulted up the cement stairs to the crumbling porch, Teller close behind. Kate brought her knuckles up to the door and rapped, keeping her voice low. "Audrey Davies?"

"Kate..." Teller's voice was urgent. Kate didn't have to look. She felt the change in the atmosphere by the way the hair on her arms rose. "There's a Z next door. He's a big sombitch, too."

Kate knocked harder.

"He's got his snout in the air... Should we take a powder?"

Becoming frantic, Kate growled against the door, "Audrey? Open up."

Teeth clacking carried in the wind. "Goddamn it, Kate!"

"I think I hear someone." From the corner of her eye, she saw Teller's stance shift. He lifted the rifle and pushed the bolt forward, aiming. The blast of the gun firing was deafening.

The Z folded.

"Who's there?" A woman's voice asked through the door.

"We heard your broadcast," Kate said. "Please, for the love of Pete, let us in!"

"You've gotta be kiddin' me." Teller nudged Kate in the ribs with an elbow. A mob of at least fifty zombies rounded the corner of Oak Street. The echo of their feet stamping and their teeth snapping heralded their arrival. "Open up, lady!"

Kate closed her eyes, reciting a prayer.

The deadbolt turned. A young red-haired woman peeked out. The zombies leading the pack landed on the front yard sidewalk and Kate squealed.

Teller put his head down like a stampeding bull and rammed his way into the house. Kate crashed the door closed, locking it just as the horde clambered up to the porch. The whole house shook.

Audrey Davies had an hourglass figure, and her hair was arranged in a flattering style which framed her perfectly made-up face. Body trembling and sherry-brown eyes dazed, she appeared near collapse. "I was l-l-locked in the bathroom. I d-didn't d-dare come out."

"Now ain't the time, lady," Teller barked, putting his gun on the carpet. Slamming his body against the door, he hunkered down beside Kate, bracing it. They bounced as the zombies beat against it. "It's gonna give!"

Bodies pummeled the front window. Kate's lips were rubbery when she demanded, "Back door?"

Teller fished the truck keys from the chest pocket of his shirt and placed them in Kate's palm. "Y'all get a head start. We'll meet at that godawful pink house on Birch—"

"No!"

"Go," Teller roared. Kate stuffed the keys into her jeans and hurried after Audrey into a compact kitchen. Audrey's hands were too unsteady to unlock the deadbolt. Kate used her hip to prod her aside and unbolted it herself. The backyard was unoccupied. Kate grabbed Audrey's arm and yanked her into the alley. She looked over her shoulder for Teller, but he wasn't there. *Fuck!*

Heart banging like a drum, Kate trotted down the alleyway toward where she'd seen the pink house. Audrey scurried to keep up. Zigzagging through a backyard, Kate slowed, disoriented. "Where is it?"

Audrey bent over, struggling to catch her breath. "Pepto Bismol pink with yellow shutters?"

"Yes! I'm all turned around."

"I know where it is. Ow!" For the first time, Kate noticed Audrey wore no shoes. In the current circumstances her fuchsia-painted toenails seemed incongruous, even comical. Kate shook her head as Audrey took the lead, picking her way through an overgrown yard, then skirting a brick house. "This street is Birch."

The pink house came into view. Teller leaned against a tree in the front yard, the rifle in one hand and a grin on his lips. Kate hurried up to him, panting.

His grin transformed into a cheesy smile. "Y'all take the scenic route?"

Buoyed by her relief at seeing him unharmed, Kate deadpanned, "You lost your Stetson, cowboy."

CHAPTER FIFTEEN

"Peaceful as it is here, best we get outta sight." Teller kept his voice low, his expression sobering.

Ax dangling from her fingers, Kate's gaze flew over the street. Cape Cod-style homes with postage stamp-sized yards lined Birch Street. Other than an occasional overturned garbage bin or the corpses rotting on a sidewalk, the neighborhood was serene. Still, the horde of Zs rampaging Audrey's house was mere blocks away. "We should be okay here for a minute. All the commotion they're making will lure others from us. I hope."

Audrey said shakily, "They'll lose interest."

Kate turned to her. Audrey's milky skin was so pale that her freckles stood out in high relief. She swayed. Kate put out a hand to steady her. *This is all we need.* "Take a deep breath."

"I'm alright," Audrey insisted, but she dropped to the curb, hugging her knees to her torso. "I-I-was out of food, so I thought I'd try my neighbor's house. I've got a key."

Teller lowered his lanky frame down next to her, observant, his rifle in his grip.

"Mary was layin' dead in the kitchen... she looked like she'd been mauled by a pack of wolves. The stank." Audrey shuddered. "Joe ran in from the other room. He was one of *them*."

Kate transferred her ax from one hand to the other, an eye on the changing sky.

"He came at me, and I tore outside. I was screeching and thrashing around. I made an unholy racket." A tinge of scarlet flooded Audrey's cheeks. "I know it was stupid of me. I got in through my back door, but by that time a couple more of them joined him."

"We heard you over my brother-in-law's radio. How did you broadcast?"

"My ex left his ham radio. Sometimes I monkey with it. I've called for help for the last week and not a peep, but I was desperate. They butted their bodies against the house, and I freaked, worrying they'd bust in."

Teller frowned. "But they didn't."

"Nuh-uh. I led Joe on a wild goose chase and was inside by the time he got into my backyard." Audrey shook her head, her red curls springy. "It's as if he sensed I was in the house but couldn't figure out how I got there. I called out on the radio then hid in the bathroom. I didn't know what else to do."

"That must've been Joe you shot," Kate told Teller.

He tsked. "I didn't have much choice but to take him out. Regardless, the result was ugly. We gotta use firearms thought-ful-like—the blast draws Zs. Audrey, you said they'll lose interest?"

She shrugged. "If enough time passes."

"I don't know the best way to handle this," Kate said, pushing a lock of hair from her face. "Do we wait 'til they disperse, chancing running into them when we do make our way back to the truck? Or do we sneak back *now*?"

Teller worked a hand at the back of his neck. "Shoot, could be they're more dangerous when *not* in a horde. If we go back to Oak Street and keep distance enough to not be detected, we can make a mad dash for the truck."

"That seems risky," Audrey murmured.

Kate volleyed her a terse look but kept her voice low. "Every option will be risky. Teller's right. The more the Zs spread out, the better the probability of encountering them. Fast is the name of the game. We'll have to read the situation as we go and adapt."

The trio made their way across the street and through a weed-choked yard, giving dead bodies a wide berth. The smell of rotting flesh assaulted Kate's nostrils. She swallowed compulsively to avoid puking. *Ugh.*

Teller held up a hand, signaling them to slow. Audrey, bringing up the rear, didn't notice and knocked into Kate.

Kate frowned at her in rebuke before turning to where Teller pointed. A chubby, middle-aged Z wearing a floral blouse shambled two houses down. *I know her.* The woman's glasses were gone, but she was recognizable from the alley when Kate came through River Heights. The zombie blood made Kate invisible then. Should they splash some on their clothes?

They flattened against a storage shed, waiting. The wind picked up, making branches of a tree flap on the roof of a nearby garage. The sky had taken on a yellowish-green hue. Ozone pervaded the air, drowning out the foul stink of the corpses littering the neighborhood. There was a deafening crack of thunder coupled with a flash of lightning. Audrey flinched and squawked. Kate whirled toward her and glowered before pivoting back to survey the Z. Unmoving, she twitched her nose like a rabbit. *Oh no.* A pellet of frozen rain boomeranged from Kate's shoulder, then another.

The skies opened, assailing them with pea-size ice.

They hugged the garage, sharing an unspoken moan. Mouth parted, Kate watched the Z. The hail seemed to confuse her. She darted from side to side as it ricocheted off her, her snorts and grunts confirming her displeasure.

Teller shook Kate's arm, whispering, "Now's our chance, while it's distracted."

Kate nodded, passing the message to Audrey. Following behind Teller, propelled by adrenaline, Kate's legs pumped, the ax moving to the rhythm of her stride. Single-minded, she outpaced Teller, her only goal reaching the safety of the truck. Heart thudding painfully in her sternum, she came to an abrupt stop in the alley behind Audrey's ranch. There were easily two dozen Zs drifting around the immediate area, their body language displaying bewilderment.

The hail's letting up. That's problematic. Soon, it would cease altogether, and their cover would be blown. Kate rocked on her heels, winded. Teller and Audrey, sweaty and out of breath, skidded to a stop beside her.

Teller mopped at his brow. "You thinkin' what I'm thinkin', girl?"

"Clue me in," Audrey pleaded.

Kate held out a palm. Barely any hail fell now. Glimpsing at Audrey's feet, she said, "We've got about thirty seconds to get to the truck before the Zs get their bearings. Keep your wits and boogie, Audrey."

Digging into her pocket, Kate chucked Teller his keys. They met eyes, and he nodded. "Go!"

Zs were in Kate's path as she sprinted through Audrey's backyard and around the side of her house. She wove around them as if on an obstacle course, suppressing a scream as she brushed one's icy arm.

The truck was just ahead—she was so damn close!

A teenage Z snatched at her, getting a handful of her shirt. It yanked with surprising strength. Kate floundered, losing her equilibrium. Teller shoved the Z away, and it fell to the grass. He grabbed Kate's hand, towing her to her feet and into the crook of his arm. Releasing her at the truck, Teller made his way around the tailgate to the driver's door. Kate grasped the passenger door handle, swinging the door wide open. The hail dwindled. Fat raindrops took its place, soaking her skin. Teller's voice was urgent. "They're gettin' aware."

Some of the Zs brought their faces to the sky, snuffling.

Audrey was almost to the truck, a Z in pursuit. Kate stepped aside to give her room to scoot in. "Hurry!"

Humming in terror, her eyes wide, Audrey shinned into the truck.

Bringing her feet shoulder width apart, Kate readied her ax. Heart slowing, she was aware only of her breathing, scarcely registering Teller yell from the periphery, "Leave it be. Get in, Kate!"

The Z was upon her. Turning the handle so the blade was parallel to the ground, she swung the ax with all her might, slicing through its neck. Black blood sprayed her shirt and Audrey shrieked, pitching back and flailing her arms. The severed head fell and rolled under the truck. Its body thudded at Kate's shoes.

As if in a trance, Kate scrambled into the truck.

Teller peeled from the curb, his fingers tight on the steering wheel as they plowed through a group of Zs. Kate put her ax on the floorboard and slouched in her seat. Spent, she was only vaguely cognizant of Audrey's sobs.

Rain pounded on the windshield as Teller made his way out of town. Body wracking, Audrey eventually quieted, hiccupping and wiping her tears and snot with the hem of her black velour hoodie.

The pelting rain and the hushed voices of Audrey and Teller as they chatted lulled Kate into a fitful sleep. She dozed until Teller put the truck into park in the overgrown lane at Mayfly Hollow's entrance.

"Aw, hell," Teller said. Something in his voice worried her. Blinking, Kate looked at him, her brow knotted. He was white as a sheet in the muted light. Her intestines turned to liquid when he gulped and brought his finger to the unadorned visor above his head. "The remote control. It's gone, Kate."

CHAPTER SIXTEEN

"What do you mean, *it's gone*?"

"I don't know how to make it any plainer," Teller said. "The remote to the fuckin' gate is gone, Kate."

Audrey put a palm up. "Can one of you tell me what exactly is going on?"

"It was clipped on the visor when we left Mayfly Hollow—I know 'cause I used it," Teller explained.

"You mean you didn't lock your truck doors?" Audrey asked. "Why not?"

Teller lifted a shoulder. "For easy access."

"A Z isn't sophisticated enough to pinch it, so it had to be a person, right?" Kate skimmed her fingers over her face, wiping away sweat and trying to rein herself in. "How did they manage it?"

"Now, let's not lose our heads here," Teller said. "I imagine either Audrey or me bumped into the visor during the fracas of you takin' that Z down, and it got unclipped. Bet it's lyin' in the street right about now."

"You're sure nobody followed us back here?" Kate demanded, turning in her seat to scan their surroundings, her heart in her throat.

"Once we were out of River Heights there was nothin' but scattered Zs here and there. Nobody woulda been able to filch the remote, Kate. There were too many Zs around. I see there ain't any guns missin' from my gun rack neither. The remote wasn't stolen."

"It's alright then," Audrey breathed.

Kate's voice came out harsh. "This time. Somebody only has to look in the glove box at the registration to obtain our address. How was I so short-sighted? Why didn't I think of removing it?" She opened the glove compartment and found the paperwork, waving it in the air.

Teller took the registration from her and stuffed it in his shirt pocket. He reasoned, "We ain't never been in a situation like this before. We're figurin' things out. I'll talk to Seth about reprogrammin' the system as a precaution. In the meantime, we can use the number pad attached to the intercom."

"And Seth will have another shit fit."

Teller rolled his window down and leaned out to punch a code into the pin pad. "Ain't no use cryin' about spilt milk. What's done is done."

"He'll blame *me*. I'm the one who pushed to go to River Heights."

Pulling through the open gate, Teller said, "I'll deal with Seth." He drove along until they were in front of Kate's cabin. "I explained to Audrey about quarantinin' for a few days. She can have the cabin next door to you, and I'll take the other one."

"Umm." Audrey shifted her gaze and fidgeted with her hoodie. "Is it okay if I share? I don't want to be alone."

The question seemed aimed more at Teller than Kate. He emitted a choking sound, his Adam's Apple juddering.

Oh really?

Taking pity on him, Kate said, "You can bunk with me."

Teller coughed. "Y'all get settled in, and I'll be over in a jiff to use your walkie."

Kate opened the door to her cabin, ushering Audrey in. She'd left the kitchen window open, but the room smelled fusty, like a tent spotted with morning dew. After listing the amenities, Kate sorted through the pile of clothes on the desk. She selected a t-shirt and a pair of sweatpants, figuring they'd fit Audrey. "Here, you should change. I'll get a garbage bag for your dirty clothes."

Without a word, Audrey took the clothes and disappeared into the bathroom. Kate quickly undressed and put on faded khakis and a printed tunic, depositing her soiled outfit into a bag from under the kitchen sink.

Sitting on the edge of the bed, Kate waited for Audrey, holding the bag open when she emerged from the bathroom. Audrey stuffed her velour tracksuit into the trash bag, then crossed her arms uncertainly over her chest. "Now what?"

Kate tied the bag closed with the drawstring. "Why don't you wash your hands while I put this on the porch?"

When she returned, Audrey was drying her hands on a kitchen towel. Kate lathered up at the sink, saying over her shoulder, "Have a seat if you'd like. Can I make you lunch?"

"Please. I haven't eaten since yesterday." Her demeanor self-conscious, Audrey perched on the edge of Kate's bed. "Teller told me this is your family's place?"

Kate opened the refrigerator and grabbed the pot of tomato and rotini soup she'd made earlier in the week after Connie sent down a cardboard box of vegetables. She set the pan on a stove burner. "My sister Connie and her husband Seth. After quarantine's over, I'll introduce you, but FYI Seth isn't the easiest person to deal with. He was opposed to helping you. I'm sure he'll be frosty to all three of us."

"Oh." Audrey came to the kitchenette and leaned on the peninsula countertop, putting her chin in her hand. "Why did you help me, Kate?"

After scrounging for tuna salad and sliced bread in the fridge, Kate snagged a tomato from beside the toaster. Facing Audrey, she shrugged. "I wouldn't be able to live with myself if I didn't."

Audrey gasped, straightening. "Hey! Tomato? Where did you get *that*?"

Amused at her astonishment, Kate placed the tuna sandwich on a plate and cut it into triangles. She pushed the plate across the counter. "My sister has bushels of them. Pretty soon you'll be as sick of tomatoes as I am."

"Oh my, this is delish," Audrey said after swallowing a bite. "I've been living on crackers and dry cereal."

Kate ladled soup into a bowl when there was a tap on the door. Teller opened it, averting his gaze. "Y'all decent?"

"Come in," Kate said. "Interested in soup and a sandwich?"

"Hell yeah, but you better give me the walkie, so I can take care of business first."

Kate scooped tuna onto bread, then gestured to her bedside table with the spoon. "Help yourself."

They listened to Teller's exchange with Connie as he explained what occurred in River Heights. He paced between the bed and bathroom as he spoke. "I left Ace in the barn. I'd be mighty thankful if you tended to him while I quarantine."

"I'll send Jamie. I'm not feeling very good. I get woozy when I stand," Connie said, weariness evident in her voice. "Seth is fit to be tied, and it's stressing me out."

Kate crossed to Teller, her palm out. "Let me talk to her." Without hesitation, he passed the walkie over. "Are you okay? Should I come up to the house?"

"No! Seth would be livid. What if you're infected? I've got my hands full up here as it is."

"At least ask Judy and Peggy to make dinner."

After a second of silence, Connie's voice came across the walkie. "I have casseroles in the deep freeze. I'll be fine. Seth wants to talk to Teller."

"And I want to talk to him," Teller said with a show of bravado. Walkie in hand, he took a deep breath and pressed the button on the side. "Seth, listen. I'm gonna need you to repro-gram the gate remotes."

Teller made the mistake of removing his finger from the button. Seth's voice was full of reproach. "I knew it! Something sinister has been brought to Mayfly Hollow. You succumbed to Satan's errand, opening the floodgates. We'll all be punished for your recklessness—"

"Phew." Teller blew through his lips, shaking his head as Seth's tirade continued. "I best take this outdoors. I'll be back."

Kate sank onto the bed, appetite wavering. A knot tightened in her innards, making her palms sweat. *Teller's getting his ass chewed out. I bet Seth can't wait to sink his teeth into mine.* How could she possibly reason with him? He seemed beyond reasoning.

"Ahem." Kate's attention skittered to Audrey. "I'm real sorry I caused all this."

"Everyone's been cloistered here since the beginning. You're the first outsider, other than me. My brother-in-law may be freaking out, but he is right about one thing. Bringing you here was reckless."

"But I had the virus." Audrey fiddled with her spoon, scraping the bottom of her bowl. "I was exposed at the beginning, at the salon where I was a stylist. Man, I was sicker than a dog for three days. I thought I was going to die."

"And I never contracted it even though I was exposed multiple times," Kate mused, chewing a nail. "I don't understand. It's so random."

"You think I can get the virus again?"

"You must've developed antibodies. I'd wager whoever fell ill and survived probably acquired some kind of... whatever you call it. Immunity."

"Then I should be immune."

"But what if you still carry the virus?"

"Oh."

"That's why bringing you to Mayfly Hollow isn't without risk. Of course, who really knows? It's all conjecture."

Teller stepped back inside, rubbing a rough hand across his

jaw. "I could use a stiff drink after the tongue lashin' I just received."

Wincing, Kate asked, "That bad?"

"Yup."

"Did he make sense?"

"Not really. Forbiddin' biblical verses dominated the conversation. He's got a lotta passages memorized."

Kate sighed. She got up and went into the kitchenette to fetch Teller's food. "You better eat on the porch since you haven't been able to change yet."

"Much obliged," Teller said in his cowpoke drawl.

Audrey bundled the rest of her sandwich in a napkin, hastening to follow as Teller went outside, her curls swinging. "I'll come along. I can't wait to hear more of your stories about the rodeo."

Index finger tapping her hip, Kate assessed Audrey with narrowed eyes. *Girlfriend's sure keen, isn't she?* Lower lip between her teeth, Kate wondered how she felt about that.

She'd filled the sink with hot, soapy water and was washing the dishes when the walkie on the bed came to life.

"Hello? Anyone there? Kate? It's Judy. Please, answer!" There was a beat of silence. "Connie's collapsed!"

CHAPTER SEVENTEEN

KATE RACED AROUND THE COUNTERTOP, WIPING HER HANDS ON HER tunic as she went. She seized the walkie from the bed. "Judy?"

No response.

"Judy?"

"I'm here—can you come up to the house? Connie's asking for you."

"I'll be right there."

Kate found Teller and Audrey loafing on the porch steps. The rain had stopped though the sky remained gloomy. When Teller caught sight of Kate in the doorway, he started, his skin suffusing scarlet.

Had he been flirting with Audrey? *Does he think I'd be upset if he were? I hardly know him. Why's he acting guilty?* As she latched the door, Kate said, "Something's wrong with Connie. I need to head up to the farmhouse. Can I use your truck? It's faster than walking."

Teller unfolded his loose-limbed frame and got to his feet, seeming eager to assist. "I'll drive you. That way you can bring your van back."

Maneuvering the truck up the lane, Teller asked, "So, what's goin' on?"

"Who knows? Could simply be stress related. I was shocked when I first saw her. She looked terrible even then. Haggard. Of course, Seth's too consumed by his delusions to notice."

Teller made a noise low in his throat. "He always thought he ran this place, but a lot of it's Connie. If she's incapacitated he'll likely spiral further. Could be an issue."

"What a lovely thought." Kate gave him side-eye.

"Yep. Concernin'." He huffed. "Golly, am I glad to escape that Audrey. She's enough to test any man's patience."

Despite her unease, Kate couldn't hold back a giggle. "You've got yourself a fan club."

Grimacing, Teller parked the truck behind Kate's van. With a word of thanks, she ran into the house.

Connie reclined on the threadbare sofa in the living room, Seth beside her, patting her hand and looking dumbfounded. His button-up shirt was filthy and his eyes red-rimmed. Kate slumped against the wall, not wanting to intrude. Judy removed a blood pressure cuff from Connie's arm. She shook her head as she rolled the cuff and put it in its case. "I'm not thrilled with your BP. Your body's commanding you slow down."

"I can't," Connie argued. "The gardens need weeding, and I have canning and freezing to do. What about the cooking, cleaning, and laundry?"

Kate stepped forward. "I'll take over the household stuff, and I'm sure Audrey will help with the gardening."

Seth launched to his feet, his eyebrows in a line. "Yeah, and she'll infect us all in the process. Who the hell do you think you are? You don't govern here—*I do.*"

"She'll stay away a few days to make sure she's not sick. And I have *zero* interest in—"

"Bullshit! Don't think I can't see what you're up to, you Jezebel—"

"Stop it!" Connie sat up, smacking a palm on the arm of the sofa. Her voice became shrill as she said, "*I* invited Kate. *I* need her. I've been ill for a week... do you want me to lose the baby?"

Seth didn't answer. The room fell silent, the tension ratcheting.

Glimpsing from person to person, Judy inched to the door by degrees, slipping out. There was the sound of the kitchen door slamming.

Connie lifted her chin, making her defiance unequivocal.

Seth roared, "A wife must submit to her husband! I won't stand for this treachery."

Kate tried to be rational. "Look, there's risk in everything we do now but—"

"You and your goddamn mouth," Seth snarled, swiveling toward her, radiating fury. Kate flinched. She retreated until she bumped into the wall. Was he going to strike her? She eyed him suspiciously. Squaring her shoulders, she prepared for attack. He was half a foot shorter than Kate, but his body quivered with rage—like his control dangled by a thread. "I see this for what it is."

Kate scoffed, "And what is it?"

"Trespass," Seth sneered, his lips twisting.

"Trespass? I was invited here." She rolled her eyes, exasperation replacing fear. *Jackass.* "Why don't you shut up?"

"I'm two seconds from throwing you out. Two seconds. Mutiny is unforgivable. Sanctuary will not be granted to a Judas!"

Connie sniffled. Volleying Seth a look, Kate shook her head. *He's unhinged.* "You need to snap out of it and focus on your wife right now."

Seth closed the distance between them, grasping her forearm roughly and jerking. He ground out between gritted teeth, "I've had about all I'm going to take from you, you little cunt."

Whoa! Kate loathed that word. She chomped down on her cheek to keep from lashing out.

"Seth, don't," Connie cried, rising unsteadily to her feet.

"Stay there, Con. It's okay," Kate murmured, boldly meeting Seth's eyes though her pulse throbbed in her temples.

Time halted. Seth's breath came out in harsh pants, his fingers convulsive on her arm. The noxious aroma of liquor emanating from him made Kate's eyes water. *Bourbon. Oof. Not good.*

"You been drinking, Seth?"

He released Kate, tossing her aside. He stalked from the room without uttering another word.

Rubbing her forearm, Kate shakily went to the sofa and collapsed on it. She kept poker-faced so Connie wouldn't see how rattled she was. Seth had never been violent before. Liquor had apparently amplified the resentment simmering between them—and his paranoia.

Connie cupped her hands over her face and sobbed. At a loss, Kate grabbed a box of tissues from the side table and put an arm around Connie's shoulders.

When she was composed, Connie turned to Kate, sniffly and despondent. "Everything's falling apart. What am I going to do?"

CHAPTER EIGHTEEN

The following days, they established an uneasy routine.

Kate moved into a spare bedroom at the farmhouse and undertook the day-to-day domestic operation. She cooked and cleaned while Connie rested in her room or on the front porch, a knitting project in her lap.

Teller and Audrey quarantined in the cabins, waiting to see if they'd fall ill after exposure to the Zs. Jamie and the farm's foreman, Otis, took up Teller's slack, working the farm. Otis's wife, Peggy, grudgingly neglected her flower gardens and helped Judy with the vegetable gardens until Audrey could assume responsibility full time. The others were polite to Kate, but circumspect, keeping their distance. She tried not to take it personally.

Seth appeared only at mealtimes. Not speaking, he'd shovel food in his mouth then disappear downstairs to the basement panic shelter. As Connie's condition improved, Seth's deteriorated. He wore the same button-up, which was rumpled and grimy. Unshaven, his eyelids baggy, he stank of liquor.

After sending Jamie to deliver a tray of dinner for Teller and Audrey, Kate stacked dishes in the dishwasher and wiped the kitchen counters. Once she began a load of laundry, she poured tumblers of iced tea, joining Connie on the front porch. Her sister sat in a rocking chair, a hand resting on her swollen midsection. A half-completed baby sweater and a yellow ball of yarn were discarded on a shabby wicker end table.

"Here," Kate said, handing Connie a glass of tea.

"Thanks. You look spent."

"I am," Kate admitted before sinking into her chair. "Cooking three meals a day for ten people is no small feat. And the washing up! How did you manage it in addition to the gardening?"

"It's all in the planning."

"Speaking of—I prepped a slow cooker oatmeal recipe for tomorrow's breakfast."

Connie said with approval, "Good, because with Teller and Audrey coming, you won't have time to cook."

"Are you sure you'll be able to show us around the farm? Teller better do it."

"I'm not an invalid, Kate. Besides, Teller doesn't know a thing about my gardens."

Tucking her hair behind her ear, Kate appraised her sister with critical eyes. Posture relaxed, Connie used her bare feet to glide her rocker back and forth. The chair drummed over the weathered planks of the porch floor, making them groan and creak. Though she wore an old pair of yoga pants and a faded t-shirt, she looked well rested, her complexion rosy.

They sat companionably, each lost in their own thoughts. The subject of Seth's mental state remained unspoken. Whenever Kate had broached the subject, Connie shut her down, unwilling to discuss him. Not wanting to further add to her sister's stress, Kate refrained from bringing him up anymore though privately she believed Connie was in deep denial.

The farmhouse sat on the crest of the hill, overlooking Kate's cabin and the entrance gate below. From their vantage, all was still. The tang of fresh grass and the manure from the pasture tinged the air. As the sun set, the chirp of cicadas and the rhythmic groan-creak of the floorboards under their rockers granted solace. Connie yawned then asked in a casual tone, "What's your opinion on Teller?"

Kate squinted at Connie. "Why?"

"I think he's besotted with you."

Kate wasn't sure how to respond. "He's a cool guy, but I'm not sure how to take him sometimes. His aww shucks cowboy routine seems like a put on."

Connie laughed. "It's not. He's the real deal."

"Not that it matters. Now's a bad time for a romance."

That made Connie laugh harder. "Kate, you're hilarious."

"What? What's so funny?"

"Because it's always a good time for romance."

"Hmm. Can we discuss something more important than my love life, please?"

"All I want is for you to be happy, Kate."

"I know." Taking a deep breath, Kate brought up what she'd been pondering all day. "I mentioned my friend, Ben."

"Yeah," Connie replied slowly. "What of him?"

"I could bring him here. He's clever, knowledgeable. He'd be an asset."

"No!" Connie's good humor melted away "You'd be gone too many days! I-I... Please, don't leave me alone with Seth."

Connie's poise had vanished. Her serenity transformed to terror, her eyes huge in her troubled face. It gave Kate pause—added to her disquiet regarding her sister's fragility and the threat Seth posed. Shaken, Kate felt encumbered, as if *she* were the elder sister. The weight of it took her breath away. She had to force herself to count to five before responding. "I'll stay."

Connie's relieved words came out in a rush. "It's just I need you here too much. You're the glue keeping things together. If you go, I don't know what will happen. Seth..."

"You're worried like I am that he's on the verge of a complete breakdown."

Connie nodded, looking down at her hands. "He's isolating

himself. The drinking… it's gotten progressively worse over the years but now it's constant."

"Hmm. Without me here, he'd feel more in control. It would give him a chance to regroup."

"But I don't want you to go!" Connie's tone hardened as she spoke. "I've had it with him. He's always been inflexible. Mule headed. Not that I need to tell you about his flaws. You always saw through him."

Wow. Connie had never uttered a single criticism of Seth in all the years they'd been married. Kate didn't respond—she didn't know what to say.

"I wanted to start a family years ago, but he said wait. It was *let's finish outfitting the bunker first.* Then, *we have to buy more solar panels before having a baby.* Then, *we need to fully stock the panic shelter.* He's been single-minded. I was fine living in this broken-down shack and wearing thrift store junk. Cutting my own hair. Ten-hour days at the office then coming home to work another four hours. Making do, so we could invest in prepping. I waited for Seth's okay to get pregnant… for what he wanted. Now look where we are!"

Deciding the best tact was levity, Kate reminded gently, "C'mon, sis. It's not as if the guy could have foreseen an invasion of the undead."

Connie grumbled, "I know I sound sulky. I just have so many regrets about always deferring to him, what he thinks is best. Kate, he's spent our whole marriage preparing for this exact scenario, and he's choking now that it's reality! I have to ask myself if my sacrifices have been worth it 'cause I'm rapidly losing respect for him. I keep praying he'll man up, but he's not capable of it! He's big on talk, but Seth Metzger is no leader."

"If that's how you feel, you're free to leave at any time, conspirator."

Rotating in her seat, Kate spotted Seth silhouetted in the open screen door.

She leaped from her chair as he unlatched the door and

stepped onto the porch, his countenance dark with anger. Standing between him and Connie, Kate motioned for him to stop. "You're drunk. Go sleep it off."

"No, Kate, it's fine." Connie lumbered to her feet. "Seth and I have plenty to discuss."

"I don't know if—"

"Leave us, Kate."

Contrary to her better judgment, Kate made her way down the porch steps. Not wanting to stray too far in case their discussion got heated and she needed to intervene, she lapped the house. Kate rounded a corner, then slowed. In the distance, she saw Teller saunter toward Audrey where she waited outside Kate's cabin. Too far away to discern details, she drew conclusions by their body language. Familiar. Friendly. Audrey put her hand in the crook of Teller's arm, her head close to him as they conversed. Their pace leisurely, they meandered down the path and along the fence line.

Were they on their way to the glade Teller had taken Kate to when they first met? It felt as if it were only yesterday they sat side by side on the log at the brook. The clearing had seemed like a secret garden—enchanting. They'd connected there. Kate recalled how the dappled sunshine lit the trees. The breeze had been mellow, just powerful enough to make the branches dance so the leaves glittered like gems. The stream had sparkled like a thousand shimmering diamonds when the sun set.

Would Teller and Audrey embrace? Perhaps share a kiss at dusk? Audrey surely had no qualms about romance during desperate times. The setting was perfect for it, too. Magical.

It's not like it's our place, is it? Teller owes me nothing. We don't even know each other. Not really. He can kiss any girl he wants.

Leaning back against the house to revel in the warmth of the brick, Kate nibbled at her cheek, wondering why such thoughts made her heart squeeze with envy.

CHAPTER NINETEEN

"Mornin', Kate," Teller said, stepping into the kitchen the following morning. His crooked smile seemed to electrify the air.

"Hey, stranger." Giddy as a teenager, Kate tried to hide her feelings as she pulled a melamine bowl from the cupboard.

Audrey straggled behind, her hair in a complicated looking updo and her manner tentative. A pathetic whine carried through the screen door. Teller hitched his thumb over his shoulder toward the sound. "Ace doesn't want to let me outta his sight now. Mutt acts like I've been gone two weeks instead of two days."

"You're early. It'll be a couple minutes before the others show up." Kate indicated the trestle table in front of the windows. "Have a seat. I'm preparing a fruit salad."

"I can help," Audrey said.

"All it entails is opening zipper bags. It's more a compote than a salad, really." Emptying a freezer baggie of strawberries into the bowl, Kate paused, hyperaware of Teller's presence. It made her oddly jittery. "Actually, something you *can* do—down the hall is a bedroom that's been converted into a pantry. Grab syrup for me, will you?"

"Sure."

When they were alone, Kate lifted the percolator from the stove and took it to the table where Teller sat, his cowboy hat on the bench beside him. Cheeks heating, she said, "I see you found another Stetson—"

At the same time, Teller asked, "How's it been?"

They both laughed, self-conscious. She poured him a cup of coffee, viewing him from under her lashes. Something was different between them, but she couldn't put her finger on exactly what. "Well. The mood here hasn't been welcoming."

Murmuring his thanks, he spooned sugar from a ceramic bowl on the table into his cup and stirred. "The folks here are nice enough—once they get to know you. I'm sure they don't mean to be cold."

"Not cold… just aloof. I've caused a shift in the power differential. They're trying not to choose a side—"

"Omigosh, that's more than a pantry!" Audrey materialized with a quart jug of syrup. "It's practically a grocery store."

Kate took the jug, watching as Teller threw Audrey an indulgent grin. "Y'all missed the sugarin' season here. It's Otis's specialty. He tapped a bunch of maples on the property and boiled down the sap over an open fire."

"My folks took me on a trip to Vermont when I was in the sixth grade. It takes ten gallons of sap to make a quart of syrup," Audrey said.

Connie appeared. Her hair was damp from a shower, and she wore her customary tee and stained yoga pants. "But it's worth the work. You must be Audrey."

Introductions were made as Otis and Peggy came in the back door. Learning Otis had a wicked sweet tooth, the day before Kate had baked him cookies, hoping to ingratiate herself. She liked his level-headed demeanor and saw him as a prospective ally. The tall, thin man was soft spoken and not easily ruffled— attributes she respected. He peeked into the slow cooker, putting his hands in his overalls. "Any chance of chocolate chips for the oatmeal?"

"I got you covered," Kate said, opening a cabinet and plucking out a bag of milk chocolate morsels.

"The doctor said you need to watch your blood sugar, love," Peggy reminded her husband. The first time Kate heard her speak, she'd been surprised by her breathy Marilyn Monroe-esque voice. It seemed at odds with her flowy tie-dye caftan and Birkenstocks. "But kudos for the steel cut oats, Kate. They are incredibly nutritious, especially sprinkled with wheat germ."

"Oh... you're welcome."

She held a glass jar of honey, a section of comb in the center. "I see you have maple syrup, but I brought this."

"How generous. Thanks, Peggy." Kate set the jar beside the bowls and silverware she'd arranged on the counter buffet style.

"Is that *honey*?" Audrey joined them, rubbing her palms together. "The food here is so yummy!" Her shyness evaporating, she greeted the newcomers with a megawatt smile. In response, they were polite but reserved. When conversation lulled and the moment turned awkward, Kate encouraged everyone to serve themselves from the buffet she'd set up.

The group assembled at the table. Kate spooned oatmeal in a bowl and sat across from Audrey, where she'd cozied up on the bench next to Teller.

"Sorry we're late," Judy said from the doorway. "We overslept and had to feed the chickens."

As a rule, Jamie spoke little, and Nora took after her father. Kate found her an unusual child, immature for her age. Clinging to her mother, she appeared bashful at Audrey's presence. Judy held her hand, leading her to the table while Jamie got breakfast at the counter. After serving Nora, he set a glass of apple juice in front of Judy.

Connie waved her hand. "Scott family, I want you to meet our guest."

They acknowledged Audrey in their taciturn way, then Judy complained to nobody in particular, "My morning sickness has been horrid—I can't wait 'til I'm done with my first trimester."

"I'll bring some ginger tea by your cabin later," Peggy offered as she sprinkled raisins on her oats.

"Can I come see your hives?" Audrey asked. "I'm interested in beekeeping."

"If you'd like."

Listening to the others chat as they ate, Kate's glance traveled around the table. She noted an absence. "Seth usually doesn't miss a meal. Where is he?"

The atmosphere became stilted. Connie cleared her throat. "He left early this morning with supplies for our bunker. It doesn't take long to get there by foot. He'll be back in a day or two."

Everyone focused on their food. When he finished eating, Otis pushed away from the table and put his bowl by the sink. "We got fences to repair. We'll be back in time for the noon meal."

With thank yous to Kate, Teller and Jamie got to their feet, following Otis outside.

It was as if Connie read Kate's mind when she said, "You know, Kate, with summer on us it's getting hotter. There's no need for a cooked meal midday. When I show you the hydroponic garden, we'll pick lettuce for a salad."

"You sure do have pretty hair. Golden, just like your mommy," Audrey said to Nora, and the little girl blushed. "Would you like me to give you a French braid?"

Nora bobbed her head and Audrey stood, moving behind Nora where she sat beside Kate. Audrey sectioned hair and deftly braided. She said brightly, "I can do haircuts for everyone too, if you have sharp scissors."

"Kind of you. But later. I'll show you around now," Connie replied with authority. Kate considered her. She'd seemed delicate the night before. Now, Connie was confident in her role as the matriarch of Clan Metzger. Her sister was a study in contrasts.

"Tell Miss Audrey thank you," Judy instructed, smiling with

approval when Nora complied. "We ought to get to our geography lesson."

Nora trudged behind Judy.

"Barn, obviously," Connie said a few minutes later, motioning toward the large, red-painted structure behind the house. "We have livestock—hogs, horses, cows. Enough for our own use."

"I love cows!" Audrey enthused. "Can I pet that black one over in that field by the pond?"

Kate bit her tongue to keep from chuckling. "That's the bull that charged Jamie yesterday. I'd keep away if I were you."

"There's the machine shed. Pole barn over there. And, this is the coop, of course." Amy, Connie's Speckled Sussex, clucked, pecking the dirt. A brown cockerel with a jaunty comb strutted toward Audrey with purpose, his beady eyes unblinking. "Lenin, shoo!"

"Gah!" Audrey jumped back as the rooster puffed out his hackles and flapped his wings at her. Connie swooped in and grabbed Lenin before he accosted Audrey, tucking him under her arm.

"His name fits," Kate said drily.

"He's a bastard." Connie advised Audrey, "Just walk away. Once you're out of his line of sight, he'll forget all about you."

After a five-minute stroll north, they came to a row of cabins much like Kate's—timber-sided with solar-paneled green metal roofs and minuscule front porches. Audrey put a hand at her forehead to shade the sun from her eyes. "This is some setup. How many acres do you have?"

"Three hundred. Follow me," Connie said. She looked at Audrey over her shoulder. "We'll check out Peggy's bees, then maybe she'll give you a detailed lesson while Kate and I pick lettuce for lunch. You and I will tour the gardens this afternoon."

The beehive was enclosed on three sides by a rickety lean-to. Without the steady hum of buzzing bees, the half-dozen crates would've looked like nothing more than a stack of wood storage containers. Hesitant to get too close, they hung back at a safe distance, observing the honeybees' comings and goings.

A colorful perennial garden was planted beside the hive, serving as a source of nectar for the bees. Blooms every hue of the rainbow were in a perfectly manicured bed. Kate bent to pick a handful of lily of the valley. She inhaled their fragrance. "Momma's favorite."

"Yes. I remember her talking about how the blossoms symbolized purity and joy. It's a nice memory," Connie replied, softening momentarily. "Hold on. I'll grab Peggy."

Leaving Audrey with Peggy, the sisters traversed back to the farm proper, their pace unhurried. Connie pointed out anything of note as they walked. Just beyond the red barn was a simple cinder block building. "Here's where the hydroponic garden is. We built it last year."

Pulling the door open, Connie led Kate inside. Artificially lit with grow lights, there were metal shelves fitted with oversized PVC pipe. Veggies grew in the pipe. Kate spotted heads of lettuce, kale, peppers, and more. "There's water inside the PVC?"

"Yes. Isn't it fabulous? I even have herbs."

Connie selected a plastic storage bin from a supply shelf, and they quickly filled it before making their way to the house. Kate sat the tote on the kitchen counter and unloaded it, her gaze feasting on the produce. She'd fix a chef salad and garlic toast. When she turned, she found Connie regarding her, her brow knit. "What's up?"

"I'm going to show you something, but you have to be discreet with what you see."

Kate said, "I'm intrigued."

Connie crooked her finger, leading Kate downstairs. It was an ordinary basement, musty and smelling of wood rot. The stone walls were discolored with streaks of lime and calcium and lined with bookshelves. Going to the largest shelving unit, Connie pulled and it rotated out, exposing a simple hollow core door.

"Everyone knows we have a panic room down here, but they don't know details."

"Oooh," Kate breathed. Connie opened the door and they stepped into a narrow passage. There were metal doors similar to those on elevator cars directly in front of them. A pin pad was affixed on the wall.

Connie punched in a code. "Two-seven-one-four. Remember that."

The doors slid open.

CHAPTER TWENTY

"Wow," Kate said after Connie switched on a light.

Rectangular-shaped LED fixtures attached to the drop ceiling illuminated the well-ordered room. The walls were drywalled and painted off-white, the floor beige and black stippled linoleum. It was immaculately clean, reminding Kate of a hospital lab.

"Not bad, huh? We've tried to maximize efficiency."

Sizable, it was perhaps thirty feet square, outfitted with a streamlined kitchen and a table with chairs. Along two walls were sets of metal bunk beds made up with green army surplus blankets. Across from the kitchen were floor-to-ceiling wardrobes and another set of elevator doors.

Kate pointed to the doors. "Where do those go?"

"To a tunnel under the barn." Connie cocked her head toward the other side of the kitchen. "There's a bathroom with a commode and shower stall over there."

"You have *running water*?"

"No, we've got a holding tank of water for the shower. The commode's a composting toilet." She bent and gestured under the nearest set of bunk beds. "See the containers of water? They're for drinking and cooking."

"This must have cost a fortune to set up!"

Connie snorted, taking a seat on a molded plastic chair at the dining table. "Now you see why we drive old cars and never take vacations—why our furniture and appliances are thirty years old even though we have a thriving accounting business."

"I'm… speechless," Kate said, dropping into a chair across from her sister.

"That doesn't happen often."

"No, it doesn't. I count twelve bunks. How long can that number of people survive in here?"

"At max capacity with strict water rationing? Three weeks to a month. Not much longer. This is a bug-out shelter. It's only for temporary use—like if we're under attack."

"Huh." Kate swept her gaze around the room. "How will you know when it's safe to come back out?"

"By watching live feed from our cameras on a laptop computer."

Kate chewed a nail thoughtfully. "But what if you run out of food and water before it's safe enough to return to the house?"

"Then we use the tunnel and evacuate through the barn."

"To the bunker Seth went to? The one his parents gifted you for your wedding?"

"Bingo." Connie gave Kate a grim smile. "Any prepper worth their salt has more than one contingency plan. If, for some reason, our bunker is inaccessible, we can work our way toward Seth's family's place. Granted, it's twenty miles away…"

"So, where exactly is your bunker?"

"I'll get to that, but you have something you're chewing over."

I guess I'm easy to read. "Yeah. You've been too tight-lipped about Seth. What went down last night?"

Connie turned obstinate. She put her hands over her midsection. Her jaw ticked. "I told him to leave and not come back 'til he gets his head on right. And I changed the code to this bunker after he left. We can't trust him."

Kate stared at her, unblinking.

"Don't look at me like that. You thought I was a pushover—see, I can be tough." She shook her head. "I may feel different later, but right now I'm beyond done."

"You really think Seth has the skillset to make it on his own?"

Connie brought up a shoulder, indifferent. Her green irises were like chips of ice. "It's not that far and he took a gun. He's a big boy."

Uh… okay. She could tell Connie was unwilling to discuss Seth any further. Changing the subject, Kate said, "Speaking of guns… they aren't the best way to handle Zs. A single gunshot can attract huge numbers of them. We must figure out something quieter—like my ax."

"You never did like firearms."

The words *ever since you found Momma and Dad's bodies* hung unspoken in the air. Pretending they didn't, Kate swallowed and briskly continued, "Swords? Bows? Unless you have any here, we'll have to scavenge for some."

"No. There are stores in River Heights that sold that type of thing."

"Unless somebody got there first. If so, we may have to venture further." Kate crossed her arms, nibbling at her lip as she deliberated. "I really think it needs to be soon. Maybe tomorrow? Of course, I'll go. Teller knows what it's like out there. I can ask him to come along. Jamie, too. He seems fit."

"If you think quieter weapons are required, then you have my blessing. But you're right. The sooner the better."

"Then it's decided. I'll talk to Teller and Jamie today."

"Is there something else, Kate?"

Kate's lip quirked. "Yeah. Two things. The first is water. Tell me what the water situation is here on the farm."

"We have a well. I'm not sure if you noticed but we have rain barrels for the vegetable gardens—and Peggy's flowers." Connie shrugged. "At this juncture, water supply's plentiful."

"The other thing is meals."

"It's a lot of work, isn't it?" Connie's tone was amused, and Kate bristled. "Now, now, don't get your feathers ruffled."

"I don't have a problem with the work, but why can't the farmhands prepare food in their own cabins?"

"You know those kitchenettes aren't exactly conducive. Part of the hands' compensation package is provided meals." She drummed her fingers on the tabletop. "However, you have more pressing matters to deal with in the coming days. I'll take over breakfast prep—"

"I don't think—"

"And we'll figure out a rotation for lunches." She gave Kate a smile, her manner unyielding. "It's time for everyone to pitch in. What else?" Kate shook her head. "Okay, let me show you the facilities."

Pushing to her feet, Connie crossed the room and swung kitchen cabinets open one by one. Simple plastic dinner and glassware were stacked in one cupboard. Others were stuffed with MREs and non-perishables. An apartment size fridge was tucked under the counter, along with tanks of water. Instead of a stove, there were hot plates and a microwave.

"You've seen the potable water stored under the beds. Go ahead and poke your head into the bathroom." Behind a wood door between a set of cots was a simple lavatory with a commode and a fiberglass shower stall. There were two water tanks. From behind Kate, Connie explained, "One tank feeds the shower, the other holds gray water."

The floor-to-ceiling wardrobes across from the kitchen contained everything from tools to bug-out bags to board games and weapons. "When you have spare time, I want you to come down here and explore. Really familiarize yourself with it all."

"I will."

Connie rooted in a kitchen drawer. "Sit down, Kate. There's something important we must go over."

Complying, Kate sat and waited, her mind racing. Notebook

and pencil in hand, Connie joined her at the table. Without speaking, she flipped to a blank page and scribbled.

"What are you drawing?"

Briefly showing her a rough sketch, Connie returned to her work. "It's a map."

Overwhelmed, Kate rubbed her temple. "A map? For what?"

Connie's emerald-green gaze flew over Kate. "To our bunker. You wanted to know how to get there, remember?" Head bent, her chestnut hair covered her cheeks as she drew. She didn't look up until the map was finished. Placing her pencil on the table, she thrust the notebook in Kate's fingers.

After examining the labyrinth of lines and squiggles for a moment, Kate scratched her head, feeling addle-brained. "How long does it take to get there?"

"It's about a ten-minute hike." Connie leaned across the table and put her hand on Kate's. "You need a break. We'll get some lemonade and sit on the front porch before you prepare lunch."

"Should I bring the map along?"

"No, leave it," Connie said firmly. "You can review it later when you come back here. You must commit it to memory then destroy it. Kate, listen…"

Setting the map aside, Kate searched her sister's eyes. "I am listening. What?"

"*Very* few people know where the bunker is." Connie clasped Kate's hand tight. "For now, I think we should keep the location under wraps."

Kate blew a raspberry. She was starting to feel claustrophobic and needed air. "You're the boss."

"Good. Come on. Let's go upstairs."

Thoughts jumbled, Kate silently followed Connie through the elevator doors and up the basement steps.

Lounging against the kitchen counter, Kate watched her sister pour tall glasses of lemonade. Voices from outside pulled her from her thoughts. "What was that?"

Without waiting for an answer, Kate hurried to the screen

door and peered out. Nora stood frozen beside the chicken coop. Unmistakably distraught, her arms hugged her slight body. Peggy and Audrey supported Judy, duckwalking her toward the farmhouse. Judy's skin was chalky.

Kate called, "What's happened?"

Then she saw the blood soaking Judy's skirt and trickling down her legs.

CHAPTER TWENTY-ONE

"Oh my God!" Kate held open the screen door, beckoning with her arm. "Bring her in and put her on the living room sofa."

"What is it?" Connie asked from behind Kate.

"Looks like Judy's having a miscarriage. You better grab some towels to put under her."

Audrey and Peggy jockeyed Judy through the door and hall. Connie put layers of old towels across the couch cushions and they lowered Judy gingerly. Connie gaped at Judy and wrung her hands. Peggy's heavily lined face was set in concern. Audrey looked green.

Anxious Audrey may pass out, Kate met her eyes and said in an even tone, "Go get Judy a glass of orange juice. Please."

Nodding dumbly, Audrey moved toward the kitchen, her steps hesitant.

Judy's eyelids flickered.

Fighting to keep her panic contained, Kate took a calming breath. "Judy, tell me what to do."

"There's nothing anyone can do. I'm past that." Judy's voice was reedy but resigned. "I've lost too much blood." She winced. "The cramping is… severe."

Her tone high-pitched, Connie asked, "Why is this happening? Did you fall?"

"No, no. Nothing like that," Peggy insisted. "We were chatting about the hens, and she had a twinge. The next thing we knew, blood was gushing down her leg."

Audrey was back with the juice. Peggy took the cup and kneeled by the sofa. She held it to Judy's lips so she could sip from it. Kate turned to Connie, wrapping her fingers around Connie's forearms. Her eyes unfocused, Connie's gaze was glued on Judy. "Con. I want you to get Nora and sit out on the porch with her. Audrey, run out to the pasture beyond the corral, and see if you can locate the guys. Fetch Jamie."

After the women left, Judy whispered, "There's nothing anyone can do…"

"I'm scared you're hemorrhaging, Judy. Please, just be still and rest."

Peggy looked up at Kate, her brown eyes enormous. "She's weak. She's already lost too much blood."

Bringing her palms up, Kate said, "Not like we can take her to the ER for a transfusion."

While Peggy encouraged Judy to drink the juice, Kate went into the kitchen and brought chairs. She sat beside the couch, holding Judy's clammy hand. Not knowing what to say, she could only mull the possible worst-case scenarios. What if the bleeding didn't stop? What if Judy developed an infection?

Pushing the cup of juice away, Judy dozed. Her skin looked colorless and paper-thin. Kate narrowed her eyes, pressing her fingers into the towels under Judy. They were saturated. It was difficult to tell whether the bleeding had slowed. She sent up a prayer that Judy would be okay.

At last, Audrey brought Jamie. He was dusty, his dishwater blond hair was coated with perspiration. Peggy and Kate got to their feet and pushed their chairs back. He came to the sofa and bent to Judy, gathering her in his arms. Kate wanted to give them privacy. She tapped Peggy on the arm, and they went into the kitchen.

Unsure what else to do, Kate dully set about preparing lunch. She put a cutting board and knife on the butcher block counter for Peggy to chop veggies. Kate washed and tore lettuce into a bowl while eggs boiled. She was dicing ham when Jamie appeared in the kitchen entryway, Judy in his arms.

"She wants me to take her to our cabin," he said in his subdued way, and Kate wiped her hands on a kitchen towel.

"Uh. Here," she said, grabbing a walkie where it charged on the counter. She tucked it in the front pocket of his shirt. "Let us know if you need us. I'll bring your lunch to you in a bit. We'll... we'll keep Nora here."

Jamie thanked them and left, Judy's body drooping against him.

"Fuck," Kate muttered, feeling tears prick her eyelids. She hated helplessness, but that was what she was—helpless. There was nothing she—or anyone else—could do. Sinking her teeth into the inside of her cheek to keep from weeping, she swallowed the lump in her throat.

Peggy put a pan of garlic bread in the oven, giving Kate a sympathetic smile. "It's permissible to cry, you know."

"It's not," Kate insisted, knowing she must gather her wits about her, to be strong. "People depend on me. What if Connie or Audrey saw me bawling? What if Nora sees?"

Peggy's wrinkled face set into a look of pity. "God has a plan for all of us, Kate."

Kate whirled on her, trying to keep her sudden burst of temper in check. "You think God's plan includes killing innocent people and turning them into bloodthirsty zombies? Really?"

"Faith isn't always easy, but—"

"Save it, okay, Peg?" Kate asked tightly. "I don't buy into religion."

"So, you've not been saved?"

Kate didn't respond. Brittle as glass, she felt as if she were teetering on the edge of a world class meltdown. She knew all it would take was a gentle nudge and she'd explode. Grinding her teeth, she grabbed plates and cutlery, avoiding Peggy's prying eyes. Since her parents' death, Kate had a thorny relationship with God. She certainly wasn't going to discuss the subject with Peggy.

The men came in a short time later, and Audrey and Connie brought Nora to the kitchen. Everyone tried to act normal for the child's sake, but their bright smiles and cheery manner didn't seem to convince her. Nora's dubious gaze volleyed between the adults.

Tummy in knots, Kate barely ate. She pushed her food around her plate and made a show of eating. Compelled to do something, she put her fork down. Kate encircled Nora's thin shoulders, squeezing. "I know you're nervous about your mom, kid. We all are. Just try your best to keep a positive attitude."

"When can I see her?" Nora asked in a tiny voice, eyes downcast.

"Not quite yet. She's resting now," Kate explained. She sought Audrey across the table. "How about if you hang out with us today?"

Audrey latched onto Kate's suggestion, as if relieved to be assigned a task. "I can give you a haircut."

"And you can help Connie by showing Audrey the vegetable gardens, right?"

"O-okay."

After cleaning the kitchen, Kate found a crate and packed plates of salad and garlic toast covered in cling film. Crate in the crook of her arm, she walked to Jamie and Judy's place. Trepidation caused her heartbeat to flutter in her ribcage as she climbed the porch steps.

Jamie answered Kate's knock right away, his face grave. His shirt was crusted with blood, infusing the air with hot metal. "I was fixing to call you on the walkie."

Mouth pursed at the odor, she handed him the food as she stepped over the threshold. "Why? Has something happened?"

"The bleeding had stopped, but it's picking up again..."

The cabin was like Kate's but larger, with two bedrooms. She found Judy supine on the bed in the master bedroom. Pausing in the doorway, Kate's nostrils flared. It couldn't be, could it?

"Kate," Judy gasped. "I need help to the bathroom. My cramps—it's like my insides are being shredded—"

Kate grasped Judy's outstretched hand and assisted her to her feet, winding her arm around Judy's waist. As she piloted her toward the door, Kate glimpsed back at the bed. Reddish-black blood drenched the quilt.

Coming to them, Jamie reached for Judy. He and Kate got her into the restroom and situated on the toilet. Judy howled in agony, her cry tortured. She bent down, her skin red and sweaty. She whimpered, "It hurts so bad."

With a final wail, there was a plop as something hit the surface of the water.

The smell in the bathroom was overpowering, making Kate's eyes and nose water. She mopped at her brow, worried she might lose consciousness. They waited until Judy caught her breath, and Kate used a hand towel to clean her up. She pursed her lips to keep from dry heaving.

Jamie grunted as he lifted Judy from the commode and helped her to the door.

Twisting in his arms, Judy tried to look in the toilet bowl. "I-I want to see..."

Jamie grimaced, his expression anguished. He averted his face. "No, Jude. No." He hustled her out, leaving Kate behind.

There was a splash in the toilet bowl. Bracing herself, Kate peered down.

Bobbing and thrashing amongst foul clots of blood, a three-inch-long fetus snapped its undeveloped jaws. Flipper limbs flailed.

Flap. Flap. Gurgle.

Kate sprang back, whacking into the wall across from the commode. She clapped her hands over her mouth to keep from shrieking.

Oh fuck. Oh fuck.

Shuddering with disgust, she flushed the monstrosity away.

CHAPTER TWENTY-TWO

Jamie and Judy don't know—they have no idea!

Kate turned on the faucet and splashed her cheeks with cold water. Locking her hands on the rim of the bathroom sink, she confronted her tormented reflection in the mirror. Her irises had darkened to a shade of murky blue-green reminiscent of a choppy sea. Water dripped down her quivering chin and onto her shirt.

What happened to Judy was *her* fault. She'd brought Audrey —and the virus—to Mayfly Hollow. Kate was shaken to her core. She was culpable.

Guilt sliced through her. Jagged. Lethal.

Kate's brain involuntarily echoed the grotesque images—the monster buoyant in the water. The flap flap of its thrashing. Fingers constricting on the sink, she fought wave after wave of nausea.

Breathe, Kate. Get control. What if Jamie comes in and sees you losing it? How would that make him feel? How would you explain?

Contaminated by what she'd witnessed, Kate took a clean towel from the vanity cabinet, her movements jerky. With more force than necessary, she scrubbed the moisture from her skin until it was raw. No matter how hard she wiped, Kate couldn't remove the shame and revulsion left behind.

Straightening her spine, she stepped from the bathroom and into the living area. Judy reclined on a loveseat, moaning and clutching her groin. Jamie knelt beside her, dabbing her sweat-sheened forehead with a cloth. Kate faltered. It seemed wrong to witness such an intimate moment.

"Ahem," Kate said. Jamie hoisted himself up, looking world-weary. Broken. "I'll strip the sheets from your bed and wash them. And Nora can stay with us overnight."

Jamie nodded. Avoiding his eyes, Kate went into their bedroom and collected the sullied bed linens dripping red-black blood. Suppressing a gag, she hurried back to the main room. Promising to look in on Judy later, she sprinted from the cabin.

Kate made it to the staff laundry building before she lost her lunch. Outside the simple cinder block structure, she vomited into the weeds until there was nothing left in her system. Insides roiling, she swabbed the puke away with the hem of her shirt. "Ugh."

There was a light switch just inside the door. Designed for functionality rather than form, the interior was sparsely furnished, containing a commercial capacity washer and dryer set, a laminate counter for folding clothes, a drying rack, and a utility tub. Generic detergent and off-brand bleach were on a wire shelf above the washer.

Humming with distaste, Kate stuffed the linens into the machine and added soap. At the utility sink, she washed her face and hands. The harsh, hostile stink of Z blood remained in her soft tissues, taunting her.

Reluctant to return to the farmhouse, Kate slumped against the counter, her thoughts racing. She wrestled the myriad of emotions warring in her chest. Her instincts were screaming, vying for her consideration. Begging her to heed their counsel. Run, they compelled. But Kate couldn't. She was stuck.

How had she become saddled with the responsibility of co-managing this place, of ensuring its occupants' well-being?

Duty. Family. Obligation. The ties that bind. The constraints chafed. She longed to flout them and flee Mayfly Hollow. To never look back. But her sister and the baby she carried tethered Kate in place. Held her captive.

Connie.

She'd have to watch to make sure Connie didn't exhibit symptoms. Shaking her head, Kate groaned. She hesitated to share what transpired in Judy and Jamie's cabin. Connie's mental state was fragile. Unpredictable. It vacillated between sensible and unstable. She'd worry herself sick. What about Teller? Should Kate confide in *him*? What was the right thing to do?

Keep it to yourself.

Once decided, Kate headed back to the farmhouse. There was laundry and cleaning to be done, and later, the evening meal to prepare. In the root garden, Nora and Audrey were on their knees weeding in the even rows of crops. Kate pasted a smile on her lips and greeted them as she walked past.

She found Connie sitting at the kitchen table, looking completely healthy but bothered. She held a pill bottle. *What now?* Kate sat on the bench and put her chin in her hand.

"How's Judy?" Connie asked, her gaze never abandoning the bottle.

"She miscarried."

Connie sighed. "The bleeding stop?"

"I think so. I told Jamie I'd come by later. That we'd keep Nora for the night."

"When you go back, ask her if she needs any pain pills. We have some in our first aid kit."

"I will. Speaking of pills—what's that, Con?"

Connie met Kate's eyes, but she was visibly shaken. "I was looking in Seth's nightstand for a pair of nail clippers, and I found this. Apparently, he hasn't been taking his meds."

"What meds?"

"Seth has... barriers. Five years ago, he received a dual diagnosis—both a mood disorder and a personality disorder." Connie presented the prescription bottle with Seth's name on the label. "These are his anti-psychotics."

"That explains a lot."

Connie was defensive. "Up until now, it's been well-controlled with pharmaceuticals."

Kate angled her head back on her neck and surveyed the ceiling, which was yellowed with age and needed dusting. *Connie has secrets, too.* When Kate spoke, she chose her words carefully. "Why didn't you tell me before? Were you ever going to?"

"You already don't get along with Seth. Do you really think the knowledge would change your relationship for the better?" Connie pulled a face. "You know there's stigma attached to mental illness. He begged me to keep mum. I couldn't betray his confidence, could I?"

"In light of the current situation, it would've been helpful information to share. I am capable of empathy, you know." Unable to muster any irritation, Kate shrugged, pragmatic. "How long?"

"This was filled before the virus. It's mostly full."

"So he quit weeks ago, in the thick of all the end-of-the-world bullshit. Why? Why would he do that?"

Connie lifted a shoulder. "Perhaps he thought he wouldn't be able to get to a pharmacy easily again and weaned himself off. Or he thought he was strong enough to do without. I don't know. He's touchy about discussing his diagnoses, considers it a liability."

"Clearly he's been abusing liquor to self-medicate. Not that it's helped much," Kate said grimly. *More issues. Just what I fucking need.*

If Seth ever made it back to Mayfly Hollow, the matter would require immediate attention. It would be an unpleasant scene. The thought of it made Kate feel incredibly tired. Everything was a goddamn mess, and there was nothing she could do about it.

Keeping her expression impassive, Kate pushed up from the table. Focusing instead on her relief that Connie wasn't showing signs of the virus, she bent to her sister, hugging her. "It'll be okay. When Seth comes back, we'll figure it out."

Connie hid her face in Kate's shirt and sniffled. Her voice was muffled when she said, "Alright."

I've gotta get out of here. Gradually pulling away, Kate patted Connie's arm. "I'm gonna take a minute. Get some air before dinner."

Connie gave her a watery smile. "You do need a breather. I'm defrosting a casserole from the deep freeze. I can put it in the oven if you aren't back in time."

THE LOG in the glade was daubed with dappled afternoon sunlight. Kate plunked down on it with a grateful sigh and stretched her legs out in front of her. The day was warm, but the clearing was lush and cool. Teller was correct in calling it a hide-away. It was a place where a person could shed their burdens and merely *be.* Kate was introspective as she listened to the rustle of the brook.

There was a whistling swoosh of wings as birds flew over-head. Then low, throaty coos joined the babble of water moving against stones in the creek by Kate's feet. She scoured the leafy branches of the trees. Spotting them in an oak next to the foot-path, her mouth curved in delight. A pair of gray and tan freckled mourning doves perched on a bare limb.

Nostalgia swelled in Kate's heart, the doves' gentle cooing evoking memories long forgotten.

Momma's long chestnut hair was tucked under a green headscarf that made her dramatic jade-colored irises even more intense than usual. She hummed as she bustled around the kitchen, tidying up after lunch. Five-year-old Kate played with wooden blocks on the aged kitchen linoleum while Momma washed dishes in the sink.

"Ohh, Katie Scarlett. You absolutely must see this," she breathed. She took her hands from the sudsy water and peeled off her lemon-yellow kitchen gloves. Lowering, she scooped Kate into her arms.

"What is it, Momma?"

"Look," she said, tapping a pink-tipped fingernail against the kitchen window above the sink. A plump gray bird sat on the windowsill outside, its round eyes intent. "It's a mourning dove."

Kate's dark, finely etched eyebrows drew together. With fascinated concentration, she studied the bird. "Mourning dove?"

"Yes, baby." Momma kissed Kate's forehead. Her perfume wafted to Kate's pert nose—lily of the valley, a flower that grew wild and plentiful outside their apartment building each spring. She loved picking them by the fistful. "I want you to remember something very important whenever you see a dove."

"What?"

Momma brought her silky-smooth cheek to Kate's. Her honeyed Savannah accent was distinct when she said, "This too shall pass, Katie Scarlett. This too shall pass."

CHAPTER TWENTY-THREE

THE DOVES FLEW AWAY AS RAPIDLY AS HER MEMORIES, THE WHISTLE of their wings reverberating in the grotto-like space. Kate shook her head to clear the clinging cobwebs.

It was inconceivable that less than two months earlier the mundane day-to-day tasks of operating her bakery had dominated her every waking moment. Her determination and hard work had just begun to pay off, too. She and Rosie were launching a second Buttercream location in the autumn, intending to eventually franchise. Everything Kate ever wanted was within her grasp. That life seemed so distant and vague now that survival was the sole goal.

She snarled in defeat. What good did it do to pout? To dwell on the past? She needed to stay grounded to the here and now instead of ruminating over what would never be.

The here and now.

As haunted as she was by Judy's miscarriage, knowing Connie had escaped unscathed took a huge weight from Kate's shoulders. The swift-acting virus had left destruction in its wake, but if Connie was to become ill, surely infection would've ravaged her hours ago, just as it had ravaged Judy.

Kate evaluated her impulse to return to the farmhouse and

confess the truth to her sister—that she'd killed Judy's baby by bringing the virus. That she may as well have stabbed Judy in the womb.

How would Connie react? Perhaps she'd lash out at Kate, rebuking her for putting all of Mayfly Hollow at risk. Maybe she'd tell Kate to leave as punishment. Connie would be right to do so.

What she'd told her about Seth gave Kate a lot to think about. Face prickling, she considered what he'd say when he learned what occurred in his absence. He'd gloat. The inevitable yet completely justified *I told you so* would blister with the heat of a thousand suns. He'd definitely kick her ass out, no doubt humiliating her in front of the others in the process. He always knew how to wield his words to get under her skin, to flay her open. Suddenly hot, Kate shucked her sweatshirt, only leaving on the tank top she used in lieu of a bra.

She'd certainly dithered enough about whether to travel to Clayton's Corners to find Ben. She ought to leave Mayfly Hollow before Seth returned.

Coward. Things get difficult and you bail... just like Dad.

Kate balled up her sweatshirt and pitched it away. Inertia caused her to lose her balance from her seat on the log. Arms flailing, she tumbled off, landing on her back in the springy grass. It was fresh-smelling and supple, cushioning her fall. The absurdity of it all made her laugh until her sides hurt.

Maybe Seth's not the only one losing his mind.

Kate extricated her legs from where they rested cockeyed on the log. Not bothered enough to get up, she laced her fingers and put her hands under her head to pillow it, pondering the heavens. The sky peeking through the tree branches had become overcast, transforming from cerulean to Palladian blue with striated oyster-colored clouds. Leaf mold and earthy loam had replaced the odor of Z blood in Kate's nostrils. The blissfully cool air relaxed her. She closed her eyes. Yawning, she settled more comfortably into the grass.

Kate was woken by a noise lapping at her subconscious. Reflexes on high alert, she vaulted up and into an attack stance.

"Whoa there, Xena Warrior Princess," Teller quipped, putting his palms up in defense. Ace stood obediently by his master's side, acknowledging Kate with a quick woof.

She let out a breath she hadn't realized she held. Her pulse lurched in her throat. "You shouldn't sneak up on me!"

"Sneak? Damn hell, girl. I've been callin' your name nigh on five minutes."

Embarrassment wormed its way through Kate's veins and painted her cheeks. She was glad the light was too dim for Teller to notice. The sun was gone, leaving it misty and chilled. The air was diffused with fog. How could she have allowed herself to fall so deeply asleep out in the open—to put herself in such a vulnerable position? Next time she might not be so lucky. Kate wondered if she ought to take to carrying her ax with her at all times.

She kept her voice from wavering when she said, "Good thing you weren't a Z."

"No shit." Teller sat on the log, motioning for Kate to join him. Ace dropped on his haunches next to Teller's boots, his snoot on his front paws. "You must've been tuckered out—you were comatose."

Shivering, Kate located her sweatshirt. She slipped it on before sitting beside Teller. It was damp and imbued with the aroma of soil, but she was happy to have it. "How late is it?"

"Well past suppertime. Connie said you needed solitude, but by sunset she was fixin' to send out a search party. I told her I had a notion where you were."

"Ugh. I should've checked on Judy hours ago. I'll go do that before it gets any later."

Teller extended a hand to still her. "Peggy's spendin' the night at Jamie and Judy's. I'm told Judy's restin'. And Audrey and Nora are bunkin' with Connie. Everything's shipshape."

Kate sighed, rolling her head in a circle. Her body felt bruised and battered—she was evidently too old to sleep on the ground.

He cleared his throat. "You know, Kate…"

Teller's voice was contemplative. Brow knit, she looked at him, but he didn't meet her eyes.

"I've got a hunch you're scoldin' yourself," he murmured, the hard planes of his face softening as vapor crept past them and suspended above the brook. "You take on too much."

"What do you mean?"

"You're battlin' yourself, but you care far more than you'd like to admit."

Thrown off-kilter by his too accurate assessment, Kate deflected by scoffing in disdain, "We barely know each other."

"I ain't blind." Teller's gaze sharpened. "And just 'cause I talk with a drawl don't mean I'm dim-witted."

"I never said—"

"We might not have been acquainted long, but *I do see you*."

Her tone was curt when Kate said, "Really? Please enlighten me with your insights into my psyche, Dr. Freud."

The noise he made threw her—it told her he knew she was full of crap. That he saw right through her façade. The realization made her stomach cartwheel.

"You're a contradiction, Kate."

"How so?"

"You have one foot outta Mayfly Hollow, but the other is firmly shackled. No amount of yearnin' for your freedom will ever defeat the hold Connie has over you." Teller's tongue clicked against his teeth. "As much as you like to think you're a loner—an outsider—you are forgin' connections with the others here. Becomin' part of the fabric of this place."

Had Connie confided in Teller about Seth's diagnoses? About him not taking his meds? Kate doubted it—and she didn't plan to tell him either, at least not yet. She grunted, shaking her head. "They're polite because I'm their boss's sister. Tolerated. The truth is I'm nothing more to them than a glorified maid."

"I disagree."

"Face it, Teller. Judy's miscarriage was my fault. Once the ugly truth comes out, I won't be welcome anymore. I can guarantee it."

"How's it your fault?"

Kate swallowed, choking on her words as she told him about what she'd seen at Jamie and Judy's cabin. Misery she couldn't contain seeped into her speech when she whispered, "The fetus was a Z."

"What?"

Throat burning with emotion, Kate bit her lip to curtail the tears brewing in her eyes.

Teller put a hand to his chin, causing little swishy sounds when he rubbed hard against the bristles of his five o'clock shadow. "Jamie and Judy don't know?"

A tear streaked down Kate's cheek. "Nuh-uh. Nobody does. But don't you see? It's my fault! I was bound and determined to go to River Heights—"

"Shoot, girl," Teller chided. "I made the decision to take you there, so that makes me just as blameworthy, don't it?"

She shook her head. Nothing anyone could say would ever change Kate's mind. She knew. "I didn't quarantine when we got back because Connie needed me. It must have been *me.*"

"I ain't buyin' it. Infection spreads like wildfire. You were there for days before Judy got sick. It was Audrey or me that exposed her—not that it matters. Pointin' fingers gets us nowhere." Teller sighed. "Sooner or later, Mayfly Hollow was gonna be affected, Kate."

He bent toward her and brought a work-calloused thumb to her cheekbone, gently brushing away the tracks of moisture. His closeness made Kate's heart skip a beat. The cells in her body sang at his scent—soap and hay—and compelled her to lean in.

Gaze rapt, Teller trailed his thumb to the curve of her mouth. "Oh, Kate."

Lips parting, she hissed at his touch, her head tilting of its own accord.

Teller's kiss was sweet. Kate entwined her arms around the strong column of his neck. Lost herself in his heat—

In the distance, faint banging echoed. Shouts rang out. Ace's posture stiffened. Spotlights posted on tall metal posts illuminated the clearing. Through the dense haze, unnatural light spilled over Kate and Teller where they sat.

Kate jerked from his embrace and sprung to her feet, adrenaline oozing from her pores. They had to get to the farmhouse and see what was going on. Once out of the clearing, Kate and Teller broke into a run, Ace in stride.

Visibility was poor. Teller reached for Kate's hand. "Cabins first," he panted. "We gotta get guns."

CHAPTER TWENTY-FOUR

THE ROLLING FOG GAVE A HAZY OTHERWORLDLY QUALITY TO THEIR surroundings. Though the spotlights blazed, the light reflected into Kate and Teller's eyes and made it all the more difficult to navigate to Kate's cabin. They didn't veer from the gravel road.

Muffled commotion carried from the direction of the farmhouse, but no more shouts. Troubled by the implication, Kate's hands curled into fists and she pumped her legs harder.

"Almost there," Teller gasped.

"The guns and ammo are hidden under my bed."

Teller took the porch stairs in one giant step and threw open the door, Ace bounding inside behind him. Kate turned on the bedside lamp and fell to her knees to yank out boxes of bullets. Teller had found a rifle like the one he'd taught her how to use in River Heights. Making certain it was loaded, he handed it to her and resumed foraging under the bed.

In the intensity of the moment, Kate swallowed her squeamishness about the rifle. Gripping it tight to her body, she snatched handfuls of extra ammunition and stuffed them into her jean pockets. She waited impatiently for Teller to do the same. "Hurry!"

"Stay, Ace," Teller commanded. The shepherd whined but didn't disobey as Teller slammed the door.

They jogged up the path to the farmyard, their firearms at the ready and their eyes squinting. That Zs could be lurking a few feet away sight unseen made Kate want to bellow in frustration. "It's like fucking pea soup out here!"

"Just keep to the gravel."

A wail filled the air, giving Kate pause. The hairs on her arms rose. She'd never heard anything quite like it. "What on earth was that?"

"Cow in distress. Whatever's goin' on—it's by the cowshed."

Unable to see more than a few feet ahead, they kept their backs to the outbuildings. Kate growled in exasperation. "I want to go to the house. Maybe somebody there can tell me what happened."

"Not alone. Lead the way."

Cautiously, Kate traversed the lane to the concrete steps leading to the kitchen door. At the bottom stair, she encountered something solid at her shins. It was a person. She crouched down, Teller following suit. She recognized Peggy's garish striped caftan. Gulping, Kate extended a hand to touch Peggy's exposed shoulder. Her skin was warm. "Help me flip her around."

With Teller's assistance, she got Peggy face-up. The stench of viscera enveloped Kate like a miasma, and she reeled backward. *Oof.*

Teller coughed, making a strangled sound. "I don't think she's breathin'. Try for a pulse real quick."

Kate's hands were coated in Peggy's sticky-slick blood, but she probed her neck joint for a pulse. Nothing. Frantically, Kate traveled her fingers down Peggy's midsection to gauge the severity of her injuries. She repressed a yelp when she was confronted with carnage. Peggy's entrails lay coiled on the ground. "She's been disemboweled. Her guts are everywhere."

From by the barn, there was clattering and a horse knickered in alarm. Kate and Teller leaped to their feet.

The kitchen door squeaked open, and Connie's voice came through the mist. "Kate? Teller?"

"It's us," Teller said.

They scrabbled up the steps. Teller unfastened the screen door. Connie stood aside to allow them passage. She held a shotgun. The hallway light was harsh on her face.

"We were in the living room and heard a disturbance outside. I opened the door to investigate." Connie's hands shook. Kate peeled Connie's fingers from the stock of the gun and leaned it against the wall.

Teller asked, "And?"

"I couldn't tell at first, then Peggy rushed up to the house. I could barely see her in the fog, but she was hollering and carrying on." Connie put her knuckles over her mouth. "The next thing I knew, Otis was on her. He was *on her*! He was one of them!"

"Shh," Kate murmured, as her sister hid her face in her shirt and keened. "Take it easy, Con."

"The terrible cries Peggy made." Connie sobbed. "Then, he smacked against the house to get to us. I-I sent Audrey and Nora upstairs and turned on the floodlights."

Kate stroked Connie's back and shushed her, but there was no consoling her. "He's still out there. Teller and I have to go—"

Connie clawed at Kate's arm, hanging onto her. "No!"

"You can stay. Time's wastin'," Teller said, starting for the door.

"Oh hell no. I'm not staying." Kate took Connie's chin in her hand. She met her sister's eyes. "It's out there killing the livestock. We have to stop it. Turn off the floodlights. Then, go upstairs with Audrey and Nora. I'll be back soon."

Prying Connie off, Kate hastened after Teller. She closed the door firmly behind her. View obscured, they lingered to listen.

Panicked nickering. Cattle lowing oddly. Teller said, "Probably workin' through the barn."

They picked their way over Peggy's body. The spotlights extinguished. Once her eyes adjusted to the change, Kate was able to make out the shape of her van parked beside the house. The chicken coop was just ahead, across the lane.

Teller stumbled as they passed the coop. "Damn hell."

"What?" Kate whispered.

"It's Amy, Connie's hen. What's left of her anyhow."

There was a thump against the inside wall of the barn then the snorting of a horse.

Teller said urgently, "When we get inside, I'm gonna flick on the light. Be prepared to shoot."

Kate readied her rifle with care. She exhaled as Teller swung the door open and turned on the overhead lights.

Otis was on his knees, face in the innards of a heifer. Kate pushed the bolt forward, aimed at the base of Otis's spine and fired. In her inexperience, she hit him between the shoulder blades instead, but it was a good shot.

The force of the bullet propelled Otis forward, and he lay splayed over the cow. Kate's ears rang. She didn't dare breathe. Was one shot enough to fully incapacitate him?

"Well done, Kate!" Teller brought the butt of his shotgun up to his collarbone, inclined his head and waited, his finger on the trigger.

Otis tottered to his feet, his nose to the air. He spun, the right side of his body dragging. He snuffled. Teeth clacking, he squatted down, ready to strike.

The shotgun shell blasted into Otis's skull. His head exploded, spraying brain matter. Slivers of bone and black-red blood painted the wall. He plummeted to the hay-covered floor. The cow twitched.

"The poor beast is still alive. Put her out of her misery," Kate pleaded. As Teller approached the animal, she staggered outside, gasping for air.

She slouched against the barn, holding her gun tight.

Another blast. Then three more, in intervals.

Teller joined her outside, sighing.

"So, he got four?" Kate asked dully.

"A horse and three cows. It's a loss for Mayfly Hollow."

"Fuck. This is a nightmare."

"You did real good back there." Light from the barn bathed Teller in yellow. He put his arm around her and brought her in close. "You alright?"

She managed a wobbly smile. "We need to check in on Jamie and Judy. But first, let's update Connie."

Connie was in the hall beside the kitchen, wringing her hands, her eyes wide.

"We got him," Teller said.

Connie shook her head, her mouth opening and closing like a trout.

Kate grabbed her hands. They were moist. "What is it?"

"T-t-the sensors on the gate h-have been activated. Someone —something—is at the entrance—trying to get in!"

CHAPTER TWENTY-FIVE

"IT'S TOO FOGGY. THE S-SECURITY CAMERAS ARE USELESS," CONNIE explained. "I walkied Jamie. He and Judy are on their way to the farmhouse. H-he insisted. He wants to be with Nora."

A zap of fear spiked through Kate, making her voice shrill. "But what if whoever—whatever—was at the gate is already inside the compound?"

"The fence..." Connie trailed off.

"As I've said before, the fence is tall and strong, but *not* impenetrable," Kate admonished.

"I wonder if Zs can climb. Betcha they can. They sure jump well enough." Teller rocked back on his heels impatiently. Kate felt the palpable tension rolling off him in surges. It was obvious he needed action.

Connie raked her fingers through her hair. "Jamie said he'd take the walkie along. I can tell him to turn back."

"They could already be halfway here by now. Just tell him to shake a leg. Shoot, I'll meet 'em. Fend off any of them things if need be," Teller said.

Putting her rifle down, Kate took Connie's hand. "We should go to the basement bunker as a precaution. I'll fetch Nora and Audrey."

Teller had the kitchen door open, his fingers wrapped around the barrel of his shotgun. "If we ain't back in ten minutes, y'all lock up tight as a drum in the bunker. You hear?"

Kate nodded, and Teller was gone. She heard Connie's tentative voice on the walkie-talkie as she hurried up the narrow, old-fashioned wood stairway. Audrey and Nora were in Seth and Connie's cramped bedroom. Audrey held Nora in her arms, and they both looked pale and terrified.

Kate hid her bloody hands behind her back. "We're going down to the basement for the night, just in case the fence has been breached."

"B-basement?" Audrey stuttered, making no move to get up.

"Yes. There's a safe room down there with everything we need. With any luck, we'll only have to stay one night." She smiled at Nora. "Your mom and dad are on their way."

Upon hearing that, Nora scrambled from the bed. Wordlessly, Audrey got to her feet and the three filed down the steps. Connie met them at the top of the basement stairs, her posture rigid.

"Six more minutes," Connie muttered, biting her lip. Little spots of red dotted her lower lip where the skin had split. Kate couldn't stop staring at the blood as they waited. Each second seemed to last forever. Just when Kate was sure they'd have to secrete themselves in the bunker without the rest of the group, the kitchen door swung inward.

Teller and Jamie were out of breath, their cheeks crimson. Judy sagged in her husband's arms, drawn and pallid, her eyes half-closed. With a sob, Nora went to her parents and hugged them. Teller extinguished the kitchen lights as the others warily made their way in the dark to the basement.

In tense silence, they lingered in the pocket-sized vestibule for Connie to key in the security code on the glowing pin pad mounted to the wall. The metal elevator doors parted and they quickly shuffled in. Connie turned on the overhead lights. The group blinked in dazed curiosity as Teller shut the wooden door firmly behind them. Once he'd stepped into the bunker, Kate pressed the button on the wall to close the sliding doors.

Kate let loose a lusty, relieved moan. They were sheltered, for the moment.

Everyone stood just inside the room, their manner uncertain, watchful. Connie was flagging. Dark circles ringed her eyes. She pulled a chair from the dinette and wilted into it. Arms on the table, she put her head down. "I'm so dog-tired."

Ace. Kate and Teller exchanged a look. She could tell he was lamenting leaving his dog behind. Resting her rifle against the wall, Kate stepped forward. She'd have to take charge. She entreated Nora and Audrey to take a seat at the table. At first, Nora didn't want to leave her mother's side, but Audrey coaxed her away with gentle reassurances.

After helping Jamie get Judy into the bottom bunk of a set of bunk beds beside the bathroom, Kate was at a loss. Fingers tapping against her thigh, she thought fast. They needed normalcy. *Tea. I'll make tea.*

She washed Peggy's blood from her hands and beckoned Teller. Opening a kitchen cabinet, Kate indicated mugs, teabags, and packets of granulated sweetener. He lined the mugs up on the counter in a neat row and added tea and sweetener while Kate filled an electric kettle with water from the tap.

Kate leaned her hip against the counter while the kettle heated. The atmosphere was strained. Ominous. She broke the silence, her voice unnatural when she asked, "Can I get anybody food?"

In turn, everyone shook their heads. Kate emptied a box of cookies on a plate anyway and put it in the center of the dinette. When the kettle whistled, the sound pierced the air, making the group flinch. Kate broadcast a reassuring smile before pouring the hot water in the mugs. Teller distributed the tea to Nora, Connie, and Audrey before taking a seat next to them at the table. Kate handed Jamie a cup where he perched on Judy's bed at her feet. Judy had fallen into a deep slumber and didn't stir.

Finding a spot beside Connie, Kate sipped her tea and ate a cookie. The hot drink was soothing. Connie drained her mug and put her head back down, yawning. Unable to stop herself, Kate yawned too, her eyelids heavy. Shaking her head to clear it, she got up and explored the floor-to-ceiling cabinetry for the laptop Connie had said was kept there.

Setting the computer on the table while it powered up, Kate slid back in her chair, stifling another yawn. Her eyes seemed gummy. With a quick glimpse in Connie's direction, she opted not to disturb her sister unless she couldn't figure out how to access the camera footage.

An icon on the home screen was labeled *security cameras*. Easy enough. A few clicks and the display filled with live feed from eight strategically posted cameras on the property.

"Dammit," Kate muttered.

Teller came to immediate attention from where he sat next to her. "What's up?"

Kate mewed, rotating the laptop so he could view the live feed for himself.

He squeezed her arm. "Hopefully the vapor'll burn off at daybreak. Nothin' else to do but try to get some shuteye."

"Yeah."

Settling in his chair, Teller extended his long arms above his head, interlacing his fingers. His knuckles popped. "We'll assess the situation in the mornin'."

There were under cabinet lights affixed to the kitchenette cupboards. Kate switched them on before flipping off the overhead fixtures. The corners of the room were shadowy. It was dark enough to sleep, but bright enough to light the way to the bathroom.

"Connie," Kate said, shaking her sister's arm. "Go tuck into bed."

She watched Connie flop onto one of the beds. Nora's eyelids drooped as she fought to stay awake. Kate put an arm around the girl's waist, helping her to a bunk near her parents. Arms crossed, Jamie snored, his head resting against the metal frame of Judy's bed.

Kate laid Nora on the mattress and removed her shoes. Arranging the army surplus blanket around her, Kate noticed the girl's somber gaze lasered on her. "We're safe here, kid," she promised. "Sleep."

Before snagging a bunk for herself, Kate grabbed her rifle. As secure as the room was, she'd rest better with her weapon at her side, although she wished she had her ax instead. She situated the open laptop beside her on the mattress. Stretching out without bothering to fold back the blanket, Kate groaned. Stress sure did wear on a body.

KATE JERKED awake what seemed moments later. The room was silent and still except the occasional snore or soft exhalation of breath. The bunker was like a deprivation tank—it was impossible to determine time of day. Squinting at the laptop, Kate sat up, rubbing her eyes. According to the display, it was after eight in the morning.

From the onscreen images she could tell it was a bright, sunny day. The fog was gone, and the images were crisp-clear. Trying to shake her grogginess, Kate clicked on the first thumbnail, seeking anything untoward. Discovering the cameras pivoted three-hundred-sixty degrees by using the keyboard's arrow buttons, she thoroughly scrutinized the compound. Other than the destruction Otis had left in his wake, the feed from cameras one through four showed everything was normal. The fifth was posted on the barn's roof and gave a vantage of the back of the farmhouse.

"Oh no," Kate whispered.

They'd left Peggy's corpse where they'd found it—at the base of the steps by the kitchen door.

All that remained on the gravel was blood and a section of entrails.

Peggy's body had vanished.

CHAPTER TWENTY-SIX

Unspent energy made Kate edgy. Dread pooled low in her belly. Her fingertips were wet with perspiration. When she put the laptop on the mattress, it almost slipped from her grasp. Pushing up from the bed, she skimmed her hands across the seat of her jeans to dry them. In Kate's haste to reach Teller where he slept on a chair at the dinette, she nearly tripped on the laptop cord.

His head was bent back, his mouth gaping as he snored. She prodded his bicep. With a start, Teller twitched awake. "What the—"

"Shh," Kate said, putting a finger to her lips. She grabbed at his hand and tugged until he got up and followed her to her bunk.

Teller flopped down, rubbing a palm over his eyes and yawning. His voice was husky when he whispered, "What now?"

Kate didn't say anything. She picked up the computer and placed it on Teller's lap. Tapping a fingernail on the screen, she gave him a meaningful glance.

He blinked. "Oh."

"She was definitely dead," Kate insisted in a hushed tone.

"Must've become one of them." His Adam's Apple bobbed in

the glow cast by the computer screen. "'Spose we should've put a bullet in her cranium to make sure she didn't turn. Hindsight."

Kate buried her face in her hands and shook her head. *Damn!* She took in a big breath to stave off the encroaching dizziness, and Teller wound his arm around her, comforting her.

"She could be in the barn or in a pasture—places where there ain't cameras. This is from camera five. You've reviewed six, seven, and eight, right?"

Kate stilled. "Uh, no… I just saw she was missing and…"

Teller clicked on the next thumbnail. Nothing out of the ordinary. Camera seven was posted on the west facing side of the farmhouse's roof. In the fringes, they saw an immobile figure in the pasture beyond the barn, like a scarecrow. Teller adjusted the camera, zooming the focus tight on the field. It was blurry, but they could make out the striped pattern of Peggy's caftan.

"Yeah, it's her," Kate said dourly. "I hope she hasn't slaughtered all the livestock. We'll have to go out and take care of her straightaway, before she does any more damage."

She began to rise, but Teller halted her. "Hold up. What about camera eight?"

The front of the farmhouse was as usual. The overgrown lane leading to the gate was undisturbed. Teller drummed his thumb against the keyboard's down arrow until the camera swept over the entrance where the combination pad to the gate was located.

Kate gasped. A man lay facedown on the gravel.

Tiptoeing, she went to the kitchen drawer for a pen and paper. She scratched out a message in case they weren't back before everyone woke up, leaving it in plain sight on the dinette.

Teller waited for Kate at the steel elevator doors. When they slid noiselessly open, she palmed her firearm and led Teller out. The basement was gloomy, the glass block windows throwing little light. The stairs creaked as they hustled up to the kitchen.

Outside, the blazing sunlight temporarily blinded Kate. Dazzled, she put a hand to her forehead to shield her eyes.

"Let's hightail it to the west pasture." Teller started toward the barn and Kate hurried to keep up with him, purposely avoiding the sight of the henhouse and the dead birds littering the ground. Teller said over his shoulder, "We can take the ATV. It's quicker."

Kate hadn't noticed the red all-terrain vehicle parked at the back side of the barn during her ranch tour. Teller got on it, putting his shotgun across his knees. Not wasting time, Kate settled in behind him, mimicking his actions and placing her rifle in her lap. With the flip of a few switches, Teller stepped on the brake and the ATV roared to life. He stretched down to adjust the choke and they were off. Kate put one hand on her gun to keep it from slipping. She closed the gap between her open thighs and Teller's back, winding her arm around Teller's side and resting her hand against his muscled abdomen.

As they got closer to the pasture, the breeze carried the metallic tang of blood. Kate swallowed, pursing her lips. She took note of the slain steers lying near the enclosure, steeling herself. Peggy was on the far side of the overgrown field, her face upturned.

Teller parked the ATV beside the barbed wire fence separating the farm from the pasture and jumped off. "She's tryin' to locate us. You prepared to cover me if necessary?"

Kate crawled off the vehicle and was beside him within seconds. "Yes."

"I'm thinkin' we let her come to us." Teller got into his stance. He flicked the safety off the shotgun and fit the buttstock into the pocket of his shoulder, readying his aim. "She's onto us like flies on a rib roast."

The figure moved as gracefully as a gazelle, the snapping of her teeth getting louder the nearer she got. When she was within shooting distance, Teller's index finger depressed the trigger. The racket of the blast caused Kate's ears to buzz. She winced, sticking a finger in her eardrum and wiggling it, but the buzzing refused to cease.

"Dang," Teller muttered. He'd hit the Z in the shoulder. The force of the shot pummeled her to the ground. Almost immediately, she bounced up again. Teller pumped the gun, but his spent cartridge didn't eject. "What the—it's jammed! I don't believe this shit!"

The panic in his voice had Kate bringing her rifle into position and racking the bolt as if on autopilot. The Z pogoed into flight, defying the laws of gravity, and sailed through the air toward them like a missile. Kate's novice actions revealed her inexperience. She moved stiffly and awkwardly as she sighted.

The Z was almost upon them. Kate pressed the trigger, but succumbing to her nerves, she shot wide and missed.

It happened as if in slow motion. Like a high jumper, the Z vaulted over the barbed wire fence. The skirt of the caftan snagged on the barbs and ripped, but it didn't do much to slow her.

Teeth making a cacophony of noise, she dove onto Kate, landing on her and pushing her off her feet. Kate fell on the packed dirt. The wind was knocked from her lungs with a hiss. Stunned, she did the only thing she could think of. She brought the gun up lengthwise under the Z's chin, holding her off. Kate's arms trembled with the effort of keeping her restrained.

Kate no longer heard the discordant melody the teeth made or Teller's cry of alarm. She was aware of nothing but the steady thrum of her pulse in her throat and the milky eyes of the Z mere inches from hers. She scarcely noticed the fetid stench or the bloody strings of saliva dripping off the Z's face and onto her cheeks.

Teller brought the butt of his shotgun against the Z's temple. The Z swayed to the side and Kate rolled away. She lay on the ground, watching in horror as Teller hammered at the Z's skull.

Whack. Whack. Whack.

Black blood and slivers of bone flew. Soon, the Z's head was completely gone, smashed and flattened.

Teller flung the shotgun away. His arms and clothes were flecked with dark droplets of foul-scented blood and gray matter. His nostrils flared. Face red and sweat stained, he wheezed. Bending, he braced his hands on his kneecaps.

Kate swiped a forearm across her cheeks to wipe away the filth that had spilled from the Z's mouth. Slowly, she sat up, bringing her knees to her torso. They stared at each other, not speaking. Once she was able to catch her breath, Kate whispered, "Thanks."

Teller appeared as unnerved by the experience as Kate was. He brushed his hands on his denims to clean them, shaking his head. "Whoa. From now on, we do a head shot to make sure a Z really is dead. That was too close a call."

"Tell me about it." An icy shiver traveled through Kate as she recollected how Peggy's brown irises had been transformed to an ethereal shade of milky blue. Her teeth had been jagged stumps, with bits of meat, skin, and fur lodged in her gums. *Ugh.*

Teller's eyes were grave as he scanned Kate. A muscle worked in his jaw as he came to her and lowered his body down to the ground. He crisscrossed his legs at the ankle and held out his arm. Gratefully, Kate put her head into the crook of his shoulder and sighed.

The kiss in the glade had changed their relationship. The pervading sense of intimacy between her and Teller hung in the atmosphere, unspoken yet tangible. Several times, Kate opened her mouth to discuss the subject, only to close it again when she couldn't summon the appropriate words.

Kate liked Teller—a lot—but was there potential for more than friendship? She preferred lovers who didn't provoke her, who didn't ask for more than she was willing to give. She was a diehard loner, right? Without even seeming to try, Teller pushed her boundaries, made her want to lose control. Never had Kate been so conflicted.

She wondered what the kiss meant for Teller, but it didn't

seem fair to ask him to divulge his feelings when she was uncertain of her own.

After a few minutes, Kate drew reluctantly away from him. It was time to get back to business—to shake off what happened with the Z. "Can you take me down to the gate on the ATV, so I can see if that guy's still alive?"

CHAPTER TWENTY-SEVEN

THE MAN HAD CRUMPLED FACING AWAY FROM THE ENTRANCE. HIS skin was dark with grime. The soles of his boots were worn, and his trousers and t-shirt tattered and grubby.

Kate clambered off the ATV and toward the fence, Teller beside her. His voice was low when he said, "He's bad injured judgin' by the blood pooled on the ground."

"Hard to tell if he's breathing from here. I'll have to check for a pulse."

"Hmm. I do not love the sound of that." Sighing, Teller shrugged. "Give me the rifle. I'll have it trained on him when you feel for a pulse."

Taking a fortifying breath, Kate punched the code into the keypad to open the gate.

She bent at the man's side, ready to spring up at the slightest warning of anything amiss. Tentatively, she reached and put her fingers on his neck behind his whiskered jaw. His skin was hot, his pulse rapid. Kate murmured, "Not dead. Unconscious and burning up with fever. Should we take him to the empty cabin next to mine, so we can evaluate his wound and tend to him?"

Teller sucked his teeth. "We're makin' a decision here that

could have lastin' ramifications, Kate. What if he's been bit by a Z? Surely that can transmit the virus."

"You're right. I'm not thinking straight. Help me turn him so we can make sure he's not."

Teller gripped the man by the shoulder and Kate took him by the leg, flipping him on his back. He was badly emaciated. What she saw made her heartbeat accelerate. "Oh my God."

He smelled of body odor and road grit. His face was caked with dirt, and his shaggy blond hair was unwashed and greasy. It was Ben.

Relief flooded through Kate, but it was fleeting. *If his wound's infected…*

"You know him." Teller's eyes narrowed as he surveyed Kate, his expression inscrutable.

"Uhh…" Kate hesitated to claim Ben as her boyfriend, but *fuckbuddy* seemed crass. "Yeah, he's a-a friend."

"Oh?"

"Yes. Ben. I have to help him, whether he's bit or not."

Teller slowly nodded, a wily expression flitting across the severe angles of his face. "Huh. Welp, we best get your *friend* here up to the cabin."

The next several minutes were spent trying to drape Ben across the seat of the ATV. He stirred, moaning and mumbling every time he was jostled. It was a torturous ordeal. Not able to witness Ben's suffering any further, Kate declared, "This isn't working."

Teller gently placed Ben on the grass. "Stay here. I'll take the ATV up to the machine shed and hitch on the trailer kept there."

Kate kneeled beside Ben, keeping an eye on him and brooding. Teller had clearly known what sort of *friend* Ben was, but if he was jealous, he'd kept it to himself. Kate recalled how she'd felt when she'd seen Audrey link arms familiarly with Teller from afar. Maybe they already had something casual going. If so, the kiss Kate and Teller shared was merely a passing fancy, a momentary lapse of judgment. Kate's jawbone ached from clenching it. She opened her mouth wide to ease the pressure.

Ben jerked restlessly, pulling Kate's attention. She shushed him and patted his shoulder, unsure what else she could do. Besides being filthy, his facial features were lined with fatigue. His neck, arms, and hands were scratched and scabbed, attesting to what surely must've been a hellish trek from Clayton's Corners.

Kate decided to see what sort of injury she was dealing with. She painstakingly pried the hem of his shirt from where it stuck to his skin.

A ragged hole was torn into the discolored flesh of his side, the injury festering with malodorous yellow pus. A gunshot wound. "Oof. That can't be good."

The sharp rank of decaying flesh overpowered the funk of Ben's body odor, hitting Kate like a slap in the face. She released the shirt, breathing through her mouth.

The sound of the ATV's motor announced Teller's arrival, and soon he rounded the corner. She got to her feet as he parked. They loaded Ben on the flat wooden trailer. Kate sat beside him for the short trip to the cabins, ensuring he didn't teeter off. Her mind raced as she tried to formulate a strategy.

After Judy's miscarriage, Kate had intended to go through the farm's first aid kit, but there'd been no opportunity. Ben would need potent antibiotics. What if he needed an IV?

Concentrate on one insurmountable task at a time!

Teller scooped Ben under the armpits, hauling him from the trailer. Jockeying him up the porch steps, Teller instructed, "Open the cabin door."

She rushed to do as Teller bid, staying out of his way as he got Ben inside and onto the bed. In the background, they heard Ace barking frantically from where he was locked in Kate's cabin. "You go ahead and get your dog—he's probably starving. I'll give Ben a sponge bath."

"I'll be back once Ace's sorted."

The cabin door closed firmly behind him. Kate gnawed at her lip for a second, contemplating. First things first. She turned on the wall-mounted AC unit to cool the room and reduce some of the damp, closed up feel of the cabin. Finding a basin in the kitchen, she filled it with warm, soapy water. Adding washcloths from the bathroom, she then placed the basin on the bedside table.

Undressing Ben proved arduous. By the time he lay naked before her, Kate was drenched in sweat. She stood back to catch her breath. He was ripe. *Phew. Revolting.* Her head throbbed from hunger, but the stench made Kate forget all about food. Ben's feet were worse than Kate's had been when she arrived at Mayfly Hollow. She'd have to apply Connie's salve.

Before washing him, she got plastic garbage bags from under the kitchen sink and rolled his body, placing the bags beneath him to protect the bedspread. She'd seen the exit wound in his back. That was something, anyway—excavating a slug from Ben's body was unimaginable. She nudged the bullet hole with her cloth, and slimy pus gushed out.

The water needed to be changed four times before Kate was satisfied Ben was clean enough. She poured the last mucky basinful down the tub drain and scrubbed her hands with soap. Sitting in an armchair across from the bed, she tried to unwind. Lightheaded from low blood sugar, she dozed until Teller entered the cabin. He'd changed and held a stack of garments.

"I ran up to the farmhouse. Connie saw me comin' and let me in the bunker. She was fixin' everyone breakfast. I clued her in to the newest developments, then I went to my place for these. Let's get your friend dressed."

Kate showed Teller Ben's injury, confiding her worry about the infection. Teller didn't say anything. He helped dress Ben in sweatpants and a t-shirt. He worked efficiently, his face a study of concentration. Throughout the ordeal, Ben had lapsed in and out of consciousness. Now, he slept peacefully, though his color was bad and his breathing shallow.

Teller took Kate by the arm and escorted her to the kitchenette. Speaking softly, he said, "Someone will have to stay here and watch him, 'cause if he passes, he may turn. We can't allow that."

Weariness and hunger made Kate despondent. Tears stung her eyes. "I know. If we can't find antibiotics, he's good as dead."

"Connie and I had a little conference. I inquired about what sort of medications she's got."

Kate's gaze flew to Teller. "And?"

"The basics are in her first aid kit, but I don't think penicillin is gonna be enough to fight off the sort of infection your friend's sufferin' from. Connie says there are physician's reference books in Seth's office. We'll have to read up and figure a course of treatment."

"What if he needs an IV? Nobody here knows how to do that." Kate wrapped her arms around her chest, hoping she didn't swoon. If she didn't eat soon, she'd be fainting.

"Shame we don't have a doctor onsite, huh?" Teller gave her a lopsided smile. "If Audrey's willin' to undertake babysittin' your friend, you and me can go scavenge the pharmacy downtown River Heights."

"We're in a race against time here—the sooner we leave the better."

Teller met her eyes, his expression sobering. "I hate to keep heapin' more problems on your plate…"

Oh great, Kate thought. She braced herself. "Just tell me, then I'm going next door to grab food."

"Judy's condition ain't improvin'. Looks like she's at death's door. What I'm gnawin' over is the possibility that not only was her baby tainted with the Z virus—so is Judy. I think it's slowly killin' her from the inside out."

CHAPTER TWENTY-EIGHT

KATE SAT AT THE ROUGH WOODEN DESK IN THE CORNER OF BEN'S cabin, eating from a family size can of tuna and washing it down with bottled water. Teller had kept an eye on Ben while she'd dashed to her cabin for food and fresh clothes. Once she'd come back, Teller had gone up to the main house to fetch the physician's reference books.

Ben was in a bad way. As Kate chewed, she monitored him, at a loss of what she could do to alleviate his discomfort. He acted as if he were in the midst of a nightmare. He tossed and turned, grunting and murmuring, sporadically crying out. Seeing Ben's distress made Kate feel sick. Abandoning her food, she went to him and lay on the bed, enfolding him in her arms and whispering words she hoped consoled him.

For a moment, Ben quieted, but it was short-lived. He thrashed and moaned in intervals. Kate forced back a sob, feeling powerless as she had so often lately. She trailed her fingertips across his forehead. His skin was dry and hot, evidence of his fever. Knowing dehydration was as deadly as septicemia, Kate went to get a bottle of water.

She jumped when Ben called from across the room, "Kate?"

Rushing back to his side, she crawled across the mattress, her heart pounding. "I'm here. We're going to find antibiotics for you. You're going to be alright. I know it." She slid an arm under his head, bringing the water to his mouth. Tipping the bottle, she encouraged, "Drink."

He coughed and some of the water spilled down his chin and on the pillowcase. At that moment, Teller entered the cabin with Audrey trooping behind. His gaze traveled over the scene in front of him where Kate cradled Ben in her arms, but his face didn't disclose his mood.

"Jeepers," Audrey said. She carried a crate, which she sat at the foot of the bed. Today her red curls were piled high on her head, accentuating the swan-like curve of her neck.

Kate frowned at the crate. "What's that?"

Teller answered as he put his armful of books down on the kitchen counter, "It's what I scrounged from the medical supplies up at the farmhouse."

Audrey picked at her nail as she examined Ben with frank curiosity. "Teller told me this guy's your boyfriend."

Ben made a groaning noise, his fingers tightening on Kate's arm. Attention shifting back to him, Kate helped him take another drink. Her voice was distracted when she responded, "I wouldn't say *boyfriend*—we went to high school together. He's a good friend. I invited him here."

"You need me to play nursemaid, right?"

Ben's eyelids slid down over his rheumy eyes. He'd lost consciousness. Kate gently pulled her arm from under him and put the half-full bottle of water on the nightstand. She swept her hair back from her face as she stood, her gaze on Teller. He slouched over the kitchen counter, his head bent above a notebook. Appearing absorbed, he pored over one of the volumes from Seth's den. Kate said to Audrey, "Come outside with me, will you?"

They took a seat in the plastic chairs on the front porch. Before Kate spoke, she surveyed Audrey. Even wearing a baggy tee, her buxom figure was evident. Her complexion was fresh-scrubbed peaches and cream. She was gorgeous.

"You think my brains are in my tits, don't you?"

The comment so startled Kate that she leaned back in her chair and hooted. "Why do you say that?"

One of Audrey's ginger eyebrows rose. "I may not have the experience you do, but I have different strengths. And I'm willing to learn."

"Who says I'm experienced?" Kate's forehead wrinkled as she searched Audrey's face. "I owned a bakery. I never even shot a gun before the shit hit the fan."

Audrey shrugged. "You take charge. Think on your feet. That isn't how I'm programmed." She squinted at Kate. "You seem fearless."

And I've made mistake after mistake! Isn't that obvious to every-one? Kate framed and rejected several rejoinders before saying, "Audrey." She paused to allow her words impact. "I don't have a fucking clue. I'm just… muddling through like everyone else."

"You hide it well."

I do?

"Teller sees my worth," Audrey mused in a rather sly way. Kate was taken aback by the calculating slant of the woman's eyes. It was a revelation. She'd made the mistake of thinking Audrey was a ditz. No more. "I've taken Nora under my wing. Your sister's impressed."

What is this? A competition? Unsure how to reply, Kate said, "Oh-kaaay." She gave Audrey a hard look. "Do you have a problem with me? 'Cause we don't really have time for this right now."

"Why would I? It's just when you and Teller brought me here, I thought you were a couple. He told me you weren't, but I could've sworn I saw attraction. Good thing your beau finally showed up." She brazenly met Kate's gaze. "Defines boundaries."

Thrown, Kate tightly smiled to cover her feelings. Confusion warred with irritation. Irritation won. *I don't need this shit.* She refrained from protesting. Why bother wasting precious minutes arguing? It wouldn't make any difference or change Audrey's perceptions.

Plainly, Kate was a rival.

Deciding the best tactic was to redirect Audrey to the matter at hand, Kate said, "Once we establish the best method to treat Ben's infection, Teller and I'll be driving into town. While we're gone, we need you to keep an eye on him."

Audrey gave her a peevish glare, as if annoyed Kate wouldn't engage. "What should I do if he wakes up?"

"Give him sips of water. Put a cool cloth on his forehead. Make sure he doesn't die."

Audrey's face drained of color. "How am I supposed to do *that*?"

"Just use your common sense, Audrey." Kate swallowed, her expression serious. "This is important. If he does die..."

Audrey waited.

"If he dies, you'll have to... dispatch him."

"*What?*" Audrey leaped from her chair, her sherry-brown eyes wide.

Kate stood and calmly pulled the revolver from her waistband. "I brought this from my cabin. It's loaded."

Grabbing Audrey's hand, Kate placed the revolver in her palm and curled her fingers around it.

CHAPTER TWENTY-NINE

TELLER POINTED TO AN UNPRONOUNCEABLE WORD HE'D SCRIBBLED IN the notebook. "This?"

"Umm." Kate leafed through the drug reference book he'd brought from Seth's den. Skimming over the text, she made a sound of aggravation. "Nope. It requires IV administration, too. I just don't think I'm up to figuring out how to do that."

"According to my research Safolinix is another antibiotic used to treat sepsis. Check that one," Teller suggested impatiently, then groused, "This is takin' too long."

"I can almost hear the clock ticking," Kate agreed. She located the entry for Safolinix and quickly read. "Common dosages to treat sepsis are five hundred milligrams to two grams, depending on severity of infection... IM. That's intramuscular injection!"

"Bingo."

"Jot down the brand names, and let's go," Kate said.

AS TELLER DROVE them into River Heights, they came upon an occasional lone Z on the highway. Nearer town, they gathered in scattered groups. Unmoving until they heard the truck's engine, they then snuffled their noses in the air, their bodies swaying as they attempted to locate their prey. Kate had insisted Teller leave the windows up, which seemed to conceal their scent enough to allow them to thread through and continue on their way.

Kate drummed her fingers anxiously on the handle of her ax. Not wanting to be unprepared, she'd kitted up with a full arsenal of weapons. She wore a leather belt with attached holsters. On her left hip was a nine-millimeter pistol and on her right was a detective's special revolver. A hunting knife was lashed to her ankle. The encounter with the Z in the pasture earlier that morning had left an indelible mark on her psyche. She'd do anything to make sure she was never in the same predicament again.

River Heights looked vastly different than when they'd come to rescue Audrey the week before. Teller whistled. "Holy annihilation."

The residential section on the west side of town was half gone. Only charred shells of homes remained in some streets. They turned on Oak. Audrey's ranch had been one of the houses leveled by fire. Even with the windows shut, the heavy stink of soot drifted into the cab of the truck.

Leaving his foot off the gas, Teller wove through the Zs. They were everywhere. Some loitered motionless, as if they were robots not yet activated. Other dead roamed freely among the rotting corpses strewn on the streets, grass, and sidewalks. The further they went, the thicker the clusters of Zs became. Teller carefully drove over the curb to avoid hitting them, navigating through yards. Kate held her breath to see if the sound of the engine would wake the Zs, but other than becoming restless and sniffing the air, there was no further reaction. Numerals and indistinguishable figures were painted on front doors, like the kind authorities left after natural disasters.

"That ain't FEMA leavin' them spray paint tags," Teller said, and Kate twisted to face him.

"Then who? Scavengers?"

"Yup. Probably keepin' track of what they've already ransacked." Teller's aquamarine eyes were serious and his mouth tense. "Food's likely gettin' scarce. Other resources, too."

"We could be watched. We're a target in this pickup." Kate nibbled at her thumbnail. "Maybe we should park it somewhere and hoof it to the business section."

"That ain't without its hazards neither."

"I don't know the correct answer," Kate grumbled, rubbing her hands across her eyes. Lack of rest was catching up with her.

"I got an idea. There's a parkin' garage about a block up from the main drag. I betcha there's some vehicles parked there we can blend in with. We can hot foot to Fairdale Drug."

Five tense minutes later, Teller entered the concrete parking structure on Sycamore Drive. The gray truck was unremarkable next to the other vehicles there.

When Kate's sneakers hit the solid concrete floor, she shivered. Though it was a warm day, it was cold and dark in the ramp. Foreboding. Spooky. Goosebumps rose on her flesh. She slipped her arms into the straps of the empty backpack Teller had brought from the ranch. Searching the surroundings, she tightened her hold on her ax.

Teller wore his backpack and had a handgun in his grip. "C'mon. We gotta get outta here."

They kept their backs to buildings as they stole toward Main Street. *Gah.* The reek of putrefaction taxed Kate's respiratory system. *Can't be healthy breathing that in.* She thought of the pathogens swirling in the air—the risk of tuberculosis and cholera. Next time they came into town, she planned to wear a mask. *Fuck that… I'll find a hazmat suit.*

A mini horde of Zs loitered in the city park at the end of Main Street. A block from Fairdale Drug, Kate spotted the chubby Z in the flowered blouse and skirt she'd seen the last two times she'd been in town. *She sure gets around.* The Z brought her face to the sky. Teller took Kate's hand before the Z could announce their presence, and they scurried to the double plate-glass doors of the drugstore.

The glass on the upper portion of the right-hand door was shattered, but the door was locked. Teller snaked his arm through the shards and turned the deadbolt. The Z's teeth snapped, and they slipped inside as fast as they could, shutting the door behind them.

Teller fastened the lock again. He whispered, "May as well. Any Z tryin' to wander in will be stopped by the metal bar across the door. Slow down people, too."

Kate nodded. The pharmacy counter was in the rear of the store. She made a beeline there, noting the evidence of prior looting. She mentally crossed her fingers that something had been left behind.

The entrance to the pharmacy was bolted. Kate set her ax by a cash register and hopped up on the counter. She swung her legs over, dropping to the other side. Teller followed suit. She faced the half-empty shelves, her hands parked on her hips, wondering where the hell to start.

With no electricity, there was no ventilation. The atmosphere was close, dense. Would the humidity mess with the drugs' effectiveness? A trickle of sweat dribbled down Kate's spine. Teller didn't seem bothered by the oppressive confines. He left Kate where she dawdled, walking along the perimeter of the room.

"The layout seems straightforward—the meds are arranged accordin' to classification." Teller gestured to shelves as he passed them. "Disinfectants, drugs for external use, infusions… Here, injectables. Looters didn't seem to want many of these."

Kate hurried to join him. The boxes and bottles were in alphabetical order. She scoured the shelves for Safolinix or any of the brand names the drug was sold under. Her anxiety hitched, escalated. "It's not here, Teller! Maybe they were taken after all."

"Or maybe not. It's a heavy-duty antibiotic. It's possible mom-and-pop corner drugstores don't stock it on the regular."

Kate's shoulders drooped. "Then we need to figure out where to try next because—"

Outside, the staccato clatter of gunshots reverberated through the street. Fairdale Drug served as an echo chamber, making it seem as if it were happening mere feet away. Kate ducked on instinct, bringing her hands up to cover her head.

"Damn hell," Teller muttered, his mouth tight. "That's semi-automatic gunfire."

"Let's peek out the front display window." Kate swallowed the lump of fear in her throat. "I want to know what's happening on Main Street."

Teller shinned up the counter and made his way smoothly over, holding out his hand for Kate. She snagged her ax from where she'd left it as she negotiated the counter. They crept to the window, hiding behind the revolving greeting card display.

A dented conversion van was parked in the street, blocking access to Kate and Teller's route back to the truck. A ragtag gang of six men and women made their way toward the city park on foot. They were dressed in leather and chains. Their body language said they were spoiling for a fight. "Christ," Kate breathed. "They're armed to the teeth."

Some swigged liquor from the bottles they carried. Others whooped and hollered as if they were having the time of their life. The hum of motorcycles reached Kate's ears. A second later, choppers roared past, then did figure eights directly in front of the drugstore. With a robust war cry, a man lifted a gun and emptied a round in the air. Kate and Teller shrank back from the window.

"What are they doing?" Kate gasped. "They're certifiable. They must have a death wish."

"Yep. Any second the Zs will be runnin' this way, boxin' us in. We gotta bounce."

Kate turned on her heel, terrified. She started for the rear of the building, hoping to find an alley exit.

Coordinated clacking mixed with the joyful howls of the

rabble rousers, the din drifting into the store. More gunfire. A stray bullet hit the display window where Kate and Teller had been moments before. It splintered, falling to the tiled floor in one large sheet. The crash was deafening. Kate squealed, glancing quickly over her shoulder.

"Hurry, Kate," Teller ground out, prodding her in her spine. The exit was at the end of a hall, past a public restroom. Taking a quick breath, Teller opened the door and peered into the alley. His chest rapidly rose and fell, his shirt speckled with perspiration. "You ready to make a break for it?"

"Yes." Lacing fingers, they sprinted out into the alley.

A Z appeared in their path, its snout in the air and jaw working. Without thinking twice, Kate pulled away from Teller. She raised her ax, darting up to the Z. It activated, getting into position to strike. With a grunt, Kate swung, slicing its head from its neck. A spurt of victory zipped through her bloodstream, giving her a needed jolt of adrenaline. Kate didn't break stride as she continued down the alley.

Eyes vigilant, they made their way into the parking garage. Teller's truck was where they left it, a shining beacon. Sanctuary. Seconds later, Teller had the doors unlocked. Breathing too heavily to speak, they scrabbled into the cab.

They were on the outer fringes of River Heights before Kate caught her breath. She rested her neck on the headrest and closed her eyes. "You know where the nearest hospital is, Teller?"

"Sure, County Memorial's over in Calhoun. Ten miles away."

"That's where we'll go... they'll surely have a fully stocked pharmacy. I just hope the scavengers haven't raided it already."

"That place'll be crawlin' with Zs. Are you out of your apple pickin' mind?" Teller's tone had Kate opening her eyes and assessing him. He looked shaken from the episode in town.

She gave him a Mona Lisa smile. "I've got a plan—but I'm just letting you know *right now*—it won't be pleasant."

CHAPTER THIRTY

Teller's mouth was set in distaste. "How'd you figure out this trick?"

They'd left the truck on the outskirts of the hospital's campus and sneaked up to the closest Z that was on its own. Enacting a two-prong plan, Kate threw a pebble nearby then trotted up to the Z, making no effort to conceal herself. Slightly disoriented, it prepared to attack her. Taking advantage of its confusion, Teller sidled behind it. He sunk the blade of Kate's knife into the base of the Z's skull. It buckled to the pavement, the hilt of the knife protruding from its head.

Once Teller tugged out the blade, Kate took over, gutting the Z from sternum to stem. Shaking his head in disbelief, Teller watched as she dabbed the Z's rank black viscera across her shirt and jeans with a handkerchief she'd gotten from the truck. Gagging, he allowed Kate to dot muck on him.

Kate wiped the knife blade on a shrub and sheathed it at her ankle. She picked up her ax from where she'd left it on the grass. "I learned this *trick* purely by accident on the trip up from Clayton's Corners."

They strode toward the hospital entrance. "If this effectively disguises us, then why the heck didn't you propose this technique when we rescued Audrey?"

"Well, a number of reasons. One, it's still in beta testing," she admitted, keeping her voice low. "Although I'm pretty confident it works. Two, it's hardly practical. Three, I'm not in a hurry to rub toxic waste on my body—what if it comes in contact with a scratch or something?"

"Still in beta testing? That don't buoy *my* confidence."

Kate's step faltered. A large cluster of Zs was within earshot. She said from the corner of her mouth, "There's like fifty of those creatures we have to wade through to get inside. You have a better idea? I'm all ears."

Teller put his hands up in surrender. "Not really. Dang, girl, you got a bigger set of balls than me."

Kate rolled her eyes. "I wouldn't advise making any extra noise as we make our way through. We've got to find a map of this joint once we get inside—there should be one somewhere in the lobby."

"Lead the way, Gunga Din."

Kate shot him a look over her shoulder. "I saw that movie on the classics channel when I was a kid, Teller." She added drily, "Things didn't end so good for Gunga, so I don't particularly appreciate the comparison."

He grimaced, waving her on.

Keeping her footfalls light and her ax at the ready, Kate inched forward into the throng. Some Zs remained in place, but others stirred and shuffled. It was impossible to predict whether they would move in front of her, no matter how meticulously she stepped. Several times, Kate came into direct contact with a Z. When their chilled flesh grazed her, it was all she could do to keep from recoiling.

The sliding glass doors were ajar, but not wide enough to walk through. Their gazes affixed on the Zs, Kate and Teller each took a side, yanking. A vein in Teller's neck emerged as the doors refused to budge. With a final wrench, the door yielded, making a high-pitched squeal. The pair stilled. Kate saw her terror reflected in Teller's eyes.

Collectively, the horde snuffled. Would their teeth clack? If so, Kate and Teller were done for. Teller urged Kate inside before they found out. There was enough space to squeeze through the doors, but her backpack strap stuck on the latch apparatus when she skidded by. With frenzied actions, Teller freed her, then propelled her into the lobby.

Bright sun streamed into the atrium-like space, making dust motes glimmer. There were no zombies within sight, but that didn't ease the tension in Kate's bones. She remained on high alert as she made her way past fake tropical plants and an empty koi pond set into the tiled floor.

The body of a woman wearing a striped smock and a volunteer badge was slumped on a rolling chair behind a reception desk. It reinforced Kate's theory that not everyone who died would become a Z. The corpse's skin was black and decayed. Kate averted her gaze as she walked by, trying to ignore the virulent stench of rotted meat hovering in the air like ether.

From the corner of her eye, she saw Teller point to a wall-mounted map. A Z shambled down the hall toward them, leading a pack of agitated creatures. Would the smeared Z blood be enough to keep her and Teller from being detected? Sidestepping the Z, Kate waited with her ax in position, but the pack passed by. *We really are invisible!* Relief replaced fear. When she noticed Teller expel a breath, she mouthed *I told you so.*

Triumph coursed through her veins. Kate trembled as she studied the map. The hallways resembled a multicolored maze. She located the *you are here* arrow. There was a gift shop to the left of the lobby. If they veered right, the hospital pharmacy was around a corner.

Kate threw Teller a significant glance, and he nonchalantly ambled behind her as she trod down the corridor, her sneakers soundless on the tile.

The top part of the Dutch door beside the pharmacy counter

was open, but the lower section was fastened shut. They hopped the counter like they had at Fairdale Drug. A portly Z wearing a pristine lab coat wandered by the consultation window, bumping into a nearby desk before making his way in a circuitous route to the drop off window. Kate viewed him with interest. He looped back and forth from one window to another as if he were programmed. *Bizarre.*

The sound of a zipper opening pulled Kate back. In the dim light of the enclosed pharmacy, Teller shoveled drugs into his backpack. Keeping an eye on the Z, Kate joined him.

She whispered, "Found it?"

Nodding, he angled the bag for her perusal. He'd amassed an impressive assortment of medications. On another shelf, Kate spied a hefty white box of syringes. She shrugged out of her backpack and stowed the box in it. What else? A plastic bedpan. Suture kits. Alcohol wipes. Wound cleanser. Gauze. Wasting no time, she went from shelf to shelf and took anything that she deemed of value. When Kate's pack was so full she could barely zip it, she smiled.

They were on the homestretch.

Winding their way through the Zs on the way back to the lobby, Kate had a thought. She put up a finger to Teller to get his attention, then hurried past the reception desk. The darkened gift shop was deserted. Giving Teller her ax to hold, Kate went over to a shelf beside the cash register and rummaged for a shopping bag with handles. She chose puzzles and a board game, topping them with candy and snacks. On the way out, she plucked a plush teddy bear off a glass display for Nora.

When they rallied at Teller's truck, they shared a celebratory high-five.

Teller sported his signature grin. "We're a helluva team."

She returned his grin before stowing her ill-gotten gains in the pickup. When Kate turned around again, Teller had shucked his shirt. His backpack and cowboy boots lay discarded on the pavement. He kicked away his denims, the sun glinting on the downy hairs of his finely corded thighs. Kate's gaze raked over his boxer briefs and the notable bulge outlined in blue cotton.

He was lean but built. His well-defined six pack and muscular chest hinted at wiry strength. With each movement his pecs rippled.

Swallowing hard, Kate tore her attention away before he caught her gawking, fixing her gaze on her sneakers. The visceral pull of desire low in her loins made her voice catch when she demanded, "*What are you doing?*"

"We ain't gettin' into my four by four with Z blood all over us," he said firmly. She felt the heat of his stare on her body and the blush blooming on her cheeks. "I got hand sanitizer in the glove box for our hands. Strip down to your skivvies."

CHAPTER THIRTY-ONE

In the days after the pharmacy run, Kate thought often of the way Teller's gaze roved her body. It was almost a caress. Even as he drove them back home, she could feel the heat of it. Was he as affected as she was? If she'd had the fortitude to look over, would she have found him aroused?

Staying at Ben's side as he slowly healed from his injury, Kate had plenty of time to ruminate and second guess herself.

She'd pretended it was no big deal to strip down to her black t-shirt bra and leopard-print panties, but Kate's cheeks had flushed, as had the responsive skin of her décolletage. Studiously keeping her concentration on the horizon, she'd stolen glances at him from under her lashes as she'd undressed. Apparently under no compulsion to look away, he casually watched. Did he want her?

Kate was drawn to him—it was as if he were a magnet. Her body begged her to heed the attraction. Go to him, it whispered, and offer your lips for a kiss. The temptation proved difficult to disobey. Like a wave engulfing her, it threatened to pull her from shore and cast her adrift.

She'd climbed in the cab of the truck and fastened her seatbelt, refusing to acknowledge the proof of what she craved—the wetness between her thighs.

Was Kate the only one that felt the desire pulsate between them? If Teller recognized it, he didn't comment on it. He'd left her at her cabin to dress, telling her to take the backpacks with her. He'd reminded her someone had to dispose of Peggy and Otis, and the dead animals—to bury or burn them.

"Kate?" Ben was awake. She scrambled from her chair and went to him, her brow furrowing and all other thoughts disappearing. He still seemed to sleep an awful lot, but his complexion had markedly improved, and his temperature was now normal.

"I'm here."

"Thirsty," he rasped.

She held a cup of broth for him. He drank deeply then collapsed back against his pillow. She put the cup on the bedside table. "It's almost time for the next dose of your medicine."

"Not another shot in my butt. Aren't I allowed any dignity?"

Laughing at his tone, she teased, "It's not your butt, it's your ventrogluteal." Kate had religiously reviewed the instructions in the manual Teller had brought from Seth's den, learning how to administer injections. Now, she readied the syringe, all business.

"You say potato..." Ben muttered, shifting in bed to his side. He winced as Kate gave him his shot.

"Tonight's dose will be your last," she promised, putting the plastic cap on the needle and chucking it in the trash can beside the nightstand. "The book said any more than a five-day course can damage your kidneys."

While he remained on his side, Kate carefully probed his wounds. He was recovering. The antibiotic had worked its magic. The surrounding skin had transformed back to a healthy hue, and there hadn't been any sign of pus for days.

"Stop fretting about the stitches. They're holding. You did a good job."

She'd used the suture kit from the hospital pharmacy to stitch his ragged entrance and exit wounds. It hadn't been pleasant. Critical of her sewing skills, she'd checked her handiwork often. Kate hadn't mentioned she was troubled, but Ben was canny enough to figure it out on his own. She helped him into a supine position. "How would you know? You were unconscious at the time."

His eyes crinkled in the corners. "Still here, aren't I?"

She returned his smile, wanting to ask him if he was ready to tell her about what occurred at his parents' farm. To inquire about his family's fate. Kate bit her tongue. Ben kept his manner sunny, but she saw the dark sorrow he hid. He'd obviously been through hell and back and needed time to come to terms with his loss. She understood his reticence. "Want me to rub more salve on your feet?"

Kate didn't wait for his response, opening the drawer in the bedside table for Connie's homemade tincture of meadowsweet and calendula. She evaluated his soles as she applied the salve. They were nearly healed. Soon, there would be nothing preventing him from getting up and moving around.

Whenever Kate had asked about his journey to Mayfly Hollow, he'd been close lipped, not wanting to discuss it. Now, she tested the waters, saying, "Your feet were worse than mine when I arrived... How much did you end up walking?"

His tone was gruff when he finally answered. "Seemed like a gazillion miles."

"What happened to your Jeep?"

"I got overrun on the interstate."

"By zombies or people?"

Ben swallowed hard. "People. Amazing how quick law-abiding citizens can turn criminal. Desperation will do that, I guess."

"Want to tell me about it?"

He shook his head. "Does it matter? I made it."

She pulled the desk chair up to the bed and sat. Ben stretched a hand to her, and after a second of hesitation, she clasped it.

"Nothing matters anymore," he whispered. "Except being here, with you."

Kate extricated her hand. It wasn't the first time that week he'd murmured tender words. "Ben."

"You know how much I care."

She avoided his eyes, keeping her gaze firmly glued to the carpet. She was compelled to say, "Yes. You want more from me than I can give."

"Why do you put up walls?"

"I'm not *putting up walls*," Kate argued. "No strings, no demands, no obligations. I've been honest with you since the beginning."

Ben palmed her knee. "I won't hurt you. I'm not your father —I won't abandon you. I'm not like your sister's asshole boyfriend either. I'd never lay a finger on you."

Kate's mouth dropped open. "What do you know about any of that?"

"The old biddies running the rumor mill in Clayton's Corners had plenty to say when Connie hauled you into town to shack up with her internet boyfriend." He squeezed her knee. "You really didn't know about the gossip?"

"Sure. I knew people talked. But how did they find out about my problems with Jared?"

"When he got some whiskey in him, you couldn't get him to shut up about you."

Kate slid off her chair and stood with her back to Ben. Unseeing, she stared out the window. It had been more than fifteen years ago, so why did it still sting to hear about being the subject of wagging tongues? Would she ever be able to shake her past? "I almost moved to New York City after I graduated high school. I should've." Putting her knuckles to her bottom lip, she added bitterly, "Small towns and their smaller minds."

Ben scoffed, "Who cares what they thought."

"Apparently *I* do." She spun on her heel, her mouth taut. "Why dredge all this up?"

"To assure you that I'm on your side, Kate. You're an amazing woman—"

Kate snorted.

"Look at how devoted you've been to me. You've nursed me back to health singlehandedly. I'd have to be a fool not to notice you've been worried sick about me."

"Of course I have," Kate acknowledged. "I invited you here. I have a responsibility to you!"

"I think it's deeper than that."

Not knowing what else to say, she clenched her teeth. "I can't talk about this right now. I-I'm tired. I've got a pregnant sister whose husband should've returned last week—he's AWOL. Her health is precarious. Since miscarrying, Judy's basically cata-tonic. Her husband is useless now. Their kid is trying to cope with losing both her mom and her dad..."

"And you're doing a remarkable job juggling all of it," Ben reassured her. "Why don't you get out of here? Go take a stroll. Clear your mind."

Her heart leaped at the prospect of solitude. "You'll be okay on your own?"

"I don't need 'round the clock care anymore, Kate. I'm getting sleepy anyway." He yawned to illustrate his words. "You go on. It's a beautiful afternoon."

She flew from the cabin, eager to escape.

CHAPTER THIRTY-TWO

THE GLADE WAS BLESSEDLY COOL, THOUGH THE DAY WAS sweltering. Kate wearily lowered to the log and watched the water swirling around algae-laced stones in the brook. Further down, there was a tranquil, shallow pool. Little bubbles broke the surface of the crystalline water. Upon closer examination, she spied a school of silver minnows. The dappled afternoon sunshine made them shimmer like platinum as they swam.

Kate inhaled deeply, trying to shake her mood. The damp earthy smell usually comforted her, but she couldn't settle.

Even speaking superficially about her past was enough to wreck her. Naturally, the scandal spurred gossip when she and Connie had moved to Clayton's Corners a month after their parents' death. The specter had haunted them wherever they went, clinging and hostile. Demonic. Kate had never been able to exorcise it, no matter how hard she'd tried. She sealed a hand over her mouth to keep from crying out, rocking back and forth. Remembering. The upsetting visits from social services. Being hounded by the press. Mentioned on the nightly local news for weeks. The salacious, cringeworthy newspaper headlines.

And, after. She hadn't known about Jared's drunken yapping to all and sundry. The shame sliced like a scalpel, although rationally she knew none of that was her fault. *Fucking Jared.* Kate should have shanked him the first time he put his filthy paws down her panties.

She thought she'd been invisible at school. When she'd bumped into Ben at Cahoots last year, he'd bought her a vodka tonic and flirted. Told Kate she'd caught his eye when they were in school. That he'd always regretted not asking her out. She'd been flattered. He was cute, successful. She'd taken him home that night and climbed him like a mountain.

Kate berated herself. For the last month of their arrangement, Ben had made his intentions clear—he wanted them to be a couple. She'd never come right out and told him no. Kate liked their pact, refused to alter it. She'd been content with their once-a-week booty calls. Had she led Ben on?

They'd agreed from the outset that it was strictly sex. It wasn't supposed to be anything more. She'd told herself what they had was mutually beneficial. And it had been, at first. Once Ben developed *feelings*, the stakes had forever changed.

Kate had taken advantage of Ben. No matter how well-intentioned she was, it was self-serving. She wasn't proud of that. Guilt flooded her guts and took root. Vined its way up to her ribcage, tightening.

Every time Ben had proposed taking things to the next level, she'd brushed it off, changed the subject. That last morning at Buttercream was the most direct she'd been. Had diplomacy been a mistake? Perhaps he'd read more into Kate's invitation to Mayfly Hollow.

She ought to be brutally honest and tell him in no uncertain terms that there was no future between them. Kate despised hurting him—couldn't help feeling his mental state was tenuous, no matter how cheerful his disposition. His optimism was surely a façade. Wasn't *everyone* fragile? The end of the world wasn't good for anyone's psychological fitness. Still, wasn't it more cruel to string someone along?

Weakness. Kate loathed it. Cursed it. She'd always thought

she was strong, but she'd lied to herself. Self-awareness was more than an inconvenient truth. It could cripple.

Ben's persuasion was endearing and sweet. Kate didn't fault his persistence. In some ways, she was enticed to give in. He was easy to be with. Caring. He didn't make her pulse hammer in her throat like Teller did. Even now, her body hummed with want. All week, whenever she'd closed her eyes she saw Teller. As someone who liked to keep men at arm's length, giving up control and indulging in her desires both excited and repelled Kate. She'd lost plenty of sleep over it.

The way the sun hit the wiry hairs on his thighs and chest. His slender but muscled physique.

It was ironic—there was no real indication that Teller felt the same. It could very well be one-sided, much like her with Ben. If Kate threw herself at Teller, would he try to let her down easy like she had Ben? That would be an unpalatable taste of karma. Mortifying. Her armpits prickled, and she felt her face heat.

They'd shared one inconsequential kiss, but it hadn't meant anything. He played up cowboy persona. The flirtatious manner was likely second nature. There was just something provocative about Teller.

Stop! The ranch was in jeopardy of collapse, and she was rhapsodizing about her love life.

Kate got up, deciding to hike to the farmhouse. She hadn't had the opportunity to see Connie since coming back from River Heights, though they spoke daily over the walkie. Audrey had stopped by Ben's cabin occasionally to bring food, apparel, or give Kate a short respite. She'd kept Kate up to date on how everyone was, but Kate wanted to check on her sister and see if Judy's condition really was as grave as she'd heard.

The day was muggy, making Kate's hair transform into frizz. She dug in her pocket and found an elastic band, arranging her hair in a ponytail as she walked. Her sneakers kicked up dust as she made her way past the entrance gate, then to the row of cabins. Kate briefly peeked in on Ben and found him sleeping.

She was out of breath by the time she ascended the hill. Following the curve of the gravel lane, Kate observed her surroundings with interest. She'd not been here since the tragedy. Amy was conspicuously absent, as was Lenin, and for some reason tears sprung to Kate's eyes. In the distance, Ace barked, but the barn was noticeably silent. Had any livestock evaded massacre?

Her minivan was where she'd left it. An arc of Peggy's dried blood painted the side like macabre artwork. *Yuck.* Connie was in the kitchen, assembling a casserole for dinner. Greeting her, Kate noted her sister's gaunt cheeks.

"Here," Kate said. "I'll do that, and you can take a load off."

Connie didn't debate. She left the spoon in the bowl where she'd been mixing canned cream of mushroom soup and crumbled, cooked ground beef. After filling a glass at the tap, she went to the trestle table. "Thanks."

Kate emptied the freezer bags of thawed corn and green beans into the bowl, then stirred until it was combined, surveying her sister over her shoulder.

"There are tater puffs for the top in the freezer. I'm dialing it in," Connie said self-consciously. "Not that anyone other than Teller has an appetite these days."

"I gather he's pretty much running the farm solo. At least from what Audrey says." Kate spread the meat and veggies in a buttered baking dish.

"She helps him every afternoon. In fact, she's out with him now. She's really stepped up. I've never seen anyone so enthusiastic."

I'll just bet. "Where's everyone else?"

"I put a DVD on for Nora in the living room. Jamie's with Judy in their cabin. He rarely leaves her side. She's not bouncing back, Kate." Connie massaged the bridge of her nose, closing her eyes. "And Jamie's so shattered he's hardly functioning. I hesitate to push him to do his share of chores. Audrey's been a godsend for both Nora and Teller."

Kate lined tater puffs in orderly rows in the baking dish and set it in the fridge, then joined Connie at the table. Not knowing what to say, Kate held Connie's hand. Her sister looked poorly. Her skin was ashen and her hair dull. She seemed to have shrunk. Connie's bulbous belly was at odds with her scrawny frame. Dread zipped up from Kate's toes, making her scalp tingle. "You been sleeping?"

Connie smiled, evidently noticing Kate's gaze on her midsection. "No position is comfy. Not even on my side. My back aches something fierce."

"How far along are you now?"

"Friday I'll be thirty-three weeks."

"Time flies," Kate said. "That means I've been here a month. I can't believe it."

"I know. In some ways it seems like yesterday... in others, forever ago." Connie stroked her bump meditatively. "I think Seth is dead, Kate."

Kate grappled with a response. She didn't want to be cavalier and airily dismiss Connie's concerns. Seth very well could've died from a Z attack or any number of reasons. *Or he could've deserted us.* She was noncommittal. "Possibly."

Connie met Kate's eyes. "I have mixed feelings about that."

"How so?" Through the screen door came the sound of the ATV.

Smile enigmatic, Connie cocked her head. "That'll be Teller and Audrey coming back. Why don't you go say hi?"

Kate lingered, tempted to press for an answer. *Leave it alone.* She gave Connie's fingers a final squeeze and left.

Teller was parking the ATV by the half-empty chicken coop. Seated behind him, Audrey's arms circled his abdomen. When she saw Kate watching, her lips curled in a smirk. Kate flouted the quick stab of jealousy and maintained her pleasant expression. Ace raced up to receive her. Kate stooped to pet him.

"Howdy," Teller said, brightening at Kate's approach. His

clothes were rumpled and his face dirt streaked. "Can I chat with you for a minute?"

"Sure, cowboy."

A look of annoyance crossed Audrey's face, but she inched off the ATV and trooped to the house without a word.

"I wanna show you somethin'," Teller said, leading her into the barn. Ace loped at his side. "Best we keep it to ourselves for now, I reckon."

Otis's brain matter remained where it had been sprayed on the wall by the feed trough. Tissue clung on the wood slats in withered clumps on streaks of black blood. Its putrid aroma imbued the interior of the barn.

"Stay, Ace." Whining, Ace sank to his haunches, glumly regarding his master.

Kate focused on climbing up the ladder to the hayloft after Teller. She liked how he treated her as his equal, sharing confidences. How he knew she could handle it. Kate also liked the way his backside filled out the seat of his denims.

"I'm thinkin' we've got a little time yet. 'Course, I could be mistaken." He extended a hand toward her once he was in the loft. "Needs monitorin'. Still, matter of time 'til it's another obstacle."

Oh goody. Another obstacle.

Once he'd pushed the shutters open at the window facing the back of the farmhouse, Teller scooped up a pair of binoculars from the hay-covered floor. He held them out to Kate. His tone serious, he instructed, "Look past the gate, to the highway."

Taking a bracing breath, Kate brought the binoculars to her eyes.

At the turn off to the farm, a massive horde of Zs congregated.

CHAPTER THIRTY-THREE

OVER THE NEXT WEEKS, THE DAY-TO-DAY OPERATION OF THE FARM descended into a new normal.

Kate and Teller monitored the zombie mob on the highway at intervals. They were watchful for any indication the horde would meander down the lane closer to Mayfly Hollow, but the Zs merely loitered at the turnoff to the lane as if heeding a signal, effectively cutting off the ranch's highway egress.

The members of the compound went through the daily tasks by rote, existing but not necessarily *living*. Kate likened it to being suspended in time, like a prehistoric insect fossilized in amber.

Steadily putting on weight, Ben regained his strength. Once he was ambulatory, Kate showed him around and introduced him to what was left of their fractured group.

Connie had a speculative gleam in her eye when she first met Ben, as if visually measuring him up for a wedding suit constructed with brother-in-law material. Audrey analyzed him like he were a specimen in a glass slide under a microscope, as did Teller. Kate often noticed the way they each scrutinized her and Ben's interactions.

At first, Teller was reserved, but Ben was a likable man. It was hard to resist his charm. By degrees, Teller thawed toward him. Ben had grown up on a farm and volunteered to help wherever he could. Teller seemed grateful—even with a diminished number of livestock, maintaining an operation the size of Mayfly Hollow was taxing.

Judy's condition hadn't worsened, but it hadn't improved either. Barely able to eat, she remained weakened. Jamie had declined Connie's invitation to move Judy to the main house. Withdrawing, he kept vigil beside her in their quarters. Nora stayed with the rest of the group. It was as if Jamie and Judy forgot they had a child. Audrey completely assumed parenting responsibilities, and Nora meekly adapted.

Kate resumed her job as cook and domestic. In the evenings when the cicadas droned, she'd laze on the front porch with Connie. The further she advanced in her pregnancy, the more Connie gave the impression of looking inward. She didn't speak of Seth. Kate hesitated to bring him up.

"Ben said the same thing happened at his folks' place. They eventually swarmed the farmhouse. You think that'll happen here?" Connie asked soberly.

Their wicker chairs moved rhythmically across the porch's worn floorboards as they rocked. Summer made the days hazy and humid, perfuming the air with flowers at twilight. Gossamer lightning bugs glowed, reminding Kate of her childhood, when she'd collected them in jelly jars.

Pinching her lip between her teeth, Kate considered the sky. Stars filled the inky atmosphere, blanketing the ridge in obscurity and disguising the zombies in the distance. "It might."

"The breeze may carry our scent, whip them up. Perhaps we shouldn't sit out here."

"It hasn't carried much of *their* stench," Kate reasoned. "Besides, Con, I need a break from being inside with everyone all the fucking time."

"I get it. Me, too. So long as we don't wander too far from the house. If the sensor is tripped on the fence, we'll have to dash down to the basement."

"Right. I don't dare go to the glade," Kate said.

"I like that clearing myself. I used to walk down there all the time… before. Imagine the months ahead of us all being cooped up together in the long-term bunker."

"*If* we go. We can't seem to come to a consensus about leaving Mayfly Hollow. What if Seth's there? We wouldn't be welcome."

Connie tossed Kate a mulish look. "That bunker is half mine. He has to share, whether he likes it or not. My point is that we can't wait too long to leave. Soon there'll be a newborn and a woman who just gave birth to schlep along."

"Even if we went now, it wouldn't be much easier. We have a dog, a ten-year-old, her invalid mother, a heavily pregnant woman, and a man easily winded by an almost fatal bout of septicemia."

"I'm just saying… if the farm gets swarmed and we bug out to the basement then can't escape through the barn, we *will* run out of food and water, no matter how closely we ration it."

"It's a dilemma, to be sure," Kate said. "And we're all getting restless."

There was the sound of the door opening behind them. The light from the hallway fixture fell across Ben's face as he unlatched the screen door, illuminating his boyishly handsome features. Cold air and the buttery scent of popcorn drifted out. "Ladies, why don't you get out of this godforsaken heat and come play Monopoly?"

Teller, Nora, and Audrey were at the kitchen table, the Monopoly board set up in the center. Teller sipped from a bottle of beer. His Stetson rested beside the bowl of popcorn. He swallowed, pointing to the newcomers. "You three against us three."

"We're the top hat," Nora volunteered in her shy way.

"And we're the race car," Ben said, helping Connie take a seat on the bench.

Kate lowered beside her sister, keenly aware of Teller's gaze on her as she propped her ax against the table leg. They rarely saw each other alone. She wondered if he missed her as much as she missed him.

"Can I get you a beer, Kate?" Teller was already on his feet.

Kate met his eyes and smiled. "Sure."

Audrey called, "Grab one for me, will you, hon?"

Hon? That's new. Kate organized the *community chest* and *chance* cards into neat piles, pretending not to notice the way her hackles rose at Audrey and Teller's familiarity. "Who's gonna be the banker?"

"Me." Ben beamed. "And my lovely and capable assistant Miss Nora will be in charge of doling out houses and hotels."

Teller twisted the tops off the beer bottles, handing one to Kate then Audrey. Audrey looked at him coquettishly, placing a hand on his forearm. "I don't typically drink more than one, but we worked so hard in the field this afternoon. I'm thirsty."

You sure are, sis. "Nora, why don't you roll the dice? Your team can go first."

SHE COULDN'T MOVE, *no matter how much she strained her muscles. Kate was locked in place. Imprisoned. She was cognizant of what it was —sleep paralysis. It was as if Kate were awake but had zero control over her limbs. Calling out was impossible. She screamed, but only on the inside.*

Kate was in her lumpy twin bed at Jared's grody little bungalow. It was the middle of the night. Connie must be working her overnight shift at the mini mart. Moonlight streamed in through the sheet tacked above the window, allowing enough light to make out the edges of the furniture crammed in the tiny room. The pressboard desk where she sat to do homework in the evenings. The discount store dresser with the wonky drawer always coming off the tracks. The milk crates stacked beside the bed used as a makeshift night table, topped with an ugly, bulky nineteen seventies lamp.

Kate shouldn't have been able to see the doorknob revolving, yet her gaze zoomed to it. She wrestled against the sleep paralysis, trying to wake. It was happening. Again. The hinges squeaked. The door swung open in slow motion. Ominous.

Silhouetted in the hallway, bathed in gold, stood Jared. He appeared almost beatific. But he was evil. At twenty-five, Jared wasn't grotesque, although his teeth were rotted from chewing tobacco, and he had a prominent beer belly. A hulk of a man, he filled the doorway, his shoulders touching each side of the doorframe.

"Katie," he sang. "I got somethin' for that tight little pussy."

Terrified, she watched Jared slide off his basketball shorts. When he half-turned to fit through the doorway, his huge hard on bobbed, mocking Kate. He put a hand to it, encircling it with his middle finger and thumb. He pumped once, twice, as he staggered to her bed.

It hurt last time. Ripped her tender flesh and made blood spot her panties the next day. No, Kate shrieked internally, please, no!

"Remember what I said. You tell Connie and I'll say you're a slut who came onto me. Or maybe I'll slit her throat in her sleep. Then you really will be an orphan." He wore a stained football jersey and a jester's grin. With his free hand, he flicked Kate's thin blanket aside. "Take off them undies and spread your legs. I want to see that cock teasing cunt."

"Stop! Stop!"

Kate bolted upright. For a moment, she didn't know where she was. Gloomy pre-dawn gray filtered through the curtains. Squinting, she identified the rocking chair in the corner and the antique chiffonier at the end of the bed. She was in her upstairs bedroom at the farmhouse.

Her jaw throbbed from gritting her teeth, and her muscles ached with strain. She rolled her head slowly and stretched her arms. Ever since her conversation with Ben about Jared, her subconscious had unearthed long buried specters—the nightmares had returned with ferocity. The same flashback plagued her each time she dreamed, relentlessly replaying like a scene of a film set on repeat.

Every night, she was back *there*. It was torture.

Did I cry out?

Reclining against the metal headboard, Kate cupped her palms over her face and growled with frustration. Would the nightmares ever cease?

She gave up on falling back asleep. She'd get up and bake. That always soothed her.

As Kate prepared a *tangzhong* starter for a batch of cinnamon rolls, she thought about the evening before. Game night had been an enjoyable diversion, despite Audrey hanging off Teller at every available opportunity, giggly and flirty. Each throaty chuckle accompanied a smug smile aimed in Kate's direction. Kate had refused to take the bait, though it cost her.

Hand kneading the dough proved therapeutic. Kate poured a mug of coffee and went to sit at the table while she waited for her dough to rise. By the time she formed the rolls and put them into the oven to bake, she was in much better spirits. When Kate set the pan of baked rolls on the counter to cool, the redolent fragrance of cinnamon infused the kitchen.

Using a whisk to combine the half-dozen eggs the remaining hens had laid, Kate then added diced onion, ham, and bell pepper to a skillet. She threw in a generous handful of leafy spinach from Connie's hydroponic garden.

She was icing the rolls when Ben came in the kitchen door, a huge bouquet of pink, purple, and red wildflowers in one fist. Kate recognized cardinal flowers, bee balm, wild bergamot, and cranesbill.

"A token of appreciation for the chef," he said, presenting the bouquet.

Kate smiled with pleasure, accepting the flowers as Teller came into the kitchen, his cowboy boots clicking against the floor. "Thank you, Ben. That was sweet of you. I'll find a vase to put them in."

Ben pecked her cheek. "Looks like breakfast's ready. I'll go let everyone know."

Blushing, Kate opened a cabinet for a glass pitcher and filled it with water from the tap. She peeked at Teller where he poured a cup of coffee from the stovetop percolator, but his face was impassive.

"I wouldn't have taken you for a flower lover," he observed, arching an eyebrow.

Something in his tone irked her. "Why wouldn't I be? Most women like being surprised with flowers."

"You're hardly *most women* though."

"Aren't I?" Kate smiled tightly, recollecting the evening before. How Teller had grinned at Audrey as she'd flirted, had guffawed at her idiotic jokes. Kate plunked the bouquet into the pitcher and water splashed out, getting on her hand. She grabbed a towel. "I bet Audrey would love for you to go out at dawn and pick her some wildflowers."

"I ain't the flower pickin' type," Teller responded, putting his mug on the counter. His gaze intent, he came to Kate, chucking the towel aside. The clean, soapy smell Kate identified as Teller reached her nose as he pinned her against the counter, his pelvis to hers.

She gasped as he gently caged her in his arms, bracing his palms on either side of the sink.

Teller brought his mouth to Kate's ear and whispered, "But now that I know *you* like flowers..."

CHAPTER THIRTY-FOUR

TELLER STEPPED INTO THE KITCHEN THE FOLLOWING MORNING AS Kate stacked blueberry pancakes on an earthenware platter.

She looked over her shoulder, pasting a blank expression on her face. Emotion made her esophagus sticky as she recalled the words he'd so softly murmured yesterday—how he'd then stepped away, breaking contact. He'd gone to the table and sipped his coffee, unbothered. Kate had been left reeling. Frustrated. Aroused. She hadn't recovered. Even now butterflies flapped their wings in her tummy.

Swiping his hat from his head, Teller declared, wide-eyed, "You won't believe it."

Kate's spatula clattered on the skillet, her heart jackhammering. "The sensors on the security gate haven't been triggered. Do we have to hurry down to the basement bunker? Should I sound the alarm?"

Teller appeared more mystified than panicked. "No, no. It's crazy, but they're gone!"

"What do you mean *they're gone*?"

"I don't know how else to make it clearer, Kate," Teller said. "They're gone—they've vanished into thin air."

Kate blinked. "Wait. There were literally hundreds of Zs there last night—same as always. They're *somewhere*."

"Not that I can see from the hayloft." Teller shrugged.

"What about the camera feed?"

"I'm on my way now. You finish with what you're doin'. I'll holler if I uncover anything of note."

Distracted by questions she had no answers for, Kate finished frying the sausage patties. With his farm responsibilities, Teller was an early riser. At daybreak, he'd climb the ladder to the hayloft and scan the property with the binoculars. Before breakfast, he'd review the cameras. He and Kate would take turns checking the horde through the day.

After placing the sausages in a shallow bowl, Kate arranged the food on the counter buffet-style. Going to the foot of the stairway, she called everyone downstairs to breakfast.

The group piled their plates with food and found their seats at the trestle table. Too keyed up to eat, Kate poured a tumbler of juice. A few minutes later, Teller entered the kitchen. At Kate's probing look, he shook his head and lifted a shoulder.

He helped himself to a tall stack of pancakes and several sausages, then lowered his loose-limbed frame to an empty chair across the table from Connie. "Welp," he said. "Y'all might be interested to know the Zs have moseyed on."

First, there was stunned silence. At once, everyone erupted into chatter, exclaiming and asking questions. Connie gestured impatiently for them to simmer down. She asked Teller, "Where?"

Teller chewed a bite of sausage and swallowed. "Your guess is as good as mine, boss lady."

"Just because they've shifted from the highway entrance doesn't mean they aren't a threat," Ben pointed out.

"Yeah... maybe they're at another section of gate where you can't see from the hayloft," Audrey said.

Teller liberally poured syrup on his pancakes. "You think I'd have brought the subject up to y'all before reviewin' the camera feed from Seth's computer? I can confirm they aren't anywhere near the perimeter of the fence."

Nora's cornflower blue gaze volleyed between the adults as they spoke. During the lull in the conversation, she asked softly, "Are you going to go look for them, Teller?"

"You know," Kate mused, tapping a nail on the table. "That's not a half bad suggestion."

"Today's laundry day, isn't it, Kate?" Audrey asked, her mouth curving into a patronizing smile. "I can go out with Teller this time since you'll be busy."

Yeah, right. As if! To stifle a cackle, Kate pretended to cough.

"No, Audrey." Nora beseeched, "You can't leave me. 'Sides, you said we have to start on fractions this morning."

"Laundry can wait but fractions cannot." Kate hid her mirth, bringing her tumbler of juice to her lips. *What's that saying about turnabout being fair play?* "Actually, I have a fantastic idea, you two. Did you know that measuring out laundry detergent is an ideal way to learn fractions?"

Audrey's cheeks turned a fiery red, and she opened her mouth to speak, but Connie said authoritatively from her seat at the head of the table, "That *is* a good idea. Audrey, you and Nora can incorporate laundry into your lesson plans today. Kill two birds with one stone."

"I wish I wasn't still so damn feeble, or I'd come along on your scouting mission," Ben said with regret. "You'll be careful, won't you, Kate? Teller, you'll keep an eye on her, yeah?"

"Always do, Benji," Teller replied easily. To those who didn't know him as well as Kate, the tinge of disdain beneath his amiable exterior would go unnoticed.

For the remainder of the meal, Audrey kept her mouth shut but threw venomous looks Kate's way.

WORRIED the sound of an engine may bring them undue attention, Kate and Teller had decided to scout on foot.

They'd applied sunscreen, and Teller stuffed a travel canister of insect repellant in his pocket. He grabbed his favorite rifle as they prepared to leave. "You've got your handguns, your knife, and your ax. Need anything else?"

"Canteens," Kate said, flapping the hem of her ruffled green tank top to demonstrate she was already overheated. "Even if we only intend to be out for a couple hours, we're going to need hydration. I'm oozing through my top."

Teller wore walking shoes instead of cowboy boots. "We may have to trek through brambles. We oughta be wearin' long sleeved shirts with our jeans."

Taking the ATV down to the main entrance, they parked it by the gate and exited the compound. Hiking through the overgrown lane toward the highway turn off, they scanned their surroundings for stray Zs.

"The air still stinks of them," Kate said, wrinkling her nose in distaste.

"Yep. Hovers quite unpleasantly, don't it? Amazin' it didn't work its way up the ridge."

At the turn off, they paused. Kate used her hand to shade her eyes. They contemplated right, then left. Kate murmured, "Unless they're after prey, they move slow as molasses. How far could they really have gotten? They were here twelve hours ago."

Teller scratched his ear, then adjusted his hat. "Somethin' had to lure 'em away, right? Or they just gave up on us volunteerin' to be their next meal."

"I guess. Which direction do you think they went?"

Left led to River Heights. Right took them into Colliers Junction proper, a once bustling village that had become a ghost town over the years. It was comprised of nothing more than a few houses, a bank, a post office, and a ramshackle tavern that had sold watered-down rotgut.

"Logic tells me that since River Heights has been decimated, they're lookin' for fresh meat, which makes me think we oughta head towards Colliers."

"Unless they were drawn back to River Heights. I mean, maybe that motorcycle gang came through again." Kate sighed then waved her hand to the scrubby pine forest in front of them. "Or they ditched the highway and went into the woods straight ahead. Let's just pick a damn direction, Teller."

"I say right."

North. Kate nodded. The terrain was flat, allowing them to see the stretch of highway ahead for three or four miles. Keeping off the road, they stayed parallel to it, their pace brisk. They didn't encounter any Zs or people. The buzz of cicadas and the twitter of birds seemed eerie in the stillness of their surroundings. *Welcome to the apocalypse.*

An hour into their journey, when the highway began to incline, Kate stopped. The mid-morning sun beat down on her head. She used the back of her hand to wipe the sweat from her forehead. Uncapping her canteen, Kate took a deep swallow. "We should've come across them by now. We have to reassess. But first, let's take five."

"I vote for that," Teller groaned.

They found a copse of trees where they were shielded from the view of the highway. Choosing trees across from each other, they sat with their backs against the trunks.

Kate bit her cheek, thinking. "They must've gone to River Heights."

"You may be right," Teller agreed. "I say we walk just a mite further. Once we get to the summit of the hill, we'll be able to see for miles."

"Okay. If we don't see anything, we head back home. After lunch we can scout south of Mayfly Hollow. Agreed?"

"Agreed. I'm gettin' mighty hungry. Pancakes are wearin' off." Teller patted his flat waist, unfolding from his sitting position. He brushed pine needles from his denims, then held a hand to Kate.

Grabbing it, she allowed him to hoist her up. She batted her eyelashes. "My hero."

Teller tipped his hat.

"Nice to know chivalry isn't dead."

Once they met the highway, Teller said, "Let's tackle that hill."

Kate was breathless as she made her way up the steep incline, her thighs burning from effort. She wasn't the only one huffing and puffing—Teller was out of breath, too.

"There they are," Teller said with grim satisfaction at the top, motioning toward the mob a half mile ahead.

Kate shook her head in awe. "I can't believe they made it that far."

"They are most assuredly headed north."

"But why?"

"Who the heck cares, Kate? All that matters is they won't be a concern at Mayfly Hollow. Mission accomplished." Teller smiled, his relief obvious and catching. He gathered her in his arms for a triumphant bear hug, lifting her from the ground and swinging her around in a wide circle.

When he set her down again, Kate glanced the way they'd come. She felt her grin melt from her face. "Uh, Teller?"

"Huh?"

She pointed a shaky finger. In the distance, another horde of shambling Zs tailed them. "We didn't see them when we finished our break and started walking again. That means they're moving."

"We're trapped," Teller whispered. "We're gonna have to hide in the forest deep enough so they don't detect us. Wait 'til they pass so we can continue south. And what if there are more hordes comin' behind them? We could be stuck out here overnight."

CHAPTER THIRTY-FIVE

HANDS LINKED, TELLER AND KATE CLAMBERED FOR THE DENSELY wooded pineland on the western side of the highway.

"Dang, Kate. It's like them Zs are on some sort of pilgrimage. So much for this bein' a quick scoutin' mission."

"Each mission we've gone on has been more complicated than we anticipated. We may have to lure a Z and splash on its blood to make it through this one," Kate muttered as she side-stepped a low-lying section of scrubby brush. "Especially if we're stuck over-fuckin'-night in the forest."

"Less talk, more walk," Teller said, urging her forward. "That other pack behind us moved swift. We better shake a leg."

After several minutes of power walking, Kate slowed, disoriented. "I thought I was keeping due west, but now I'm turned around."

"I believe we're on course but," he fished in his jean pocket, "I did have the foresight to bring this along."

He held a metal compass in the palm of his hand.

"Any chance you got a sixteen-ounce T-bone in your pocket, too?" Kate asked, her digestive tract grumbling.

"That I do not." Teller snorted. "Keep your eyes peeled for berry bushes. Wild strawberries are in season right about now."

They hiked until the earth sloped into a tall, broad ridge. "I'm *not* scaling that Everest," Kate asserted, hunger making her short-tempered. "So I hope this is far enough from the horde."

"I reckon so, but if the Zs come in this way we may have no choice but to scale it."

"Well, consult your compass, Sir Edmund Hillary. We should head south now, don't you think? That way at least we're traveling in the right direction for Mayfly Hollow."

"I'll make sure of it."

Kate watched for strawberry patches but found none. She sipped from her canteen to mollify her stomach with something. Clouds covered the sun, making it seem as if it were dusk instead of lunchtime.

Ahead, Kate identified the outline of a structure. Could it be? Yes, it was. A cabin. "Teller, look."

"Hot damn!"

They advanced on the dilapidated dwelling with an abundance of caution. The timbers were blackened with age and rot, but the cabin appeared sturdy enough. It was perhaps fifteen feet square with modest fitted glass windows. Crumbling wooden steps led to a rough-hewn door.

Teller put his hand on the piece of wood serving as a latch, but Kate stopped him, hissing, "Listen."

There was a distinct thump. "Could be a squirrel."

"Or a Z. I'll peek in the window." She marched to the far side of the cabin, where a window was closer to the ground. Standing on tiptoe, she squinted into the darkened interior. When she joined Teller again, she asked somberly, "You want the good news or the bad news?"

"Good first."

"There is a huge strawberry bush kitty corner from the rear of the cabin."

"And the bad news?"

"It's not a squirrel." Kate plucked her ax from the loop attached to her belt. "You open the door, and I'll stand off to

191

the side. When the Z emerges, I'll do my signature move, okay?"

"You got it."

They got into position. Kate adjusted her ax, gripping it so the blade was horizontal. She sent up a prayer that she'd calculated the Z's height correctly. She dipped her chin. Teller unlatched the door, and it swung wide open.

Boots scuffed against the floor. Snuffling. Then, the snapping of teeth.

Gauging its speed, Kate counted to three. She let out a breath, bringing the ax back. Slammed it forward. The blade connected with the Z's forehead, knocking it off its feet. It landed hard on the stairs.

There was a gaping gash on the Z's temple, but Kate's blow hadn't been enough to fully incapacitate it. *Dammit!* Before the Z could spring back up, Kate straddled it and brought the ax down with a grunt. The blade landed squarely between its eyes and cut through its nasal cavity.

The Z no longer moved.

Kate met Teller's gaze. "Wow. Between the eyes is my new favorite spot—easy to get through and barely any mess! No muss, no fuss."

"Congratulations," Teller said drily. "I'll drag him from the steps."

"Don't take him too far."

Kate scrambled up the crumbling stairs, eager to scope out their digs. The interior was shadowy. It smelled of mildew and lingering Z. A full-size bed covered in a threadbare chenille bedspread took up most of the space. A Hoosier cabinet rested against a wall next to a mounted cast iron sink with an old-fashioned metal water pump. "No way!"

Teller appeared in the doorway. "What's wrong?"

"Nothing, especially if this sucker's functional." She lifted the handle and cranked up and down. At first, she thought it wouldn't work, but then water flowed into the basin. "Woohoo!"

Kate washed her hands and splashed the icy water on her face. Bliss. She stood aside so Teller could have a turn.

Face dripping, Teller said, "I'm not sure I trust this water for drinkin'."

"Me either." Kate removed the canteen attached to her belt loop and unscrewed the top. Half full.

"I got about a third left. We'll have to ration."

Kate opened the Hoosier cabinet. A metal bowl was on a shelf. She rinsed it using the water pump and dried it with the hem of her tank top. "Let's fill this with strawberries. Then, we'll hunker down for a few hours."

After picking berries, Teller barricaded the front door with the cabinet. Kate perched on the bed, mindful of cobwebs and spots of mold on the chenille spread. She popped a strawberry in her mouth with relish, chewing slowly and moaning. "My God, this is the best thing I've ever eaten."

"Not bad."

When the bowl was empty and their fingers stained with berry juice, they shifted into a more comfortable sitting position, with their spines against the wood slat wall. Kate smothered a sneeze. "How long should we wait?"

"I figure we can reassess before suppertime. If we can't leave then, we're better off spendin' the night here and startin' for home first thing."

The windows threw little light into the cabin, but Kate could make out the lines of Teller's face clearly. "Too bad we can't call the farm to let them know. They'll be worried."

"I never had much use for cell phones myself," Teller said. "But they sure were convenient."

Kate tweaked the sodden neckline of her top, which stuck to her like a second skin.

"Penny for your thoughts? Five bucks if they're dirty ones."

Chuckling, Kate admitted, "I'm bummed I didn't book that Caribbean cruise like I wanted to. I could be on a white sand beach right now, but I didn't want to add to my credit card debt."

"You'd be snackin' on pineapple instead of strawberries." Teller smiled, tracing a pattern on his pant leg with his thumbnail. "I hope it ain't been too terrible spendin' the end of the world with me."

The soft-spoken comment had Kate's pulse gathering speed. She cleared her throat to cover her discomfiture. "It's been fun."

"I'm not one for sappy sentiments, but I want you to know... I admire you greatly, Kate."

She felt a blush creeping up her neck. "You do?"

"I've embarrassed you," Teller said, his voice shrewd.

"No. I'm... flattered... I just don't understand *why* you admire me."

"Why wouldn't I?"

"I'm far from perfect, that's for sure," Kate replied huskily. "I'm prickly and judgmental. Often unreasonable. Trying to do the noble thing but blundering, making misstep after misstep." She'd resolved to be more open about her feelings but hesitated. *Easier said than done.* "You know when Ben gave me that bouquet yesterday?"

"Yeah?"

"As sweet as the gesture was, it triggered... remorse. Because all I can think of whenever I look at it is Peggy—how she'd been so devoted to her flower garden and how disapproving I was of her for that devotion. I came down hard on her for not contributing more around the farm. I was wrong. I'd apologize to her, if I could."

"Speakin' of comin' down hard on someone," Teller mused. "I think you come down harder on yourself than you ever could on others."

"But don't you see? Peggy understood beauty and joy. In this world—that's something to be celebrated, not scorned. I need to do better. Otherwise, what's there to look forward to? What's the payback for the struggle?"

"Sure, but—"

"No. She didn't deserve my criticism. Let's not forget who brought the virus to Mayfly Hollow. It's my fault she and Otis are gone."

"We've been through this," Teller reproached. "Nothin' you've done can ever change my feelin's about you. You're a helluva good person."

An ember of frustration ignited Kate's bloodstream. She was no angel. "I'm not a *good person*, Teller. You'll definitely have a change of heart once I tell you a few things..."

CHAPTER THIRTY-SIX

"WE ALL HAVE A PAST OF SOME SORT, KATE."

Kate shook her head, her intestines churning. She just couldn't make herself look at Teller. *Should I? Gotta open up to someone sometime.* The thought of it made it hard to breathe. Clasping her hands in her lap to keep from fidgeting, Kate forced herself to inhale and exhale evenly. Before she could change her mind, she asked, "Connie ever tell you about our parents?"

"Other than they passed the summer she turned eighteen, no."

Kate murmured, "You know that word vivacious? If you looked it up in a dictionary, I swear my momma's photo would be there. She wasn't only stunning, she was full of life—made the air crackle. I guess it would be called charisma. People gravitated toward her. God, she was lovely."

"That's not hard to believe, lookin' at you. Connie's mentioned your ma modeled in her teens."

Kate felt her face flame at his compliment. But as far as she was concerned, she was a bland facsimile of her mother. "Only for a few catalogs. She wanted to go to Hollywood after graduation, but she got pregnant with Connie senior year. Her folks were conservative, upright southerners. They insisted she marry my dad. They wed at the courthouse a week after she received her diploma."

"She didn't want to marry?"

Kate shrugged. "She wanted to be an actress more than a housewife and mother. It was her dream. And Momma could've been famous. She had star quality."

"She turn bitter?"

"No, not bitter. Resigned, maybe? Nevertheless, she was a wonderful mother. Did her best. Lavished us with love and attention, but I always knew she secretly longed for something... bigger."

Though Kate didn't meet Teller's eyes, she knew his rapt gaze never left her.

"What about your daddy?"

"Dad was older than Momma. He owned a string of furniture stores on the east coast. They met when he was vacationing one summer in Savannah. He would've been considered a good catch. He was handsome. College educated. Moderately successful."

"Somethin' tells me it wasn't the happiest of marriages."

"It wasn't *bad*, but it had its challenges. Around the time I was born, Dad got into financial trouble. The economy wasn't great, and he'd become overextended. People were tightening their belts, curbing their discretionary spending. A new sofa isn't essential when you're having trouble putting food on the table."

"True."

"Dad declared bankruptcy. Restructured his debt. Lost half his stores."

"How old were you then?"

"I was just a baby, but Dad couldn't recover. I never knew him as a carefree, successful man. I only knew him sad and broken. By the time I was a toddler, all his stores had closed except the scratch and dent liquidator in Fenton. Even that one was failing though."

"Fenton? Just north of Colliers?"

"Yes. He had to sell our house to keep it afloat. He found us a cheap apartment in Colliers Junction and assumed the day-to-day operations at the remaining store. From a gracious five-thousand-square-foot Colonial to a five-hundred-foot hovel. It bruised his ego. He coped by hitting the bottle."

"He became an alcoholic?"

"Basically. A functioning alcoholic but an alcoholic. Three martini lunches. Wine at dinner. Scotch and soda after."

"How did your mother cope?"

"Momma discovered internet chatrooms."

"Ah." Teller said astutely, "The internet was still kinda new and fascinatin' then. It opened up the world, but many a relationship went bust as a result of those chatroom conversations."

Kate pushed her fingers through her hair.

"And? Somethin' happened."

"My mother was always animated and bubbly, but a few weeks before my thirteenth birthday... it was like somebody turned a lightbulb on inside her. I mean, she glowed from within. I was looking in her dresser, to borrow a pair of socks... and I discovered this packet."

"What was it?"

"A contract. She'd been offered a role in an off-Broadway revival of *The Glass Menagerie*. Amanda Wingfield."

"Starring role, right?"

"Yeah. Even off-Broadway, it's a big deal. I confronted her. She confessed she'd met a guy online who owned a theater. When Connie and I were at school, she'd take the train and meet him halfway for rendezvous. They were *in love*. Naturally, he bestowed the leading role upon her. He wanted her to move into his townhouse in Bay Ridge. We girls would come stay with them on weekends. Momma explained she was like a bird. Her wings had been clipped. She needed to be free to grow and spread them. She asked me to let her break the news to Dad herself... and I agreed."

"You're gettin' agitated. Your breathin's erratic," Teller

observed. He enclosed Kate's hand in his. "Dang, girl. Your palm's clammy as hell. You ain't havin' a panic attack, are you?"

Tears puddled in Kate's eyes. She blinked them away, shaking her head. Her voice strangled, she said, "I lied to my mother. I went straight to my father and told him what she planned! I-I didn't want her to leave! I thought he'd stop her, and things would stay the same—"

"Oh Lord," Teller whispered. He drew Kate into his embrace, stroking her hair and making shushing noises. "Hush now. Hush."

Sniffling, Kate hiccupped as she tried to get control. His soothing actions and tender murmurings were a balm to her tattered soul. After a minute, she sat up, scrubbing her tears away with shaky fingers. She'd never told anyone about what happened. Not Connie. Not the social workers. Not anyone. "Sorry."

Teller only smiled for a moment, then said, "I'm waitin' for the end of the story—whenever you're so inclined."

Kate rested her back against the wall, not noticing how the rough slats dug into her shoulder blades. She looked up at the dark, cobwebbed ceiling. "It was Saturday. Connie was at a friend's house. Dad yanked Momma into their bedroom. Slammed the door. There was arguing. Yelling. Banging. They tussled. Momma came out with a black eye and a bloodied lip. She wouldn't look at me. I knew why—I'd betrayed her. I felt shame. Dismay. When Dad walked through the living room, he had the contract in his hands. He tore it up. Threw it in the trash.

"The next couple weeks were awful. Connie didn't understand what was going on. Momma and Dad claimed everything was fine. I played dumb when she asked me. Workdays, Dad began phoning the apartment every hour to check in on Momma, coming home unexpectedly to keep her on her toes. Took away her wallet and car keys. He even trashed the computer. Pitched it right into the dumpster."

"Shit."

"Yeah. She was hostage. I saw black-and-blue marks on Momma's arms. She didn't speak. It was like she wilted. She was no longer luminous and lovely—she was a husk."

Kate quit talking. The pain made her want to curl into a fetal position, to weep like a child. Instead, she crossed her arms protectively over her chest.

"You alright?"

She whispered, "He came home one afternoon, and she was packing a suitcase... apparently, she'd had enough. She was going to run away. Dad kept a loaded gun under the bed, in case of burglars." Dully, she met Teller's eyes. "They say he chased her into the living room. Hunted her down like a goddamn animal. He blew her brains out, then turned the gun on himself. I found them when I got home from school."

"Oh no," Teller breathed, "Oh Kate. No wonder you had such an aversion to guns. I'm so sorry."

He rested a consoling hand on her forearm, but Kate pushed it away. "I don't deserve your sympathy. I betrayed my mother's confidence. I may as well have pulled the trigger myself."

CHAPTER THIRTY-SEVEN

"Knock it off right now," Teller commanded. "You weren't but a kid, Kate. Nobody's responsible for your folks' death but your father."

"I wish I could believe that," Kate said hoarsely. She tightened her jaw to keep it from quivering.

"You don't think the truth woulda come out on its own eventually?" Teller reached over and gripped her chin, making her turn to him. His face was serious. *"You were not responsible. You were a child.* Hear me?"

Kate didn't answer, noticing something of interest—breathing wasn't quite so arduous. While the weight that normally compressed her chest when she thought about her parents wasn't absent, it was less heavy. It mystified her. She stilled. Breathed in and out. Yes, it was definitely less.

"What?"

She looked at her hands in her lap. "I've never ever, *ever* told that to anybody, Teller... I think it was... what's the word? Cathartic."

"Well, there you go. Aren't you glad you shared with me?"

"Yeah. I think so." Kate shook her head, pulling herself back to the present. She yawned. "But it wore me out."

"Can I tell you something *I've* never told anyone?"

Kate swiveled her head toward him. "Of course. Anything."

Teller smiled, then scratched his nose, sheepish. "My first name is Horatio."

For a second Kate was nonplussed, then she snickered. Teller joined her.

"Horatio Teller?"

"The one and only," he replied. "Ma was a Shakespeare lover."

Teller seemed to know just what to say to lighten the mood. Kate's lips relaxed into a grateful smile. There was more she wanted to share with him, but she was too sleepy to broach any further sensitive subjects. *Like Jared.*

When she yawned again, Teller put an arm around her shoulders and tucked her into his side. "Take a nap. When you wake up, we'll decide if it's time to brave the hike back to Mayfly Hollow."

Within seconds, Kate fell into a sound sleep.

SHE COULDN'T MOVE, *no matter how much she strained her muscles. Kate was locked in place. Imprisoned. It was as if she were awake but had zero control over her limbs. Calling out was impossible. Kate screamed, but only on the inside...*

"Kate? Wake up, Kate."

She bolted upright, her heart thudding and blood pounding in her temples.

"You were thrashin' about. I figured you were havin' a nightmare."

"Yeah. Phew." She swallowed and put a palm to her forehead. "Again."

"So it's recurrin'?"

"Used to be. I hadn't had one in years, then they started up again recently."

"You know I'm a good listener," Teller replied, his voice kind.

"You are. But you've heard enough of my true confessions today. I think it's *your* turn to confide."

"Hmm." Teller reflected. "That's fair. I'll tell you a story about when I was probably five, six."

"Okay." Groggy, Kate stretched her neck to work out the kinks.

"Welp, we lived on a farm. No shocker there, huh? Funny thing was my ma wouldn't allow me to have a dog. She didn't like 'em. Imagine, a boy livin' on a farm with no dog. One day, I walked over to the neighbors' place to play with their little girl. She and her folks weren't home, but there was a puppy on the porch. A yellow lab. He ran up to me, tail waggin'. Somehow I got the notion if I could get him to follow me home, Ma would let me keep him. I cajoled him the whole way back to my house and lemme tell you—it was hard work. Once I arrived, I explained the dog wanted me to be his new owner. She was amused."

Kate replied, "But she didn't let you keep him."

"Naw. She said that was Jessica's puppy, and I needed to take him back. That task was grueling enough to teach me never to pull a stunt like that again. And once I got him back, he didn't want to stay! I had to sneak away like a thief. But the sad part came a week or so later." Teller heaved a sigh. Then his mouth set in a straight line.

"The sad part?"

"We were shoppin' at the grocery store in town, and another neighbor stopped Ma and me by the produce section. She said she'd seen me on the road coaxin' that dog to follow me. Shook her finger at me and said I'd taught the puppy to leave the farm. That it was hit by a car and it was *all my fault*."

"What a bitch! If I was your mom, I would've slapped her. What did she do?"

"She was caught off guard. She didn't say too much. Whisked me out of there, and we didn't speak of it again. But it sure did make me feel low as the soles of my boots," Teller acknowledged.

"You poor thing!" Kate leaned over and impetuously kissed Teller's cheek.

"Will I get a smooch for any story I tell you? Or just the tragic ones?"

Rolling her eyes, Kate shook her head. "Should we start back for the farm?"

"I'm thinkin' we oughta spend the night here, head back at first light. Why don't you tell me about that nightmare? I have a suspicion it's somethin' else that might be *cathartic.*"

Kate shot him a look, but she knew he was right. She thought she'd shown strength when refusing to confront old ghosts—in truth, it would take Herculean effort to face them head on. Maybe it was time.

"Jared often smacked me around. Even for small transgressions. Connie worked overnights, so we were alone together a lot. It started innocent enough—he'd brush against me and pretend it was an accident. Then he began... touching me. I realize now, of course, he was grooming me. Seeing how far he could push things."

"Sounds like a damn pedo," Teller spit.

"Could've been. Connie doesn't know, but he raped me twice. The third time he came in my room in the wee hours, I had a kitchen knife ready under my pillow."

"Holy shit."

"I grabbed his dick and stuck the tip of the knife into his ball-sack." Kate's mouth contorted in a sadistic smirk. "I just held it there. I still remember the blood trickling on the wood floor. *Drip, drip.*"

"You changed him from a rooster to a hen in one swipe, didn't you? I reckon you're badass enough to have."

Kate laughed without humor. "Regretfully, no. And I sure didn't feel badass at the time. I thought I'd pass out I was so terrified. I was shaking like a leaf! However, I threatened him good. Told him I'd de-nut him while he slept. From then on he left me alone—but the damage was done. It really scarred me."

"Understandable."

"Couple months later, he kicked us out, and Connie found a new boyfriend for us to live with. It became a set routine. We'd wear out our welcome with the new guy, and she'd find another. They became progressively more unsavory. I didn't get along with any of them."

"They touch on you?"

"Some tried, but I wasn't putting up with anyone's shit anymore," Kate said. "I kept my head down. Went to school, made respectable grades. As soon as I was old enough, I got a job in a little bakery. At sun-up, I'd help mix doughs for rolls and pastries. I'd go back after my last class and clean and prep for the next morning. By that time, we were in an efficiency of our own. We never would've survived without my pitiful salary. Connie was always a bit wild, but she'd gotten heavy into alcohol and drugs. As soon as she started a job, she'd lose it for missing shifts or coming to work high. It was like I became *her* guardian."

"Connie? Really?" It was late afternoon. A shaft of sunlight came in through one of the cabin's windows, kissing Teller's face. His eyes glittered like gems, his dark brow wrinkled. He added incredulously, "Hard to picture. Anyhow, y'all seem tight now."

"We're the closest we've ever been," Kate conceded. "If it wasn't for Armageddon, we'd likely still be estranged."

"So you learned the bakery business at your high school job."

"Yeah. I worked there all through school and after gradua-tion. I took a few business courses at community college, and when my boss retired, my co-worker and I took the bakery over. Not too riveting of a story."

"Oh, I think it is. I like learnin' about people's pasts," Teller said. "I wish I would've known you then."

"Believe me, you wouldn't have liked me after high school. I was a royal bitch. Cynical. Embittered. I was what you'd call a man-hater." Kate looked down, dusting a cobweb from the knee of her jeans to avoid Teller's gaze. "No. A *man-eater*. After graduation, I went through a self-destructive phase. You see, I realized I could make guys fall in love with me. When they did, I'd break up with them and sleep with their best friends, their fathers. Really manipulative stuff. It gave me cheap thrills to destroy people. It was a sick, sick game, but I liked the sense of control it gave me. The power."

"Hurt and anger often manifests into such things," Teller said sagely.

"I was a shitty person, consumed by jealousy. It had festered all through school—other people had such a cushy upbringing. Why did *I* have to go through all the crap I did? Thankfully, by twenty, I was over feeling so damn angry all the time. I shifted my energy to building my career instead."

Teller observed. "That served you well. Connie says Buttercream got rave reviews."

Kate gave him a rueful smile. "Career-wise, I did achieve a measure of success. My personal life? Not so much. I only know how to keep people at arm's length. I'm awkward."

"Shoot," Teller said, "I think you're bein' tough on yourself. Look how you've opened up to me. Look how you were able to repair your relationship with Connie."

"Repair? I don't know if that's the right term. We've put a bandage on the old hurts—we don't talk about Momma and Dad or any of the other crap."

"Hmm. Maybe you oughta consider healin' them wounds," Teller suggested, "before you don't have the chance. I wish I could've with my dad."

"How so?"

Teller lifted a shoulder, his expression pragmatic. "He wanted me to take over the farm. I scarpered off to the rodeo circuit instead. I needed to make my own way in the world, and doin' my own thing was more important than carryin' on his legacy.

Since I was his only kid it must've cut him deep. He turned real cold towards me. He never was the same after Ma died of cancer anyhow."

"That's sad, too," Kate said.

"That mean I earned another smooch?" He chuckled, and she gave him side-eye. "You know, Kate, I treasure our relationship."

Her heart panged. Before she could reply, there was a solid thud against the side of the cabin. Kate froze.

"What the hell," Teller said softly.

Kate whispered, "Something's out there."

They listened for a moment.

Could be a wild animal. I left the Z into some brush on that side of the cabin."

Great.

Teller slid to the edge of the bed and got to his feet and Kate followed. In tandem, they crept to the window. Kate got up to her tiptoes. In the late afternoon gloom, she made out a recognizable form rooting in the scrubby underbrush. Black bear.

"He's eating the Z! Why?" Kate asked, keeping her voice low.

"Black bears like their veggies, but they've been known to feed on carrion."

"Normal carrion, sure, but a Z? It stinks so bad." Kate shuddered in distaste.

"Your guess is as good as mine. He don't look to be starvin' either. Actually looks like a healthy adult. Maybe about three hundred pounds," Teller said as he scratched at his five o'clock shadow. "We leave him be, he'll likely wander away of his own accord. I've heard black bears are plenty timid unless frightened."

"Teller," Kate said pointedly.

He turned to her. "What?"

"He's *feasting on a Z's corpse.*"

"What of it?"

"Call me crazy, but I can't help worrying the bear will become infected."

"You really think that can happen? The cattle Peggy killed in the pasture didn't turn."

"But *she* killed the animals. The animals didn't devour her rotted flesh." Kate pinched the bridge of her nose. "Fuck if I know whether it'll become infected. My friend's cat died of the virus, and while I haven't seen any animals turn, we have to be prepared for every contingency. Can you imagine a zombified Smokey the Bear?"

CHAPTER THIRTY-EIGHT

HE STARED AT HER, AGHAST. "I DON'T WANNA IMAGINE IT. I GUESS the only thing we can do is see what happens. Maybe he'll lose interest fast and mosey along."

For the next several tense minutes, they observed the bear. Through the thin pane of glass, they heard him chew, sniff, and snort. When they were sure he'd never leave, the bear got on its hind legs and stretched. Black blood stained his tan muzzle. He made a plaintive sound like a whiny wolf, then he dropped back down on all fours.

Evidently finished with his meal, the bear ambled away from the cabin and into the woods.

"He's goin' the right way—that's north. We'll be headed the opposite direction in the morning," Teller said.

"I don't know. What if he turns between now and dawn? Comes back to the cabin?"

"We adapt, Kate. Just like always. If we gotta hunt zombie bear, we hunt zombie bear."

"Well, we definitely aren't going out for more berries now, no matter how hungry we are," Kate said firmly.

"By daybreak, our bellies will really be demandin' sustenance. Best we try to get some shuteye now. Put this night behind us."

They took a seat again on the bed. Slouching down, Teller rested his spine against the wall. He crisscrossed his ankles, then his arms. Within a few minutes, he was snoring.

Kate wasn't able to unwind. She shifted to find a comfortable position. At last, the silence of the dim cabin lulled her. Leaning into Teller, she drifted into a doze, dreaming of Smokey the Bear warning her of the dangers of forest fires.

Sleeping fitfully most the night, Kate's subconscious was on high alert for any noises outside the cabin. Finally, exhaustion prevailed, and she sank into a deep slumber.

"Kate?"

"Mm?"

"It's near dawn. Best we get up and move on."

Kate rubbed the crust from her eyes. "Damn. I feel like I'm a hundred and ten."

"Rough night, wasn't it?" Teller shimmied to the edge of the bed and stood. His joints creaked as he stretched. "I'm gonna move this here cupboard. Then we'll scope our surroundin's out."

Gripping her ax, Kate watched Teller push the Hoosier cabinet back by the sink. He withdrew his knife from its sheath attached to his belt and flipped up the wooden door latch. When the door swung outward, he jumped out, scanning the woods. Kate hurdled over the steps, landing beside him.

Although it wasn't yet dawn, the mugginess in the air settled on Kate like a fine mist. She whispered, "Ugh. Mayflies."

"'Tis the season." The winged insects clung to the cabin, seemingly covering every spare inch. "Must be a body of water nearby for 'em to be this abundant."

Kate inched her way around the corner of the cabin, surveilling. "We're good in this direction."

"Fine here, too," Teller called softly in the hush of the forest. "Grab that metal bowl, and let's get it filled with berries."

Dish in hand, Kate closed the cabin door and joined Teller where he waited at the strawberry patch, eating berries while keeping an eye out for any threats. He chewed and swallowed. "Wish I had one of your cinnamon rolls right about now."

"These will have to do 'til we get back home."

Vigilant for anything unusual, Kate and Teller walked in a south-eastern direction, hoping the Zs had long passed by. When it was apparent they were completely alone, they relaxed. Teller put his compass in his jean pocket and helped himself to a straw-berry from the bowl Kate held. When they finished the berries, she abandoned the dish on the ground.

The night before, they'd tackled some hefty subjects, but Teller didn't react the way Kate expected. She was surprised— she thought for sure he'd reel back in horror at her revelations, but he was as happy-go-lucky as usual. He was the same old Teller, and Kate was relieved. Between that and the fact they'd soon be home, her mood lightened.

They hiked with purpose. The ground was saturated with mayflies. Kate and Teller's shoes made crunching sounds as they stepped.

"I can't believe your sister actually likes these pests," Teller said, wiping his berry-stained fingers against a dew-covered bush to clean them. He used the front of his shirt as a towel. "Crazy that she named the farm after 'em."

"While lots of people like dragonflies or butterflies, you don't hear a lot about mayflies being a favorite, do you?"

"I asked her once about it."

"What did she say?"

"She listed their attributes. How remarkable it is they've been around three-hundred-million years and that some species' larvae spend up to two years in the water to hatch and only live ninety minutes. That they're a good indicator of water quality."

"I prefer the more romantic description. Some say mayflies are symbolic," Kate said as they came to an open area.

Teller laughed. "I don't really associate insects with romance."

"Okay, then. How about magical?" Kate asked, giving him a grin. "My mother was keen on fairy-tales and allegory. According to her, every object in the natural world signified something else, usually with a much deeper, spiritual meaning."

"Do tell."

She thought a minute, remembering what her mother had taught her and Connie. Kate's voice was pensive when she said, "Momma was in awe of their biological drive—their lifecycle is fleeting but mesmerizing. They mate in flight, then die. Their sole function is to produce offspring and pass along their genes."

"Sounds depressin' as hell."

"Momma explained it much better than I am. I recall her saying a mayfly nymph emerges from the water and transforms in movement. She likened it to the birth of a child—the way an embryo becomes a fetus and then infancy progresses into child-hood, and so on. Cyclical. The intensity of the mayfly's transfor-mation truly encapsulates living in the moment."

"Welp. 'Spose that's the bit that made Connie choose the name Mayfly Hollow. It's a nice thought—livin' in the moment." Teller looked over and met her eyes. "We ought to do more of that."

The warmth in Teller's eyes made the air leave Kate's lungs. "I'm trying."

"The cycle of life must be on Connie's mind nowadays. Only weeks 'til her baby's due." He tsked. "Not that I can fathom bringin' a kid into this mess."

Kate told herself it was low blood sugar that caused her heartbeat to flutter when she asked, "You ever want to have kids? I mean, before."

"Not when I was younger. I was a randy young buck, only seekin' a good time. When I hit my mid-twenties, I thought about havin' a family." Teller came to a stop when they were in sight of the highway. The sun hovered above the horizon, a vibrant pink orb. There were plenty of mayflies on the moisture-darkened surface of the road but no indication of Zs. "I knew my rodeoin' days were numbered the closer I got to thirty. I met Gina in Saskatchewan—she was a cowboy groupie, but I thought she was different from the rest. More fool me. When I got injured, I retired from the biz. We moved down here, where her folks lived."

So her name's Gina. Keeping her expression blank, Kate appraised Teller's face for any hint of his feelings. She waited for him to speak again as they made their way along the highway toward home.

With a lift of his shoulder, he threw Kate a matter-of-fact grin. "Turns out Gina wasn't the settlin' down sort. I was newly single, jobless, down on my luck. Stayin' at a fleabag motel. Then I saw the ad Connie placed for a farmhand. And the rest, as they say, is ancient history. What about you? You want kids?"

Kate hooted with laughter. "Are you joking? I have the maternal instincts of a rock. I don't know how to act around kids, what to say. Even with Nora I get all awkward and weird, and she's like a miniature adult."

"Nora's definitely serious-minded," Teller agreed.

Changing the subject, Kate said, "Seems we don't need to worry about zombified bears after all."

"Nope." Teller uncapped his canteen and took a sip. "There's *nothin'* out here."

They continued on amicably, the only sound the buzz of insects and the occasional rumble of their stomachs. As they drew closer to the turn off to Mayfly Hollow's driveway lane, Kate said, "We really need to do that trip for weapons now that we don't have a horde trapping us."

"But River Heights is picked clean. We'll have to go further afield. Could be hazardous."

"Teller, the longer we delay it, the greater the chance somebody else will get to them first. We need quieter weapons—fact. We have to find swords and crossbows somewhere."

"Don't think I'm not of the same mind," Teller said. "We gotta strategize."

"I didn't tell you, but I put all those hours I sat at Ben's bedside to good use."

As they approached the gate, Teller turned to her, an eyebrow arched. His tone was teasing. "What did you do?"

"I made a half-dozen simple canvas ponchos. I lined them with plastic shower curtains Connie had in her stash. I figured we can paint them with Z guts. It'll still be gross, but we won't mess up our clothes if we need the camouflage."

"I like the way you think, girl. No wonder we're such an awesome team."

Face heating at his praise, Kate put a hand to Teller's arm, stilling him from punching in the security code at the entrance. "We better prepare ourselves before we go in. Who knows what's happened in our absence?"

Teller solemnly agreed before entering the code into the pad.

CHAPTER THIRTY-NINE

To Kate's relief, all was serene at the farm. Teller drove them up to the farmhouse on the ATV, the sound of the engine rousing everyone from their beds. When Kate and Teller came into the kitchen, they all waited there, yawning and still in their pajamas. Ace's body wriggled with enthusiasm when he greeted Teller.

"Thank God you're home safe," Connie said, enveloping Kate in a brief hug.

After Kate and Teller petted Ace, Audrey threw her arms around Teller's neck, planting a bold kiss on his lips. "I was so worried!"

"I thought the trip was meant to be a quick, simple scouting operation," Ben scolded lightly, putting his arm around Kate's waist. As soon as she could without openly offending him, Kate retreated, diverting her gaze so she wouldn't see his expression inevitably tighten.

Rubbing sleep from her eyes, Connie demanded, "Tell us what happened."

Kate was desperate for a hot shower and a meal, but she and Teller took turns recounting their adventures.

"The horde is no longer an issue?" Ben asked when they finished.

Kate replied, "Not the one that was camped out front."

"Unless more mobs pass by—the ones we saw seemed committed to journey north," Teller added.

"Strange," Connie said, pensive.

"That's what I thought," Kate acknowledged. "But who knows why they're heading that direction en masse. Could be important. Could mean nothing. Time'll tell."

"Bet you're hungry after eating nothing but some piddly strawberries." Audrey gave Teller a brilliant smile. "I know what a big appetite you have. How about I prepare breakfast while you shower?"

Though Audrey spoke only to Teller, Kate was quick to say, "Audrey, how darling of you! I'm dying for a shower."

Connie smiled warmly. "We have leftover ribeyes I grilled for last night's dinner. How about we reheat those, and I'll see what the hens have produced for us?"

Audrey's gaze jetted daggers in Kate's direction.

AFTER BREAKFAST, Kate brought up the subject of venturing out for weapons.

"I hate the idea," Ben said, shaking his head. "It's not fair you two get saddled with it."

"I don't mind," Kate replied.

"Still, perhaps I should come this time."

"Ben," Connie said authoritatively from her seat at the head of the table. "You aren't recovered yet. I don't want you to overdo."

"Connie's right." Teller drained the coffee from his mug and poured more. "You'll only slow us down."

Kate caught the irritation that passed over Ben's face at Teller's breezy dismissal and quickly said, "You'll have your chance to go out, when the time's right."

"Okay," Ben conceded. "But I've hunted for years, so I'll be undertaking instructor duties when you get back with the crossbows."

"Good," Kate said. "Because I have a lot to learn."

With a wily smile, Audrey said, "I'll be tagging along."

Kate's first impulse was to object. She tamped down her objections and asked, "Why would you want to do that? You were petrified in River Heights."

"You don't have anythin' you need to prove to us, Audrey," Teller drawled in his soft-spoken way. "You do plenty to pull your weight 'round here."

"Ben isn't the only one who knows his way around a quiver." Audrey lifted her chin in Kate's direction. "My high school boyfriend was into bowhunting competitions and got me into the sport. It's been a while, but I'm a damn good shot."

Not only a cursory knowledge of ham radio but experience with bows and arrows. Huh. I didn't foresee that.

After breakfast, Connie unearthed a phone directory from Seth's office, along with a road atlas. Kate sat at the kitchen table with a notebook and pen, Teller beside her, and Ace at his feet.

"The directory is a few years old," Connie said as she set the books on the table.

"I'm just happy you kept it." Kate opened the volume, her sinuses itching from the dust.

"Mergenville's our best bet. It's about eight miles southeast of here. There'll be a gun shop. I recollect a decent-sized pawnshop, too," Teller said.

"I know Mergenville." Thinking of her trek to Mayfly Hollow, Kate thumbed through the yellow pages. Jones Brothers was on Roosevelt Avenue and advertised guns, ammo, and supplies for *all your bowhunting needs.*

Teller watched Kate scribble the address on her notebook.

"You wanted a sword. The pawnshop might have some. I think it's on Taft Street."

After scouring listings, Kate said, "Here it is. Ad says collectible swords and knives."

Teller shrugged. "That works. After morning chores and breakfast tomorrow, we'll take my truck. Best pack food and water in case we get stuck overnight."

"Nora and I will be making farmer's cheese today," Connie announced as Teller, Kate, and Audrey prepared to leave the following morning. "The leftover whey will be used for bread dough."

Kate gave her sister a look. "Don't overexert yourself."

"I'll make sure she doesn't," Ben assured Kate. "This afternoon, while Connie naps, Nora and I'll weed in the garden and pick berries."

"If we end up not gettin' back 'til tomorrow, you'll be able to manage the chores, right?" Teller asked Ben.

"Nora said she'd help me. She offered to mind Ace, too," Ben replied, grinning fondly at Nora where she stroked Ace's ears.

During the drive, Audrey was bubbly. She sat between Teller and Kate on the bench seat, chattering about how excited she was to leave the farm. Kate listened with half-attention, keeping a look out for any possible threats as they traversed the secluded area. Teller stayed on back roads. Occasionally, they came across small groups of Zs or a lone straggler, but the hum of the truck's engine did nothing more than make them lift their noses in the air.

"Can we drive through River Heights on the way back? I want to see my house," Audrey said wistfully.

Kate cleared her throat, the devastation on Oak Street coming to mind.

"Sorry," Teller said. "We didn't tell you, but when we went

into town for Ben's medicine... most of the residential section is gone. The only thing left of your place was the foundation."

After a moment, Audrey persisted, "I want to see."

"This isn't a Sunday drive, Audrey," Kate reminded her, keeping her tone courteous. "River Heights is a war zone."

Kate guessed Audrey seethed by the way her jaw ticked, but the woman didn't quarrel.

Teller entered the city limits, slowing the truck until they coasted. With a population of fifteen thousand, Mergenville was an unremarkable and modest municipality. He observed, "Don't seem too bad here. We may just find what we're seekin'."

Audrey pinched her nose. "Smells awful."

Welcome to the new world order. Better buckle up, buttercup.

"Dead bodies and Zs." Kate shrugged, used to the stench. She was the navigator on this trip. She consulted the atlas. Streets were designed grid-like, businesses and residences inter-mingled in a curious way. "Jones Brothers and the pawnshop are only four blocks apart. Turn right on Indiana."

"We've had good luck parkin' and goin' on foot, though we're limited to what we can carry," Teller said. "Let's find a spot somewhere between the two."

Kate pointed to a tan brick apartment complex with a half-filled parking lot. "This is about the midpoint. The truck should blend in."

"Plenty of Z corpses to choose from," Teller said.

Audrey's gaze alternated between Teller and Kate. "What do you mean *corpses to choose from?*"

"We need camouflage. We'll be slicing a Z's innards open and slathering them on the canvas ponchos I made. Here—you're in charge of doling them out. I'm not afraid of taking on the job of slicing and dicing." Kate couldn't keep the smugness from her face when she lifted the backpack from the floorboard and shoved it into Audrey's hands.

CHAPTER FORTY

"You're nuts, lady," Audrey hissed, her face a fiery wash of crimson, "if you think I'll allow you to smear zombie guts anywhere near me."

"Now, Audrey—"

"No, Teller, allow me," Kate interrupted. Eyes narrowing, she met Audrey's belligerent gaze. "You got your way about coming with us, but you are *not* in charge here. You do what the fuck I say, or you'll stay in the truck. *Capiche?*"

Audrey huffed before turning to Teller. He gave her a sheepish look and put his palms up. "It works. I know Z guts ain't agreeable, but we gotta do what we gotta do."

"Fine," Audrey bit out.

Kate exited the truck. There was a dead Z on the sidewalk ahead. "Poncho, please."

Audrey unzipped the backpack and selected a green canvas square, handing it to Kate with snappish movements. Kate unfolded it and slipped it over her head. The poncho was a modified design, shortened to allow full range arm movement. Steeling herself for the unpleasantness to come, Kate stooped down to remove her knife from the sheath at her ankle.

Plunging the blade into the Z's navel, Kate dragged it up to the sternum. Black blood gushed, along with the familiar reek of rotted meat. She heard Audrey vomiting into the bushes behind her. "I need the zipper bag with the paint brush."

Teller rooted in the backpack Audrey had discarded on the asphalt, then passed Kate the zipper bag.

"Go ahead and put your ponchos on," Kate said, breathing through her mouth.

"C'mon, Audrey," Teller ordered curtly as he pulled on his poncho. "We ain't got time to dawdle. I see a Z down the block."

Audrey stumbled to her feet. Her face had gone from crimson to alabaster. She feebly accepted the folded canvas from Teller.

"Bet you wish you hadn't been so insistent on *tagging along*," Kate drawled in a mild tone as she adjusted her poncho.

Audrey lobbed her a spiteful glare.

Kate dipped the brush in the Z's stomach cavity, then across the canvas on her chest before painting Audrey and Teller's ponchos in turn. "Fortunately, it doesn't take much to disguise us."

Putting the used paintbrush back in its baggie and stowing it in the zippered pocket of her pack, Kate then found her ax in the truck. She slipped it into the loop on her belt.

Shrugging into the straps of their backpacks, they walked through the parking lot. Sun sizzled on their heads as they made their way down the sidewalk toward Jones Brothers. Whenever possible, they stayed in the shade of the trees planted along the boulevard. From her peripheral vision, Kate saw flashes of scattered houses, a bar, and a church, but she focused on the path ahead. Numerous Zs wandered near the trio, often shambling into them. Each time she was touched, Audrey squeaked, compelling the Zs to raise their snouts.

Sweat beading on her brow from both heat and apprehension, Kate elbowed Audrey in her ribs as a warning.

It seemed eons later when they arrived at Jones Brothers, a nondescript brown building with bars on the windows. The door latch was broken, and the door wobbled when the breeze whipped up.

One hand on her ax at her hip, Kate carefully opened the door and peeked around the corner. The shop appeared unoccupied. Her breaths coming in rapid puffs, Kate gestured for Teller and Audrey to follow her.

In the silence of the store, Teller murmured, "Welp. Picked over."

"No." Audrey stepped forward, her face knit in concentration. "There's plenty of compound bows, which are relatively easy to use with practice. Grab a couple each. I'll use one of these duffels for arrows. We need broadheads for serious shooting. I'll just pack anything I think'll be useful, like sight pins and string wax."

Maybe it wasn't such a bad idea letting her come. Kate caught the pleased glance Teller threw Audrey and felt a swish of jealousy. She shook it off, studying the weapons affixed to the wall with brackets.

"No longswords here," Teller said to Kate, slipping off his backpack and moving behind a glass enclosure. "But there are some Bowie knives I'm covetin'. Why don't you roam about, and see what you can find?"

Ammo shelves were bare except a box of gunshot shells and two boxes of bullets. Kate stuffed them into her pack, then chose weapon holsters from the mounted racks across from the cash register.

"Ready?" Teller asked, a dark gray compound bow in each hand.

"Sure." Kate collected the two remaining bows off the wall. They were constructed of aluminum and fiberglass and were much lighter than she expected.

Teller held the door open for Kate and Audrey. "You still want to see if the pawnshop has swords?"

Adjusting her grip on the bows, Kate nodded.

"We'll be returnin' to Mayfly Hollow in record time," Teller said. "This has been a walk in the park. Best not dally, or we're invitin' trouble."

Heeding Teller's words, they speedwalked back to his pickup, eager to get on the road. The heavy fabric of Kate's poncho was a sweatbox. Her clothes were soaked. She thought longingly of a cool shower and a glass of iced tea.

After depositing what they'd scavenged in the truck, Teller spread a dark blanket on the backseat to hide the weapons. Pushing the door closed, he locked the truck. "Now, we gotta go past the apartments in the opposite direction."

The atmosphere was viscous with humidity, making it difficult to take in air. Feeling very much like a wilted flower, Kate gamely led the group past the complex's stone-pavered courtyard, sidestepping the corpses in her way. "What's it called again?"

"*Pawnshop*, remember? Creative, I know," Teller whispered, panting.

Wiping her hands on the seat of her jeans to dry them, Kate kept to the shaded portion of the sidewalk. Teller and Audrey did the same, trailing her in single file.

Oversize yellow signage on metal poles outside a windowless square building proclaimed *Pawnshop*. The glass had been broken out of the front door. Teller reached through to unbolt it. Stepping over the threshold, he abruptly came to a halt.

A stocky Z wearing a pearl-buttoned shirt and elastic suspenders paced the interior. His nametag read *Fred*. Waiting until he passed by, they skirted the racks of DVDs and the jewelry kiosk. The collectibles section was in the far corner.

Few knives remained in the display case, but Kate's gaze zeroed on the black hilted katana and its scabbard displayed on a wood stand on a high shelf. She gestured to Teller, standing aside as he stretched to grasp the hilt. As he pulled the sword down, the scabbard fell. It smashed against the corner of the glass case before clattering to the cement floor. Audrey cried out. Fred stopped his shuffling. His head tilted. Lifted. Without thinking, Kate took the katana from Teller. It was weighty, solid.

Fred snapped his teeth together, as if in Morse Code.

Wrapping both hands around the hilt of the katana, Kate strode toward him. Wielding it the way she'd seen in Samurai movies, she sliced the blade across Fred's throat. Blood squirted, hitting Kate's poncho. His head tumbled to the floor and rolled toward Audrey, who shrieked.

Jaw hinge working, it nipped at her ankles.

Audrey kicked it away, shuddering and hyperventilating.

Kate growled, "Keep your cool, Audrey." Using her booted foot, Kate stepped on Fred's fleshy cheekbone, bracing the head tight against the tile. She dipped the blade of her sword into Fred's ear. The jaw stilled.

"You don't have to be so snotty," Audrey whined, tears streaming down her face.

Kate felt a twinge of repentance and exhaled slowly. She knew she was too tough on people. "Look, I don't mean to be so harsh. You just witnessed how sound gets them het up. You've gotta keep it together, or you'll bring a shitstorm down on us."

"If it wasn't for me, you wouldn't have known what bows to get. You could at least say thank you," Audrey blubbered.

"Of course Kate's appreciative. We both are," Teller said. "It's only that she's intent on the goal—which we all should be. No more squabblin'."

Kate hurried to scoop up the scabbard, sheathing the katana. "Right. Let's move."

Still sniffling, Audrey followed Kate and Teller, pausing to swipe handfuls of jewelry from the velvet trays she passed.

They jogged back toward the parking lot. They'd just stowed Audrey and Teller's packs in the pickup when noises echoed from ahead. Motorcycle engines. Angry voices.

Shit.

As if on autopilot, Kate quietly pressed the truck door closed. Snatching up her sword, she gestured for the others to come along with her. She ducked into the courtyard of the apartment complex, her chest constricting. Teller and Audrey were hot on her heels, their faces mirroring her distress.

"It's that goldamn motorcycle gang boxin' us in again," Teller spit. "We're gonna have to hide 'til they pass."

"What gang?" Audrey demanded.

Disregarding her, Kate said, "So much for this trip being a walk in the park."

CHAPTER FORTY-ONE

"They're gettin' closer," Teller said hoarsely.

Biting her lip, Kate quickly glanced around, evaluating. "I want to see what's happening. Let's get somewhere higher, so we have a better vantage."

Audrey tapped Teller's arm. "Look."

A window was ajar in an apartment directly across the courtyard.

"Maybe a kitchen window? I'll cut the screen. You want to go in?" Kate asked Audrey. When she didn't receive an answer, Kate lifted a shoulder. "Forget it. I'll do it. I should fit. Teller, can you give me a leg up?"

Kate ran the tip of the katana around the perimeter of the window screen. With a nod to Teller, he bent and laced his fingers into a cup. After sheathing her sword and leaning it against the building, Kate put one foot in his cupped hands. At the same time, Teller boosted her up and forward. Clinging to the windowsill, grunting with effort, Kate crawled through the window. Her backpack cumbersome, she lost her equilibrium and tumbled. Her hip slammed against the sink, the ax attached at her belt digging painfully into her flesh. She gritted her teeth to fight the wave of agony. Why hadn't she taken time to remove her pack? Wincing, she rolled off the counter.

As soon as her feet hit the linoleum, she whirled, her hand fumbling to grip her ax in case she came upon the apartment's occupant.

"Kate?" Teller called.

"I'm okay. I'll open the sliders in a sec, after I make sure we're alone."

In a bedroom, a decaying corpse lay on the floor. Kate shut the door firmly before hurrying back into the living room to let Audrey and Teller in.

"We heard you fall. You sure you're alright?" Teller asked urgently, but Kate brushed his concerns aside.

Teller held her katana. Kate reached for it. "Now that we're inside, we need to find the stairwell." She hustled toward the door by the kitchen, which led to an interior corridor. "If it's locked, we're screwed."

Fortunately, access to the stairwell didn't require a key. It was stuffy and lit by thin shafts of light streaming through glass block windows. Ignoring the pain radiating down her side, Kate took the stairs two at a time. They came across three Zs as they climbed to the top floor. Without faltering, Kate dispatched them with her sword before continuing on her way.

"Dang, girl," Teller breathed.

Winded, Kate paused at the top floor. "Cross your fingers that we find an unlocked *and* unoccupied east-facing apartment."

"Yep," Teller agreed.

Audrey didn't speak. Her eyes were round with fear and her skin pallid.

Kate tried each door along the hallway but all were bolted. Soon, she became impatient and short-tempered. "By the time we get into an apartment they'll have left."

Teller said, "It's only been about ten minutes since we got into the building."

Kate turned the corner. Four corpses lay in their path. At an end unit, one was sprawled in a doorway, propping the door open. *Yes!* She gave Teller a smile and picked her way around the dead bodies. Kate scoped out the interior of the apartment. A typical reasonably priced one-bedroom unit, it consisted of a galley kitchen and a combo dining and living area across from the bathroom. A bedroom was at the end of the hallway. Keeping her voice low, Kate said, "Clear."

Teller dragged the corpse into the corridor, and he and Audrey came inside. He secured the door behind them. "Best place to watch is from the bedroom window."

Once in the bedroom, the trio viewed the scene below. A half-dozen choppers were parked at the end of the block. The riders, an assortment of coarse-looking men and women, had gathered on the blacktop, conferring. By their body language, Kate guessed they were amped up, intoxicated. Audrey and Teller lingered beside her as she slowly slid the window aside, listening.

The voices carried, easily distinguishable.

A man in a leather vest clipped a walkie to his jean loop. "Vonda says they're almost at the rally point."

The rest of the group whooped, lifting bottles and flasks. Kate and Teller exchanged a baffled look.

For the next several minutes, the men and women loitered, joking, drinking, and horsing around. When a straggler Z posed a threat, they coolly lifted machetes and metal baseball bats and waited. One member would draw the Z and another would bring it to the ground. Once the Z was on the asphalt, they surrounded it, giving it a beatdown while laughing. They didn't seem bothered in the least when black blood splattered their faces.

"Eww," Audrey muttered.

Voice subdued, Kate asked, "You think this is the same MC from in front of the pharmacy, Teller?"

"Hmm. Maybe. No conversion van to be seen, and I don't recognize any of 'em, but that don't mean a thing."

Cheers and hollers preceded the rumble of forthcoming motorcycles. Four choppers came into view, cruising at a low speed. Men with their hands tied behind their back were tethered to the bikes by lengths of rope. They struggled to keep the motorcycles' pace. Their clothes were streaked with dirt and their faces and arms scratched, suggesting they may have been dragged along the road at some juncture.

"Oh my God." Kate recognized one of the bound men—it was her carjacker.

Parking their bikes, the riders swung their legs over their seats. The prisoners frantically squirmed, trying to loosen their bonds.

A skinny woman wearing aviator glasses, her white hair in a braid, proclaimed in a folksy manner, "Y'all evidently aren't aware this here is Falcon territory. Unfortunately for you, we have a zero-tolerance policy."

"You tell 'em, Vonda!" A craggy-faced blonde with a blue bandana kerchief on her matted hair saluted Vonda with her bottle of whiskey.

Vonda circled the hostages. "Fellas, Mergenville belongs to us. Takin' what's not yours ain't allowed. Our bylaws state that stealin' from the club is punishable by death."

Audrey gasped as Vonda pulled a long-barreled revolver from a leather holster around her narrow hips. Movements unwavering, she brought the gun to the carjacker's temple and fired. Putting her hands over her ears, Audrey buckled to the carpet, making a humming sound.

Her gaze cemented on Vonda, Kate clapped a palm on her mouth, appalled. Shouts of approval rang out and the gang applauded. The remaining three prisoners sobbed. One begged for mercy. Another, a Black man, apologized. She was vaguely aware of Teller murmuring, "This can't be real life..."

Vonda kicked the next prisoner to his knees. Kate looked

away, unable to watch. Another gunshot. More cheers. Teller gathered Kate in his arms.

"Now, boy. Y'all tell me where the other three are—the cowboy and the ladies."

Kate pulled away from Teller and looked up, meeting his vivid blue eyes. "She means *you, me, and Audrey.*"

"It was just us four, I swear," the Black man cried. The other stood as if frozen in place, bewilderment etched on his face. He didn't speak.

"Why should I believe you? Maybe your friend'll tell me the truth and I'll spare *him.*"

"He can't. He can't hear or speak."

Vonda angled her head, considering. "I see. Well, I don't know sign language." Wheeling around, Vonda shot the deaf prisoner executioner style. "Hurley, come on over and untie this lucky fella. I want him to spread the word about how you don't mess with the Falcons."

A squat, brick-shaped man hurried to do Vonda's bidding. Once freed, the prisoner fled, glancing back often to ensure he wasn't pursued.

Vonda holstered her revolver. "Anyone heard from Purdue lately?"

The man with the walkie came forward. "Not since he reported seeing the other looters skulkin'."

The blonde woman chortled. "Knowing that freak, he probably got distracted by a dead. A pack of smokes says he's got a lady dead tied to a tree and is fucking her in the ass right now."

"I told him he's gonna end up with scrot rot screwing them," a dark-skinned woman in leather chaps said.

The brick-shaped man clutched his crotch and ground his hips against the dark-skinned woman. She cackled, kneeing him in the groin. He curled like a shrimp, then reared back. He punched her on the chin. They fell to the pavement, wrestling.

Stride determined, Vonda advanced forward, kicking the squat man hard in the spine.

The man got up slowly, rubbing his tailbone and casting a baleful look at Vonda.

Vonda asserted, "Hurley, you, Bev, Mikey, and Arthur search outside the city limits for them other thieves. The rest of us will tool around Mergenville and see if we can find any sign of 'em."

CHAPTER FORTY-TWO

Kate gingerly shut the window and lowered the vinyl blinds. Swallowing, she sank down on the bed. "I think we miscalculated. The real menace isn't the Zs. It's the survivors."

Audrey's cheeks were wet with tears. She pulled her knees to her chest, looking miserable.

"I doubt they're gonna break into every unit in this place," Teller reasoned. "As soon as the coast is clear, we're outta here. I know all the back roads."

Kate tried to summon optimism. "The mornings have been misty lately. The fog will help conceal us."

"I feel sick to my stomach," Audrey said.

Kate thought about her carjacker, how he'd been murdered in front of her very eyes. No matter how angry she'd been that he'd stolen her van and fired shots at her when she took it back, he didn't deserve to be executed. "So do I."

Teller marched from one end of the room to another, austere-faced.

Unspent adrenaline made Kate tremble. Her voice shook when she said huskily, "Sit down. You're making me tense with all the pacing."

He perched on the edge of the bed, his posture revealing his discontent.

"Is this the way it'll always be now?" Audrey wondered aloud, and Kate scanned her face. She had mixed feelings about the woman, but now all Kate felt was melancholy. Audrey sniffled. "That group, or another, raiding the farm... it's like a hamster wheel in my brain. I can't stop picturing it."

The thought of invasion had entered Kate's mind often, but she knew someone needed to assuage Audrey's despair, or it would spark an inferno, consuming them all. "Sure, if people know about the farm, we'd be in jeopardy. I'm not going to serve up platitudes—it'd be a disservice to fool ourselves into a false sense of security." She paused significantly. "That being said—we're sitting damn good. We're in a secluded location. We've got clean water, food, solar panels, cameras, a fence."

"I'm just gonna put it out there." Teller ran his hands roughly across his face. "I believe it's only a matter of time 'til trouble comes a knockin' there. Especially when there ain't no more stores and houses to pillage. Even God-fearin' folk turn violent when hungry."

"You're correct. No doubt about that." Kate took a moment to choose her words. "Let's look at this rationally. There's plenty to fear. Yes. I can't argue there isn't. But, again, *we're sitting damn good*. We have an impressive stock of firearms already. Now, we've acquired bows. We'll learn how to use them. If, and when, we get raided at Mayfly Hollow, we'll decide whether to retreat."

Teller asked, "Fight or flight at its most fundamental, huh?"

"We have to fight," Audrey said. "The last place I want to go is Connie's underground bunker."

"Plus, Seth could have bivouacked there already," Teller added.

"Connie doesn't have much to say about her missing husband," Audrey pointed out in a calculating sort of way, and Kate felt her hackles rise.

"It's not for us to speculate," she chided. "Relationships are tricky."

Teller chuckled gruffly. "Amen to that."

"We're stuck here all night, so we may as well relax. This apartment is an improvement on the cabin the other day, isn't it, Teller?"

"I'll say. You think we ought to barricade that door? I could push the fridge in front of it."

"If it doesn't make a bunch of noise," Kate said.

Teller stood. "I'll try. I need to do somethin' useful—I'm chock full of nerves."

Realizing she still wore her backpack and poncho, Kate got to her feet and shucked the pack. Unzipping it, she fished for the plastic bag for the ponchos. "Give me your canvas, Audrey."

After folding the ponchos and packing them away, Kate joined Teller in the kitchen. He'd unplugged the fridge. It made a squealing sound as it scraped the floor. Kate cringed.

"Nope. Ain't worth the risk. Likely better we have fast access to the exit anyhow."

"I'll take your poncho," Kate offered, and Teller plucked the canvas garment over his head.

"You've got food in your pack, right?"

"Yes. And water."

"Sandwiches?"

"Peanut butter and grape jelly. Under the stuff from the pawnshop. Probably smooshed by now."

She and Teller returned to the bedroom. Audrey was stretched crosswise on the bed, sleeping. Kate unearthed a bottle of water and a bag of sandwiches, placing them on the bedside table without waking her.

"Living room?" Teller asked.

After closing the drapes across the sliding glass door, Kate sat her backpack on the coffee table and foraged for her packet of wet wipes before taking a seat on the overstuffed sofa. As she scrupulously cleaned her fingernails with a wipe, she said, "This couch is heaven compared to the one at the farm."

His gaze roving over the tidy, well-decorated space, Teller responded, "From the photos, it looks like the gal who lived here was once an attendant on chartered flights for the rich and famous. All sorts of shots of her and celebrities in the eighties."

She handed Teller a wet wipe then unwrapped her sandwich. "Well, she had first-class taste. It's cozy. If we had AC, this place would be an ideal hideout."

"The farm wins on that score. Can't complain about the central air there."

"About the farm..."

Teller chewed a bite of his sandwich, one eyebrow lifting.

"What if we recruited survivors? Made a community? A *real* community."

"Would Connie go for that?"

"Who knows?" Kate shrugged. "But to fortify the place, we don't just require weapons and fences. We need people. Families, too."

"Hmm."

Frowning, Kate asked, "You don't like what I'm proposing? I didn't anticipate that."

"It ain't that I dislike it." He took a sip of water. "But how do we vet the good folks from the bad?"

"That's something we'll have to think on. One thing I know with certainty—I agree with Audrey. I'd rather stay at the farm permanently instead of living underground."

Teller put his feet up on the coffee table. "All of us would, I reckon."

"We should drive around to other farms. Nick anything useful before others do. If we could replace some of the livestock Otis and Peggy killed..." Kate put her water on the table, getting up. She walked the length of the room, her sore hip unnoticed. "Don't you want to build something, Teller? Something lasting? Something meaningful?"

"You seem to be becomin' a mite agitated, Kate," Teller observed mildly, crumpling his sandwich wrapper. He tossed it on the side table and interlocked his knuckles behind his head.

"I am. There's just so little we have control of these days. Planning nurtures hope. If all we have to look forward to is being zombie prey or trying to outrun murderous gangs bent on turf wars..." Kate faltered, massaging her temple. "I'd rather put a bullet in my brain than live a life *like that*."

"We're gonna be fine, Kate. I promise," Teller said. He held an arm out, beckoning her to come to him. "Once back home, you and Connie can discuss your idea. Whatever's decided, I'll be there to back you up. Always."

Kate flopped down on the sofa and allowed Teller to fold her into the crook of his arm. She yawned, suddenly drained. "You really don't think they'll comb through the apartment complex?"

"I don't." Teller's voice became husky. "You've been a tower of strength for both me and Audrey this whole trip. Lay down your armor now. It's *my* turn to keep *you* safe, sweet girl."

CHAPTER FORTY-THREE

KATE WAS AWAKE WELL BEFORE DAYBREAK. USING A PENLIGHT FROM her pack, she went to use the restroom. Before pulling up her jeans, she examined her hip. Livid purple bruises marred her skin. She brought a fingertip to the marks and whistled. *Ouch.*

Rummaging in the kitchen cabinets, Kate found canned soup and soda crackers. Breakfast. She shook Teller to wake him, then went to the bedroom to fetch Audrey. The walk-in closet's louvered doors gaped open. Clothing lay on the carpet. While Kate and Teller slept, the woman must've played dress up.

An unzipped overnight bag was at Kate's ankles. It was stuffed with jewelry, cosmetics, and bottles of nail polish. An open suitcase rested on an occasional chair in the corner, stacked with clothes and shoes. Curious, Kate swept the penlight over it for a closer inspection. Silk. Lace. Stiletto heels. There were no swanky nightclubs anymore. Perhaps Audrey planned on wearing the frills for Teller.

But I was the one who woke up in his arms.

"Audrey," Kate said, prodding her chiffon-covered leg. She'd changed into the sort of peignoir dames in 1930s cinema donned before being informed their rich old husband had died of mysterious circumstances. Heeled marabou mules were next to her on the mattress. Kate rolled her eyes. Sometimes the woman was such a dingbat. "What are you wearing?"

"Huh?"

Was that makeup on her face? And nail polish on her toenails? Yes, it was. "Get up. After we eat, we're leaving."

THEY'D PUT their ponchos back on. Audrey held Kate's ax in one hand, the suitcase in the other, and the overnight bag's strap was slung over a shoulder. Kate wielded her sword and wore her pack. Teller had a dagger in his grip. Stepping into the corridor, Kate softly shut the door to the apartment, then straightened her shoulders as if for battle. Through the hallway windows, it looked like a typical predawn summer morning. Dewy fog made the air ghostly and opaque.

Kate in the lead, they traced the path they'd used the day before but in reverse. Hurrying down the stairwell and through the ground floor apartment overlooking the stone-pavered court-yard, they exited through the sliding glass doors. Kate put a finger to her lips, listening. The waking calls of birds. The slackening chorus of insects. The croak of a distant bullfrog. Nothing else. The bikers must be sleeping off hangovers.

Linking gazes with Teller, Kate dipped her chin.

Mayflies carpeted the pavers and clung to the surface of the building. Pack heavy on her back, Kate trod delicately. The crunching of the mayflies under the soles of their shoes was deafening in the muted stillness.

The truck was coated with condensation and scores of mayflies but otherwise undisturbed. Kate flicked the insects from the door handle. She gestured Audrey inside before taking off her pack and climbing into the cab.

"Here goes nothin'," Teller whispered, turning the key in the ignition.

Kate held her breath, squinting into the haze of the parking lot for any signs they weren't alone. Something stirred in the fringes. She pressed the button to lower the window, putting her head out. A Z emerged from behind a car, shuffled into the shrubs, and fell. "It's okay."

Teller kept his foot off the gas as he steered onto Roosevelt. He explained, "I don't wanna accelerate. Gotta keep as quiet-like as possible."

Audrey gasped.

The men Vonda had shot were strung up by their necks on decorative streetlamps lining the boulevard. Cardboard signs with crude lettering declaring *looters* were propped on their bound wrists. Kate gulped. "I guess somebody hanged them while we slept."

"Sure sends a message," Teller said as they drove past.

It was a chilling tableau. Kate contorted in her seat, her gaze riveted on the corpses. Though there was little wind, they swayed from their nooses. The more distance Teller put between them, the less distinct they became. Fog rolled across Roosevelt, obscuring the view, but Kate still shivered.

Once on the outskirts of Mergenville, the tension in Kate's gut lessened. The perfume Audrey had put on made her windpipe swell. She rolled her window fully down, though the air was muggy. Grateful to be alive, she murmured, "Those motorcyclists are barbarians."

"At least we got what we needed," Audrey said. "And escaped without them tailing us."

Kate glimpsed at the suitcase on Audrey's knees and the polka dot sundress she wore. "You certainly made out like a bandit."

Audrey flushed under Kate's scrutiny. "It's not like the lady that lived there will ever be back. She had fabulous clothes. Everything fit me, too. Even shoes. Shame to let such an expensive wardrobe go to waste."

"Hmm." Kate gave her side-eye then turned back to the window. She stared at the passing scenery, contemplative. It was soundless enough to hear the restive twitter of birdsong. The gray bleakness of the sky was being replaced with warm tones of rose and orange. A cockerel crowed faintly, rousing Kate from her reverie. "Teller, stop!"

He slowed to a halt, a question in his eyes.

The cockerel squawked once again. "Rooster. I want it. I think there's a farm somewhere just ahead."

"Could be further away than you imagine," Teller cautioned.

Audrey asked, "Can't we go straight home? I need a shower. I stink."

"You do," Kate agreed drily. "You've bathed in that horrid eau de cologne. Please, Teller?"

"You sure you wanna tilt at windmills here? We may be pushin' our luck. After all, we accomplished what we originally set out to do."

"Haven't you had enough adventure?" Audrey asked in a snappish tone.

Kate lifted an eyebrow. "You two fancy fried chicken this winter? Homemade noodle soup? Chicken with dumplings?"

"Shucks. Since you put it that way…" Teller threw her a good-natured grin before stepping on the gas. "But we ain't gonna spend all day stalkin' poultry. Even if these are back roads, we could still cross them biker goons."

"Agreed. If we can't find it in a timely fashion, we'll head home." A quarter mile ahead, Kate spotted a driveway. "Try left there."

It was a small-scale hobby farm. A charming cottage with trellises dripping purple clematis blooms sat on the ridge.

"There's the hen house." Audrey pointed to a white-painted wooden coop with an attached screened-in run. Three russet-feathered hens pecked at the ground outside the cleverly constructed coop. "I wonder where the rooster is. Connie told me they like to be up high when they can."

"Lenin preferred the hen house roof." Kate gasped with delight. "Look, a turkey! It's a tom. Wow, that would be a score."

Teller protested, "Not sure how I feel about transportin' a buncha live birds in my pickup."

"It's a short trip home," Kate cajoled. "*I'll* clean up any messes they make. The rooster is a necessity. And if we can get the turkey, Thanksgiving will taste like we remember, like before."

Audrey brightened. "I love turkey. I can try to catch him."

Regarding Audrey's impractical outfit with skepticism, Kate shrugged. "He may be skittish. Corner him if possible." She opened the truck door and slid out, grabbing her sword in the process. Fastening the scabbard to her belt loop with its attached clip, Kate said, "You guys gather all you can. I'll hunt for the rooster."

"Now, hold up. I'll come with," Teller called after her, but Kate waved him away.

"I'll be fine."

Convinced the cockerel wouldn't have strayed too far from the hens, Kate crept past the coop and rounded the cottage. Nothing. She made her way toward a metal machine shed further up the hill beyond the hen house.

After investigating the perimeter of the shed, Kate stood with her fists on her hips. Not wishing to be rash, she put off entering the gloomy interior. She perused the grounds below and the dense woodland surrounding them, but there was no sign of anything untoward. Action by the cottage caught her eye. Teller had snagged the turkey. He held it in the air with a show of triumph while carrying it to his pickup. Following, Audrey had two hens by the feet, keeping them away from her body as they wrangled for freedom. Kate watched them deposit the birds in the backseat of the truck.

There was a reverberation from inside the shed. Kate listened. Wings flapped. She trailed along the side of the building until she came to the entrance. The sliding barn door stood a few feet ajar. Mouth pursed with determination, Kate forced it fully open. It made a jarring shriek as it hurtled along the rusted track.

The interior was still far too dim for Kate's liking, but she edged inside, staying against the wall as her eyes adjusted. There he was! He stood on the hood of an ancient lawn tractor. Kate recognized his breed, the same as Lenin—Rhode Island Red. She tiptoed toward him, her arms outstretched.

With a cluck of alarm, he beat his wings, taking flight. He escaped to the far side of the shed. As she chased him, Kate said, "That wasn't a smart place to go, birdbrain. Now, your goose is cooked…"

With a quick lunge, Kate swooped, seizing him. He was displeased by his confinement. She tucked him in her armpit to ward off any pecks as he fought her. "Oh no, you don't! You're not going anywhere."

In her eagerness to capture the rooster, she hadn't noticed she was no longer alone. There was the clacking of teeth then a *swish* of movement.

Spinning around, Kate registered the arrival of the Z as it vaulted across the lawn tractor and landed in front of her, cutting off access to the exit. With a cry, Kate scrambled to the opposite corner of the shed, tightening her grip on the rooster. She clumsily unsheathed her sword with her free hand as she ran.

The pudgy Z wore a flowered apron. It sniffed the air, trying to home in on Kate's new position. It squatted. Just as it sprang up, Teller dashed into the shed, gripping Kate's ax. With a growl, he plunged the blade in the back of the Z's cranium. It slumped to the dirt floor with a thud.

Dust motes sparkled in the sunlight spilling through the door, washing over Teller's lean figure. Black liquid dripped from the ax blade. Wheezing, Teller shook his head. "When you get a bug up your butt… damn hell. I've never met a more headstrong, reckless—"

Sagging against the cold metal of the wall, Kate inhaled. Her heart seemed ready to burst from her sternum. "I'm sorry. The blood on my poncho must not be smelly enough anymore. Next time I'll—"

"I can't believe you ain't caused my hair to turn snow white yet," Teller declared, marching up to her and grasping her by her forearm. "You coulda been killed."

Kate adjusted the writhing rooster, then looked up at Teller, contrite. "I said sorry."

"Fool-headed woman," he whispered, his expression savage but his eyes smoldering with tenderness. Passion. He hauled her body forcefully against his chest, bending his head. Bringing his lips to hers, Teller kissed her thoroughly.

CHAPTER FORTY-FOUR

KATE SAT BACK IN HER CHAIR AT THE HEAD OF THE KITCHEN TABLE, the mug of tea in front of her long forgotten. "You two need to be completely aware of what we face. I want to be proactive rather than reactive."

Teller cleared his throat, and Connie's and Ben's gazes fixed on him. "Now, there was no indication we were pursued. We don't think the threat is necessarily imminent. Maybe the bikers will never happen upon us at all."

"Right," Kate agreed. "But *somebody* will, eventually. We must protect what's ours. Now's the time to focus on defense."

"I said I'd teach everyone to shoot bows. Audrey said she would, too," Ben reminded her.

Kate nodded. "That'll be a great start. We'll do drills, target practice, spar with my sword—"

"And engage in hand-to-hand combat," Teller added, petting Ace's head where it lay in his lap. "We'll create scenarios, action plans—what to do if we're overrun by invaders—either Zs or people. We all gotta be on the same page. Even Nora has to train."

Connie's cheeks were pale, but she nodded in agreement. "I'll give permission for her to. The poor lamb doesn't have parents anymore."

Kate felt a pang of empathy for Nora. "When was the last time Jamie or Judy asked after her?"

"They don't. Well, Jamie doesn't. Judy doesn't speak. She's too weak, all skin and bone. Jamie spoons her broth since she's not able to feed herself. Every time I take Jamie's dinner down to their cabin, they both look worse. He hasn't coped well with Judy's sickness. It's aged him terribly." Connie made a tsking noise.

"So you don't think Jamie's fit enough to participate in training?" Ben asked. "We could use another able-bodied person to defend this place."

"No. He's useless for anything other than nursing Judy. I wouldn't bother asking him," Connie said. She repositioned in her seat, grunting.

Kate sat up at attention. "You okay, Con?"

"My tailbone is just aching from sitting on this wood bench."

"Your *tailbone's aching*?" Kate asked, her eyes widening then narrowing.

Connie laughed. "You should see the look on your face, Kate. You've been reading too many of those pregnancy and childbirth books. I'm not in labor. I'm still weeks away from my due date."

"One day you'll be grateful I've pored over those books," Kate groused.

"I do appreciate your concern," Connie said. "Just as I appreciate you guys bringing the birds. We'll have a plentiful stock of poultry again soon."

"Can I get anyone more tea?" Ben offered, rising. At their nods, he went to heat another pot of water. "I'll go into the TV room and see if Audrey wants a refill. Her and Nora's movie must be near done by now."

"Connie," Kate began.

Giving her sister an astute look, Connie smiled. "You've got something up your sleeve."

"I guess you could say that. To piggyback what Ben said about having more able-bodied people around the farm…"

"Yeah," Connie said slowly.

Teller unfolded from the bench, getting to his feet. "Believe I'll give y'all a chance to chat."

Teller left the kitchen, whistling for Ace. Obeying without hesitation, the shepherd loped after his master. Formulating the right words, Kate said, "I have an idea. I want you to hear me out."

"I will."

"I'd like to bring more survivors to Mayfly Hollow."

"I don't know if—"

"You said you'd hear me out."

With a mew of protest, Connie closed her mouth.

"There are still good people out there, but if they don't find refuge, they'll all die off. Then only the ruthless will be left. We've got more than enough resources here, and we'll replace the livestock we lost."

"It's decent of you to want to give survivors sanctuary." Connie put her hand on Kate's and squeezed. "I'm proud of you and your principles."

"Altruism has its virtues," Kate said, snorting, "but you give me way too much credit. It's practicality. Safety in numbers. With a larger community, we could build a watchtower over-looking the property. Assign people to monitor it in shifts. And 'round the clock patrols along the fence."

The kettle whistled. Connie went to turn off the cooktop. "You've put some thought into this."

"Yeah."

"How do you intend to recruit these new members? How will you assure their motives are pure?"

"I'm still figuring out that part," Kate said, joining Connie. She opened the tea canister and took out fresh bags. "I wanted your consent. You own the farm. I don't."

Connie leaned a hip against the counter, her face unreadable.

Finally, she groaned in frustration. "It's so tough making choices in this world. I'm not sure what to do."

"We could build a cooperative here, Con." Kate paused, emotion clogging her throat. She didn't meet her sister's eyes. "There can still be a future. Families. Kids. A chance to thrive, for all of us. Don't you want that for the baby?"

"You know I do. I'm just... fearful we'll let in the wrong people." Connie's voice softened. "This is vitally important to you, isn't it?"

Kate flattened her hands at her sides to keep from fidgeting. Yes, it was. She bobbed her head.

"I'll mull it over."

***

KATE WAS SITTING on the porch that evening when Ben stepped out of the house. He closed the door and took a seat in the wicker swing. Without preamble, he said brusquely, "I don't think it's a wise idea to usher in a slew of outsiders."

"Connie mentioned my proposal."

"Teller did. He knows all about it. Quite the dynamic duo you two make. The Napoleon and Josephine of Mayfly Hollow."

Kate swiveled in her seat, her brows knitting in consternation. She appraised Ben's face in the dusky light. Her tummy dropped at the ire she discovered there. "What are you talking about?"

"I was under the impression Teller was merely a hired hand. Seems to me he does more than milk cows and labor in the hayfield. In fact, he thinks he's your partner here. Is that true?"

Kate weighed her response, puzzled by Ben's wrath. Apparently, she'd been *too* diplomatic with him. "I do view him as my partner, yes. The farm couldn't function without him."

"You've known this guy, what—two, two and a half months?" Ben argued. "He's a stranger. I want you to stop spending so much time with him."

Who does Ben think he is? He's not my keeper.

"I know Teller better than I know you," Kate said coldly. "And I'll keep company with whomever I choose."

"Is that so?" Ben's jaw became rigid, and his face reddened. "Have you fucked him, Kate?"

"I beg your pardon!" Kate leaped to her feet, her rocking chair knocking against the brick. She counted to ten to temper the roar of her anger. "That's none of your goddamn business."

"Hell yes, it is." He got up from the swing, his teeth gnashed.

"No, it's *not*. We aren't a couple, Ben. We never were," Kate said firmly.

"So I was just a stiff cock for you to bounce on whenever you had an itch needing to be scratched?"

"Don't be vulgar."

"You really feel nothing for me, do you?"

Kate sighed. "Of course, I care for you! I wouldn't have invited you here if I didn't. I wouldn't have risked my life to get you antibiotics if I didn't. You're my friend!"

"Friend?" Ben said the word as if it tasted sour. "After everything we've shared, that's the best you can do?"

"Hey, I'm not obligated to be your girlfriend just because we slept together for six months." She lowered her voice. "I apologize if you feel I've led you on. I never meant to."

"I thought you'd changed," Ben spat. "Boy, was I wrong. You're still a selfish slut. That'll never change. The people here will learn that soon enough."

His words wounded, maimed. Hurt trickled through Kate's veins, then built into a crescendo, almost drowning her. She wobbled, vaguely wondering if she'd swoon. "Stop it."

He came to her, put his face near hers. Scorn graced his lips. "You're trash."

"And you're a fucking asshole!" Without thinking, Kate reared on her heels and slapped Ben across the chops.

She bolted down the steps and into the night, leaving him holding his cheek and glaring after her.

CHAPTER FORTY-FIVE

KATE DIDN'T STOP RUNNING UNTIL SHE WAS IN THE GLADE. HER chest ached from her heart battering against it. Palm stinging and legs like gelatin, she collapsed to the log beside the brook. She covered her face with her hands. Allowed the tears to fall.

Once spent, Kate chose a comfy spot in the lush grass beside the creek and lay on her back, studying the sky. The babble of water and the soporific buzz of cicadas soothed her. Despite being enveloped by darkness, she wasn't frightened—it sheltered her like a woolen cocoon. Through the canopy of the pine branches, stars dotted the pitch-black sky. Kate identified the only constellation she knew, The Big Dipper, her mind straying back to the row with Ben.

No doubt they'd been due for a blowout. He'd called Kate out, and his scorn stung. It caught Kate off guard, but she should've foreseen it. The status quo between them had become untenable the chummier she got with Teller. Wearied of constantly walking on eggshells whenever around Ben, Kate courted disaster by merely exercising tact. She was wrong to skirt it. She resolved to no longer shy away from tackling tough issues.

She'd learned a lot about herself these last months. Instead of dealing with her parents' deaths, Kate had buried the trauma. Spent years acting out. She'd been convinced if she got counseling about her childhood she'd be retraumatized, yet the wound festered and infected her whole life—until Teller smoothly and skillfully penetrated her defenses. Sharing her burden had produced a curious effect. Vulnerability had fostered strength.

Was that what healing felt like?

Ben wouldn't have lashed out unless he was heartbroken. How would they continue on? Perhaps he'd leave Mayfly Hollow. It would be a loss, one that Kate would mourn.

"Stargazin'?" Teller asked from the edge of the clearing, and Kate sat up. At his approach, she saw the outline of her ax in his grip. He scolded, "When you vamoosed, you neglected to take this. It was by the rocking chair on the porch."

"Oh."

He passed her the ax then dropped down near her. "Not like you to be forgetful."

"Wasn't thinking," Kate said quietly, setting the ax on the grass. "Needed to get away."

"You left a nice red handprint across Ben's cheek." Teller sounded amused, and Kate turned her head toward him. It was too dark to make out his expression.

Super. "How much did you hear?"

"Enough."

Kate put her palms to her flaming face, humiliated. "Everyone else get an earful, too?"

"Naw. I was alone in the livin' room. Connie was makin' somethin' in the kitchen, and Audrey and Nora were upstairs preparin' for bed. They may have heard the disagreement, but I doubt they could distinguish what was said."

"Small mercies," Kate mumbled into her cupped hands.

"What?"

Kate relaxed back into the grass, locking her fingers over her midsection. "I said small mercies."

"Me and Ben had words." Teller cleared his throat. "He, uh, might have a shiner in the mornin'."

"*What?*" Kate flipped on her side, facing Teller, disregarding the pain as a rock dug into the bruise on her hip. Squinting, she demanded, "You hit Ben?"

"I might have punched him once. Or twice."

Kate predicted a rush of indignation swelling in her breast. For her lips to part of their own accord and the objections to spill out unheeding—*I can take care of myself. I can fight my own battles. Back off.* But the objections didn't materialize. Kate realized this was the first time she welcomed a man standing up for her. Warmth spread from the middle of her chest, radiating outward. It was a peculiar sensation... but pleasing. One she could get used to.

"You ain't too talkative," Teller said, remorse tinging his speech, "so I gather you're cross with me."

"No, it's not that..." Kate replied faintly, her mind preoccupied as she grappled with a novel sensation much greater than mere affection.

"I overstepped. 'Spose I should've minded my business, but I couldn't abide him beratin' you." Teller sounded as if he were talking more to himself than her when he added, "I gotta bear in mind it ain't my place."

"Teller, I—"

His tone resolute, he spoke quickly, as if he wanted to get the words out, "From the moment I saw you through the window in that cabin, I felt a connection to you. But once Ben showed up... I tried backin' off. Told myself you're not mine. I shouldn't have kissed you."

Kate snorted. "First of all, it's not like I discouraged you—"

"Maybe not, but I just couldn't hold back from insertin' myself between y'all. It was a mistake. So was comin' down here. I don't know what's wrong with me—I'm all knotted up inside these days. I should go." He started to get up, but Kate pulled him back.

"Stay. Please."

Kate guessed Teller was chewing something over by the way he sighed, keeping his gaze directed to the brook. She clamped her mouth shut and waited as he worked through what bothered him. It was her turn to listen, a kindness he'd done for her so many times.

"I've mentioned my fiancée, Gina."

The non sequitur threw Kate for a second. "Yeah, you did, but not that you two were *engaged*."

He grumbled, "Only for about ten minutes. Then she cheated on me with an ex. Claimed they had unfinished business that required attendin'." Teller shrugged, lifted a hand. "I see similarities here, Kate, so I'm gonna have to bow out, withdraw—"

"Nuh-uh," Kate interrupted. "I am not like Gina."

"You misunderstand. I see similarities in the situation, not with you and Gina—you couldn't be more dissimilar. It's the unfinished business between you and Ben that unsettles me. I gotta grant y'all space and privacy to attend to it. To not interfere."

Kate's heart panged. Tears sprang to her eyes. "*You* misunderstand, Teller! You're wrong about me and Ben. I don't love him. I never did. What I feel for you, it's different. Special."

Teller began to speak, but his voice cracked. He coughed to clear his throat. Whispering, he asked, "What are you sayin' exactly? For once and for all, tell me true."

"I..." Kate expelled a shuddering breath as her diaphragm constricted. "This sort of stuff isn't easy to..."

He entangled his fingers with hers. "My God, your palm is sweaty as hell... and you're tremblin'. You're actually nervous."

She acknowledged, "I am. I'm scared."

"You're *scared*?" Teller chuckled gently. "I've seen you slay three Zs in a row without battin' an eyelash. You're a warrior, girl. Courageous. Badass. Tough as fuckin' nails."

"I don't feel that way," Kate confessed.

He brought her hand to his mouth, brushing his lips against her knuckles. "Ain't I been your soft place to fall?"

A zap of desire zoomed straight to Kate's loins. She closed her eyes. Nodded. Inhaled the clean soapy scent of him—the smell of home.

"Kate," Teller said, enunciating each word against her knuckles, "just *tell me true.*"

She closed her eyes. Exhaled. "All I know is... I-I'd be miserable without you in my life..." She swallowed the lump in her esophagus, admitting, "I've never felt this way with any man. I-Is this love? I think it is."

Teller's breathing hitched. He tilted his head back, addressing the heavens. "At last. Thank you, Jesus." Gathering Kate in his arms, he tugged her onto his lap. His hands tight on her ribcage, he buried his face in the crook of her neck, kissed her. Branded her as his. "Kate... I love you. I love you."

CHAPTER FORTY-SIX

"I... I LOVE YOU, TOO." BODY THRUMMING WITH URGENCY, KATE offered her mouth. Teller captured it, threading his hands in her hair, deepening the kiss. His tongue coaxed, slipping between her lips, explorative.

Kate moaned, rubbing her face against his bristly five o'clock shadow. Nuzzling the column of his throat, she tasted the skin there. Her fingertips running reverently over his broad shoulders, she traveled the breadth of his chest. Felt the ridges of his musculature through the fabric of his shirt. She slipped her hand under the hem, skimming her fingertips against his heated flesh the exact way she'd fantasized.

Teller fondled the soft flesh of her breast. When his thumb grazed her pebbled nipple, Kate gasped. Lifting her chin, she granted him access to the sensitive flesh at her collarbone. His tongue leaving her mouth, he moved down her neck and across her collarbone. He nipped her, licking and sucking.

Kate put a hand to his solar plexus, forcing him to the grass. She climbed atop him. Straddled him. Balancing over the bulge in his denims, she braced her palms on his arms to pin him in place. Rotating her pelvis, she ground her hips against him.

"Fuck," Teller said thickly, arching up toward her.

Mouth sealed over his, she kissed him as she rode him. When she couldn't wait any longer, she sat upright, her impatient fingers hunting for his belt buckle. Teller stopped her by putting a hand over hers.

Panting, she asked, "What is it?"

"No protection," he rasped, his frustration clear. "Continuin' on can have some serious ramifications I don't cotton either of us are ready for."

He was right. The last thing they needed was a kid. But her body craved release. "There are... other things we can do."

"Mm." Kate heard the smile in his voice. "That sure is an encin' proposition."

"But?"

Sighing, Teller shifted into a sitting position, adjusting her so she remained in his lap, straddling him. His arousal jutted against her center, tangible proof of his desire. He cupped her face, outlining the curve of her jawline with a calloused thumb. Leisurely sweeping it along her bottom lip, he kissed her, but it was a chaste kiss. "As much as I'd like to undress you... taste and caress and savor every single inch of you..."

Kate whispered, "Yes?"

"I want to be a gentleman. Court you proper-like once." He pecked the corner of her mouth. "Then," he trailed the tip of his tongue across her jaw, following the track his thumb had traveled. "When the time comes..." He whispered into her ear, "When I finally get to worship your body the way it deserves, the waitin' will make it all the sweeter."

"I'm not good at waiting," Kate warned, shivering. The ache at her core was almost a physical pain.

"I promise it'll be worth your while."

His arm around her midriff possessive as they strolled back to the farmhouse, Teller asked softly, "Are you ready for everyone to know we're an item?"

Kate smiled. "If I said I wasn't, would you be willing to hold off until I was?"

Teller's step faltered. She looked up at him. His face was inscrutable in the moonlight. She sensed his disappointment when he said, "'Course. If that was what you wished."

"Thank you." She snatched a kiss before they continued on. "However, I think I'm ready to stake my claim, cowboy."

Teller exhaled. "I'm glad."

"I am expecting Audrey to challenge me to a duel though."

"Naw, she's harmless." Teller laughed, waving away Kate's concerns.

"Hmm. There were a few interactions between you two that made me wonder just how much you liked her."

"She's likeable if a mite ditzy. And vain. But she never stood a chance. You've had my heart since the first time we talked. I've just been bidin' my time, hopin' someday you'd feel the same."

Escorting Kate upstairs, Teller seemed reluctant to leave her. He backed her up against the wall outside her bedroom. In the darkness of the house, with only the hallway nightlight glowing, he murmured in her ear, "You lovin' me... it seems almost too good to be true. When I wake up in my bed tomorrow, will I find tonight was all just a dream?"

Tipping her head to investigate the shadowed, angular planes of Teller's face, Kate met his eyes. Drank in the sight of the love shining there, the yearning. She inked the moment to memory, emotion sticking to her throat. What would it be like to sleep with a man she actually loved? Instinctively, Kate knew it would be intense, surpassing every expectation. "Come inside, and you can wake in *my* bed tomorrow."

Teller grinned. "Siren."

"If you change your mind..."

He tucked a strand of hair behind Kate's ear, then kissed her forehead. "Sweet dreams."

THE NEXT MORNING, Kate hummed as she mixed batter for blueberry muffins. She'd scarcely slept but was buoyed by an emotion she'd not felt in too long—happiness. It was as if she floated on a cloud. She couldn't believe it, but she was *in love* with Teller.

A cough from behind her made Kate drop the rubber scraper and whirl around. Ben. His face was adorned with a sheepish expression and a black eye. She felt her smile evaporate, a frown replacing it. "Oh. Uh, good morning."

"I'm a jackass," he said with unexpected candor.

"Yeah. Your words were cruel and callous—they hurt. Nevertheless, I am sorry for slapping you."

"I provoked you. That slap was warranted." Putting a palm out to stop her from protesting, Ben shook his head. "I was raised better than I acted. I laid awake last night, ashamed by what I said. I was off base." He pointed to his bruised eye. "This was definitely warranted, too."

"We agreed that first night at Cahoots that we were only looking for a fling," Kate reminded him, leveling him with a sober look. "I admit I should've been firmer with setting you straight rather than tap dancing around it, but if I led you on, it was unintentional."

Ben's gaze shifted, making him appear uncomfortable. "You and Teller, when I see you two together… it's obvious it's more than mutual attraction."

"Yes." She slouched against the counter, crossing her arms over her chest. "Respect. Admiration. Affection. Love."

Feigning interest in the linoleum floor, Ben said, "I never could woo you into a relationship. You fell for him so effortlessly. My male pride was dinged."

"What'll you do?"

"What do you mean? Haven't I fallen on my sword adequately?"

"No, Ben. It's not that. Not at all. I mean if Teller and I are a couple, will you stay at Mayfly Hollow?"

He glanced up, met her eyes. "Do you want me to leave?"

"No. But would you be... uncomfortable?"

"I like you, Kate, but it's not as if you're the *only* woman left in the world," Ben said, his mouth quirking.

Kate knew his blasé attitude was an act, but she played along. "There's always Audrey, I suppose."

"That would be incestuous. She's like an annoying kid sister to me." He rolled his eyes. "Romance in the time of the apocalypse. Speed dating's out. Can't go to a singles bar. Where do I find all these women?"

"Slim pickings here, but I'm sure there are more prospects outside the fence," Kate said without hesitation.

Ben took a deep breath. "I know. We do need more people to keep the farm operating, too."

"And for defense."

"I've got some ideas for training that I want to talk to everybody about at breakfast," he said. "I made notes when I couldn't sleep last night."

"Oh?"

"I've sketched out an obstacle course of sorts. We can construct it in the side yard. Hay bales for target shooting, an area for swordplay, another for sparring. I'd like to set it up today and begin drills tomorrow."

"You have been busy," Kate said.

"This is my home. I'm contributing." Ben shrugged. "I also have a recruitment strategy in process. I'm going to sit in the office now that I've formally expressed regret about our altercation. Do some thinking before breakfast."

"Okay." She watched him walk out of the kitchen, relieved he was staying—and that he was willing to assist with both training and recruitment. It was a big undertaking. Questioning if things would be weird between them, she went back to her muffin batter.

Kate had just put the muffin tins in the oven when she heard the screen door and the *tap tap* of Ace's nails on the floor. A minute later, Teller's arms wrapped around her waist. He kissed the nape of her neck and tendrils of desire lapped at Kate's center.

"'Mornin', beautiful," Teller whispered. "Still in love with me?"

Beaming, she turned, twining her arms around his neck and offering her lips.

He kissed her until they were both gasping. When he drew slowly away, Teller asked with his customary lopsided grin, "I wondered durin' chorin' if you'd changed your mind about us. After that smooch, don't break my heart by tellin' me you're not as crazy about me as I am about you."

"I wouldn't dare."

He stole another kiss, his work-roughened hands spanning her backside and bringing her pelvis to his so she could feel how much he wanted her. "Good."

Kate heard voices drift from the other room and jerked away, her face heating. Voice higher pitched than normal, she asked, "Want a cup of coffee?"

Clearly enjoying his effect on her, Teller said, "Dyin' for one."

He waited while she poured the coffee and added sugar, accepting it with a wink. "After breakfast, I'm gonna hitch the trailer on my pickup and venture out to the neighborin' farms. I'll gather whatever livestock's still alive."

"You want help?" Kate used a wire whisk to beat eggs in a melamine bowl.

"Actually, I'm takin' Audrey with me."

Brow furrowed, Kate stilled, glimpsing at him over her shoulder. "Really. Why Audrey?"

"Green-eyed monster got you, girl?" Teller teased.

She ignored the blush she felt deepening on her cheeks. He could read her like a book. Kate *was* envious, and she didn't like it. Navigating new love seemed slippery.

"You know I'm head over heels for you, right?"

Kate pulled a face. "Still don't like you two having heart-to-hearts."

"Look. She ain't surreptitious about her crush on me. I wanna let her down easy. It's the fittin' thing to do, Kate."

Abandoning the bowl, Kate went to cuddle Teller, her cheek against his chest. She lingered there, listening to the reassuring beat of his heart and inhaling his soapy scent. "And that's exactly why I love you."

CHAPTER FORTY-SEVEN

TELLER AND AUDREY RETURNED AT LUNCHTIME WITH THREE GOATS, a brood of ducklings, a half-dozen hens, and a barn cat. The marmalade tom was friendly, purring and rubbing against Kate's ankles as she and Connie observed the menagerie.

"We needed a cat," Kate said. "I can't believe you didn't have any here at the farm to keep the rodent population under control."

"I wanted a couple, but Seth doesn't—didn't—like cats. As usual, he got his own way."

"Oh."

Connie didn't often speak of Seth. Kate waited to see if she would say more but to no avail. Instead, Connie asked Teller, "Where'd you locate all this?"

"The Schneiders' place. And Deacon's farm. There were a few head of cattle in his pasture as well. I'll collect 'em later."

"You and I can go before dinner if you'd like. I've got a roast in the slow cooker, so I'll have time." Aware of Audrey's gaze on her, Kate met the woman's eyes. Her mouth compressed tight, Audrey regarded Kate with brazen displeasure. *So she's going to be obstinate.* Kate internally sighed but kept her expression blank, asking, "You two notice what we've been working on while you were gone?"

"Sure did," Teller said. "How'd y'all get them hay bales in the side yard?"

"I attached the little flatbed trailer to the ATV. Kate, Ben, and Nora dragged them one at a time onto the trailer with rope, and I ferried them over." Connie stooped down to pet the cat, her swollen belly making her ungainly. "He's a friendly fella, isn't he?"

"He came right up to me, so I decided to bring him back with us," Audrey said, swiping sweat from her forehead with the back of her hand. "I wasn't about chasing after him."

"I'm famished," Teller declared, his words directed at Kate. "What's on the menu?"

The fire she found in his eyes made her fidgety. "Chicken salad. After we eat, Ben wants to begin training with the compound bows."

Connie called out to Ben and Nora where they spray painted orange bullseyes on the ends of the round hay bales. "Come and eat, you guys!"

Teller joined Kate as the group made their way to the house. Without a word, he clasped her hand in his and brought it to his lips. Kate noted Connie's raised eyebrows, but her sister said nothing.

AFTER A HASTY LUNCH, Teller, Connie, Kate, and Nora sat on rectangular bales of hay in the side yard. Ben and Audrey stood in front of them like college professors at an auditorium lecture.

"Any of you ever shot a bow?" Ben asked. The group shook their heads. "It's fine. We'll be giving you an introductory lesson. You may feel intimidated, but once you have the basics down, it'll be a breeze."

"Those bows look way too big for Nora," Connie said, indicating the waif-like girl sitting beside her.

"They are, but these were the only ones left at the shop," Audrey responded testily. She'd been in a foul mood since returning to the farm with Teller. "I still want her to try to shoot."

Ben said, "Crossbows tend to be easier for newbies, but Audrey was lucky to score enough bow slings and anchor points for everyone, so that'll help."

"You'll each be assigned your own bow." Audrey's confidence was apparent as she put on a Velcro wristband with a thin cord hanging from it. There was a plastic clip on the end of the cord. She picked up the bow at her feet. Flexing the string on the bow with a finger, she demonstrated its elasticity. "Each time you take your bow out to practice, inspect the bowstring for any issues because you don't want to shoot with a frayed one. If you apply string wax occasionally, it'll last years. Now, I'm going to show you proper stance, and Ben will break down each step as I go."

Facing a hay bale with a spray-painted target, Audrey looped a braided strap attached to the bow over her wrist.

"That's a bow sling, and you put it on the wrist of your dominant hand—the hand that you'll use to hold the bow," Ben explained. "Basically, it stabilizes the apparatus and prevents you from dropping it after shooting."

Audrey held out her free hand. "Arrow, please."

Ben bent to grab an arrow from the duffle bag resting on a hay bale next to him. "These colored feather-looking things on the nonbusiness end are called vanes. There are three vanes. The white one helps remind you how to load the arrow on the bow's rail, the channel-looking deal. You put the white vane side down in the rail."

Taking the arrow, Audrey tilted the bow so they could see how she placed the arrow in the rail. "It's easy to load," she assured them. "There's a little V-shaped niche in the end of the arrow. When the bowstring clicks into the niche, you'll know it's properly nocked." She affixed the clip hanging from her wristband into the bowstring-nocked arrow.

"That's the trigger release, which is a handy-dandy way to draw back your bowstring." Ben waited for Audrey to pull the string back using the cord attached to her wrist. "It's okay to grip the bow tight as you draw the bowstring back, but once in position, loosen your hold on it a bit. Breathe. Like when firing a gun, you must get into a Zen-like zone."

Audrey stood in position, waiting for Ben to finish speaking. The bowstring remained drawn back, and the trigger release was still clipped on the bowstring nocked at the end of the arrow. She held the string attached to her wristband at the side of her mouth.

"That circle thing on the string? That's a kisser button. See how she's got the kisser button tucked into the corner of her mouth? That's what Audrey uses as a trigger point. Some people hold the string differently, but we'll be teaching it this way, for simplicity's sake. Vital to practice the same way every time, in my opinion, for accuracy and consistency."

Audrey squinted at the target.

"She's using that circular shaped sight on the side of the bow to take aim. Don't focus on the dots—the pins—in the scope. Focus on where you want to hit your target, and let the pins stay in your periphery, as a guide. Aim small, hit small," Ben instructed.

Moving her index finger from behind the trigger to the top of the trigger point, Audrey flicked the trigger back. The arrow released. It sailed toward the bale, hitting just outside the target. After a second, Audrey lowered the bow, grimacing. "I'm rusty."

"Some drills, and you'll be back in top form. Your stance is perfect," Ben said.

Teller, his brow knit in concentration, asked, "How far can an arrow go?"

"Depends on the person, but on average thirty to sixty yards.

Once you master closer targets, we'll start practicing further back." Ben added, "We like being as far away from our adversary as possible."

"Why do you use that little string trigger wristband thingy instead of just pulling the bowstring back with your fingers?" Kate asked.

"Better control, better balance," Audrey answered. "It's a light, smooth trigger. You barely need to press to get it to release."

Connie threw Kate a confused expression. "It looks complicated, don't you think? Too many components to learn."

"I'm overwhelmed," Kate affirmed, kneading the tension from her neck with the pads of her fingertips.

Ben reassured them, "If you can shoot a rifle, you can shoot a bow. The best way to learn is by doing. Connie, you first. Grab your bow and come with me. Nora, Audrey will help you."

"I DON'T THINK archery is for me," Kate said as Teller drove them to Deacon's farm five minutes south of Mayfly Hollow. "You're a natural already."

Teller chuckled. "They ain't wrong when they say it's like shootin' a rifle."

"I prefer my ax. Or my katana."

"I know you do. Best we get proficient in as many weapons as we can though."

Taking a right off the highway, Teller piloted his truck along a lengthy gravel driveway and over a set of ridges. They went through an open metal fence, which seemed more decorative than functional. A large letter *M* in a circle was welded on the header. "Circle M Ranch?"

Teller nodded. "Deacon Mulroney. At one time this was a sizable operation, but once the Mulroney kids grew up, Deacon semi-retired. Kept much fewer livestock. Feels deserted, and I didn't come across him or his wife earlier today, but keep your eyes peeled on the off-chance."

They passed a brick farmhouse much like Connie's place then a rundown barn. "You said the cows are in the pasture?"

"Yeah. The ones that were locked in the barn starved to death. We should've come a lot sooner."

"That is a pity," Kate said.

The pickup made its way across the bumpy track, the trailer behind making squeaking noises. "Not much longer," Teller promised.

It was a sultry day. The rays of late afternoon sun made the air shimmer, but a hot breeze blew through Kate's open window.

A fenced field came into view. "See them fences up yonder?" Teller pointed to metal panels arranged in a penned corridor of sorts with gates on each end. "Here's my plan. We're gonna drive them cattle to the passageway enclosure and trap 'em inside. Then, I'll back this rig up to the outside gate and funnel them into the trailer. Shouldn't be too tough. Can you hop out and open the pasture entry? Fasten it again before gettin' back in."

"Sure." Kate slipped out of the truck. Swinging the gate wide so Teller could drive through, she marveled at how different her life was post-apocalypse. Learning how to operate a compound bow and rustling cows in the space of five hours made for a scintillating afternoon.

"Okay," Teller said once Kate was back. "Fortunately, this pasture ain't too big. I'll drive closer to the cattle, then I'll have you get behind the wheel."

Kate felt a little zip of alarm. "What do I do?"

"Just keep behind me. Go real slow and maintain a little distance. I'm gonna encourage them to follow me to the pen."

"How will you do that? In films cowboys are always on horseback."

"The cattle have been through this countless times. Watch me shepherd 'em." He winked. "You'll be awestruck by my cowboyin' talents."

A cluster of four cattle came into sight a moment later. Teller turned the truck so it faced the direction they needed to drive the livestock. Stepping from the cab, he made his way toward the cattle, his posture relaxed. Kate slid into the driver's seat, observing Teller in the rearview mirror as he approached the cows. He put his arms out, and the animals began to move obediently. "Wow."

Teller made herding cattle look easy. Like homing pigeons coming to roost, they ambled toward the enclosure. Not rushing them, Teller walked alongside then ushered them into the pen, shutting the gate to keep them contained.

Kate put the truck in park and scooted back in her seat.

Teller climbed into the cab, adjusted his Stetson, and flashed her grin. "And that is how it's done. I think I deserve a smooch for doin' such an expert job, don't ya think?"

CHAPTER FORTY-EIGHT

LATER THAT WEEK, POP MUSIC PLAYING FROM A PORTABLE CD player next to the kitchen sink, Kate perched on a step ladder. With a paintbrush, she cut in robin's egg blue paint along the top of the wall where it met the ceiling. Wearing jeans and a ratty t-shirt, she hummed along with the upbeat song.

"What are you doin', girl?" Teller asked from behind her, his tone tickled.

Kate smiled over her shoulder. "Painting, obviously." Setting the paintbrush in the tray, she descended the ladder.

"You're avoidin' bow practice," he said cannily. Hands on his hips, Teller wore an entertained expression, which faded as his unhurried gaze roved her tight-fitting tee.

"Busted." Kate giggled, and his attention skittered to her face. She grabbed her iced tea from the counter, taking a swig. "Ben and Audrey are like fucking drill sergeants with their *drop and give me twenty* shit."

"Ain't that the truth." Teller motioned toward the kitchen table. "Looks like you've been busy. Ready for a break?"

She took a seat on the bench facing the window.

Teller poured a glass of tea before joining her. "Between the fresh paint and no curtains on the windows it sure is brighter in here."

"I know. The curtains are in the laundry. They're practically rags. Too bad I can't order some new ones online. Along with a set of rugs. Pot and pans. Dishes. Everything is so mismatched and worn out."

"Ya know," Teller said thoughtfully, "there's a Save-A-Bunch discount store on the west side of Fenton…"

Kate volleyed him a startled look. "That's a solid fifteen-minute drive from here. Doesn't it seem silly to put ourselves in danger just to forage for housewares?"

"Before I answer that, why don't you tell me why you're botherin' to spiff up this kitchen?"

She shook her head, laughing. "Because Connie has gallons of paint in the basement she bought ages ago. May as well use them."

"That ain't why. And avoidin' drills with the group ain't really why neither."

Kate put her hand under her chin, resting her elbow on the table. "Hmm. Are you trying to have a deep, meaningful moment here, cowboy?"

"Only tryin' to get to the real motive."

"Alright. I'll bite." Kate lifted a shoulder, attempting noncha-lance. "That apartment in Mergenville was a stark contrast to this farmhouse. Shouldn't a home be snug and inviting?"

"I agree completely. A nest should be feathered proper."

"You agree?"

"You surprised? Fact is, it'll raise everyone's spirits. Cover up that paint tray and make one of your famous to-do lists. I'll get our packs and a lunch ready. I'm takin' you on a date to the Save-A-Bunch."

Scanning the corpse strewn parking lot, Kate rolled her eyes. The main entrance stood ajar, evidence of looting apparent. "This has to be our most harebrained excursion yet."

An elderly Z stumbled in front of the truck, but Teller didn't brake. He used the vehicle like a bulldozer, knocking the zombie down and easing over the body as if it were nothing more than a speed bump.

"Weather's to our advantage. Any minute there'll be a downpour. I figure the MC won't likely be out in a thunderstorm. And wearin' the ponchos, the Zs inside are no real threat. This is actually the best time for a shoppin' excursion," Teller said easily. Avoiding the abandoned cars in his way, he rounded the corner of the huge discount store. A sign with an arrow on the boulevard said *Shipping and Receiving*. "Still, we'll exercise due caution by goin' in the back."

Kate glanced up at the sky. Pewter clouds were rolling in their direction, promising rain. "Let's be out of here within an hour."

"Sounds good." Reversing, Teller backed up so the pickup bed was only a couple feet from the double doors.

After putting on her poncho, Kate handed Teller another from her pack before getting out of the truck. Stuffing the baggie containing the paintbrush in her jean pocket, Kate then took her knife from her ankle holster. She cut into the Z splayed over the curb next to the dumpster and used the paintbrush to apply black blood to her poncho.

Teller had used Kate's ax to break a window in one of the doors. He waited for her, an industrial strength flashlight in hand. Dunking her paintbrush into the Z, Kate carried it to Teller and swept the bristles across his poncho.

Stowing the brush in the baggie, Kate hurriedly shed her backpack and put away the paintbrush then scrounged for her flashlight. Shrugging into her pack, she followed Teller into the building. The storeroom was pitch-black except for the swathe of light from Teller's torch. She switched on her light.

He whispered, "Doesn't feel like there's anybody here, but be careful."

Dipping her chin to acknowledge his words, Kate beamed her flashlight over their surroundings. Metal shelving. Boxes. A forklift. Teller signaled her with his torch, and she hurried to keep up with his brisk pace. Beside the swinging doors leading to the store proper, he pointed to a wheeled utility cart with a flat surface, stowing Kate's ax in his belt loop. One hand gripping his flashlight, he seized the cart. It moved noiselessly over the tiled floor as he negotiated through the doors she held open for him.

The roof above was studded with skylights, which brightened the interior enough to allow them to see without the aid of their flashlights. They flicked them off and sat them in the plastic basket attached to the cart's handle. Pausing for a second, Kate looked around. The back of the store appeared undisturbed. Save-A-Bunches were typically laid out the same, with home goods in the rear left corner of the building. On a mission, she headed in that direction, Teller following.

The aisles they passed were a mess, discarded merchandise flung about, some shelves completely emptied. Fortunately, housewares didn't seem in demand during the apocalypse. When Kate came to a stop in front of a display with small appliances, Teller helped her stack a microwave, a toaster, and a coffeepot on the cart. As quickly as she could, Kate gathered dishes, hand towels, and pots and pans while Teller chose anything that struck his fancy. Tapping a fingernail against her thigh, she considered curtains and drapes.

After piling her selections on the flat bed, Kate waggled a finger in the air to alert Teller that she intended to look elsewhere.

Kate tiptoed to the pharmacy. A Z shuffled by, uninterested in their presence, exiting out the front doors. Kate searched the shelves. Where were they? Victorious, she filled her arms with as many of the small boxes she could. When she turned around Teller was grinning wide.

He mouthed, "Rubbers?"

Kate simply smiled.

She'd just finished putting the packages on their cart when they heard a crash from the opposite corner of the store. Something glass hit the floor and shattered, followed by a sharp, "Goddammit!"

On high alert, Kate drew her sword and crept forward.

"Kate," Teller growled softly. "Leave it be."

She put a finger to her lips, continuing to the food market near the front entrance. With a resigned huff, Teller drew the pistol from his holster. Kate skirted the aisles, stopping at each end cap, peeking around them to make sure the coast was clear before advancing.

A Black man was in the condiment section, a broken jar of gherkins at his feet. He held a can of olives. Bracing it on the empty shelf, he attempted to pierce the top with his Bowie knife. He cursed colorfully.

Stepping forward, Kate snagged a handheld can opener from a rack by the end cap. "This may help."

The man jumped back, olives forgotten. He dropped into a defensive pose, wielding his knife. "Keep back. You can have the olives. I don't want trouble, miss."

"Kate, what are you doin'?" Teller asked, pulling her back with one hand on her forearm then moving to shield her.

"Holster your gun. We know him. You aren't recognizing him because of his full beard." Peering out from behind Teller, she directed her words to the man. "We witnessed what happened to you and your friends in Mergenville. What the bikers did. I just want to talk, I swear."

The man frowned at them, uncertain. He didn't lower his weapon.

As a gesture of goodwill, Kate sheathed her sword. Maintaining eye contact, she crouched down and slid the can opener across the tile. It hit the toe of his boot, halting. He tucked the hilt of his knife into his armpit and snatched the opener. "Not an inch closer. Neither of you."

"We just want to talk," Kate maintained. They put their hands up in surrender. The man opened the can and brought it to his lips, drinking the brine thirstily. He tipped the can and chewed olives by the mouthful. He looked emaciated. Kate wondered when he'd last eaten.

When the can was empty, he set it on the shelf then brandished his knife again, as if unwilling to let his guard down fully. "You must be the cowboy and one of the ladies the MC saw."

"Yes," Kate said. "Do you know if they travel this far north?"

"Not yet, so far as I've seen."

"How many are there?" Teller asked.

He shrugged. "Not more than a dozen unless they've gained new members."

Kate leaned up against the shelf, purposely laidback. "You come across other survivors?"

"Here and there. I didn't used to see any. But now that a lot of the roamers migrated, people feel safer venturing out. Roamers are still dangerous, but it's easier fighting off one or two rather than a pack."

Teller nodded. "Where are the rest of your folks?"

"What folks?" The man scoffed. "Every-fucking-body I know is dead or a roamer. I'm living in a bad sci-fi thriller."

Kate looked pointedly at the empty shelves. "Food seems in short supply. Had any luck?"

"Lady, I've got nothing to steal," he spat. "You can try some houses for nonperishables but most are picked clean. Those olives are the biggest meal I've had in days."

Worrying at her lip, Kate hoped she read the situation accurately. That she hadn't made a decision that she'd later regret. "We were about to eat lunch. You're welcome to be our guest."

CHAPTER FORTY-NINE

KATE AND TELLER SAT CROSS-LEGGED ON THE PAVEMENT BESIDE Teller's truck under the canopy the overhanging roof provided. The rain had slowed to a drizzle. A picnic hamper was between them and the man, who they learned was named Adam. The trio had managed a shaky truce, but Teller's firearm was within his reach as part reminder and part warning.

When Kate unpacked the plastic storage container of fried chicken from the cooler, Adam's eyes bulged. She passed him a thigh, opting for a drumstick, observing as he wolfed down his food.

Glancing away momentarily, she met Teller's gaze to make sure they were on the same page. He nodded almost imperceptibly, affirming they were.

"I trust Kate's instincts, or I wouldn't have allowed this," Teller said, wiping his hands with a paper napkin. "I'm also a fair judge of character myself. What are your intentions, Adam?"

Adam threw the bone in the bushes, licking his fingers. "Beyond eating as many pieces of chicken as you're willing to share?"

Kate chuckled at the humor in Adam's tone. She liked him. "Here, have more."

He smiled his thanks, choosing a breast from the plastic container and taking a hearty bite.

"I meant beyond this repast," Teller drawled, sipping from a bottle of water.

Once he finished chewing and swallowing, Adam said, "To be honest, I'm occupied with the now. Living like I am? Tomorrow's indeterminate. You rely on the quantifiable—your next drink of water or mouthful of food. Where you can lay your head. Isn't easy finding a secure place. I rarely sleep."

His eyes were smudged with exhaustion. Kate guessed that beneath the caked-on grime and scruffy facial hair, Adam wasn't a bad looking guy. He probably wasn't much older than she was. She handed him a bottle of water, which he chugged.

"Ice in the cooler. Fried chicken. Your situation is patently worlds apart from mine. You all are fortunate," Adam said. "In any case, I appreciate your hospitality."

Teller tipped his hat. "You're mighty welcome."

Adam grasped his bag of belongings from where he'd left it on the pavement and got up. "I better keep on trucking. Pleasure to meet you both. It's encouraging to learn there are still civilized people alive."

Kate stood, hugging the building to stay dry. Her hair had frizzed in the humidity and a trickle of sweat worked its way down her spine. Mind already made up, she knew her impulsivity would likely irk Connie, but she had faith in her intuition. "Adam. Would you mind answering a few more questions before you go?"

He slouched against the building. "It's the least I can do to repay your generosity."

"If the bikers show up here, what's your plan?"

Adam sighed, and it seemed as if the world weighed heavy on his soul. "Leave. Just like I did when my house was overrun by roamers in Upper Bremer. Like I did in Mergenville when I came up against the MC. I suppose I'll always be moving from place to place."

"You don't want to be with other people?"

"Humans are social animals, who prefer to put down roots. It's tough being alone, but those guys that the bikers killed? We weren't buddies. I didn't even know them. We met on the road and teamed up together to survive. The deaf guy was nice but the other two? Eh. I didn't trust them, and trust is paramount, especially in these times."

"Have you killed anyone? People, I mean?"

Adam looked at Kate, askance. "God, no. And I pray I never have to."

"But you'd defend yourself if you were under attack? You'd be prepared to do what was necessary?"

Several seconds elapsed before Adam replied, "The world we live in will demand it of me, no question. I wager if I wasn't willing to fight for survival, I would've slit my throat weeks ago."

Kate closed the distance between them, searching the depths of his dark irises. She detected humanity. Integrity.

She invited Adam to Mayfly Hollow.

ONCE HE WAS REASSURED Kate and Teller wouldn't confiscate his weapon, Adam seemed to trust them more. He helped them load the truck bed with what they'd scavenged. He was reserved, as if he didn't want to get his hopes up that Mayfly Hollow was the utopia they claimed. Silently, he listened to Kate and Teller chit chat on the way back to the farm, not chiming in unless spoken to directly.

"I still think we should've stopped at Bubba's Furniture and Appliance for a new sofa," Teller groused. "The one at home is about as comfortable as sittin' on a field of boulders and cowpats."

Kate gave him side-eye. "It wouldn't fit in the truck."

"It would on the trailer. I can hitch it up and hightail it to

Bubba's. Come on, Kate," Teller coaxed in his easygoing way. "The sign on the window said free sixty-five-inch television with a purchase of three thousand dollars or more. How can we pass up that deal?"

"Maybe for your birthday," she said.

At the gate, Teller leaned out and entered the code into the pin pad. The gate slid open. He continued to the last cabin in the row, parking in front of the porch. "This'll be your place, Adam. As we said, you can stay there all by your lonesome after your two-day quarantine or move up to the farmhouse with the rest of us. Completely up to you."

"I'll show you around really quick," Kate said. Teller waited for her in his pickup while she went inside with Adam.

It didn't take Kate long to point out the amenities. "There are clean clothes in the dresser. Take a hot shower. After you catch up on sleep, feel free to take a stroll. Explore. The fence keeps us protected. There are cans of soup in the kitchen cabinets for when you're hungry."

When Adam didn't respond, Kate studied him. He swallowed hard, tears swimming in his eyes. "I... I'm grateful."

"I felt the same after arriving," she said softly. "I couldn't believe I was finally safe. I was so relieved I kissed the ground. I'll check in on you tomorrow, okay?"

At his nod, she left, rejoining Teller in the truck.

"He sorted?"

"Yeah. He's shell-shocked."

"He'll be fine." Teller reached over and squeezed her knee. Navigating the truck up the lane to the farmhouse, he said, "He's a plumber—never know when that'll come in handy."

Kate was rueful when she replied, "Maybe that fact will keep Connie from being pissed that I brought somebody here without waiting for her seal of approval. Making Adam quarantine was mostly just to give me a chance to break the news to her—we probably all have immunity by now."

"There she is, weedin'. Why don't you *break the news* while I

277

unload the truck? I'll help you finish paintin' the kitchen when you're done chattin'."

Kate stretched over to kiss him before getting out. Connie got clumsily to her feet, a hand at the small of her back as she waited for Kate. "Found what you wanted?"

"We have a truckful of stuff. Rugs, curtains, towels, microwave. Even bed linens. Teller has his heart set on going back to pick out a new sofa," Kate said. Biting her tongue to refrain from scolding Connie about toiling in the garden while so heavily pregnant, she added, "I wouldn't mind replacing ours."

Connie swiped at her pants, trying to remove mud from the knees. "Me either. What we have was purchased at a tag sale years ago. It's junk. We could use new end tables, too. And a crib for the baby."

"You don't have a crib yet?"

"I didn't have an opportunity to buy one."

"Well, maybe Teller and Ben can go out tomorrow for it. The MC hasn't saturated Fenton yet. We don't want to wait in case they do," Kate said, eyeing the even rows of string beans and cucumbers on metal lattices staked into the ground.

"Kate," Connie mused. "I'm not one to toss out compliments willy nilly, but I commend what you're doing."

Kate met her sister's emerald eyes, which were so like her own. "Oh?"

"I've told you before, I'm the first to admit the house could use sprucing up." Connie averted her gaze, looking almost bashful. "You're taking an interest in making Mayfly Hollow home. It means a lot."

Wait until she hears about Adam. She may not feel as charitable. As they started for the house, Kate cleared her throat. "Um, Con. The guy we mentioned the bikers let go in Mergenville?"

"What of him?"

"Uh, we came across him at the Save-A-Bunch. It turns out he's a plumber. And a pleasant guy. I know I should've run it past you ahead of time... but I brought him here. He's in one of the cabins." When Connie didn't respond, Kate asked, "Are you angry with me?"

Her sister smiled, surprising Kate. "No, I'm not angry."

"You aren't?"

"I've been coming around to recruiting outsiders. Though I really would've preferred you consulted me before bringing him—"

"I kinda had to make a decision. I went with my gut."

"Yes, I understand." Connie stopped. She tweaked her lip, as if taking painstaking care with her words. "If it wasn't for you and Teller, we wouldn't be prospering the way we are, Kate. You have no idea how much I value you. Depend on you. You've earned my blessing with whatever you wish to do."

It wasn't like Connie to open up, to express emotion. To tell Kate she valued her. Kate was touched. She wrapped her arms around her sister and hugged her tight.

CHAPTER FIFTY

The following morning, Teller and Ben set out for Bubba's Furniture and Appliance. Kate had almost gone along, but decided to stay behind to help Connie, Audrey, and Nora paint the kitchen ceiling and cabinets from the stock of white paint stacked in the basement.

A CD of Motown tunes playing on the portable boombox, they sang along, laughing and conversing as they worked.

When they took a coffee break waiting for the second coat of paint to dry, Audrey said, "It almost feels like it used to... like *before*, doesn't it? Normal and everyday."

Connie nodded. "It's awesome."

"Doesn't it seem like it's taking Teller and Ben a long time to come home?" Nora asked, blushing, and Kate suppressed a grin. The girl had a serious case of puppy love for Ben. He'd taken her under his wing, tutoring her with operating a bow and including her in running safety drills during the previous week. She'd flourished under his coaching. Kate respected Nora's grit and determination as she concentrated on hitting the center of the bullseye or beating her best time getting through the obstacle course.

With a quick glance at the wall clock from Save-A-Bunch,

Kate said, "The store is only fifteen minutes away, and it's been hours. I hope they didn't come across trouble."

"Now you're experiencing the proverbial taste of your own medicine—what I felt waiting for you to come back each time you left." Connie scrubbed paint from her hands at the kitchen sink. "Not easy being left behind."

"Guess not," Kate said dolefully, scratching the nape of her neck.

The mood turned dismal as they touched-up the cabinets and removed the painter's tape Kate had applied.

Voice infused with cheerfulness, Connie enthused, "The butcher block countertops are handsome with the blue walls and white cupboards, aren't they? They're due for an oiling. I'll take care of that tomorrow."

Kate said, "The satisfying part will be putting down the rugs and hanging up the curtains—the finished product."

"You made excellent choices with the décor, Kate," Audrey said with grudging approval. She'd been irritable since her talk with Teller but was gradually coming around.

"I'm happy you think so. I just grabbed whatever." Kate stood back and appraised the paint job. "We have to let the insides of the cabinets cure a bit before putting everything away."

They washed brushes and paint trays and affixed the lids on the leftover paint. Connie switched off the CD player. "Hmm. Let's relax with lemonade on the porch. Watch for Teller and Ben to arrive."

Kate poured glasses of lemonade, placing them on a tray. Connie held the door open for her as she carried it outside to the porch and set it on the wicker side table. Anxiety twisted in Kate's belly as she distributed the drinks. She should've gone along to the furniture store. What if Teller and Ben got distracted by loading the couch on the trailer and were attacked by Zs? What if the bikers caught them? Strung them up? She'd never forgive herself if something terrible befell them. What if they didn't return by dinnertime? *Then you'll climb in your van and look for them. You won't come home again until you find them.*

The heat of midday cut by the fans on the porch ceiling, the women made stilted small talk and sipped lemonade. A half hour later, Nora exclaimed, "Teller's truck's at the gate!"

Palms propped against the porch railing, Kate observed the gray 4x4 with its attached trailer enter the complex and wind its way up the gravel road. The sun glinted off the kitchen appliances packed into the pickup's bed when the vehicle stopped in front of Adam's cabin. Teller went inside.

"That's a stainless-steel fridge," Connie announced, "and a matching stove... maybe a dishwasher, too?"

"Yes." Kate's relief was evident when she said, "There's so much stacked in the truck bed that it looks like the jalopy the Beverly Hillbillies drove. I see a box and a mattress wedged in one side. That must be the crib."

Audrey said, "Teller must be asking that guy Adam to come help."

Teller and Adam got into the pickup, and it continued up the lane. Rushing down the porch steps, Kate and the others went around the house, waiting for Teller to park at the kitchen door. He stepped from the truck, looking sweaty but pleased. Kate's heart soared at finding him uninjured. She hurried to him, seizing him in an embrace.

The force of it rocked Teller on his heels. He laughed when he took off his hat, warning, "I'm drenched. Reckon I stink, too."

"You are. You do. I don't care," Kate said against his perspiration-dampened shirt. "I'm just so delighted you're home."

"I oughta go away more often," Teller whispered into her hair, "if this is the type of reception I'll get upon returnin'."

Head slanted back, Kate drank in the sight of him. His technicolor blue eyes shone in the sunshine, the planes of his face softening as he smiled. *My God, I love this man.* The depth of it shook her. Trying to be nonchalant, she pecked his cheek. "I'm not letting you scavenge without me again."

"Come on, you two lovebirds. Break it up," Ben ribbed. "Don't you want to introduce Adam to everyone?"

Feeling a flush sweep her face, Kate pulled away, letting Teller take the lead in making acquaintances.

Adam's expression was unguarded and friendly as he greeted the women. "Mayfly Hollow is exactly as Kate and Teller described. It's nirvana. I'm indebted to you all—"

Ben brushed aside Adam's gratitude, saying, "You can earn your keep by hooking up the icemaker on the new refrigerator. Teller said you're a plumber. I think we've got all the materials."

"I'll assist any way I can," Adam said.

"Sorry we were gone so long. Between findin' rope and bungee cords and all, it became complicated. Plus, I had to drive real ginger 'cause the truck's overloaded, and I didn't want to bust a strut." Teller hitched a thumb toward the trailer. "Anyhow. Let's get to work."

"Kate, why don't you and Audrey put the living room furniture against a wall so it's not in the way of us putting the sectional sofa together?" Ben suggested as he unlatched the trailer doors.

Kate nodded, hurrying inside with Audrey.

STANDING ASIDE, they watched the men jostle chocolate-brown leather sofa pieces through the arched doorway to the living room. There were four sections. Kate helped Teller link them together using the brackets embedded on the sides. It made an L shape once connected.

Kate plopped down, sinking into the deep cushion. Audrey did the same, exclaiming, "Heaven!"

Just then, Adam and Ben brought in a box containing an oversize flat screen television.

"Seriously, Teller?" Kate asked drily as they set it down.

He put his palms up. "It was part of the special."

"Uh-huh." She rolled her eyes heavenward.

"Let's take the old sofa out now," Ben suggested. "Then we'll bring in the area rug."

"Area rug?" Connie asked from the hall.

"The showroom had a buncha displays set up, so I chose the one I thought would go with the recliners we already have here," Teller said, gesturing toward the pair of upholstered chairs Kate had shoved to the wall. "I brought the whole shebang."

"It was the largest sectional there," Ben added.

Connie laughed. "How did you get it all to fit inside the trailer?"

"Remember the game Tetris?" Ben asked. "I was a champion player."

Ben and Adam set the rug in front of the sofa and unrolled it across the hardwood floor. Plush, it was patterned with muted shades of brown, blue, and rust and took up most of the room.

Connie said, "It's gorgeous."

Once the wooden coffee table and side tables were in position, Teller plugged in the matching lamps. He assessed the room. "There are a few decorative geegaws in the truck cab, but I think it looks swell."

"I love it," Kate agreed.

"And I'm ravenous. How about we finish everything else after lunch?" Ben asked, taking a seat on the sofa and propping his feet on the coffee table.

Kate arranged the recliners so they flanked the table. "I'll prepare a quick salad."

She was shredding lettuce into a large bowl when Teller came into the kitchen. Hip against the counter, he said, "Y'all were productive while we were in town."

"I can't believe the difference paint makes."

"You're quite the domestic goddess," Teller observed.

Kate snorted. "As if."

"I'd like to take you on a date tonight."

"Another *date*?" Kate asked, laughing. "What did you have in mind, cowboy?"

"A picnic. The others can fetch their own supper for once. I'll take care of organizin' everything." Teller's eyes were warm when he bent to kiss her cheek. "How 'bout you meet me in the glade at six?"

CHAPTER FIFTY-ONE

"OH MY GOODNESS," KATE SAID AS SHE ENTERED THE CLEARING that evening.

Teller had spread a red and black buffalo plaid blanket beside the brook. A wicker picnic basket was on the grass and a bottle of Connie's homemade rhubarb wine was next two glass goblets.

"Your timin' is impeccable." He held a smartphone.

"What are you doing with that?"

"I'm gonna use it to play my music collection—only thing it's good for these days."

Teller had changed into dark denims with sharp creases and a fresh button-up, making Kate wish she had a frilly dress to wear. She'd borrowed a sleeveless blouse from Audrey, pairing it with jean cutoffs.

Selecting a song, Teller set the phone on the blanket and beckoned her. "Dance?"

She went to him, taking his hand but warning, "I'm not very graceful."

He gathered her close, saying into her hair, "Just follow my lead."

Exhaling, Kate leaned into him, swaying with his movements

as he two-stepped. She smiled as he hummed along to the country ballad. "Such a pretty song. Excellent choice."

"You're so good when you're bad," Teller sang off key during the refrain. He whispered, "I've been waitin' for this for so long... Charley Pride croonin', and you in my arms. I couldn't ask for anything better."

The song began again, and Kate looked up at him, her smile widening. "You set it on repeat, didn't you?"

"Damn right. I wanna savor this moment. Make it last."

Kate kissed him then nestled into his embrace, enchanted by his words and the steady, sure sound of his heartbeat beneath her cheek. "I love you, Teller."

His hold tightened and he bent to tuck his face in the crook of her neck. He sighed, his breath warm against her sensitive skin. Under Kate's ear, Teller's heartbeat accelerated. "You fit so perfect it's like God made you for me."

"I wish we'd met sooner," Kate said wistfully. "Before the world ended."

Teller clucked, "Don't concern yourself with what's in the rearview mirror. Pay attention to what's ahead." He paused significantly. "Truth is, I reckon my life didn't fully begin 'til I met you."

She didn't notice the sound of the water swirling against stones in the stream, the gentle breeze rustling the pine boughs, or the melody of the cicadas in the background. Kate was immersed in the clean scent of Teller's cologne and the feel of his kisses on her throat.

He sought her mouth, sealing his lips over hers. Kate moaned as he teased her with his tongue. She coiled her arms around his neck, burying her fingers in his hair. When Teller deepened the kiss, her knees weakened, and she clung to him, breathless.

Teller broke away, his eyes heavy lidded, filled with desire. He panted, "Phew. You drive me to distraction."

Itching for more, Kate glided a palm over the bulge encased

in his denims. He hissed, his pupils dilating. She asked, "So when are you going to let me take you to bed, cowboy?"

Teller licked his lips. "Soon."

She considered the blanket beside the brook and wiggled her eyebrow suggestively. "You got big plans for me tonight?"

"Maybe," he said, his mouth curving into a roguish grin. "How about some wine?"

"Alright."

Sitting cross-legged, Kate accepted a goblet of blush colored liquid. She wasn't much of a drinker, but the wine was sweet, with hints of lemon, and it went down smooth as silk.

"Here," Teller said, refilling her glass. He opened the hamper and brought out a bowl of strawberries, offering her one.

Kate chewed, relishing the taste of the sun ripened berry, then took a sip of wine. "I'm impressed. Very romantic."

"I had help," Teller admitted, popping a strawberry in his mouth. "Connie gave suggestions."

"Really?"

He nodded. "She ask you about us?"

"She mentioned once a while ago that she thought you liked me. She's accepted us as a couple, like it was the most natural thing in the world."

Teller laughed. "It *is* the most natural thing in the world."

"You think so?" She evaluated him over the rim of her goblet. Being around Teller was as uncomplicated as always, but the concept of couplehood was peculiar.

"Sure. You don't?"

Kate tapped a fingernail on the glass, thinking about her past relationships. Finally, she admitted in a rueful tone, "I've never been in love before, Teller. The whole *better half* thing... it's not unnatural but kind of... different."

Not exactly sure what she expected of Teller's reaction, she was mildly startled at his entertained but benevolent expression. "Different good or different bad?"

She felt her face pinken. "Definitely good."

"I've had more than my share of girlfriends," Teller confessed, lifting a shoulder, "but—"

"All the girls love a cowboy," Kate teased.

"Now, let me finish. I just wanna say the other day at the Save-A-Bunch? I've never enjoyed shoppin', but that was fun. Must've been 'cause you were by my side."

"You're only saying that because I got seven hundred boxes of condoms."

A shaft of waning sun shone through the tree branches, making Teller's eyes twinkle. "Welp. It sure don't hurt."

Kate giggled, wondering if she were drunk.

"Ready for supper?" He didn't wait for her to respond, taking a loaf of French bread and a cling film covered platter of sliced meat and cheese from the basket.

Nursing her wine, Kate lounged as Teller unpacked plates and piled sliced summer sausage and farmer's cheese on them. She was both languid and vitally alive, which was a heady combination.

When he handed Kate her food, he said, "You're daydreamin'."

"I think it's called contentment." She took a bite of sausage then lobbed him a wry look. "Could also be intoxication. Two glasses of wine are probably my limit."

"Cheap date, huh?" Teller kidded. Putting his plate on the blanket, he lay on his side next to Kate, supporting his weight with one elbow. He studied her as he chewed, his expression serious.

Feeling a mixture of vulnerable and self-conscious at his scrutiny, Kate asked, "What are *you* thinking?"

"Just in awe that a bum like me has a lady like you," he said without guile.

"You're making me blush."

"I'm not bullshittin' you. I'm tellin' you true."

Kate believed him—he was the most genuine person she'd ever met. She gave him an affectionate smile, then leaned down to peck his cheek. "Thank you for going to the trouble of organizing all this. You really know how to treat a lady."

While they ate, Kate appreciated the verdant green of the clearing, the birds that fluttered from branch to branch, the way the light caught the water in the creek and glinted on Teller's coal black hair. Her empty plate balanced on her lap, Kate closed her eyes, and put her head back, breathing deeply. When she opened her eyes again, Teller was on his knee beside her, a ring resting in the center of his work-roughened palm.

Mouth parting, Kate's gaze flew to Teller's. She didn't hide her consternation.

"It was my ma's. I've held onto it all these years, waitin' for the right woman to come into my life. A worthy woman—"

"I…"

"If you'd prefer a diamond, I'll get you one," he said in earnest.

Kate set down her wineglass, averting her gaze as she scrambled to make sense of what was happening. "I'm a mess, Teller. I have so much baggage. You've placed me on a pedestal. I'm not *worthy*, I'm—"

"Kate." Teller reached to gently grasp her chin, forcing her to meet his eyes. "We *all* have baggage. Everyone. The way to start sortin' through it is to find someone who loves you enough to help you unpack. That's *me*. *I* love you that way. Can't you see that?"

She swallowed, tears pooling in her eyes. Kate's heart twinged, heat spreading through her sternum. That was Teller. Thawing and demolishing icy dams built up over the years that no one else could. "I never believed I'd marry. I'm not sure what kind of wife I'd make you. I may bake brownies, but I'm *not* a domestic goddess. Or maternal…"

Teller laced his fingers with hers. "Is that what's botherin' you? What kind of wife you'd make? Kate, you're my home."

Time slowed as she shut her eyes. Regulated her breathing to temper the rhythm of her pulse. Teller didn't press her. Like usual, he allowed her the space she needed, undemanding. Devoted. Steadfast.

Was she prepared to take the plunge? What precisely was she frightened of? The apocalypse had its perils, but loving Teller wasn't one of them. After all, they weren't guaranteed anything —they could lose each other tomorrow. So… why wait?

Kate would be a damn fool to let him go.

When she spoke, her voice didn't waver. "Yes. I'll marry you."

CHAPTER FIFTY-TWO

THREE DAYS LATER, ADAM, BEN, AUDREY, CONNIE, AND NORA donned their Sunday best.

Audrey had generously lent Kate a dress she'd filched from the flight attendant's closet in Mergenville. Constructed with snow-white eyelet fabric, the V-necked and cap-sleeved sundress had a smocked bodice, which was a smidge too baggy across Kate's bosom. The floaty skirt was lined in bleached muslin and reached her kneecaps. She'd allowed Audrey to gather her hair into a messy topknot. Connie had gifted her a necklace with a fire opal pendant that had once belonged to their mother.

The morning had been scorching. Oppressive. They'd eaten dinner before strolling down to the clearing. The heat had mellowed to something akin to tropical balminess, making the atmosphere indolent. Now, the setting sun's rays reflected off the landscape, painting them like an artist's brush against canvas. Idyllic. Ace scampered ahead of them, barking, Nora his companion. Kate dawdled for just a moment before entering the glade, lifting her face to the sky. Etching the moment to memory.

She was about to become Teller's wife.

Connie was posed in front of the brook, hands clasped beneath her swollen midsection. A sheen of sweat on her upper lip, strands of chestnut hair shot with gray stuck to her neck though the clearing was cool. Kate and Teller met her there, Ace beside them.

Perfume of summer redolent and evocative, Kate welcomed the wafting damp earthiness as Connie said to those assembled, "I'm not a minister. I've not been ordained by any church. When Kate and Teller asked me to perform this service, at first I wondered how I could possibly do justice to such an important occasion. A ceremony may be nothing more than a formality, but I don't have any higher authority. Am I capable? I'm not one for soliloquies or flowery sonnets or romance novels. I'm hardly poetic. I'm certainly no expert on love…

"Then I set aside my misgivings. Reflected. We here at Mayfly Hollow are more blessed than most. Still, we've all lost plenty. The virus has robbed us of friends, loved ones, even basic freedoms. I won't let it steal our culture, our rites of passage. We'll be celebrating birthdays and holidays. Marriages and births. I'll be damned if I let the darkness outside the gates curtail our joy. Our traditions.

"Teller and Kate are two of the finest people I've the honor to know. I praise God every day that I have them in my life—that *we* have them in *our* lives. Simply, Mayfly Hollow wouldn't exist without them. Teller," Connie said, bestowing him a radiant smile, "I thank my lucky stars that you saw my advertisement for a farmhand. You've proven yourself a thousandfold as reliable, honest, and trustworthy. Thank you for being the sort of man my sister deserves.

"Kate." Connie reached for Kate's hand, tears glistening in the corners of her eyes. "Where do I begin, my darling? Where do I begin?" Connie's voice broke, and she cleared it. Swallowed. She wiped away the tear as it rolled down her cheek. "My sister, my rock. A woman who's guided by a sense, a belief, in doing the right thing, even when it means personal sacrifice. Kate, you have a heart of gold. You may not believe when I say it, but you possess wisdom beyond your years. You're a visionary. Under your leadership, Mayfly Hollow *will* continue to prosper. That I know."

Connie said, "You two make love look effortless. Yin and yang. Synchronicity. Harmony. It's there. I love you both, and I wish you every happiness."

"Thank you," Kate murmured, enfolding Connie in a hug. Ace barked, patting Kate's hip with his paw, as if to remind her he was there. She laughed and bent to quickly pet him.

Digging in her skirt pocket, Connie produced Teller's mom's ring, a pear cut ruby studded with diamonds on a delicate gold band. She pressed it in Teller's palm. "Now, we'll recite the vows. I'll start with Teller."

Feeling as if she were dreaming, Kate met Teller's eyes as he took her hand in his. Irises blue-green and shining with emotion, his voice low and solemn, Teller proclaimed his oath to love and cherish Kate. When he noticed her fighting tears, he gave her fingers a reassuring squeeze.

Connie instructed, "Kate, repeat after me..."

Pulse fluttering in her neck, Kate recited when prompted, "I, Kate, take thee, Teller, to be my wedded husband. To have and to hold from this day forward. For better, for worse. For richer, for poorer. In sickness and in health. 'Til death do us part, I pledge thee my faith."

Without waiting for Connie to declare them man and wife, Teller swept Kate into his arms and kissed her soundly.

IN THE FARMHOUSE KITCHEN, they assembled to eat the tiered cake Kate had baked the day before. She'd frosted it with vanilla buttercream that morning, decorating the top with roses, anemone, and sweet pea from Peggy's flower garden. Cutting it ceremonially, Kate and Teller fed each other morsels of cake, posing for Connie to snap their photo with a digital camera.

The newlyweds were toasted with dandelion wine, then

Teller grabbed their packed suitcase. Calling farewell, they made their way up the path to Teller's cabin. Feeling tipsy from the wine, Kate observed the layers of mauve and fuchsia swirling in the twilight sky, marveling, "Our engagement was probably the shortest on record. I can't believe I'm someone's *wife*."

Teller laughed. "And I'm someone's *husband*. Surreal as hell."

"Ace seemed sad when we left him behind."

"This is our honeymoon, such as it is," Teller said, "and my cabin's tiny. Him watchin' from his dog bed as I'm balls deep in my bride would be a mood killer."

"Teller!" Kate snorted.

A shadow of a grin pulled at his lips as he wound his arm around Kate's waist. "In all seriousness, I regret I can't take you somewhere for a *real* honeymoon—a fancy schmancy hotel or an island paradise. You ain't disappointed, are you?"

"No. All newlyweds really require is seclusion."

The porch light glowed from Teller's cabin, like a beacon. He set her suitcase by the welcome mat before asking Kate, "Ready for me to carry you over the threshold?"

Without hesitation, he swooped her into his arms, and she squealed. Teller brought her into the cabin. The interior was softly lit by a single lamp. The wall-mounted air-conditioning unit hummed. Identical to Kate's cabin, it consisted of one large room sectioned into living and sleeping areas, a kitchenette and bathroom tucked into the back. The décor spartan, it was extremely neat. A bottle of wine was in a champagne bucket next to a pair of goblets on a nightstand.

After Teller put her on her feet, Kate squinted at the maroon bedspread. "Scattered rose petals?"

Teller closed the distance between them, coming to stand behind her. He encircled her midsection, splaying his hands over her stomach. Lips in the crook of her neck, he murmured, "I had to set a scene for seduction. It is our first time after all."

Dizzy with anticipation, Kate said huskily, "Trust me, I'm a sure thing."

Teller's fingers stole down her thigh, rucking up the hem of her dress. Flicking it aside. He caressed her bare thigh, his touch leaving a fiery trail on her skin. He blazed his way to the elastic band of her panties. Kate's breath quickened as he skimmed a calloused finger under the sleek fabric. Palming her dampened sex beneath her panties, he explored her chestnut curls. Found her slit. When he teased her there, brushing a fingertip along her seam but not delving further, she cried out, bucking against him to urge him on.

His teeth grazing Kate's throat where her pulse throbbed, he lazily circled her clit in a figure eight pattern. She squirmed, and he pulled her hard against his pelvis, where she felt the ridge of his arousal in the small of her back. "Oh God."

Sliding two fingers into her slick folds, he worked her, the pace of his strokes unhurried. Kate honed on the tension building low in her belly. His other hand had slipped into the bodice of her dress and beneath her bra, plucking her nipples into pebbled peaks.

Her heartbeat roared in her ears as Teller's tempo increased. He pressed his thumbnail *ever so* against her nub. Kate moaned, arching her back. She hovered on the edge of the precipice, so close to shattering into a billion pieces. It was a thirst she desperately needed to quench. A whimper escaped her. She called out Teller's name. His mouth hot against her neck, he added a third finger to his strokes. There it was—a ripple of pleasure. It caught. Intensified until it engulfed her. Delicious sensations radiated from Kate's center, coursing down to her toes and back like ocean waves lapping the shore.

Breathless, her legs trembling, Kate slumped against Teller. He helped her over to the bed. She planted herself on the edge of the mattress, resting her forehead against his stomach.

Dragging the pins from her updo, he deposited them on the nightstand. Her hair cascaded over her shoulders. Teller played with the tendrils. Cupping the back of her head, the pads of his fingers massaged her scalp. "Feelin' good?"

"Better than good. That was mind-blowing. My soul left my body. I think I saw Jesus," Kate whispered, and Teller chuckled.

Emboldened by the arousal straining against his denims, she unfastened his belt buckle then unbuttoned and unzipped his fly. She tugged down the denims. Gaze rapt on the spot of moisture on his tented boxer briefs, she licked her lips. Bringing her face to the bulge, she rubbed her cheek against it. Teller groaned, and his swollen flesh convulsed. Kate inched his briefs down. He sprang free. Tracing her tongue along his length, she slurped the beaded moisture from the tip. Teller's hips jerked, his fingers knotting in her hair.

Taking him fully in her mouth, she sucked, sliding up and down his shaft. Kate raked her nails up his legs, cupping his backside. Teller's muscles tensed. She pulled away, and he popped from her mouth. Lingering a moment to give more attention to his tip, she then got to her feet, shucking her dress, bra, and panties. He stripped off his shirt, his eyes drinking in her nakedness, and his expression frank with appreciation. She felt a flush stain her cheeks.

"You're like a dream, Kate," Teller said. He opened the drawer in the bedside table, setting a package of condoms next to the champagne bucket.

She nudged him until the back of his knees bumped the mattress. Planting a hand against his torso, she pushed. He fell back on the bed, his gaze not leaving hers. Kate picked up the condoms. Opening the box, she fished out a foil square. Using her teeth, she tore it open. Reaching for him, she slowly unrolled the condom over his arousal, smiling at his quick intakes of breath.

Straddling Teller's hips, Kate lowered herself, sheathing him tight. She set a deliberate rhythm, grinding and undulating. Within moments, Teller shuddered his release.

Pulling her to the mattress, he folded her into his side, his lips on her forehead. "I love you, Kate."

CHAPTER FIFTY-THREE

KATE AND TELLER RARELY LEFT HIS BED OVER THEIR HONEYMOON except to take lengthy walks, usually keeping to the fence line and ending up in the glade.

When hungry, they heated canned food on his apartment-sized stove. Sitting with legs crossed on the bed while they ate, they talked. Kate thought she knew a lot about Teller, but with each conversation she learned more. They discussed books and movies, played cards, listened to music—and made their way through two packages of condoms.

The morning they would be returning to the group arrived too quickly. After showering, Kate and Teller packed their belongings. They'd made the decision to continue living in the farmhouse with Connie though Kate knew she'd miss the privacy of Teller's cabin.

"You're lookin' morose," Teller said in his sage way as he folded a pair of underwear.

She shrugged. "Returning to reality, you know."

"They say time flies when you're havin' fun…"

Glumly, Kate gathered their toiletries and tucked them into the zippered compartment inside the case. "Sure does."

"Maybe we should've taken more than a week." Teller grabbed her from behind, bringing his lips to her ear. "How 'bout we go back at lunchtime instead of breakfast?"

"That is tempting," Kate murmured, lacing her fingers with his at her midriff. Lover Teller was worlds apart from easygoing Teller—lustful, libidinous, insatiable. It was difficult to ignore the exquisite, heavy ache low in her loins at his suggestion. "But Connie's organizing a celebratory brunch."

Teller made a grumbling noise in the back of his throat. He slid a hand to the apex of her thighs. Kate squirmed when he raked his fingernails along the fly of her jeans, teasing. Nibbling her earlobe, he said, "We can sneak off for a quickie later."

"Here are the newlyweds," Connie exclaimed when Kate and Teller entered the kitchen. She came forward to embrace them. The air was scented with the aroma of bacon and cinnamon, and Kate's stomach growled at the thought of *real* food.

"Smells great," Teller said as he set their suitcase down. Ace barked from the living room at Teller's voice. He trotted out, nails pitter-pattering on the floor, and jumped on Teller in greeting. Teller stooped down and ruffled the dog's ears, laughing. "Hey, fella."

"Nora's done a super job caring for Ace," Ben praised Nora from where he supervised her at the stove. She held a spatula and flipped French toast in a skillet.

"I'll bring coffee to the table. Go sit," Connie ordered.

While they ate, Audrey and Ben discussed how the security drills had gone during Kate and Teller's absence.

Ben took a sip of coffee. "We've added two more scenarios."

"With the alternate option on each, we're lookin' at a dozen total plays." Teller cautioned, "Any more than that will be impossible to remember."

"That's exactly my thought," Connie agreed. "Simplicity's key. Without streamlining, we'll panic during an attack."

Audrey removed a strip of fat from a slice of bacon, discarding it on her plate. "It sounds more complicated than it is. Last night I put a binder together. Between reviewing that and the daily training, we'll be fine."

"I hit the bullseye eight times out of ten yesterday during target practice," Nora said proudly. Crimson spots appeared on her cheeks under Kate's scrutiny.

Audrey put an arm around Nora. "That's my girl."

She was shocked to hear Nora speak up, but Kate didn't want to embarrass Nora further. "Wow! Good job, kid. I'm hopeless with the bow. You'll have to give me some tips."

Teller wiped his mouth with a napkin, crumpling it before dropping it on his empty plate. "How you fittin' in, Adam?"

Adam had been quiet through the meal but ate heartily. Clean shaven, he seemed well-rested. He looked less gaunt, too. "Really good." He beamed. "I love it here. Everyone's friendly."

Nodding, Teller said, "Mighty glad to hear it."

"He's pitched in with chores," Ben said, clapping Adam on the back. "I've appreciated the help."

"What's on the agenda for today?" Kate asked, resting her elbows on the table.

"Target practice and sparring this morning. Drills in the afternoon," Connie said. "Tomorrow I want to work on my list of projects."

"Projects?" Teller asked.

"There are sheets of galvanized metal in the barn that I want attached to the hayloft walls. If Ben's positioned there with his bow during a siege, he needs to be shielded. And bedroom furniture should be rearranged so there'll be clear pathways to the windows."

"I'll wash up and start the dishwasher," Kate said, getting to her feet. "You all go target shooting. I'll join you when I'm done."

KATE ZIPPERED her jeans and brushed hair from her face, catching sight of herself in the bathroom mirror. She scanned over her scarlet cheeks and kiss-swollen lips.

Teller's eyes met hers in the reflection. He grasped her by the forearm, spinning her so she faced him. He put his mouth to hers and said, "Tough waitin' all day to bend you over and have my wicked way with you."

She licked his bottom lip. "Was it worth the wait?"

"Without a doubt."

She sighed. "And now we have to go and complete drills."

"I ain't lookin' forward to it either," Teller said. He gave her another kiss before drawing away.

They straightened their clothes. Kate stuck her ax in her belt loop, and Teller belted his holster. With a final inspection in the mirror, they left the bathroom, trying to appear casual as they walked into the kitchen. Connie was assembling a tray with a bowl of broth and plate of chicken casserole. When she noticed Kate and Teller, she grinned perceptively. "What were you two up to?"

Kate threw her sister an innocent smile, knowing full well the musky stink of sex clung to her and Teller. "We're on our way to run through the newest drills."

"Sure, Kate, sure." Eyes dancing with merriment, Connie poured a cup of milk from a glass pitcher, placing it beside the plate. "Would you do me a favor and drop this supper tray off at Jamie and Judy's cabin?"

"See y'all outside." Teller winked at Kate before disappearing down the hall.

"I can take it. That's no problem." Kate put her arms over her chest and propped a hip against the counter. "What I'm more bothered about is how much longer are we gonna keep this up— delivering trays every evening? Why can't Jamie come up here and eat? Take Judy's broth when he returns to his cabin?"

"He's not in his right mind," Connie tsked. "He doesn't shower. The cabin's filthy. I almost threw up last night when I handed him the tray at the door. He's secretive, too. Won't let me in."

"Oh no. How does Judy seem? Worse?"

"I haven't seen her for... I don't know... maybe a week and a half? I think she's totally bedridden."

"What can we do?"

"Honestly, Kate, I don't believe there's anything we *can* do other than continue as we have been. I have a bad feeling in the pit of my stomach. I fear Judy's near death."

Kate pinched her lip between her teeth. "If she dies, she could turn. Become a liability not only to Jamie but all of us. Has he forgotten Otis and Peggy?"

"He's resistant to discussion."

"Some tough love is in order. We can't allow him to be secretive. He wouldn't get aggressive with me if *I* broach the subject with him, would he?"

"He seems off but not volatile. It's a shame, really. He's a shell of his former self." Connie used a washrag to wipe the counter, shaking her head. "Fortunately, Nora's thriving despite the neglect."

"Let me see what I can do," Kate said, lifting the tray.

As she made her way past the side yard where everyone was assembled, Teller called out, "Want me to drive you over?"

"No, it's okay. It's only a five-minute walk." In truth, Kate was relieved to put off drill practice longer—though necessary, it was tedious. Besides, she needed time to formulate a strategy. If Jamie were as fragile as Kate suspected, she'd have to handle him with kid gloves.

Juggling the tray, Kate knocked on the cabin door. When nobody answered, she frowned. The door wasn't locked when she tried it. It swung open. Fetid air trickled out. Kate identified the stench—unwashed bodies and feces. *Oof.* "Jamie?"

Entering the shadowy cabin, Kate cleared a spot on the coffee table and set the tray down, then flicked on the overhead light. The living, dining, and kitchen areas were piled with soiled clothes, dishes, and refuse. There was no sign of Jamie or Judy, but the master bedroom door was closed. That was where they must be. She detected the sound of movement. What was going on in there?

Sliding her ax from her belt loop, Kate tiptoed to the door and put her ear to it. If they were having sex, she was going to feel mortified for interrupting, but that seemed highly unlikely in Judy's condition. Ax in one hand, Kate slowly opened the door.

She recoiled, her throat burning and eyes stinging. She knew that smell.

Eyesight adjusting, Kate's gaze zeroed in on the bed. Judy's mouth was gagged with a cloth. Her wrists were bound to the wrought iron headboard and her ankles to the footboard. She jerked and twisted. Backbone arched and pelvis in the air, Judy fiercely struggled to free herself.

Kate came closer, narrowed her gaze. Judy was a Z. Kate murmured, "What the actual fuck?"

How long had Jamie concealed his Z virus infected wife?

Wherever he was, he'd surely be returning soon. Kate must dispatch the Z immediately. Judy was moving too much—Kate would have to subdue her. She climbed on the bed, getting her bearings as her sneakers sank into the mattress. Straddling Judy's thighs, Kate brought her ankles together, restraining her. She raised her ax, directing the blade toward Judy's forehead. Putting her out of her misery.

Panting, Kate pried the blade from Judy's skull, stilling when she sensed she was no longer alone. Turning, she realized her mistake. She should've searched the cabin. Jamie must've been there somewhere all along—Nora's room or the bathroom. More fool her for merely assuming he'd left.

Figure outlined in the doorway, the light haloed him. Kate made out his greasy hair and full beard. His stained shirt. Was that a bandage on his forearm? Had Judy bitten him?

"Jamie? You alright?"

He put his head back and sniffed the air. Cognizance rocketed through Kate, instinct impelling her to ready her ax.

Jamie launched toward the bed, landing on the corner. The motion knocked Kate from her stance. She fell against the headboard, the ax sailing from her grip. "Augh!"

Before Kate could recover, Jamie slammed into her, and they tumbled to the floor. His teeth snapping, he dove for her neck. With a cry of alarm, Kate braced her palms on either side of his collarbone. She grunted as she strained to hold him off. Shaking with effort, she understood the limits of her stamina. *Think, Kate, think! You've trained for this.* Recalling a technique they'd practiced, she took a quick, sharp breath and rotated her body, propelling her shoulder up.

Jamie was flung aside, smacking into the wall.

Kate clambered to her feet, groping for the dagger lashed to her ankle. The bedroom door was *right there.* If only she could get to it, trap Jamie in the room. Escape unscathed. She didn't look back to gauge his progress as she stumbled forward.

Just as Kate drew the knife from its sheath, Jamie hurdled over the bed. Almost missing Kate, his body bumped into her enough to make her lose her footing. She tightened her grip on the hilt of her knife, planting face first on the floor. Kate rolled, getting on her back but not able to stand before Jamie regrouped.

He pogoed, landing on her. Breath knocked out, Kate's head connected with the corner of the dresser. Pinpricks of light threatening her vision, she scrabbled, attempting to bring her knife up.

Jamie was on her chest, pinning her to the floor. Mouth working, as if in slow motion, he went in for the kill.

Kate was vaguely aware of the snuffling noise he made as his canines met with the skin at her clavicle.

Then the zinging pain as he ripped into her flesh.

Shrieking, Kate freed her arm. In an arc-like movement, she threw the knife up and in. Buried the blade in the base of his skull.

Jamie collapsed on her.

CHAPTER FIFTY-FOUR

FOR A SECOND, KATE LAY IN A DAZE.

"Oh boy." Head woozy, Kate shimmied her way out from under Jamie's body. Holding onto the dresser, she clumsily got to her feet. She put her hand to her clavicle. It was an odd combination of slippery and sticky, which baffled Kate. Blood saturated her top.

He got her good.

Robotically, she yanked the knife from Jamie's cranium. Wiped the blade against the bedspread. Sheathed it. Where was her ax? Kate found it under the bedside table, managed to put it in her belt loop.

She felt so hot. Something was bad wrong—worse than a whack on the noggin. Was Kate infected with the zombie virus? What if it killed her, and she turned in the cabin? Teller would come looking for her—find her a Z. What if she bit *him*?

"No! I have to warn Teller… Connie…" Kate mumbled to the emptiness of the cabin.

Veins ablaze and vision blurring, Kate staggered outside, leaning on the porch railing to keep from fainting.

Have to warn them. Hurry!

Nearly tripping down the stairs, she stumbled into a jog. Her brain was boiling in her skull, making the nerve endings up and down her body electrify and crackle. The pain was excruciating. Kate ground her teeth, determined to make it to Teller before passing out.

The farmhouse came in view. Kate staggered, righting herself. *Almost there. Just a little more, and they'll see you.* The fire was consuming her now, and her vision transformed from blurred to hazy then black. She was blinded. Still, she could tell she was on the right track by the gravel under her sneakers. Doggedly staying on course, Kate ignored the way her pulse screamed in her ears. Everything hurt.

"Kate?" She heard someone yell in the distance. Relief coursed through her. *They saw.* She swayed, crashing to her knees.

"She's bleedin'. Stay back!" Teller ordered, his voice coming closer. Kate felt him grab her, push her shirt collar aside. "Fuck."

"Jamie... bit me. Can't see." Her mouth was so dry her tongue stuck to the roof of her mouth. "Killed him."

"You can't see?"

"Blind... I'm infected. Dying. I k-know it."

His hands were spasmodic as he held her. "You're burnin' up."

Kate whispered, "Promise you'll shoot me, T-t-teller. Don't wanna turn. Promise!"

"Kate..."

Her eyeballs were like two smoldering coals. There was so much pressure inside her head she was sure at any second her brain would explode. Her muscles seized, quivered. Teller put her on the gravel—Kate felt it beneath her. She moaned, jaw clenched, as her fingernails clawed at her skin.

"What's wrong with her?" Connie hollered from the fringes.

"I think she's havin' a fit. Don't come no closer. I mean it, Connie."

"We have to do something," Ben protested. "We can't just let her die!"

Teller retorted, "Get the leftover antibiotics we used on you. I'll load her in her van and drive her to her cabin. We'll tend her there. Hurry, for chrissake!"

BEING TRANSPORTED. *Placed somewhere. It was soft. Bed. She sizzled. Would the mattress start on fire?*

Jared was unzipping her jeans. "No! No!"

"It's okay, Kate," Teller soothed. She slackened against the pillow, groaning. Her head was imploding.

The prick of a needle in her backside.

"Ventrogluteal," Kate murmured.

"I TOLD YOU, Connie. It ain't safe for you to be here. Kate would skin me alive if I let you inside." Teller's voice was muffled.

"I need to see her! I have things I need to say... so many things."

"You're nearly thirty-nine weeks pregnant. You gotta think about your baby."

Connie sobbed.

MOMMA DABBED *at her brow with a cool cloth. So blessedly cool.*

"Katie Scarlett. Remember the doves?"

"I remember, Momma..."

"This too shall pass. You never forget that. Your story isn't over. Not yet, baby girl."

"Momma, stay with me..." Tears slipped from her eyes, pooled in her ears. "Momma, I'm sorry..."

Momma's lips on her cheek.

"I*T'S* BEEN *three days of constant doses. Are there no signs of improvement?" Ben.*

"*None. Three days of a one-hundred-four-degree fever." Teller sounded exhausted. "Can a body survive that?"*

"*But she hasn't had a convulsion for two days. She's a survivor. She's strong, Teller."*

"*I ain't. She tosses and turns, cryin' for her ma, havin' nightmares. It's about killin' me."*

"*You're beat. Go take a shower, man. Eat. Nap. I'll stay with her."*

S*OMEBODY SPOONING HER BROTH, helping her sip icy water.*

A *FIGURE KNEELED beside the bed, making the mattress dip. "Please God." Teller. "I've never asked you for nothin' but I'm askin' now. If I ain't got her, I..."*

"B*EN SAID HER FEVER'S BETTER." Connie from a distance. "Let me in, goddammit."*

"*She ain't outta the woods yet." Teller. He sighed. "Fine. I don't have no fight left in me."*

"*Kate. My God." Connie's palms running over her face. Urgent fingers exploring her wound. "It's healing. She's going to make it, Teller. She's too stubborn not to."*

"*I don't dare inject any more antibiotic—it's been five days." Teller sounded so beat. "The reference book says anything more than a five-day course can mess with organs. And she may never regain her sight even if she lives."*

"*Kate, if you can hear me... don't you give in to this. You hear me? I want to talk to you... I want to apologize..." Connie's voice broke.*

"Con," Teller said gently. "Kate knows. She knows."

"I BROUGHT *you a bouquet of flowers. Nora picked them for you. She drew you a picture of your favorite flower, too—lily of the valley." Ben. He kissed her forehead. "I owe you, Kate. If it weren't for you, I'd be dead. Don't think I don't know that. I've got faith you'll pull through."*

IN MUSCULAR ARMS. *She recognized Teller's scent. His body quaked with sobs, but his lips were at her temple. "I need you to wake up, Kate... Please... Please... I can't live this life without you..."*

HER EYELIDS FLUTTERED. It was too bright and her head felt like a freight train chugged through it. Where was she? She shut her eyes. Her entire body was a giant ache. Hand trembling, Kate inched fingers toward her wound, probing it. Someone whimpered. It was her.

"Kate? Sweet Jesus!" Teller scooped her up, cradled her against his chest. He peppered kisses on her cheek, her forehead, the crown of her head. "I don't deserve such mercy. Thank you. Thank you..."

CHAPTER FIFTY-FIVE

"Now, just stay in bed, Kate," Teller scolded as he stepped into the cabin with a lunch tray.

Busted. She lowered back down, pouting. "I'm bored. And I need to rebuild my strength."

"It's only been a few days since you regained consciousness. You ain't ready." Teller put the tray over her lap, his expression softening. "After you eat, we'll walk you around a bit. But only if you eat every last speck of food on that plate."

"Yessir." Kate volleyed him a cheesy smile, then brought her hand up to mock salute him.

"Saucy little wench," Teller said. He grasped her chin with his thumb and index fingers. Made her meet his eyes. "You better get your strength back fast. You got wifely duties to perform."

A little thrill zipped through her at the thought. Teller pecked her lips then sat on a chair at the bedside. Lacing his fingers, he cupped the back of his head. He watched her pick up her sandwich, his grin lopsided but his eyes shining with adoration.

Kate winked flirtatiously as she chewed.

"I CAN'T BELIEVE how weak I am," Kate breathed as Teller helped her to the edge of the mattress. "Once around the cabin wiped me out."

"Dang hell, woman. You about died last week. Stop rushin' things. What if your condition worsens?"

"It won't," Kate said with confidence. "I'm on the mend."

"You're a goldamn miracle. I can't believe your sight came back. Adam said he's never seen someone get bit and *not* turn. Without gettin' those antibiotics into your bloodstream so quick I don't know if you woulda pulled through."

"Who knows if the Safolinix made any difference at all?" Kate lifted a hand. "It could've. It's powerful. We'll hold onto the remaining doses in case anyone else gets bitten. Something else occurs to me though..."

Teller took a seat beside her on the mattress. "What's that?"

"I made enough noise for Jamie to hear me come into the cabin. Why the delay in attacking me?"

"Huh." Teller scratched his neck. "Hope the Zs ain't evolvin' into somethin' more human-like. That would be a terrifyin' prospect."

"No kidding. The only certain thing about the virus is that *nothing* is certain—there's no discernible pattern to any of this. My bite may be healing," Kate indicated the wound on her clavicle, "but the infection could remain dormant in my bloodstream. I think we need to bear that in mind."

"Welp. I don't think it's in your saliva—we kissed often enough since you've woken up."

"Still." Kate coughed, clearing her throat. Avoided his gaze. "It could be passed... to a child, for example."

Teller's voice was gruff when he said, "We'll cross that bridge when it comes time. Let's focus on today, 'kay?"

She nodded.

"I do think you're ready to move back up to the farmhouse this afternoon. How would you like that?"

Kate brightened. She *would* like that. She missed everyone

and the comfort of routine. She even missed daily drill practice. Although it would be a while before she was strong enough to participate, she looked forward to being physically able to again.

"Remember Momma's peach cobbler?" Connie asked the next day as she rolled pastry for a blueberry pie.

Nostalgia blossomed in Kate's chest, warm and gratifying. "I do. What I wouldn't give for a dish of it right now."

"I've got some canned peaches in the pantry. We'll try to recreate her recipe sometime." The color was high in Connie's cheeks, and Kate felt a zip of conscience.

"You should be on the sofa with your feet up," Kate protested. "You're due in days, after all. I'll make the cobbler for Sunday supper—you'll probably be in labor."

"I don't know about that. I have so much energy right now." She emptied a jar of homemade blueberry pie filling into the prepared shell and laid a sheet of pastry on top.

"Yeah, that's a thing that often happens before giving birth. I read it in one of the books."

"You and those books." Connie crimped the edges of the crust. "I'm not sure you're ready to cook. You're weak as a kitten."

"I'm getting stronger every day!"

"Still..."

"I can almost taste Momma's cobbler. It'll be worth pushing myself."

Connie laughed. "It was a childhood favorite."

"Connie," Kate started, then paused as anxiety welled. The words disappeared from her tongue though the subject of Momma being introduced was just the opportunity she'd needed. Kate mustn't let it pass. Swallowing her misgivings, she asked her sister to take a seat after putting the pie in the preheated oven.

Expression grave, Connie eased her body down on the bench across from Kate. "Why do I have the feeling you're working up to talking about something... heavy?"

Kate nodded. Rubbed a hand across the bridge of her nose. Toyed with her hair. She fastened her hands in her lap to keep them from fidgeting further.

"A year ago, we'd never be sitting here having heartfelt exchanges. We've come far, Kate."

"We have. But there are some things—it's high time for some plain speaking." Breath shaky, Kate blinked away tears. "I-I should've thanked you for taking me on after Dad and Momma died. I never gave you enough credit, Con."

"You don't need to—"

"I do," Kate asserted. "It was all too easy for me to forget that you were practically a kid yourself. That you were grieving, too."

"You would've been better off in foster care. I admit that. You would've been taken care of better. Would've been safer..." Connie's nose reddened. A teardrop traveled down her cheek. "When you told me Jared molested you. I wanted to strangle him."

"A-about that." Kate looked down to the tabletop. Cleared her throat. "Uhh... Jared did way more than simply molest me..."

"What? Not, not—"

"Yeah. That." Kate hitched her good shoulder. "I was embarrassed. I didn't want anyone to know. I felt complicit. *Dirty.*"

"God." Connie crumpled. She brought her hands up to cover her face, but a cry escaped. "I'm so sorry. All those nights I left you alone with him!"

Kate grabbed one of Connie's hands, interlocking their fingers. "I'm not confiding to hurt you. Or to compel you to make an apology. I only want you to understand that... what happened with Jared made me all mixed up funny inside. It stigmatized me. I lashed out at you because I didn't know how to sort it out in my own head."

"It's all my fault. Damn." Connie pursed her lips, her forehead creasing. "All I wanted was to escape with whatever drug I could get my mitts on. Christ, I was wild back then—hardly present and available. How selfish I was!"

"Yeah, well, I was wild in my own way for a while, too. We were both effed up."

"Then I met Seth and let him fix me."

"Wait. *You* overcame your addictions. That was *all you*."

"It wasn't easy."

"Exactly, so give yourself credit. It's admirable," Kate replied, squeezing her hand. "Con, sometimes I think you've punished yourself. Like you're paying a debt that doesn't exist. Even your marriage—it seemed like a penance of sorts."

"Perhaps so. I had a lot to atone for. I think I wanted a father figure. In many ways Seth was that. He was good at telling me what to do."

"Being married to him was atonement enough. Besides, your sins are nothing compared to mine." Kate paused. "This conversation is a critical part of dealing with my issues. Of healing. I-I'm hoping it'll heal you, too. And give us a sense of closure. A fresh start."

"Of course it will," Connie said kindly. "I'm honored you trust me enough now to confide about the extent of... Jared. I can only imagine how trying it was for you to talk about."

"It was trying." Kate nodded. "But freeing, you know?"

"I get it. But it doesn't lessen my guilt. I'm going to have to live with it."

"You think I'm a stranger to guilt? I'm not. I don't want you to suffer from the same self-reproach I do!"

"Any anger or resentment you feel toward me is justified. You shouldn't feel guilty for it. Kate, I accept the part I played."

"No! This isn't about me resenting you. I don't. Not anymore. That isn't what I'm saying—we're at cross purposes here. I have guilt about something else. Something I need to come clean about." Before Kate could think twice, she charged forward. Words spilled from her lips as she admitted her part in the events leading up to their parents' murder suicide. When she was finished, she asked uncertainly, "Do you hate me?"

Connie put her head back, studied the newly painted kitchen ceiling as if collecting her thoughts.

Her heart sank. "You *do* think their deaths are my fault."

Connie snorted, shaking her head. "No, of course not! You were a baby. So you've carried this secret for nearly twenty years?"

With a sniffle, Kate wiped the back of her hand across her nose. Nodded.

"Ugh. Dammit, Kate."

"I'm sorry!"

"I'm not angry." Connie's smile was sympathetic when she met Kate's eyes. "You should have told me sooner. Will you promise me something—that you'll never keep anything from me ever again?"

Kate's shoulders slumped with relief. "I promise."

CHAPTER FIFTY-SIX

CONNIE'S DUE DATE CAME AND WENT. KATE WATCHED HER SISTER like she was a ticking time bomb ready to detonate at any second.

Though Kate felt far from one hundred percent, she was well enough to prepare Sunday supper. She tossed canned peaches with sugar and flour in a baking dish, her gaze often straying to Connie. From the kitchen table where she thumbed through an old magazine, Connie protested, "Will you stop looking at me like that?"

"Er... sorry." Kate cut butter and flour with a pastry blender for the cobbler's topping. "I can't help it."

"Well, you're making me nervous, dammit!"

Kate narrowed her eyes at Connie. "You seem rather *too* unruffled, if you ask me."

Connie laughed, saying tartly, "I didn't ask you. Just chill. The crib's set up in the corner of my bedroom. The layette's organized in the dresser. I've got the plastic sheet on the bed... I'm as ready as I'm likely to get."

Kate slid the baking dish into the oven next to the tray of breaded pork chops, biting her tongue. She couldn't shake her disturbed mood. What the hell was wrong with her? Why the presentiment of foreboding? "I'll be back. I'm gonna see if Teller's done picking the peas."

"Yes, please do. You're driving me batty," Connie rebuked in a good-natured way after her.

Kate met Teller by the chicken coop. He handed her the metal colander of peapods, then removed his hat to wipe away the sweat beaded on the sides of his face. "Phew. Another hot one. What's ailin' you?"

"I don't… know," Kate said, biting at her thumbnail.

"Let's set on the steps for a spell. We can shell these peas and have a chin wag."

Once seated, Kate kept her tone low though the air-conditioning unit beside the steps hummed enough to obscure their voices. "I've got a weird tingly feeling in my gut."

"Indigestion?"

She threw him side-eye. "I'm not joking."

"Okay, okay. No offense intended."

"I woke up this way. It's not fading. I have to heed it."

"You do appear a tad tightly wound. Ain't like you to be this jumpy. Anything I can do?"

Kate's mouth was as dry as the Sahara. She shook her head, brow puckered. Putting a hand to the nape of her neck, she rubbed the taut muscles there. "My intuition has never steered me wrong before. Just… prepare yourself."

KATE TOOK a bite of peach cobbler. It was exactly how she remembered Momma's cobbler tasting. From across the table, Connie mewed in appreciation as she chewed.

The speaker box mounted on the hallway wall emitted a high-pitched whine, alerting them to a disturbance at the gate. Kate leaped up, her spoon clattering as it hit her plate and her chair knocking over. "I knew it!"

Teller was on his feet. The others sat frozen, their mouths gaping and eyes wide. Kate hastened to the office. Perching on the edge of the swivel chair, she reviewed the live video feed. No… it couldn't be.

The alarm silenced. Teller must've switched it off. The farmhouse was now deathly still. He appeared in the office doorway, apprehension shaping his features.

"Teller, you'll never believe—"

"Why has the security code been changed?" Seth's voice rang out over the hallway intercom.

Connie peeked around Teller. Her green eyes were enormous in her face, a stark contrast to her bloodless complexion. "Kate?"

"The MC's with him. Maybe ten or twelve altogether," Kate said shakily. Her hands were trembling. She balled them into fists.

Teller asked, "But is he an ally or a hostage?"

"If you think we won't force our way inside, you're fucking wrong." Seth's tone was scathing. "Let us in. Immediately."

Goddamn Seth. Kate got up. Strode around the desk, mouth compressed. As she passed Teller and Connie in the doorway she said, "Doesn't sound like a hostage to me. Get everyone in position." She paused, thinking of which scenario was appropriate. "Option two B. I'll take the lead. Uh, make sure they all have their walkies. This isn't a drill!"

Then Teller and Connie disappeared into the kitchen, leaving Kate in the hall. Her breath came in short gasps. She swallowed hard. Pressed the button on the intercom. Kept her voice steady. "What do you want, Seth?"

"Kathryn. You're still there."

Kate barely noticed the activity around her as bodies filed past. Teller called for Ace, closing him into the basement. Some people hurried to other parts of the house. Others went out the back door. She needed to stall Seth, give everyone a chance to get to their posts. "Yes, I'm here. Where have *you* been?"

"Around."

"Found some new friends, have you?"

Seth laughed. "Sure have."

"Are you gonna tell me what you want?"

"Mayfly Hollow. What else? Why doesn't my code work, Kathryn?"

Ben had read the manual for the system weeks ago, changing it. Kate weighed her response, but before she could speak Seth said, "The farm belongs to me—to us. We'll take it by force if necessary."

She fingered the pistol holstered at her waist. "I think it's better if we have this discussion in person. I'll be there in a minute."

"Hurry. Clock's counting down."

Kate turned, finding Teller lingering. "You should be preparing!"

"I have a notion this won't end well." He bent to brush his lips against hers. "I love you, Kate. Be safe. Keep to the plan. Remember, I've got your back."

Then he was gone.

Knowing she couldn't lollygag, Kate grabbed her lone rifle from the gun rack by the front door. She went outside, moving as rapidly as possible. Her heart pounded with the physical exertion, reminding her of her limitations. Relieved to be able to sit, she climbed on the ATV parked outside the barn. Slinging the rifle strap over her good shoulder, she started the engine and adjusted the choke. As she passed the hen house, Kate noticed Adam crouched low at the corner of the cinder block building housing Connie's hydroponic garden. Expression grim, he gripped his rifle. He nodded as she drove past.

The ATV zoomed down the lane, gravel flying from its wheels. Seth waited at the entrance, his arms over his chest and his face set in displeasure. He wore a leather jacket over a white tee and jeans. He looked weathered—the lines around his eyes had deepened and his glasses were taped together at the bridge.

ı

Skin stretched tight across his cheekbones lent him a rawboned appearance. "About fucking time."

Behind him, Kate saw Vonda, recognized the brick-shaped man, Hurley, and the craggy-faced blonde. Everyone they'd seen in Mergenville was there. Kate hoped there weren't more members lying in wait outside the fence. Prayed they'd underestimated the farm's occupants. Licking her lips, Kate kept to the script though her pulse fluttered in her neck and made her feel faint. "I'm sure we can work something out, Seth."

"We ain't workin' *something out*," Vonda spit from her chopper. "You can hand over this place, or we'll come back with heavy equipment and bulldoze our way in."

"You don't care you'd destroy the gate in the process?"

"Nope."

Kate met Seth's eyes. They were cold. Emotionless. "What about Connie?"

Seth shrugged. "She made her choices. She's no longer my concern."

"You gonna let us in?" Hurley asked, unholstering his firearm. "This is your only chance, sugar tits."

"Discipline *your* tits, Hurley. I'm interested in a peaceful transfer of power." Vonda smirked, revealing dazzling white teeth. "Seth told me you were a firecracker... I'm sure you and me can strike up an *agreement* if you'd like to stay." Her lecherous gaze slithered up Kate's body.

Firecracker, huh? I'd love to light a fuse under her bony ass.

The writing was on the wall now. They didn't even know how serious shit was about to get. Stomach coiling into a corkscrew, bile rose in Kate's windpipe. She swallowed it back.

Was she recovered enough? Did she have the stamina? Could she do what was necessary? She must. Kate painted her expression with abject defeat. Put her hands up in concession. "Okay. Alright. You win. We surrender—we're not fighters here. We'll leave, but you have to give us time to at least pack a suitcase."

"I'll allow that," Vonda said magnanimously, her expression triumphant, "but under my direct observation. Let us in now, sexy."

Kate nodded. Skimmed her sweaty palms over her blue jeans before removing the remote control from the ATV's cup holder. She clicked the button, and the gate slowly slid open. "Come in. Follow me up to the house."

Not waiting for them, Kate revved the ATV. She kept the speed sedate, as to not alert the MC anything was amiss. She heard the choppers fire up, crunching over the gravel lane as she led the procession. With a surreptitious glance, she ensured everyone cleared the gate. Before she was out of range, she used the remote to shut it. Now they were trapped inside the compound.

Her cabin came into view. It was almost time. Rounding the bend just beyond the last cabin in the row, Kate flicked the head-light switch, flashing the lights in quick succession. Mentally crossing her fingers everyone had their binoculars up and hadn't missed the signal, Kate punched the ATV. She rocketed, leaving a wake of dust as she peeled away from the road. Teeth gritted, she steeled herself for gunshots sure to come, not daring to break pace to look behind her.

There were shouts from the gang as they realized something was afoot—that they'd been duped. Kate headed to the safety of a metal outbuilding to rally with Teller. There was gunfire, and a bullet whizzed past Kate's ear. Squealing, she ducked. She steered in a zigzag pattern, hoping it was enough to dodge their bullets. She sensed somebody chasing her on their bike.

Teller stepped out from behind the outbuilding, rifle butt against his shoulder. He sighted, fired. Gave her cover.

Kate drove past him, parking the ATV behind the building. Her legs were jelly as she crawled off, adrenaline leaking from every pore. Her armpits were ringed with stress sweat. She brought her rifle up as she scurried to join Teller. He kneeled, concealed by the corner of the building.

The blonde was off her bike, her face contorted in rage. Her arms were held out straight, her revolver leveled. She shrieked like a banshee as she advanced toward Kate and Teller, shooting in a haphazard fashion.

"Get down, Kate," Teller yelled as her shots littered the building. He squinted through his scope. Exhaled. Calmly squeezed the trigger. The woman buckled, blood spreading across her shirt.

She landed on the grass, not moving.

Kate assessed the scene. Choppers lay on the gravel. Two men and a woman were prone, arrows protruding from their bodies. Seth was nowhere to be found.

Vonda was crouched behind her bike, using it as a shield as she discharged her pistol, shooting toward the farmhouse. An arrow sailed in the air in a downward trajectory, implanting in Vonda's temple. A confounded look passed over her face. She slumped dead to the gravel.

"We gotta motor. Stay behind me," Teller ordered, his jaw ticking.

They crept closer to the farmhouse, using the outbuildings as protection. Kate struggled to keep up with Teller. She saw Ben in the hayloft window, his forehead creased in concentration as he used his trigger release to draw his bowstring back.

Kate sought where he aimed. "Oh shit!"

"Why is she outside?" Teller asked, getting his rifle in position.

Nora was in a balanced stance by the stairs leading to the kitchen door, clasping her compound bow in position, string pulled. Her sundress was splattered with blood. Face determined, she stared down Hurley. He had a semi-automatic weapon directed at her.

"I'm the big bad wolf, Goldilocks. I'll huff and puff and I'll—"

"You killed Audrey!"

Ben's arrow flew into Hurley's eardrum. Hurley fell forward

but as he did, his finger depressed the trigger, raining fire. Nora cried out as she was struck. She tumbled back against the steps.

"No!" Kate ignored Teller's command to stay put as she dashed from behind the building and made for Nora.

CHAPTER FIFTY-SEVEN

Focused solely on Nora, Kate barely noticed anything else as she ran.

She reached the girl's side, fingers probing Nora's body to evaluate her injuries. She'd been grazed in the thigh. The more concerning wound was near her ribcage. Grunting with effort, Kate gathered Nora in her arms. Opening the screen door, Kate carried her inside, wavering as her vision blackened. She leaned against the wall for a second until it cleared. The sound of gunfire drifted from upstairs. "Connie? Connie!"

Breathlessly, Kate stumbled into the kitchen and laid Nora on the trestle table, pushing the supper dishes aside. She grabbed a towel from the counter to stanch the blood seeping from her tiny body. Lips white, Nora whispered, "That guy shot Audrey through the eye... She's dead, Kate."

Kate shushed her.

"Oh no!" Connie said from the entryway. Her breaths came out in puffs. "How did that happen?"

"She broke the rules and left the house. Come help," Kate instructed. Taking a steadying breath, she tore from the kitchen to the laundry room, fetching the first aid kit from the shelf above the washer, along with an armful of clean bath sheets.

Nora had lost consciousness, but the bleeding hadn't slackened. Connie held the kitchen rag to Nora's side, her expression frantic. Putting the kit and bath sheets on the table, Kate shared an agonized look with her sister. Before returning outside, she pressed her rifle in Connie's free hand.

Ben, Adam, and Teller were in conference beside the barn, whole and unharmed. Their gazes roved over their surroundings as they spoke, on the lookout for movement. When they noticed Kate loitering by the back door, her revolver unholstered, they motioned her over.

Kate went as quick as she could across the gravel lane to meet them, asking, "What's going on?"

"Seth's still loose," Teller said, his face glistening with perspiration. "I think we got all the others. You look spent, Kate. You best set this one out."

"No. I'll be alright. Seth's desperate. We've gotta find him before he creates further havoc," Kate said, mouth tense.

Ben nodded. "What's he look like?"

Kate confirmed the chamber of her gun was fully loaded. "Balding, with glasses and a paunch."

"Okay," Adam said. "We'll fan out. Search the buildings inside and out."

Ben hitched a thumb toward the barn, shifting his bow. "He's definitely not in there. I scoped it out."

Teller patted his empty pockets. "No more ammo for my rifle. I'll have to swap to my pistol," he said. "You two keep together, and I'll stick with Kate. Walkie if you find him."

They parted ways. Ben and Adam headed toward the laundry building and staff cabins. Kate and Teller started for the structure containing Connie's hydroponic garden.

Seth hid in a shadowy corner beside wire shelving holding gardening tools and empty buckets.

"He must be out of bullets or he'd be shooting at us." Kate sneered, "Come out, coward."

Seth complied. Holding his hands palm out, he didn't speak, but his eyes glittered with malevolence.

"Why did you betray us, Seth?" Teller asked. "What have we ever done to you to justify such a thing?"

Seth's lips twisted, his hatred obvious. "*Me* betray *you*? That's rich."

"We'll have to take him to the house," Kate shakily said to Teller, ignoring Seth. "Decide what to do with him as a group."

"*This is my farm!* How dare you, whore of the antichrist? Blasphemer!" Seth scoffed, pugnacious as his tone gained fervor. "You brought this pestilence upon Mayfly Hollow. Like a swarm of locusts hailing the Four Horsemen of the Apocalypse you begat the destruction with your witchy ways—"

"Shut your trap," Teller snapped, his face darkening with ire, "you ravin' lunatic."

"He's off his meds," Kate said, her tone indifferent.

"Bewitched him from the start! The righteous shall overcome," Seth roared. He lurched toward Kate, spittle erupting from his mouth as he cried, "As Bathsheba aforesaid to the Israelites—"

Teller inserted his body between Kate and Seth, restraining him with an outstretched arm. "Cool it, Metzger!"

Stepping forward, Kate used the butt of her revolver to knock Seth out cold.

TELLER HAD PROPPED Seth in a chair at the head of the kitchen table. Slouched down, his chin on his chest, he remained unconscious.

Adam carried Nora upstairs to the master bedroom where Connie sat vigil at her bedside. He came back down with Audrey's lifeless form cradled in his arms. Teller had swiped his hat from his head, bowing in respect as Adam took her body out.

Now there were sporadic gunshots outside as Ben, Teller, and

Adam shot the dead in their brains to keep them from turning into Zs. Closing her eyes momentarily, Kate thought of the destruction. Bullet holes scarred the surface of the buildings. Some of the farmhouse's windows had been shattered, too. The atmosphere still vibrated with death. It was jarring. Unsettling.

Nora's spilled blood began to coagulate on the table, perfuming the air with an unpleasant coppery tang that made Kate want to heave. She wet a kitchen rag and scrubbed ineffectually at the wooden surface. Her muscles didn't want to cooperate.

The men entered the house, their expressions somber.

Teller gripped the back of his neck, his face pale. "It's done. They won't turn now."

"We stacked them behind the barn..." Ben's voice broke. He sniffed to curb his emotions. "We'll give Audrey a... proper... burial tomorrow."

Adam clapped Ben on his back, his eyes sad.

Tears brewing, Kate nodded. She swept up the bloodied towels, taking them to the laundry room. She added detergent and turned on the washer, her throat thick with misery. Resting against the machine, she thought about Audrey. And Nora... would she be okay?

"Kate! Connie! Seth's comin' to," Teller called.

Kate went to join Teller, allowing him to pull her into his side. Like a sponge, she absorbed the comfort he provided.

Connie's steps were ungainly as she entered the kitchen. Her breathing labored, her cheeks were wet and her eyes were pink.

"Is Nora okay?" Ben asked quickly.

Connie's voice was flat. "She's alive. More than could be said for Audrey."

Seth moaned, his eyelids flickering. He blinked. Connie walked up to the side of the table opposite him, her spine rigid. Kate and Teller backed away to the kitchen counter with Ben and Adam, wanting to allow the couple a modicum of privacy.

"How could you, Seth?" Connie cried, her mouth quivering. "How could you?"

Hand on his head where Kate had struck him, he got slowly to his feet. "You drew the line in the sand. You chose her instead of me."

"I-I didn't choose anyone! You know how you get when you don't take your meds. Are you hearing voices like before?" Connie swallowed. Nipped her lips with her teeth as if torn between rage and compassion.

"Those pills were blinders. Without them, I've never seen things so clearly," Seth replied, his expression mocking.

"I—where did you go?"

"You thought you were punishing me, didn't you? Sending me away. I was ecstatic to leave. You hear? Ecstatic."

"Seth, please—"

"You had me fooled. Latching on me like you did. Claws in me." Seth lifted his chin in defiance. "You were a waste of my time. I'm delighting in my newfound freedom."

Connie seemed to shrivel. Mouth opening to object, Kate stepped forward to intercede, but Teller's hand stopped her. He murmured, "Let 'em say their piece."

"What about the b-baby?" Connie asked hesitantly.

"Another parasite!" Seth angled his head back, laughing maniacally. "Satan slinked into our bedroom one night and fucked you. That spawn isn't mine—it's his."

Connie placed a hand on the table for support, but her spine remained stiff and ramrod straight. "No, it's *mine*. You never wanted it." She paused, like she was marshalling her courage. "You think you can waltz back here after deserting us and just give Mayfly Hollow away? I put my blood, sweat, and tears into this place." She smacked the table. "I worked myself to the bone!"

Seth merely smirked.

"You could've left us alone. If you wanted to appease the gang, why not hand over the long-term shelter instead?" Connie demanded, tears spilling from her eyes. "You wanted to punish *me*, didn't you?"

"You deserve to be punished, bitch," he spat.

Like a film in slo-mo, Connie brandished a Bowie knife she'd had hidden at her side.

With a battle cry, she charged Seth.

CHAPTER FIFTY-EIGHT

THE EXCESS BULK AT HER ABDOMEN MADE CONNIE WEEBLE-WOBBLE as she assailed Seth, knife raised.

Seth put a hand up, clutching her wrist tight.

Her extra weight gave Connie the advantage. She fell on Seth and they toppled to the floor. Wrestling, they tussled over the knife. It was a free-for-all.

Kate cried, "Jesus Christ... stop!"

Ben tried to pull Connie away, but she slipped from his grasp, intent on brawling. She pitched forward, slapping Seth inelegantly across the face. He punched her in response. They scuffled, rolling on the floor. Connie raked her nails down Seth's cheek, and Seth howled, his fingers encircling Connie's neck and squeezing. Teller tried several times to get a hold on Seth, finally hooking his hands under Seth's armpits and dragging him off Connie.

"Stop fighting! What's wrong with you—" Kate stilled, speech forgotten as she noticed Seth's clothing was saturated with red liquid. Blood. The knife was abandoned on the linoleum. Her gaze cut to Connie where she lay, wheezing.

Connie was covered in blood.

Kate went to her sister as if in a dream. Dropped to her knees. Checked Connie. "You're hurt!"

"I'm fine, Kate," Connie insisted. Her eyes were huge. Dazed.

"No, you're not!"

Connie had been stabbed on her side, the puncture sizeable. Kate stared in horror at the blood pouring out in a constant stream. It puddled around Connie, drenching Kate's jeans. Had the baby been killed? Kate looked at Seth. His mouth was curved in satisfaction. Fury made her head buzz with the drone of a million bees.

Without thinking twice, Kate reached for the knife on the floor. Her fingers wrapped around the hilt. She launched to her feet. Her movements seemed involuntary as she sprang at Seth.

Scream tearing from her throat, she plunged the knife into his gut and rotated the blade.

"Kate!" Teller gasped, sounding as taken aback as Kate was by her own actions.

Seth folded to the floor. Like an automaton, Kate wheeled back to Connie. Adam had found a towel and held it at Connie's gash, but her color was poor and her breathing shallow.

Stumbling to her knees, Kate grasped Connie's hand, brought it to her cheek. "Seth will never hurt you again…"

Connie's gaze met Kate's, her eyes trusting. Loving. "You're good, Kate. Strong. True." She gave Kate a melancholic smile. "But we both know this is it."

"Shut up. Don't talk like that," Kate blubbered, her tears combining with snot from her nose. She sniffled. "I'm gonna take care of you. I won't let you die."

"No…" Connie coughed, and blood flooded her mouth. Adam put the towel to her lips, and she spit the blood into it. "I feel the baby moving, Kate. It may have gotten scratched but it's alive…"

"The bleeding will stop," Kate insisted. Teller came to her and put an arm around her. "And—"

"You need to accept it, dammit…" Connie's words were

harsh, but her tone was feeble. Her life force seemed to be draining away by degrees. "When I die... you must cut the baby out, Kate..."

"No!"

"You have to... save it. If I turn... it may become infected. Don't waste time..."

"I can't. I can't!"

"You can. You've read all the books. Taken endless notes." Her bloodless lips quirked in a ghost of a smile. "I know you're going to make Mayfly Hollow everything you've dreamed."

"Connie—"

Connie took a breath, her ribcage convulsing. "Swear you'll raise the baby... as your own..."

"Oh God. Oh God. Of course, I swear."

"If it's a girl... name it after Momma..."

Connie's gaze shifted to somewhere over Kate's head. Her eyes widened, focused... then she was gone. Bawling, Kate bundled Connie into her arms. "No. *No!*"

Teller's hand was on her back. His voice was filled with anguish when he said, "Kate. She was right. We gotta get that baby out fast."

Kate moved back and forth, keening.

"I can do it," Ben offered almost inaudibly, wiping tears from his cheeks. He grabbed a bottle of rubbing alcohol from the counter where Kate had placed the first aid kit. Unsheathing the knife from his belt, he dribbled alcohol over the blade.

Kate looked up at the knife then closed her eyes. Connie had asked it of her... how could she not honor one of her sister's dying wishes? She mopped her sleeve against her face, fortifying for the task ahead. "I made promises. Give me the blade."

"You sure?" Teller asked uncertainly. "You're lookin' frail."

Kate nodded. Ben handed her the knife. Adam peeled Connie's shirt away, baring her belly. Ben poured some rubbing alcohol over it. Kate repositioned so she was at the correct angle. Taking a tremulous breath, she poised the tip of the knife at

Connie's belly button, the way the books instructed for a classical vertical incision.

Kate bit back a gag, tentatively dipping the knifepoint into Connie's flesh, guiding it down to the pubic bone. The epidermis parted, exposing a layer of fat. Blood welled, dotting the white tissue. Kate hesitated, fighting a wave of wooziness.

"You alright?" Teller asked, his voice strained. Ben and Adam had turned away, apparently unable to watch.

Kate swallowed the saliva accumulating on her tongue, nodding assent, though she wasn't sure. She worked the knife through the fatty tissue, and liquid gushed. Kate remembered what she'd read. She guessed she'd pierced the amniotic sac. She knew she was almost there. Had to be careful not to go too deep and cut the baby. Just a little more.

Was that the baby? Yes, dark hair. The baby's head. Kate passed the knife to Teller. Tipping the bottle of rubbing alcohol in her palm, she emptied it. Rubbed her hands together. Brow knit, Kate delved into Connie's still-warm abdomen, grasping at the baby's shoulders. The skin was slimy, tricky to grip. Kate's fingers slipped as she tugged. The shoulders came out with a slurping sound, then the baby was freed.

"Oh fuck!" someone said, and Kate realized it was her.

"Here." Ben held a clean bath sheet.

Kate used the towel to wipe the baby's rosy face. She quickly inspected its body. There was a small puncture on its arm, but otherwise it looked perfect. Without Kate asking, Teller used the knife to slice through the umbilical cord.

He asked, "Why ain't it cryin'?"

"Hold on…" Kate hooked an index finger in its mouth, sweeping its airway. Then she put her lips to the baby's nostrils, sucking out the mucus. Kate spit as she lifted the baby to her chest. She massaged the baby's back. "Come on. Come on. Breathe!"

A thin wail filled the air.

Grace flowed through Kate's bloodstream, intoxicating as

any drug. She put her head down and said a silent prayer of gratitude to the almighty.

Teller draped the bath towel around Kate and the newborn. Tone laced with wonder, he asked, "What's her name?"

Kate comprehended that tears streamed down her face. Her lips were rubbery, moving of their own volition when she murmured, "Margaret Kathryn... Maggie."

CHAPTER FIFTY-NINE

At dawn the next morning, Kate numbly sat in a rocking chair in Connie's bedroom beside the bed where Nora slept. The child was fighting for her life, her small chest rising and falling in ragged, intermittent respirations.

Connie and Seth had been taken from the house. Adam and Ben scrupulously cleaned the kitchen, seeming eager to put things in order. To tidy and keep busy lest they be vulnerable to mulling over the devastation of the day. Kate understood that. She was haunted. Whenever she shut her eyes all she could picture was Connie dead. As fatigued as she was, sleep eluded her.

And Seth... Kate shook her head. She wasn't capable of dealing with the ugly reality—that she'd committed murder. Maybe it had been justified. Maybe not. What was done was done. But it would be a long time until Kate could unearth peace with her deed.

She cradled Maggie's tiny, swaddled body as she rocked. The infant was solemn, her eyes unfocused but watchful. When Kate studied the depths of Maggie's dark irises, she felt like she was seeing the future. An era had ended, but with Maggie's birth a new one had begun. Kate was amazed when her throat tightened, aching, foretelling waterworks. She was sure she hadn't a single drop of moisture left in her system, but a tear escaped from the corner of her eye nonetheless.

Kate thought back to when she first came to Mayfly Hollow. How the burden of familial ties was almost unbearable—how she had ardently wished to shrug off the shackle keeping her tethered to her sister, to this place. Now it was the center of her world and everything she held dear.

She contemplated the babe in her arms. It wasn't obligation to fulfill Connie's dying wish that bound her to Maggie. It was more than that—it was love. Kate thought of the threads linking them all together—her and Maggie with Connie and Momma—intricate and gossamer. Maggie was no burden. She was a gift, a tangible connection. Kate knew she would give her last breath to protect her. That was unshakeable certainty.

Teller was at the door, the hallway light casting over his tall, lithe form. He'd showered and changed into a long-sleeved tee and pajama bottoms. Lifting a bottle, he said, "I warmed some formula for Maggie."

"Thanks," Kate said hoarsely, the ache in her throat now ever-present.

He came in, passing Kate the bottle before bending over the bed. Scrutinizing Nora's bandages, he brushed a lock of golden hair back from her forehead. "I think she's gonna make it."

Kate brought the rubber nipple to Maggie's lips, enticing her to suckle it. "I hope so. Audrey's death will leave scars as much as her injuries do."

"Welp. We'll all carry scars." Teller's voice was soft, introspective, as he sat at the edge of the mattress beside the rocking chair. "What matters is we're alive, Kate. We live to see another day. That means everything."

Maggie pulled thirstily at the bottle. It was the only sound in the hushed room, other than their breathing. "You think more members of the gang are on their way?"

"If there are more, they'll likely be too wary to come lookin' for trouble. They'll realize we ain't to be trifled with."

Kate searched his face in the shadowy light spilling in from the hall, cursing herself for needing reassurance. "So... we're out of harm's way?"

"Yeah. We are."

"Until the next threat."

"Kate," Teller reproached. "We can't ask to be dealt a new hand. We have to play the cards we've been given. You know that. We'll manage."

Sighing, Kate said, "Are you... disappointed in me? About... Seth?"

Teller put his large, warm hand on her knee, his expression grave. "No. 'Course not. I know it was a spur of the moment thing. Are you agonizin' over it?"

"Yes... no. Yes." She exhaled, brooding. "What do Ben and Adam say?"

"You won't get condemnation from either of them after the hateful shit Seth spewed. They got a samplin' of Seth Metzger. It wasn't a pleasant one." Teller brought his hand up, caressing Maggie's cheek with one finger. "We'll teach her about her Ma, but we're her parents now."

Kate met his eyes. "You prepared for all that entails? It's an immense responsibility. We've not been married long. I wouldn't blame you if you turned tail and left us."

Smiling, he leaned forward to kiss her. "You're not gettin' rid of me that easy. *For better or for worse*, remember?"

EPILOGUE

The Following Year

MAGGIE ATTACHED to her chest with a patterned cotton baby sling, Kate plucked a fat cucumber from the vine, dropping it in an old plastic ice cream bucket.

"Kate, is this enough for supper, do you think?" Sofia, a plump twenty-something new to Mayfly Hollow, held out a half-filled bowl of green beans.

"Might as well fill it to the brim," Kate said easily, stooping to pick another cucumber. Usually good-natured Maggie fussed. Kate adjusted her bonnet over her silky chestnut curls, kissing her head. "It's almost lunchtime, pumpkin. I know your tummy's getting hungry."

The sound of children at play wafted to the garden, along with Ace's joyful woofs. Kate used her hand as a visor, squinting toward the side yard where Nora and three others were engrossed in a lighthearted game of tag. Ace darted from kid to kid, his tongue lolling and tail wagging. The oldest of the group and gangly, Nora towered over her friends. As she sprinted from a squat-figured little boy intent on catching her, Nora's blonde ponytail swung, sunshine glinting on the golden strands. The Indian boy, Ravi, tackled Nora, and she squealed as they hit the grass.

As she puttered in the garden, Kate's mind wandered to six months earlier, when she and Teller found Ravi in Fenton on a scouting trip. Orphaned, he'd been on the verge of starvation when Kate spied him cowering in a shop doorway. He still had nightmares occasionally, but he'd come a long way since arriving at the farm.

"I know you intend to can those, but I have a recipe for cucumber salad that you may like," Sofia said, pulling Kate from her thoughts.

She smiled politely at the woman. "With mayo, onion, and sugar?"

"No, marinated in a cilantro lime dressing. It's a South American dish from where my mom was born. She made it a lot when I was growing up." Sofia put her knuckles to her hourglass-shaped waist and arched her back. "Oh, wait. I forgot we wouldn't have any limes here."

"There's some powdered lime juice in the pantry."

"Great. I'm on the rota to cook tomorrow's supper. If you pick extra, I'll make it as a side dish."

"Sure. I'd love to try it."

Edna, an elderly lady who'd been with them for several months, asked from where she weeded a row over, "Did I hear you discussin' cucumber salad, Sof?"

"Yeah, a recipe from Ecuador. It's very refreshing to eat during hot weather."

"Sounds good," Edna said. She launched into a story about the origins of cold vegetable salad. Edna was a long-retired schoolteacher and full of random tidbits of trivia.

Nora rushed over to Kate, holding the hand of a girl called Gretchen. "Kate, Gretchen skinned her knee!"

Kate bent to examine Gretchen's scrape. Nora extended a finger to Maggie and Maggie reached from the sling, grasping it in her chubby fist, her pleasure evident. She adored Nora. Kate gave Gretchen an earnest look. "Ow. That must hurt. Why don't you go inside and ask Rob to wash it? I'll bet he has a bandage he can stick on it."

Gretchen and Nora skipped toward the house, and Kate resumed harvesting veggies.

Arms enveloped Kate's waist, clasping under the baby sling. Kate tilted her head and Teller kissed her in his favorite spot, the crook of her neck. Kate whispered, "Hey."

"You miss me while I was out in the field?" Teller smelled of fresh hay and summer days.

Kate bit her lip, smiled. "I did miss you. You ready for our date in the glade tonight?"

"Heck yeah, I am." Maggie squawked and kicked her legs, vying for Teller's attention. "I see you, little girl. How's my baby?"

"Want to take her?" Kate asked.

"'Course." He warned, "I'm a mite dusty though."

"She won't mind." Kate set the bucket down. Putting a forearm under Maggie's rump and holding her firmly to her breast, Kate unwound the fabric of the sling. She gave the baby a smooch on her rounded cheek before passing her over.

Teller lifted Maggie, gliding her through the air like she was a plane. She squealed with delight. Her ruffled bonnet fell off her head. Kate grabbed it before it hit the ground.

"Adam, Ben, and I got a lotta hayin' done this mornin'. I worked up a mean appetite. Know what's for lunch?"

"It's Rob's turn to cook." Kate grimaced. "Probably peanut butter and jelly, knowing him."

"Welp, he's a doctor, not a chef." Teller shifted Maggie to a hip, pulling Kate into his other.

Adam approached Ravi and another child where they sat in the grass, petting Ace. A baseball was in his fist, and two mitts were tucked under his arm. Kate and Teller silently observed

Adam and the kids play catch. Ravi's laughter drifted over when Ace snatched the ball mid-air and took off with it.

Sighing, Kate leaned her cheek on Teller's chest, threading her fingers in his where his hand rested at her waist. Sofia and Edna meandered further down the row, deep in conversation, and Ben joined them, a boyish grin on his face.

Kate's voice was knowing when she declared, "Oh, there's definitely a romance brewing between Ben and Sofia. Her face is as red as a beetroot. And look at their body language."

"You may be right." Teller placed his lips on the top of Kate's head. "You happy?"

She closed her eyes. "Mmm."

"But you're thinkin' about Connie."

He always could read her. Kate's smile melted, the corners of her mouth turning down. Her heart panged. The debilitating sense of loss never seemed to slacken, but with time, the sting of it became more bearable. "I can still see her here, weeding in this garden."

"She'd be mighty pleased with what we've done at Mayfly Hollow, Kate," he said gently.

She nodded.

"You know…"

"What?"

Teller was serious. "You never made a mystery about your feelin's. That you ain't mother material, that you fret the Z virus is in your bloodstream and you may pass it along…"

She worried at the fleshy part of her cheek. Avoided his all-seeing gaze.

"I watch you with Maggie. I know your heart." He cleared his throat. "Now that we got Rob here, does that set you to ease a bit? Would you consider growin' our family? Tryin' for a baby?"

Shutting her eyes again, Kate took a deep breath. Held it. They hadn't spoken of expanding their family for months, but she *had* considered it. It crossed her thoughts from time to time.

Fear of the unknown had stopped her before. Now, she remembered when Teller last asked her to take a plunge, to trust him.

Had he ever led her astray before?

"Kate?"

Eyelids fluttering open, Kate stared into his aquamarine irises —irises the color of a tropical sea on a calm day. Would their child have eyes the same shade? Exhaling slowly, Kate whispered, "What would you say if I said yes, cowboy?"

Teller whooped. He pulled his Stetson from his head and flung it heavenward with abandon.

Kate giggled and Maggie clapped her hands. Ben, Sofia, and Edna stopped talking, their expressions inquisitive.

His grip tight on her waist and his lips urgent on hers, Teller commanded, "Now kiss me, Kate."

THE END

AUTHOR'S NOTE:

If you enjoyed Mayfly Hollow, please consider leaving an Amazon or a Goodreads review. Thank you for supporting indie authors!

JUNIPER RISE

ENJOY THIS EXCERPT OF BOOK TWO OF THE MAYFLY HOLLOW SERIES

Chapter One

"THREE HUNDRED SIXTY-FOUR FUCKING DAYS."

Raindrops pelted against the plexiglass skylights, making the usually dim warehouse even dimmer. The interior was shrouded in shadows. Ghostly. But Sofia was accustomed to that now. The rows of floor-to-ceiling shelving stood like soldiers in formation, the dust-covered forklift facing them resembling a stern drill sergeant.

Squinting at the newest hash mark she'd scribbled on the

concrete wall, Sofia capped the Magic Marker. She pinched her lip between her teeth and chafed her arms for warmth.

Three hundred sixty-four days in seclusion, not daring to depart the confines of her haven. No human interaction. Sweltering temperatures during the summer. Arctic conditions in the winter. Mornings spent pacing the aisles, sure she was losing her sanity. Reading the magazines she'd taken from the employee breakroom aloud just to hear a voice. Eating tinned soup straight from the can. Washing with a rag in the staff restroom, the water freezing.

A crack of thunder reverberated, then bursts of lightning illuminated the warehouse through the skylights like a strobe light. It jolted Sofia back to the present. Hefting her plastic crate from the shipping and receiving counter, she climbed the metal stairs to the manager's office—Howard's office—which overlooked the hushed warehouse. The stacked pallets that served as her bed were situated between the desk and the wall. Sofia lowered wearily to it. Draping her tattered foil blanket around her shoulders, she sniffled from both cold and emotion.

Was anyone alive out in the real world? What if she was the only survivor? The crates of food would spoil before she could eat it all. Then what? Starvation?

Rubbing her hands to create friction for heat, Sofia reflected. She had tried contacting her friends repeatedly, her cell charging in the outlet behind Howard's desk. Her calls and texts went unanswered. Sofia had been certain that after a couple of days things would blow over. That Mama and Daddy would phone to let her know they were booking a flight. They hadn't.

For a while, the internet functioned though her social media platforms were down—Sofia had no way to connect with her followers. She scoured the results of her searches. News outlets were apparently defunct. Instead of articles and broadcast news, Sofia found shocking MeTube videos. Uploaded by a panicked populace, they highlighted anarchy—looting, disorder, lawlessness. Random violence. Brawls over resources. Once victorious, the winner abandoned their battered adversary on the pavement, their wounds leaking lifeblood that flowed into the gutter like a scarlet river.

What if somebody saw the entrance to Spenser Suppliers and, nosy, broke in to investigate? Once they realized it was filled to the brim with nonperishable foodstuffs, Sofia would be in grave danger. They'd see her as merely an obstacle. She'd be as disposable as the people in the videos. The thought terrified her.

Why hadn't she had the foresight to comb Daddy's den for his gun before driving to the warehouse?

Sofia had watched in horror, biting her knuckles to keep from shrieking at the savage inhumanity unfolding onscreen. When she was sure there was nothing worse to be seen, more recordings were uploaded that left her blinking in disbelief.

Vloggers, dumbfounded, editorialized and documented *the dead awakening.*

Bodies supine on the streets lurched to their feet. Their faces lifted to the heavens. They loudly snuffled the air. Then, they stilled. Squatted. The creatures launched up as they fixed on a target in the crowd. People scrambled to evade them, trampling those unfortunate enough to lose their footing. The slowest of the bunch were picked off first.

Before long, there were no more uploads. Sofia refreshed the screen obsessively, desperate for more information. It was almost a blessing when her phone stopped finding a signal.

The warehouse, first Sofia's salvation, became her prison. Submerging into a profound depression, she'd curled up on the carpeted floor in Howard's office and slumbered. What else was there to do but sleep and hope that when she woke the nightmare would be over? Hours blended into days which stretched to weeks, the hash marks on the wall the only confirmation of the passage of time.

One day, Sofia dreamed of Mama.

"I didn't raise you to give up, *querida,*" Mama whispered

softly, patting Sofia's cheek. "This won't last forever. You're resourceful. Strong. You'll survive. You have to."

The dream roused and renewed Sofia's determination. As she scribbled her sixtieth hash mark on the wall, she vowed to take her car, to look for others. There was plenty to share at the warehouse.

Weaponless, Sofia took a nine iron from the golf bag in the corner of Howard's office, intending to hunt for the keys to the lobby entrance.

She'd never heard any indication that what happened to the dead online had happened to Howard the Creep, but Sofia decided to be wary.

Metal double doors led to the lobby, where she'd left his corpse. Gripping the golf club, she tentatively opened one of the doors, her heart beating hard in her sternum. The sun shining through the plate-glass windows facing the parking lot was blinding. Gagging against the sickening stench that drifted to her, Sofia put a hand over her mouth and peeked into the lobby. Shuffling, a clack of teeth, then a flash of movement.

"Gah!"

Howard barreled toward Sofia, the sunlight encompassing his form in a gilded aura. He traversed the lobby in seconds. Stinking of rotted meat, his flesh was mottled. His once brown irises were now milky white.

Releasing her golf club, Sofia used both hands to force the door shut. It wouldn't latch. Howard rammed against it. It smacked Sofia's forehead. Stunned, she lost purchase, her feet skating across the floor. She clung to the doorknob as she stumbled.

Howard's fingers slithered around the edge of the door jamb. Snatched at her. Sofia screamed, recoiled. Clambered to get her bearings. Put her shoulder to the door and used her body weight. The door bounced against the jamb.

Why wouldn't the damn thing close?

The golf club's handle was in the way.

Sofia kicked at it but missed. Howard's icy fingers touched her wrist. He was milliseconds from getting in! Doing the only thing she could think of, Sofia let the door go. Positioned herself in the opening. Bringing up a foot, she booted Howard in the family jewels. He teetered back.

The club! The toe of Sofia's sandal connected with it, and it skittered into the lobby. She slammed the door just as Howard rebounded, his fingers curling around the jamb. Red-black blood sprayed Sofia's dress as his fingers were sliced clean from his hand. The digits plummeted to the concrete floor near her feet.

Stomach heaving, she bent. Vomited. Wiping her hand against her mouth, Sofia straightened. Tears and snot tracked down her face as she bawled. Howard struck the metal doors. Would he get in? If he did, she was dead.

Like an automaton, Sofia unbuckled the belt from her dress and tied it around the doorknobs. She prayed it would be enough to keep him out.

The doors rocked in their frames. Sofia backed away.

Moments lasted an eternity but Howard quieted, his interest waning. Sofia sensed him pressed against the metal. Swallowing, she tiptoed over and brought her ear to the door. He snuffled as he sniffed at her scent.

A goose egg was forming on Sofia's forehead—her brain felt muzzy. There was a bulky wooden shelf overflowing with office equipment and printer apparatus. Inching the shelf over until it blocked the doors, she then sagged against it.

Howard possessed the keys to the lobby entrance, the only logical egress. Although there an exit by the shipping counter, Sofia was leery about traipsing all the way around the perimeter of the building to the parking lot. More of those things could be out there—she'd be too vulnerable. Plus, no keys meant she couldn't secure the door behind her.

Howard had become her prison guard, keeping her incarcerated. Sofia wouldn't be going anywhere anytime soon. Tears in her eyes, she cursed her weakness. Her fear.

Dejected, she went to the restroom to wash.

———

ELECTRICITY HAD QUIT WORKING on day sixty-seven, the boiler along with it. The summer had been awful, but winter was interminable. Agonizing. Teeth chattering, Sofia had shivered as she layered up in every outfit from her suitcase. A foraging exploration netted a first aid kit with a throwaway foil blanket. It proved inadequate. Suffering terribly night after night, Sofia questioned whether she'd live to see another day. Her only companion was her sore rib cage from an unrelenting, barking cough.

Now, the cusp of spring pledged a reprieve from the frosty temps, along with the first anniversary of her confinement. Something in her bones told her Mama and Daddy were dead. That everyone she'd known was dead. She didn't know *how* she knew, *but she knew.*

Sofia was an orphan. She wore the crushing melancholy and loneliness like a weighty shawl.

Sitting on her pallet bed with her legs crossed, Sofia toyed with the last present her parents had gifted her—a charm bracelet, crafted from Ecuadorian gold mined from the village where her mother had been born—and remembered Mama's words.

EXPRESSION DETERMINED, Sofia took a cardboard packet from the plastic crate. Unwrapping the chocolate iced Little Sallie snack cake, she said, "Happy twenty-first birthday. You're gettin' out of this place. Soon."

Chapter Two

THERE WERE NO IFS, ands, or buts about it. Sofia *must* get the keys. No way would she leave the door by shipping and receiving accessible. The warehouse was hers. She wasn't going to make entry easy for any scavengers that may discover the place.

The keyring was probably in Howard the Creep's trouser pocket or on the front reception desk. He'd have to be *dealt with*. Once he was, she could take the direct route outside to the parking lot through the lobby. Again, she regretted not bringing Daddy's gun.

Maybe she could bash in Howard's cranium with one of the golf clubs? But that meant she'd have to allow him within arm's reach. Sofia's mouth pinched in distaste. Could she do it? She wasn't sure.

That night, Sofia bit her nails to nubs as she attempted to envisage a plan, to rally courage. Slaying Howard was a mandatory litmus test, one she couldn't fail—she was liable to come across other bloodthirsty creatures outside. If she couldn't put Howard down, how could she possibly hope to stay alive?

Sofia's posh life hadn't prepared her for this—she'd never had to *fight*. Anxiety caused her tummy to burn, her legs to shake. When she did doze, it was in fits, and she was awake long before dawn.

Pacing the length of the office, Sofia psyched herself up. Bravery eluded her until she thought of Mama's words in her dream. They galvanized her into action.

You're resourceful. Strong. You'll survive. You have to.

Sofia propped the eight iron from the golf bag against the cinder block wall. Hunkering down, she put her back to the supply shelf obstructing the double doors. She used her legs to scootch it. It screeched as it dragged across the concrete.

Pausing to catch her breath, she heard the unmistakable shuffle of Howard approaching the metal doors. Then, the warehouse echoed as his fists beat against them.

"This may be the dumbest idea you've ever had, Sofia," she muttered as she considered her belt on the doorknobs.

With a steeling breath, she unknotted the belt and let it drop.

Sofia twisted the doorknob. The door cracked open. Swiveling, she seized the golf club. Retreated. Keeping to her plan, she dashed to the shipping counter. Waited. She mustn't get boxed in.

Hinges squeaked. Howard appeared. He shouldered the door further ajar, huffing the air. The early morning shafts of sun flooded the corridor through the opening. Dust motes swirled around his pudgy profile like stardust.

His footsteps were halting. Then, the snuffling ceased, and Howard's teeth crashed together. *Clack-clack-clack-clack-clack.* The door banged closed. He squatted.

"Oh shit…" Sofia exchanged the eight iron for the fire extinguisher she'd placed on the shipping counter.

Howard sprang up and forward, like he was on a pogo stick.

Hands sweaty, Sofia grasped the pin on the handle. Fumbled. She yanked it out. Aimed the nozzle. When Howard was almost on her, she squeezed the handles together and sprayed the thick foam directly in his face.

Disoriented, he paused. Faltered.

With a war cry, Sofia threw the extinguisher at Howard's head. It ricocheted off his temple and hit the floor. He staggered.

Clutching her club, Sofia swung with all her might. With a hollow clunk, it connected at Howard's brow bone, the momentum of it taking him from his feet.

"Oh fuck, oh fuck," Sofia gasped as she pummeled him with the eight iron. His revolting blood splattered her clothes, her skin. The smell inundated her sinuses, making her eyes stream. "Ugh!"

The force of her blows had bowed the eight iron. Dizzy, Sofia dropped it, slumping to her knees. Would she faint?

Howard's flattened head on the concrete sickened her. Bits of brain tissue and slivers of bone littered the floor, clung to her hair. Sofia swiped at the strands, feeling defiled.

"Don't freak out... don't freak out... don't freak out..." She scrabbled back like a crab until her spine connected with a wall. Half-shrieking and half-sobbing, Sofia covered her face with her palms and howled.

When her sobs had reduced to hiccups, she used the hem of her shirt to dry her tears. As much as she disliked the man in real life, she'd never wanted to physically injure him... Was she now a killer?

Sofia shook her head. No. Howard wasn't Howard anymore. Feeling much older than her years, she stood. After washing in the restroom, she climbed the stairs to the office to change her clothes and fetch the seven iron. She'd packed a tote bag with snacks, water, and the miniature fire extinguisher from the staff breakroom. It waited on her pallet bed.

Slinging the straps over her shoulder, Sofia returned downstairs. Quivering with adrenaline and wobbly-legged, she contemplated digging in Howard's trouser pocket to search for the keys. Repulsed, she opted to check the reception desk for his keyring first.

Sofia timidly opened the metal door leading to the lobby. Howard's stink lingered, watery sunlight saturating the room with radiance. Curious, she went to the plate-glass windows. Her car was where she'd left it. Howard had driven a company car, a hybrid. Electric cars were one of Daddy's green initiatives. Last year, Sofia had plugged the car into the solar-powered charging dock next to Howard's parking spot—just in case.

Her gaze scanned the blacktop, the surrounding forest. Mother Nature had begun to reclaim what was rightfully hers— the grass had grown three feet tall. Unchecked, glossy vines stretched across the parking lot like greedy tentacles. A crow flew past, landing on a tree limb. It was wild but unnaturally still.

"Strange," Sofia whispered. Wearied by her sleepless night and grossly overwhelmed by the quest that lay ahead of her, she worked her neck muscles with her hand.

Howard's keyring was on the reception desk beside the computer. Pulse thrumming, Sofia tucked her club under her arm and shifted the tote. Keys in hand, she marched to the entrance.

It was too late to second guess herself now.

Closing her eyes momentarily, she summoned strength then located the correct key. Legs shaking, Sofia unfastened the dead-bolt and stepped outside.

Chapter Three

THERE WERE NO IFS, ands, or buts about it. Sofia *must* get the keys. No way would she leave the door by shipping and receiving accessible. The warehouse was hers. She wasn't going to make entry easy for any scavengers that may discover the place.

The keyring was probably in Howard the Creep's trouser pocket or on the front reception desk. He'd have to be *dealt with*. Once he was, she could take the direct route outside to the parking lot through the lobby. Again, she regretted not bringing Daddy's gun.

Maybe she could bash in Howard's cranium with one of the golf clubs? But that meant she'd have to allow him within arm's reach. Sofia's mouth pinched in distaste. Could she do it? She wasn't sure.

That night, Sofia bit her nails to nubs as she attempted to envisage a plan, to rally courage. Slaying Howard was a mandatory litmus test, one she couldn't fail—she was liable to come across other bloodthirsty creatures outside. If she couldn't put Howard down, how could she possibly hope to stay alive?

Sofia's posh life hadn't prepared her for this—she'd never had to *fight*. Anxiety caused her tummy to burn, her legs to shake. When she did doze, it was in fits, and she was awake long before dawn.

Pacing the length of the office, Sofia psyched herself up. Bravery eluded her until she thought of Mama's words in her dream. They galvanized her into action.

You're resourceful. Strong. You'll survive. You have to.

Sofia propped the eight iron from the golf bag against the cinder block wall. Hunkering down, she put her back to the supply shelf obstructing the double doors. She used her legs to scootch it. It screeched as it dragged across the concrete.

Pausing to catch her breath, she heard the unmistakable shuffle of Howard approaching the metal doors. Then, the warehouse echoed as his fists beat against them.

"This may be the dumbest idea you've ever had, Sofia," she muttered as she considered her belt on the doorknobs.

With a steeling breath, she unknotted the belt and let it drop.

Sofia twisted the doorknob. The door cracked open. Swiveling, she seized the golf club. Retreated. Keeping to her plan, she dashed to the shipping counter. Waited. She mustn't get boxed in.

Hinges squeaked. Howard appeared. He shouldered the door further ajar, huffing the air. The early morning shafts of sun flooded the corridor through the opening. Dust motes swirled around his pudgy profile like stardust.

His footsteps were halting. Then, the snuffling ceased, and Howard's teeth crashed together. *Clack-clack-clack-clack-clack.* The door banged closed. He squatted.

"Oh shit…" Sofia exchanged the eight iron for the fire extinguisher she'd placed on the shipping counter.

Howard sprang up and forward, like he was on a pogo stick.

Hands sweaty, Sofia grasped the pin on the handle. Fumbled. She yanked it out. Aimed the nozzle. When Howard was almost on her, she squeezed the handles together and sprayed the thick foam directly in his face.

Disoriented, he paused. Faltered.

With a war cry, Sofia threw the extinguisher at Howard's head. It ricocheted off his temple and hit the floor. He staggered.

Clutching her club, Sofia swung with all her might. With a hollow clunk, it connected at Howard's brow bone, the momentum of it taking him from his feet.

"Oh fuck, oh fuck," Sofia gasped as she pummeled him with the eight iron. His revolting blood splattered her clothes, her skin. The smell inundated her sinuses, making her eyes stream. "Ugh!"

The force of her blows had bowed the eight iron. Dizzy, Sofia dropped it, slumping to her knees. Would she faint?

Howard's flattened head on the concrete sickened her. Bits of brain tissue and slivers of bone littered the floor, clung to her hair. Sofia swiped at the strands, feeling defiled.

"Don't freak out... don't freak out... don't freak out..." She scrabbled back like a crab until her spine connected with a wall. Half-shrieking and half-sobbing, Sofia covered her face with her palms and howled.

When her sobs had reduced to hiccups, she used the hem of her shirt to dry her tears. As much as she disliked the man in real life, she'd never wanted to physically injure him... Was she now a killer?

Sofia shook her head. No. Howard wasn't Howard anymore. Feeling much older than her years, she stood. After washing in the restroom, she climbed the stairs to the office to change her clothes and fetch the seven iron. She'd packed a tote bag with snacks, water, and the miniature fire extinguisher from the staff breakroom. It waited on her pallet bed.

Slinging the straps over her shoulder, Sofia returned downstairs. Quivering with adrenaline and wobbly-legged, she contemplated digging in Howard's trouser pocket to search for the keys. Repulsed, she opted to check the reception desk for his keyring first.

Sofia timidly opened the metal door leading to the lobby. Howard's stink lingered, watery sunlight saturating the room with radiance. Curious, she went to the plate-glass windows. Her car was where she'd left it. Howard had driven a company car, a hybrid. Electric cars were one of Daddy's green initiatives. Last year, Sofia had plugged the car into the solar-powered charging dock next to Howard's parking spot—just in case.

Her gaze scanned the blacktop, the surrounding forest. Mother Nature had begun to reclaim what was rightfully hers— the grass had grown three feet tall. Unchecked, glossy vines stretched across the parking lot like greedy tentacles. A crow flew past, landing on a tree limb. It was wild but unnaturally still.

"Strange," Sofia whispered. Wearied by her sleepless night and grossly overwhelmed by the quest that lay ahead of her, she worked her neck muscles with her hand.

Howard's keyring was on the reception desk beside the computer. Pulse thrumming, Sofia tucked her club under her arm and shifted the tote. Keys in hand, she marched to the entrance.

It was too late to second guess herself now.

Closing her eyes momentarily, she summoned strength then located the correct key. Legs shaking, Sofia unfastened the dead-bolt and stepped outside.

JUNIPER RISE IS available now on ebook and paperback at Amazon, or read free with Kindle Unlimited.

OTHER BOOKS BY ANNE LUCY-SHANLEY:

Meeting the Past

A PAST LOVER OFFERS A SAFE HAVEN—AT A SUBSTANTIAL PRICE.
Dangerous wrong-side-of-the-tracks bad boy Jake Carter is definitely Eve Shawcross's Mr. Wrong. She's been playing with fire, and only after getting burned has she learned a painful lesson—no-strings-attached sex ain't for her, no matter how sizzling it is. Craving a real relationship with the promise of a future, Eve vows to find her Mr. Right, a man who can give her what she so desperately wants—love, marriage, and children.

Ten years later, Eve is left reeling when Mr. Right's sordid secret life is exposed. Shattered by his bitter betrayal, she tries to pick up the pieces. When his duplicity jeopardizes her safety, survival becomes her sole focus. Just when Eve thinks she's avoided peril, she comes face-to-face with sexy Mr. Wrong—and their complicated past.

The tables have turned. Now wealthy and powerful, Jake's determined to tempt her back into his bed. He proposes an arrangement, but she's thrown by the terms in his contract. The stakes are high. Knowing her traitorous body and how persuasive Jake can be, Eve isn't sure she can play the game by his rules. Her gut cautions that all is not what it seems, but the passion she once found with him can no longer be denied.

CAN Eve abide by Jake's terms? Or will desire evolve into love?

MEETING THE PAST EXCERPT

"AM I IN *THE TWILIGHT ZONE*?" Eve cried, half-expecting Rod Serling to materialize. "You're the Carter of Carter Consolidated?"

This cannot be happening! Memories flashed of the first time they met. The scorching heat. The undeniable pull. It was still there, humming below the surface. The knowledge terrified her. His smirk told her he guessed what she felt. Move, her brain squawked. "This isn't right... I'm leaving."

"Stay where you are," Jake ordered. Always intense, now he was downright imposing. "I'm in charge this time."

Her voice was strangled when she asked, "Why am I here?"

"I have a business proposition for you."

Eve's breath came in gasps. She was sinking, as if in quicksand. "I already work for you. Or I did."

"Wendy says you're a wonderful addition to the center," Jake said in a sensible tone, his expression mild. "I've no intention of firing you."

"You think I should continue working here? With you as my boss?" Eve managed a dry laugh, remembering how angry he'd been when she broke up with him.

"It would be exceedingly foolish for you to throw away a perfectly good job because you want to avoid me, wouldn't it?"

Eve framed and rejected several rejoinders, sensing resentment simmering beneath Jake's controlled façade. *What is he playing at?* He chuckled, leaning back in his chair. The crooked smile exposed his dimple. They locked gazes, and the tension in the air ratcheted.

Eve made the mistake of looking at his mouth. She moistened her lips with the tip of her tongue, remembering the pleasure his mouth brought her once upon a time. Her body remembered, too. She shifted in her seat.

"You're exquisite. That hasn't changed," Jake purred, expression turning predatory.

Eve quashed the urge to run from the room. "Did you hear I was back in town and engineer this?"

"*This?*" he mimicked, his head cocked to the side, as if having fun at her expense.

"Yes, the job. This meeting. Is it a setup?" She waited for his response, pulse racing, but his face was impassive. "I don't know what you have in mind... but, whatever it is, it won't work."

Jake nodded to the rings on her left hand. "Because you're married?"

"Yes," Eve said, defiant, clasping her hands in her lap. *Keep your cool. Don't let him see he's rattled you.*

"Martin Pierce. A topic we should address." His tone glib, a muscle worked in his jaw. *He's still pissed at me, after all these years.* Eve shook her head, stomach churning. No, she didn't want to talk about Martin, especially not with Jake. "I know your husband's dead."

Eve's lips parted. A myriad of emotions blossomed in her chest. She struggled to decide which was the strongest, which to latch onto. *Fear? Confusion? Anger? Frustration?*

"And, I know about the mess you're in."

"Explain," Eve demanded, her teeth gnashed.

"I've kept tabs on you the last ten years, Angie. I've waited for you to be free again."

Eve moved to the edge of her seat. "Did you have something to do with Martin's death?"

Tipping his head back, Jake laughed. "Don't be ridiculous."

"That's reassuring," Eve snapped. "I'm comforted by your declaration of innocence."

"You're delectable, but you flatter yourself if you think I'd assassinate your husband to get you back. Your marriage wasn't destined to last. Widow or divorcée... it makes no difference to me." Jake raised a hand in a placating gesture. "Don't be angry with me. Pierce got himself in trouble."

Eve bit her tongue to keep from arguing. She'd get nowhere lashing out. Sitting back in her seat, she crossed her arms. "Tell me what you know."

"I don't know why your husband needed money, but he borrowed a lot from the wrong people." He shrugged.

"A lot?"

"Into the millions," Jake said with grim satisfaction.

Oh, why not? I should've figured. I'll bet Barbee's the tip of the iceberg. Darkness closed in. Defiance gone, Eve put her head between her knees, her coat and purse falling to the floor.

"I'm surprised you haven't been leaned on yet."

Eve sat up, rubbing her temple with shaking fingers. "Who says I haven't been?"

"So you know the characters Pierce borrowed from are mobsters. They'll make your life unpleasant until they receive payment."

Eve gulped, insisting, "My house will sell and I'll chip away at the debt."

"You think the type of people you owe will be patient?"

"Then my father will help... I have friends who'll help."

Jake's smile looked smug. "I doubt your pride would allow you to ask him—or your friends—for the astronomical amount you need."

"You have all the answers," Eve snarled. "What do you suggest?"

"You need a benefactor. I need someone to manage my home and accompany me on social occasions with none of the obligatory romantic rubbish. No syrupy sentiments, no expectations or proclamations of love. A business arrangement free of entanglements. I propose marriage."

MEETING THE PAST *is available for purchase on ebook or paperback on Amazon.*

ABOUT ANNE LUCY-SHANLEY

CRAZY CAT LADY. FAN OF THE OXFORD COMMA. AUTHOR.

WITH DEGREES in education and psychology, Anne Lucy-Shanley is a novelist based in the American Midwest. An enthusiast of all things written, Anne dabbles in dystopian, young adult, and non-fiction writing. As a firm believer in happily-ever-afters, contemporary romance remains her favorite genre.

• • •

SOME OF ANNE'S pastimes include drinking whiskey, sharing dirty memes, and coming up with captivating storylines while soaking in the tub. When not embracing the quiet life with a book and a cat on her lap, she occasionally travels with her husband of twenty years.

ANNE LOVES CONNECTING with her readers! Come join the fun at her Facebook group, Saucy Society. Sign up for her monthly newsletter The Saucy Gossip at www.annelucyshanley.com. You'll receive updates on her books, info about giveaways, and reading recommendations delivered straight to your inbox.

www.ingramcontent.com/pod-product-compliance
Lightning Source LLC
Chambersburg PA
CBHW021134260626
47169CB00005B/1606